Amanda Brookfield worked in advertising before becoming a freelance journalist. She has lived in China, Germany, Sweden, Argentina and America and currently lives in Dulwich with her husband and children.

Also by Amanda Brookfield

Alice Alone
A Cast of Smiles
Walls of Glass

A Summer Affair

Amanda Brookfield

FLAME

Hodder & Stoughton

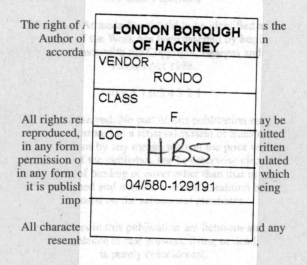

A CIP catalogue record for this title is available
from the British Library.

ISBN 0 340 62341 1

Typeset by Palimpsest Book Production Limited
Polmont, Stirlingshire
Printed and bound in Great Britain by
Mackays of Chatham plc, Chatham, Kent

Hodder and Stoughton
A division of Hodder Headline
338 Euston Road
London NW1 3BH

For Jane and Fi

Nicholas put his head in his hands and rubbed his finger-tips in the bristly dryness of his hair, massaging his scalp with small circular motions so that his nails scraped the gritty surface of the skin. A miniature snowstorm of white specks floated down onto the grey keyboard of his computer, accompanied by several hairs. Faintly repulsed, but intrigued, Nicholas began to move his hands more vigorously, causing even greater quantities of dry skin to float down onto his desk. Craning his neck to one side and swivelling his eyeballs mercilessly, he then entered upon an anxious investigation of his shoulders, squinting to make out any signs of skin-flakes on its busy pattern of white and blue. Pencil-points danced before his eyes, while the whirls of blue and white heaved of their own accord. Nicholas removed his glasses and rubbed his eyelids with his knuckles, causing the black spots to be replaced by slashes of vivid green and orange.

Kate had given him the shirt for his birthday; the colours were good – even Nicholas could perceive that they sharpened the otherwise hesitant blue of his eyes – though he still worried about the lack of a collar. Only T-shirts should be without collars, he felt, especially if the wearer was forty-something and had donned ties and long-sleeved shirts for every day of his working life. But Kate had been very certain about the neckline, undoing the top two buttons with her cool fingers and shaking her head in a kind of teasing admiration that he couldn't help liking even though it filled him with distrust.

His screen flashed at him, hinting that it required fresh fodder of some kind. Nicholas sighed heavily, causing a flurry of skin flecks to fly at the screen. He pushed the return key and the flashing stopped.

He began tapping at the keys, using one hand only, moving slowly and without conviction; the words dutifully appeared on the screen, under a lengthy description of a kitchen:

'I'm fed up with eating cornflakes every morning; what about some fresh croissants or a plate of cheese and ham?'

After staring glumly at this sentence for a few minutes Nicholas deleted the clause about croissants and inserted the world *'fucking'* before *'cornflakes'*. *'I'm fed up with eating fucking cornflakes every morning'* was, Nicholas felt, a much more incisive representation of the mood of his character: so much bolder, more assertive, more like a man of passion and guts.

Any desire to develop this sentence, however, was drummed out by the need to confront the disquieting fact that the emotions it expressed were almost identical to those voiced by Nicholas himself at breakfast that morning as he dolloped milk into his cereal bowl and carved out a space to lay his newspaper amongst the usual debris on the kitchen table. 'I'm fed up with cornflakes,' he had remarked, without swearing, because of the children, and Kate who didn't like it, before turning his attention to headlines about terrorists and plane crashes.

Whatever fizzle of inspiration Nicholas might have had was flattened by the suspicion that such petty pilfering from one's own existence might not be the hallmark of a great literary talent. His screen had started flashing at him again, apparently having digested the cornflakes and in need of something more substantial. Nicholas typed *'bugger off'* and got up to inspect himself in the tiny pearl-encrusted mirror that hung beside the door of his study. The mirror, which had belonged to Kate's grandmother, was so small that only sections of his face could be studied at any one time. His nose came into view first: long and rather wide at the bottom, each nostril looking as though it had been ever so slightly stretched to one side. It was a comical nose, bordering on the ugly, and best regarded in context with his mouth which was pleasantly wide, with full lips that curled in the corners, as if permanently on the verge of a smile. His teeth were okay too, Nicholas decided, shifting his position to view them more clearly, and running the tip of his tongue round their edges, feeling the small gaps which had slowly reappeared weeks after he had completed a six-year course of prescription braces. At least he'd fared better than Alison, he thought with a rueful smile, tugging a curly-edged postcard from behind the mirror and studying the faded picture of Sydney Opera House, its towering concrete folds looking like the pipes of a mammoth organ. His sister, Alison, who was two years older than him and whose mouth still retained something of the look of a badly organised graveyard in spite of the best efforts of teams of orthodontists during her teens, had resided for some years in Melbourne, Australia, where she was married to a landscape gardener with four children and five dogs. Three of the children came from a previous partnership on his side, though the dogs were all their own. For no particular reason it irked Nicholas that Alison should send postcards of Sydney when she lived in Melbourne; there was an illogicality to it that was typical of her, he thought, bending his knees to see if he could get a good angle on any part of his shoulders.

'How's it going in there?' came Kate's voice from the other side of the door, together with a brisk rap that made Nicholas jump.

Having conceded a warning knock, Kate felt little compunction at flinging open the door, with the result that Nicholas found himself pinioned against the wall just as he was attempting to skip back behind his desk.

'Sorry to interrupt, darling,' she said with a quizzical smile, but managing not to ask why he was apparently undertaking an investigation of door hinges instead of cracking on with his beloved play. 'Just to say that I'm on my way out now. I've got a couple of things to get for supper – thought I'd treat us to that liver thing with bacon and mushrooms – and then I promised I'd help Mary Sullivan with some flowers.' Kate wrestled with a wide-patterned scarf while she spoke, tossing it over her shoulders and deftly pinning it to one side of her linen jacket so that all the spare folds hung attractively down her back and front. 'James said he's got a lift back from cricket, so don't worry about that and I can pick Grace up on my way home because she said they won't be done till at least three – the last rehearsal ran two hours over. Millie's upstairs in her room – I've told her I'm off. Lunch is on the table. Baked potatoes in the oven, they should be done in an hour or so. Okay?' She stopped suddenly, as if pausing for breath, her brown eyes shining with the pleasure of being hectic but in control.

'Absolutely.' Nicholas stood there with his hands in his pockets, looking as if he was waiting for her to go, which only made Kate linger, wondering what was wrong, whether it was serious, whether she had time to probe for an explanation before the local shop shut up for the weekend and Mary started a series of panic phone-calls about wilting orchids and who should sit on the left and the right.

'Darling, I've really got to run.' She stepped forward and kissed him tenderly, wanting to make up for her rush. 'I should be back by tea,' she added, wiping away the faint smudge of pink she had left on his lips.

As she pulled back Nicholas slipped his arms around her waist, interlocking his fingers to prevent her from breaking free. 'You're wearing perfume,' he said, his voice sounding ungenerous and accusing while his mind admired, as it had so many many times, the intriguing attractions of the creature he had married nearly twenty years before. Kate Latimer was one of those women about whom, in physical terms at least, the effect of the whole was considerably more impressive than a close scrutiny of the parts. Apart from her eyes, which were a deep glossy brown, very round and unafraid-looking, there was no feature that stood out particularly. Her hair, though full, was rather dry and fly-away; while her nose was clearly a shade too long for her face and could look quite Roman when she was cross. Her skin, which had always been a natural olive colour, was these days laced with the tell-tale hair-lines of middle-age, egged on slightly in Kate's case by the fact that she spent so much time in the garden and couldn't be bothered with the paraphernalia of hats and sun-creams. Yet the overall impression of her, this morning as every morning, was stunning, bordering on the voluptuous.

'Not perfume, just a pongy new shampoo. It was on special offer. It's got eggs in it – and lemons, I think.' Kate pushed his arms down. 'I'm late and you've got loads to do – two thousand words, if you meant what you said last night. Look, it's bleeping.' She frowned at his computer.

They both turned towards the screen, which, if left to its

own devices for long enough, started up an intermittent hum that synchronised perfectly with its light-flashing trick. Nicholas edged reluctantly back to his desk chair. Kate had almost closed the door when he called her back.

'Nicholas, really . . .' Her impatience was undisguised now, all the fun swept from her eyes.

'Have you noticed whether . . . do I have dandruff?'

'Dandruff?'

He patted his shoulders. 'You know, embarrassing white heaps on dark jackets.' He made a face, sticking out his chin and sucking in his cheeks. 'Tell me, I'll take it like a man.'

'No, darling, no.' Kate spoke slowly, as if to a testing child. 'I hadn't noticed anything to worry about during the last decade or two – not in that area at least,' she teased. 'If you're worried, try my eggy stuff,' she added as a parting shot, 'it's supposed to work wonders.' And with that she closed the door.   .

Nicholas moved the cursor to the beginning of his cornflakes sentence and pressed the delete button. Overhead Millie began practising her ballet.

Nicholas Latimer had some basis for believing that he could write, though he wished more and more these days that he hadn't. It had all started with a short story, a quirk of inspiration following an unusually idlyllic trip to the coast a few summers before, when Millie, then a precocious five year-old, had befriended a raggedy old man combing the shore with a rusted metal detector. Having promised the story as nothing more than a gimmicky memento for his youngest daughter, Nicholas found that during the writing of the tale it somehow transformed itself into something rather grown-up and meaningful which, at Kate's suggestion, he had sent to the BBC. Expecting nothing, his elation at having it accepted had been immeasurable. They read out his words, all six thousand and forty-two of them during the slot between Kaleidoscope and the PM news programme. Nicholas, giddy with success, then took the dubiously generous step of sending his own precious, crackling tape of this momentous event to several of those unfortunates who had been unable to tune in at the time, including, finally, his sister in Australia. While Nicholas took care to package the only tangible evidence of his literary triumph (he had meant to make a copy but had never got round to it) within the womb-like security of a padded box and no less than two sturdy jiffy bags for its journey across the globe, Alison had seen fit to return it several months later in nothing more than a slim brown envelope. As a result, the interference on the opening section of the soundtrack, which had once been acceptable, had mushroomed to sandstorm proportions; and five minutes into the story the tape stuck completely, at the same point every time, the thin strip of brown cellophane having twisted to the width of button thread.

Nicholas, eyeing this battered testimony to his authorial debut, now gathering dust on the overcrowded bookshelf to the right of his desk, often now imagined that its sad demise at the hands of the international postal service was meant as a sign. He should have given up long ago, instead of clinging to the hook of a notion that writing could somehow offer that inscrutable added extra to life, something to make up for all the other tawdry business of growing old, of cocking things up, of never having enough money, of being so wretchedly uncertain even though one was forty-six and had fully expected certainty to be one of the few recompenses for approaching such a terrible age.

'Dad, I'm starving. When's lunch? Mum said I could have sweets after. I want the chocolate buttons – the white ones this time – they're a trillion times nicer than the brown ones.'

Nicholas' youngest daughter twirled in through the doorway of his study, pirouetting furiously, her frizzy curls flying as she leapt. She was decked in full ballet gear, her long twiggy legs sticking out from under her tutu like disconnected things. It still amazed Nicholas that he and Kate had managed to produce this child with her silvery ringlets and gangly stick of a body. Genetically speaking, the first two fell much more neatly into line, what with Grace's thick dark hair and Kate-like sallow skin, the doubtful gift of Nicholas' stiff brush of a hair-do and tall but innately ungainly looking figure having fallen to the unfortunate James. Compared to such obvious chromosomal connections, Millie, their wild and beloved nine-year-old, was something of a changeling.

'Millie, love, it's not lunchtime yet. You only had breakfast five minutes ago.'

'Didn't.' Millie did a balletic leap and landed at his side. 'Can I help? Can I do something? I could press the buttons for you.' She climbed into his chair and wedged herself onto his lap, blocking both his view of the screen and any possibility of operating the keyboard. 'I could write a story for you – I've loads of ideas.'

Nicholas didn't even try to be angry, though he suspected perhaps he should. Sending Millie away would generate two obvious problems: some predictable raging from her, which might be stressful, and, more daunting still, the necessity of returning to the depressing progress of his maligned cornflakes.

After countless rejections on the short story front Nicholas had announced his decision to apply himself to the more appealing challenge of a full-length play. Drama offered better prospects for a second career, he had said, during those heady months before euphoria had been replaced by the hangover of failure, those months when he had hinted to anyone prepared to listen, that product research had never really been his thing anyway.

Millie embarked on a rambling tale about a giraffe and a monkey while Nicholas tried not to mind the discomfort of her bony bottom on his knees and thought gloomily about the prolonged absence of his muse. *The Old Treasure Seeker* had taken three days to write, or rather three evenings; it had been a laugh, nothing more, a little scribble after work, with a pad on his knee and a drink in his hand, with Kate reading bits over his shoulder and telling him to hurry up because supper was getting cold. That had been three years ago. If nothing changed, all he had to look forward to was seventeen more years as a research director at Freeman Lyle. Nicholas sighed, pressing his forehead against his daughter's back. The path of his working life often seemed more like a series of accidents than a career. Product research had been something to start off in, something which – however vaguely – seemed related to a degree in chemistry. But one thing led to another, one job to another, one promotion to the next, until suddenly a change of careers looked absurdly hard. Then the Freeman Lyle offer had come along, with all its irresistible promises of annual minimum bonuses, guaranteed promotions and spanking new offices in a rural location just outside the Surrey commuter belt. It had been the chance he and Kate were looking for. They moved down to Elhurst from their end-of-terrace house on the acceptable side of Tooting without so much as a glance backwards, welcoming the change of life-style with open arms. Not even when Nicholas discovered that his calculations about his journey time had been seriously optimistic and that it would take not twenty but forty-five minutes to drive to work – not even then did he experience a whiff of a second thought. Commuting across London had taken twice as long and been infinitely more unpleasant, whereas cruising across country in his purring new Honda, listening to the radio, having time to notice the weather, to breathe air that contained narratives of something other than inner-city pollution had felt like a luxury indeed. Where had all that enthusiasm gone, he wondered now, all that fresh-faced eagerness for self-fulfilment? The only sustaining thought at the back of his mind these days was his pension.

Nicholas nuzzled his head into the silky back of Millie's costume as if to rub the troubles from his mind. He closed his eyes, trying to conjure up words to describe what she smelt of, how warm and vibrant she felt.

'Hey, that tickles.' Millie scrambled down from her perch and skipped out of the room, all thoughts of giraffes and chocolate buttons apparently forgotten, leaving her father feeling bereft and gloomier than ever.

2

Kate dawdled over the box of glossy field mushrooms in Mr Edwards' cramped but beautifully fresh vegetable section, carefully picking out those with the plumpest, blackest gills and sleekest skins. She handled each one very gently, almost reverently, before placing it in the bottom of one of Mr Edwards' lovely brown paper bags. She moved onto lettuce after that. There was no need for salad – she already had French beans and a cauliflower planned, together with some wild rice, perfect for soaking up the juice from the liver – but the sight of the shiny fresh green heads of lettuce was too much for her. She bought some of the curly purple-tipped kind as well, seeing with an artist's eye how the colours would look, the mingling bright and ruddy greens, perhaps with dashes of red from a pepper thrown in.

Mr Edwards, a rosy dumpling of a man who had run Elhurst General Stores for more than fifty years, gave her a wink and a grin as he totted up her purchases at the till. Kate Latimer was one of his very best local customers, well known to be a fine cook. She'd made the cake for his Dorothy's wedding a couple of years back – the most perfect fragile tower of a thing with ribbons of pink roses hemming every tier. Kate smiled back. Though she tried to shop sensibly during her weekly whiz round the massive superstore on the other side of Westbury Hill, she always seemed to end up popping down the road with shopping lists of one kind or another.

Kate hurried out of the shop scrabbling amongst her basket of brown bags for her car keys. Elhurst, though only a smattering of a town, lodged in the foothills of the South Downs, suffered terribly from lying along a slip road between two heavily used single carriageways that fed into the main arterial links up to London. Given its ancient origins – Elhurst House, which overlooked the town from its princely position on the lump of land behind the church, was said to have been built on the site of an old Roman fort – Kate often felt that the place deserved less of a daily onslaught by the ugly traffic of modern life. Their own house, safely tucked away down the lane that led past the pub through Elhurst woods and on to Chivers Farm, was mercifully out of the way of such things.

Having found her keys wedged into a side slat of her basket, she was forced to perch on the edge of the pavement for several minutes before daring to sidle round the side of her illegally parked Ford Fiesta without fear of her life. A few years back there had been much talk of a bypass, but locals, worried for the effects on their lovely patchwork of farms and hedgerows had put up a successful stand. Kate herself had been in two minds about signing the petition, brought with much aplomb to her front door by Mary Sullivan and a couple of pillars-of-the-community types whom she usually took care to avoid. There was no doubt in Kate's mind that the never-ending procession of speeding lorries in search of the ever elusive short-cut and caravanners, scouring the countryside for a picnic spot or a toilet seat, robbed Elhurst of its heart and that an alternative of some kind was definitely called for. Emboldened by tea, which she only served because of Mary being there looking so peaky and distressed, she had dared to say as much, causing the women to shake their heads in sad agreement, though not to remove the petition from her kitchen table. What Kate did not say, and felt quite cowardly about for several months afterwards, was that she thought some bypasses could look almost nice, sweeping round the swell of hills, reaching smoothly through the countryside like dark, outstretched arms. But in those days they were too recently arrived in Elhurst for Kate to feel comfortable about expressing such anarchic views; even their house still seemed to be regarded by some of the locals as belonging to old Dr Morrison, who had gladly sold up to the Latimers and retired to a cottage in Wales where the fishing was better and the closest thing to an HGV was the school bus.

Mary and Angus Sullivan lived several miles out on the other side of town in an ostentatious conversion of a fifteenth-century farmhouse whose only claim to the fifteenth century that Kate and Nicholas could detect were three or four of the roof beams running across the ceilings of the downstairs rooms. There was a fine driveway up to the front door, flanked on each side by lines of great oaks, sentinels for the rolling fields behind, which the Sullivans let out to various horse-lovers with less generous properties of their own.

Kate accelerated up the tarmac drive with a little rush of pleasure, to do with driving a shade too fast and the silky feel of the warm wind blasting through her open window, flinging her hair across her cheeks and mouth in a way that made her feel quite reckless and free. Even though it was only May, summer had definitely arrived. The sun beamed down on the crook of her arm where it rested on the edge of her lowered window. Driving with one hand Kate stretched her free arm right out of the window, turning the palm against the onrush of air, wanting in some way to welcome the belting blue of the sky and the shimmering colours of the Sullivans' uncut fields. It was still only Saturday morning. There was just Mary to get through, she told herself, then Grace to collect from St Alberry's, then the whole of the rest of the weekend to enjoy. But on remembering Nicholas' mood after breakfast Kate frowned as she pulled up behind Mary's shiny red Toshiba. He hadn't been himself lately and she couldn't work out why. While minding about this for healthy reasons to do with a robust affection for her husband of nineteen years, Kate could not entirely suppress a flicker of impatience too. Nicholas, to her mind, had nothing to be grumpy about. And being a creature who, by and large, got on with life's pitfalls and challenges without allowing herself to be submerged by any of them, she had had a tendency towards intolerance for those not prepared or able to do the same. But what Kate hated more than anything was having loose emotional threads about the place; not because she was mean-hearted, but because she was a great believer in problems of every kind having sources and solutions. Helping Mary Sullivan, which had become something of a reflex over the years – albeit a reflex laced with fondness – ultimately derived from a similiar instinct for setting things to rights.

Mary, for all her chintzy curtains, fifteenth-century beams and polished cars, was a woman who had aroused Kate's sympathy from the start. Her husband, Angus, a successful wine merchant who had clearly decided that the produce of vineyards was more interesting – or perhaps more gratifying – than his wife, treated Mary really rather harshly, even in front of other people, which seemed to Kate to be worse than being horrid in private, though she knew that it was probably no better at all. There were no children; a fact which Mary sometimes referred to, but always in the context of God whom Kate sometimes thought she had taken on as a kind of substitute husband – someone to love and look up to on a daily basis, but whose innate silence and invisibility precluded certain disappointments.

Mary waved from a window in the red-tiled roof of the barn, whose spacious rafters had been skilfully and tastefully converted into a set of carpeted guest rooms, complete with its own kitchen, bathroom and sitting room.

'Come up,' she called, motioning with a yellow-gloved hand and a duster at the little stairwell that curled up to the entrance. 'I'm cleaning,' she added, a little unnecessarily, given the gloves and cloth and because cleaning was how Mary spent most of her mornings. Partly as a way of apologising to God for the worldly extravagance of her surroundings, and partly, Kate suspected, because she would not know what to do otherwise, Mary steadfastly refused to employ any form of domestic help in her enormous house, not even when – as now – Angus had one of his major entertaining sessions coming up when hordes of his 'wine people', as Mary called them, came to stay for lavish sessions of tasting and buying. During these times Mary's role was reduced to little more than a glorified cook and maid, a burden which she assumed with irritating resignation and even a dash of pride. Though she liked to cook she was not, as Kate almost guiltily knew herself to be, someone who found it easy or who had the confidence to do anything in the kitchen without a proven recipe. Mary's idea of preparing a meal was to plan it weeks in advance after a thorough survey of all her cookbooks, to shop carefully and precisely several days before, to follow the recipe through to its minutest detail and then freeze the whole thing so that it could be extracted ready-made and perfect for a few seconds in the microwave before being placed on the table. Kate, who loved the last-minute chaos, the mingling smells of throwing a meal together, the ideas that came for merging this and that as she stirred and chopped and sieved, found it hard to progress beyond anything but sympathy for such a contrastingly clinical approach. But she kept all such thoughts, even the sympathetic ones, as well hidden as she could, an unsettlingly vivid impression of married life with such a man as Angus Sullivan making her see that all sorts of forgivable defences might have to be raised in the interests of survival.

'It looks lovely,' enthused Kate, stepping onto the soft pile floor of the barn living room and looking round appreciatively. 'You have worked hard.'

'It's too hot, don't you think?' Mary pushed a faded fair curl of hair out of her eyes with the back of her glove, revealing more of her broad white forehead, which, like the rest of her pale face was faintly freckled, like mottled china. 'It's from being so high up, with these windows, I suppose – and of course hot air rises, doesn't it? And on a day like this . . .' She peeled her rubber gloves off and laid them carefully over the edge of a bucket which was neatly filled with various aerosols and folded cloths.

'What about these flowers then?' said Kate kindly, thinking the barn room was indeed incredibly stuffy, and wanting to get on with all the other things lined up in her day.

'They are all in the utility room – there are so many I had to use both sinks and several buckets – but I wanted to keep them fresh. I think there might be enough for two vasefuls up here as well as all round the main house. It's so kind of you to help out, Kate, really it is,' she went on, leading the way down the steps, taking them cautiously with one hand on the rail. 'But it's so important to give these people a good impression. Detail really matters,' she said, unwittingly echoing sentiments frequently expressed by her husband.

Kate followed her across the gravel and into a side door of the house. 'And you know me and flowers,' Mary added meekly, now reaching out to touch the delicate, bowed heads of some irises, causing a little sneeze of yellow powder to fall from their fine arched stamens. 'I really ought to do a course of some kind,' she went on rubbing the yellow dust from her fingers, 'I saw a card about Chinese flower arranging courses in Westbury library last week – what do you think?' Kate, who thought that composing flowers into lovely shapes was something you had to love rather than learn to do, but who also thought that Mary deserved and needed to get out of the house more, said she thought it sounded marvellous.

Nicholas was wondering dreamily whether the pleasantly strong smell of cooking potato meant that he could justify leaving his study five minutes before the deadline he had promised himself, when a violent screeching from upstairs pressed all the parental alarm buttons which had mysteriously taken root in his system from the moment of James's birth seventeen years before. 'Coming,' he roared, leaping from his chair, his mind racing through a medley of possibilities involving grim-faced surgeons and mortuary attendants. In his haste to leave the room he tripped over the loose bit of carpet by the door and lurched sideways, striking his hip sharply on the exercise bike which, thanks to some unnecessary furniture reshuffling by Kate the week before, had been transplanted from a conveniently unattended corner of their bedroom to take up a limbo existence in the hall.

Nicholas, swearing in guttural whispers, hobbled on up the stairs, pulling on the banisters for added speed with one hand and rubbing his bruised hip with the other. By the time he reached the landing an ominous silence had fallen, though instinct of some indefinable kind propelled him towards Kate's and his bedroom.

He found her draped over one end of the radiator, her bony shoulders heaving in dramatic, but by now quite soundless despair.

'Millie, darling, what on earth has happened? Did you fall? Where does it hurt? It's all right, Daddy's here now.' He tried to hug her to him, but she clung to the radiator. He brushed back the bounce of hair behind her ears, keeping an eye out for signs of injury and still trying to prise her away from the wall.

'Whatever is it, Millie?' he persisted, suspicions as to the genuine urgency of her need now well stirred.

'Down there,' she hiccoughed, straightening up enough to point to the two-inch gap between the back of the radiator and the wall, 'it's stuck down there – forever.' With this last word she emitted a dramatic howl and threw herself across Nicholas and Kate's bed, kicking off her ballet shoes and burying her head in the pillows.

Nicholas peered down into the narrow dark space. After a few seconds he could make out the glimmer of something amidst the dingy dust of the skirting-board ledge.

'It's stuck forever,' said Millie matter-of-factly, now sitting up in the middle of the bed picking at a loose stitch in the counterpane.

'What is? What on earth is it?' Nicholas, knowing now that he had been conned into a massive and unnecessary overdose of adrenalin, could not keep the annoyance from his voice.

'Don't be cross.'

'I'm trying not to be, Millie,' he said tightly, 'but if you tell me what exactly is stuck it might give me a little clue as to the best method of extracting it.'

Millie tossed her head in the direction of Kate's dressing table. Whereupon Nicholas noticed that the green leather jewellery case which had belonged to Kate's mother was open, and all its contents scattered amongst Kate's tidy line-up of brushes and combs and pots.

'Oh Christ, Millie, what have you been up to?'

'I was just looking,' she retorted, not sounding remotely penitent. 'I was just looking,' she said again, more uncertainly this time since her father had not uttered a word and she was beginning to feel that serious trouble might be at hand.

'If you were just looking,' he said curtly, 'then perhaps you could explain the magic trick that induced a piece of your mother's jewellery to lodge itself between the radiator and the wall.'

For a second Millie hoped that he was trying to be funny, that everything was going to be forgotten and forgiven terribly quickly. But his tone of voice suggested otherwise. 'You can come and put all of this away – at once.' He gestured angrily at the mess on the dressing table. 'Now, what is it that's fallen down there?'

'An earring,' she mumbled, edging off the bed. 'The other one of these.' She held up a large pearl from which hung a triangular, solid gold pendant inlaid with a solitaire diamond. Nicholas felt his pulse quickening again. There weren't many items of Kate's jewel box that he could have so easily identified. But he knew those earrings only too well. They had been given to Kate by her mother on the morning of their wedding day, which, as it turned out, was just a few months before she died of cancer.

'Bloody hell, Millie.' He opened the wardrobe door and pulled out a metal coat hanger which he began to unbend and shape into something resembling a long metal hook. Millie, having carefully laid Kate's largely valueless trinkets back in the box, put her head in her hands and watched Nicholas with increasing admiration.

'You're a star, Dad,' she remarked, 'brilliant plan.'

He eyed her with a look that was supposed to be stern, but which was so full of love that she knew the worst was past.

Some twenty minutes later the two of them were toasting their success with glassfuls of Kate's homemade lemonade and platefuls of meatloaf and salad. Millie turned her freckled nose up at the dehydrated appearance of her baked potato so Nicholas ate hers too, filling each half with lavish portions of butter and mayonnaise. After all the frustrations of a fruitless morning at his computer, the episode with the earring had filled him with a perverse satisfaction; it had been retrieved – after the application of considerable skill and determination – and placed safely back alongside its partner in its cotton wool bed inside the left section of Kate's jewel box. All his anger at Millie had been replaced by a faint glow of achievement, which, even as he experienced it, he knew to be of dubious worth.

They had just chiselled out a carton of strawberry ice-cream from the back of the freezer when James strolled in, still in his cricket whites, with his bat under one arm.

'Good match?' asked Nicholas, pushing a plate and a glass at his son.

James scowled. 'It was only nets and I've hurt my hand.'

'Let's have a look,' piped Millie.

'Get off.' James pulled his hand away and put it in his trouser pocket. 'Where's Mum?' He scattered a heaped teaspoon of sugar onto a large lettuce leaf and rolled it into something resembling a green sausage roll. The crunching of granules was audible as he chewed.

Nicholas, who had for some time found it hard to establish any satisfactory lines of communication with his seventeen-year-old son, and who, since Kate had bullied him about it, was in a phase of trying to resist the frequent temptation to criticise him, got up to inspect the dishwasher, replying as he did so, aggravation nudging its way into his tone, that their mother would be back around tea time.

'Christ, this spud has undergone some pretty severe torture,' James laughed, dropping it from a height of several inches onto his plate. 'Was it nuked or what?' He made a face, sticking out his tongue in a fair simulation of being strangled from behind. Millie, adoring and dutiful, collapsed amidst peels of laughter. Nicholas, who felt the full weight of responsibility for the blackened remains of the potato and who had established the irritating fact that the dishwasher was clean and full and could not therefore be loaded without considerable investment of time and effort, straightened and stiffened. The desire to shout at his son was almost overwhelming. Shoving a pile of dirty plates out of the way, Nicholas took a firm hold of the kettle and filled it with water, the sound of the tap drowning out for a few blissful seconds the noisy tomfoolery going on at the table behind him.

'Could you two clear the lunch things away, please,' he said, turning his back on them, heading for the sitting room, coffee in one hand and no less than eight squares of dark chocolate in the other, robbed from one of Kate's endless cooking jars, high on a shelf behind bags of sugar and flour, where she hoped it might be safe. There was some good cricket on the telly, so good that Nicholas forgot about most of the things that had been annoying him and even treated himself to a whisky from the drinks cupboard. It was the weekend after all, and he needed to relax. Kate should relax more too, he told himself, as he poured himself the other half some forty minutes later and propped himself up lengthways on the sofa against one of her beautifully embroidered cushions. It wasn't right, he thought, with a tic of self-pity, for her to be out of the house pandering to the Marys of this world while her family muddled along alone. She had got noticeably busier over the last year or so – always dashing off to something or other, though Nicholas never quite managed to remember what.

She could have a lover, for all I know, he thought morosely, tipping his head back so that the last drops of whisky could trickle down onto his lips.

3

Harry Melford, Kate's younger brother, lay at full stretch on the green behind his ball, his handsome, pointed nose so close to the ground that he could smell the cool musk of the earth. The hole looked deceptively close when viewed from behind, though he knew the distance to be six feet at least and could see now that there was a teasing slope to the left before the green flattened out for the last couple of feet before the flag.

'Get on with it,' growled his father, leaning his tall but now somewhat stooping frame on his putter and giving a wink to Beth who was sitting on her knees on the grass behind Harry, trying to be still and quiet as George had often had to remind her she should be. Even the most casual of matches seemed to require the stiffest code of etiquette from these British golfing men. For Beth, who was American and whose natural inclination was to express whatever thoughts passed through her mind if she judged them to be either interesting, relevant or witty, it had been a hard lesson to learn. Harder even than her sessions at the golfing range down the road with a retired Spanish pro who made her feel goofy and inept, but who was an old friend of George's who had cut her tuition fees to half his usual rate. Beth had hoped that George might allow her the occasional swing during the afternoon, since it was only Harry whom he was playing and they were all family, so to speak. But the set of her husband's face, only minutes into the game, after he had skewed his first drive twenty yards to the right of the fairway – though at a distance from the tee that would have left Beth breathless with satisfaction – warned her that such hopes were not to be fulfilled.

It was five years since she had met George at a conference on lung tissue in Baltimore, during the days when she had still been charging round as strategic assistant to the great Professor Elias, the job description simply being a nice way of saying that he couldn't afford to pay her very much for typing, walking his spaniels, feeding his meter and keeping the local dry-cleaners in business. Being so active, even in such a menial way, suited Beth's nature, as well as providing much needed support in helping her to emerge from a bruising and acrimonious divorce from her first husband, one Joe Kenny, who sold car insurance.

One of the more interesting facets of Beth's employment was to take notes for the professor during the numerous conferences that he chaired; though it was often quite a demanding role, requiring considerable powers of selection and comprehension, she had mastered it to such a degree that she instinctively knew when to switch in and out of full concentration, when she could afford to look round the room and study the faces of the other delegates. Looking across the putting green at Dr George Melford now, she was reminded of her first impression of him round one of those polished conference tables, the oddly appealing tightness of his austere English face, with its high cheekbones and long nose, the thick white hair brushed straight back off his face, the sides falling forward only when he made a particularly vehement point.

'Would you mind?' Harry was asking, now standing parallel to his ball and swinging his arms like a pendulum.

'Sure.' Beth got to her feet, pulling her T-shirt down over her track suit bottoms and bouncing on her trainers. 'What can I do?' She rubbed her hands and grinned, exposing two protuberant front teeth which, under less relaxing circumstances, she kept firmly encased behind her lips. 'Anything to help beat up old George.'

George pretended to scowl, enjoying, as he always did, Beth's show of aggression. She was very competitive, his American wife, it kept him on his toes.

'The flag,' said Harry, languidly, 'could you hold the flag? I don't trust his nibs over there.'

Harry, who had in fact taken several holes to overcome his

irritation that his father had brought Beth along too, when he had anticipated a men-only sort of afternoon, was determined that his stepmother should sense none of his reserve. Any antagonism towards Beth, implicit or otherwise, led to the most fearful scenes with George, as Harry during the early days, when this stepmother had been flung at him and Kate like some kind of misguided birthday surprise, had learnt to his cost. There had been a period of not speaking, several months in fact, which, even given that Harry was well into his thirties and intensely independent, had made him profoundly unhappy.

'Would you mind moving a bit to the right, Beth?' he asked sweetly, flicking an elegant tress of very fair hair from the corner of his eye. 'It's your shadow, you see, it's falling across my ball-line.'

Beth, looking down and seeing a great black and not altogether flattering image of herself slanting across the sunlit tablecloth of grass, immediately hopped to one side. 'Sorry, honey.' She waved the flag pole at George, brandishing it like a spear. 'I was right across his ball-line,' she called, 'but now he's got a clear run.'

George, smiling, put his finger to his lips and took a couple of steps forward to watch his son. They had agreed to go double or quits on the last hole. If Harry sank the put he would win the third successive victory over his father in as many years. They did not play often, but when they did it was always tense. George couldn't help himself: he liked to win, he always liked to win, whether it was squash or tennis – in the days when he could still play such taxing games – or a simple hand of cards with Beth. He squinted into the sun, watching Harry's inscrutable face as he took his putter back and started the move forward.

'Miss, damn you,' George hissed, clenching his fists behind his back.

But Harry, whose acclaimed performances across a wide range of activities throughout school, university and now in the city where he worked as a headhunter had always been based on a very real love of pressure of any kind, felt in no danger of missing. The ball moved steadily but surely, pursuing the most delicate of arcs, towards its intended destination, hiccoughing only once and very minutely over a bobble of earth before disappearing with a satisfying thud into the hole.

'Bravo, Harry,' cheered Beth, waving her flag pole and doing a little dance.

'Shot,' said George, trying not to look crestfallen and taking longer than was strictly necessary to file away his golf club into his trolley before offering Harry his hand.

Beth came up and put a consoling arm round her husband, sufficiently acquainted with his ways to realise that the time for teasing was over and that discreet doses of silent sympathy were called for instead. She kept her arm round him in a canoodling way throughout the trek back to the clubhouse, causing Harry, who walked behind them, a few customary frissons of distaste. Even though it was a very long time since his mother had died, he still found it hard to consider his father as the lover of another woman, especially one with a ginger rinse to her hair; one who, though she was well over fifty, liked to pout and wheedle like a flirting girl. Harry, who had devoted a considerable portion of his life to entertaining throngs of stunning girlfriends without managing to want to marry any of them, would never have stood for such skittish behaviour himself, not in public anyway.

Since Beth was not allowed into the members' bar, George suggested they drive straight back to the house for supper. Harry, whose thirst raged but who suddenly found that he could not bear the prospect of several more hours of George and Beth, especially not over one of Beth's heavy pasta dishes, loaded with extraordinary – and to Harry quite irreconcilable – ingredients like avocados and anchovies, invariably coated in hot glutinous cheese, found himself protesting that he had to get back to London forthwith. Something had cropped up that morning, he lied – he hadn't wanted to mention it before – but he really had a ton of phonecalls to make and a deal to clinch.

'You mean you don't like my low alcohol lager,' teased Beth, who could be quite perceptive sometimes.

'Not at all, how silly, dear Beth – I'm driving after all.'

'Sure you are,' she replied in an irritatingly knowing way, offering up a faintly rouged cheek for a farewell kiss.

'As you like, dear boy,' said George, still too ruffled from his loss to bother with any nuances that might lie behind Harry's apologies. He held out his hand, which his son took briefly but firmly.

'An honourable defeat, Dad, thanks,' he said before lowering himself into his small silver car and pulling on his Italian leather gloves and peaked leather driving cap. As George and Beth waved him off, Harry couldn't help thinking how much of an old couple they looked these days, standing together and nodding their heads like car toys, their images shrinking fast in his rearview mirror.

The drive back to London was tediously familiar, more so somehow since it was a Sunday evening and a route that Harry had taken after many a weekend with his parents in the Oxfordshire countryside. Following his first wife's death, George had moved house, but only from one village to the next, to a slightly smaller cottage with less of a garden and more of a view. With his work at the John Radcliffe and his passion for the city where he had studied for his degree, George would never have considered living anywhere more than a ten-mile radius from the place. Though ever since Beth and her cats had appeared on the scene they had been murmuring about finding somewhere bigger, like a young married couple sharing pipe dreams about the perfect future. Harry shuddered just thinking about it. The problem wasn't simply that the image of his quiet, self-contained mother lay forever at the back of his mind, challenging the wisdom of such a brash replacement, but more that he couldn't help thinking the whole business of so-called love between Beth and George, all their ear-kissing and finger-twining, was nothing but a sham. He simply couldn't bring himself to believe it was real, not between people of their ages. Kate and Nicholas had never been like that, he reasoned, and they seemed pretty solid after countless years.

As he turned onto the M40 and slipped into fifth gear, Harry found himself thinking fondly of his sister, one of the few mortals to whom he felt he could speak freely. Enduring the same co-educational boarding school together had been the start of it all, the sense of being in league against parents and teachers and the world in general. And then after that, when Kate went on to sell outrageously expensive clothes in the King's Road and Harry started at London University they shared a flat in Pimlico together for almost three years, right up until Nicholas appeared on the scene.

Roadworks squeezing the by now heavy end-of-weekend traffic into a single lane had reduced the progress of Harry's Porsche to an unglamorous crawl. He pulled off his cap and ran his fingers through his sleek fair hair. Like George, he kept it swept back off his face, but several inches longer, so that the sides fell permanently about his handsome cheekbones. Though his father thought – and sometimes said – that it looked poncy, Harry was usually quite pleased at the effect; it gave him something of the Hugh Grant look, he felt, elegant but casual. Having killed a few minutes assessing his reflection, he reached down and dialled Kate's number.

'Hello, Nicholas Latimer speaking.'

'Nicholas, hello. Harry here.'

'Are you calling from Peru? Where the hell are you? – bloody awful line – perhaps it's us.'

'I'm in my car. Is Kate there?' Harry asked, raising his voice and fiddling with the phone's small aerial.

'I'll see. Hang on.' He heard Nicholas call for Kate, saying it's your dear brother on the line, which struck Harry as unnecessarily sarcastic. Even after twenty years, he hadn't quite got the measure of his brother-in-law. There was something a shade hostile in his attitude, something that related back perhaps to that very first meeting at the flat, when he mistook Harry for a rival lover.

'Katie, I'm stuck in the most boring traffic jam after an unspeakable game of golf with Dad and Beth trailing round like the proverbial lovesick cow and I thought what I need is someone to cheer me up.'

'Poor Harry. Tell me all about it.'

'What?' Harry began rifling through the glove pocket. '*And* I've run out of fucking cigarettes. How are you lot anyway? How's sunny Elhurst and all who sail in her?'

'Christ, you are bored,' said Kate teasingly, well used to Harry and his ways and being unavoidably fond of them, even the most antisocial ones. Though he was only two and a half years younger than her, she had always regarded Harry as very much more of a little brother than their age-gap warranted. The sense of looking after him, of making the allowances which had once been necessary, had never worn off. Even though Harry had long since made more money in his head-hunting business than she or Nicholas could ever dream of; he lived in a spacious flat in Fulham, with ceiling lights and revolving mirrors and giant plants that didn't need watering; his phone performed more tricks than Nicholas' computer and beside it lived a dark red filofax reserved for women and dinner-dates.

'By the way Alicia, my latest, was out for one thing and one thing only.' He had found a battered but salvageable cigarette under the passenger seat and was now groping in the pocket of his flannels for his lighter.

'Oh dear, Harry, couldn't you stand the pace?' Kate mocked, enjoying herself and motioning at Millie, who was holding up a book on ballerinas, to go and consult her father. She reached out and kicked the kitchen door shut with her foot.

'I mean marriage, you dope. She suddenly turned from being an incredibly fun-loving, beautiful creature into this wild-eyed, screechy thing, who talked about sharing and commitment. It all happened terribly fast. I tell you, Katie, it was scary.'

Kate, who knew well enough that if she ever allowed herself to become personally acquainted with any of Harry's women, she would almost certainly be inclined to side with them against him, felt free to laugh openly. 'You're horrid. Lots of men want sharing and commitment too, you know. It's just shits like you that prove the exception.'

'You always say the sweetest things.' He blew a small smoke ring at the windscreen, watching it curl and stretch against the glass. 'Any chance of meeting up?'

Kate thought for a minute, swinging her legs under the table like a schoolgirl. 'We're having a barbecue next weekend – some local friends – come along and make it jolly.'

'Sounds irresistible,' he drawled, knowing she wouldn't be offended. 'Come to London instead – wouldn't that be more fun? Dearly though I love your family.'

'They all adore you,' she said, thinking that it was certainly true of the children, with whom Uncle Harry was a great favourite, largely because he swore and smoked and asked them questions like had they tried drugs yet and if not why not.

'Lunch on me,' went on Harry, tossing his cigarette out of the car and accelerating happily into the three lanes which had, at last, opened up in front of him. 'Somewhere posh.'

'How could I refuse?' she laughed, both of them knowing that a long family joke about Harry's stinginess was being raised. 'Wednesday is good for me because Millie does ballet after school and Jamie usually has a match.' The interference on the line was getting worse. Harry's response came back in a zigzag of sound, forcing Kate to put a finger in one ear and close her eyes in order to hear anything at all.

'Great . . . my office . . . one o clock . . .' He was driving very fast now, one hand on the wheel, the speedometer springing back and forth round the 100 mph mark.

'See you on Wednesday,' Kate shouted, feeling as if her voice was being projected down a wind tunnel. She got off the table and put the phone back on the window sill. It would be nice to go up to London for the purely indulgent purpose of having lunch with her brother. Not so long ago such luxuries had been impossible without a momentous amount of plotting and planning round school runs and tea-exchanges with a consortium of other mothers. Now the children were old enough – though Millie had to be accompanied and they did not always rejoice at the prospect – to take the bus.

She crossed her arms and went to stand at the back door, looking out onto the big square of a garden which she had finally wrested under almost perfect control. Wisteria crawled along the huge side walls, a writhing backdrop of purple, lilac and green for the broad beds of flowers that skirted along its edges. Though summer was obviously the best time of year for colour, she had taken care to ensure that something bloomed every month, even if it was only a clutch of holly berries and some winter jasmine.

Family life was not quite such a manageable entity, she mused, leaning her head on the door frame and thinking back to how hard it had been, after years of accustoming herself to the rigorous demands of motherhood, to readjust back again. Not being needed so much at home, at least not in the hour-by-hour sense induced by three young children, had at first been bewildering. After a decade of longing for more time to herself, she found that when the freedom came, instead of relishing it, she had wandered round feeling dispossessed and unfocused. So much so that there had even been a time, not so very long ago, when another baby had seemed the only answer, something to make her forties glower less fiercely, something to mark the final passage of all those clever hormones before they disappeared completely. Kate was always the first at the school gates during that time, eyeing pushchairs and swaddled infants with unhealthy longing, her heart pounding with a shameful yearning for the uniquely reassuring love of a tiny child. She would never forget how kind Nicholas had been, nursing her through with repetitive but reassuring refrains about being needed still, about waiting and seeing, and taking things day by day.

Kate sighed, hugging herself, glad that such emotions were no more than a memory. She loved her time to herself now and was getting rather good at filling it. Apart from the multifarious demands of running house and family she did quite a bit of cooking these days – an activity which made her very little money but which she enjoyed enormously. To discover that filling time need not be a chore had been a bit like rediscovering an old friend, one that for a while she feared had been lost for good; it offered a way forward, a possibility of being happy that stretched beyond Millie's A levels.

There was something about a walled garden, the secret safeness of it, which Kate loved. Though in fact the wall itself was almost certainly far from safe, since the embracing wisteria provided an elegant screen for many a crumbling brick and gaping spy-hole through into the Chivers' fields beside them. But Kate hadn't bothered to mention wall repairs to Nicholas yet; not just because the garden was very much her domain and he didn't notice detail beyond whether the roses were in bloom, but also because, without even asking Billy Shore for an estimate, she knew that the cost of repointing and repairing three sections of such a high old wall could only provide fuel for Nicholas' bad mood.

She turned and stepped back into the kitchen, taking her favourite oatmeal cotton cardigan from off the back of a chair and pulling it round her shoulders against the chill of the evening.

*   *   *

'I'm having lunch with Harry on Wednesday,' she said, when Nicholas came in a few minutes later, looking something like the caricature of a crazed academic, with his small glasses perched on the end of his nose and his stiff hair sticking up at the front.

'All right for some', he mumbled, yanking open the drawer in the kitchen table, which was supposed to accommodate useful household gadgets and adhesives, but which was invariably in a state of such advanced disorder that nothing could ever be found at the precise moment it was required.

'What are you looking for?' she asked, bristling at his inexcusable gruffness. The shadow cast by the events of the day before was still very much upon them. Kate's attempt at fetching Grace from St Alberry's had been thwarted: after waiting ages for the rehearsal to end her daughter had begged to be allowed to spend the rest of her day with Megan Williams, a surly black-eyed classmate with punctured ear-lobes and nostrils for whom Grace was showing alarming and increasing signs of deference in everything. Kate, who believed that the best way to counter an enemy was by first befriending it, was summoning the courage to agree to such a plan, when Megan's mother swooped down on them, all teeth and flying black hair, offering glib chit-chat about buns for tea and dropping Grace back at half past nine. The irritation which had started then was not appeased by the sight of her kitchen: amongst the detritus of open crisp packets and dirty crockery sat flies, rubbing their front legs with leisurely complacency over platefuls of curly-edged salami and slabs of meatloaf, while wasps supped lazily on blobs of mayonnaise and pools of split lemonade. Clenching her face in annoyance, Kate had made her way into the sitting room, only to be confronted by Nicholas lying flat out on the sofa, mouth open, glasses pushed up onto his forehead, one arm trailing elegantly on the carpet beside an empty glass, while Millie sprawled on her stomach, her freckled nose just inches from the television screen, apparently enraptured by the afternoon's horse-racing results. James, to judge from a muffled thumping sound, was upstairs. Kate, who had been looking forward to a relaxing pot of tea, perhaps sitting outside in the garden with the magazine bit of the paper and a slice of the honey shortbread she had made the day before, picked up the *Radio Times* and gave Nicholas a sharp rap on the head.

'Your wife has returned,' she had declared, before marching over to switch off the television and turning round to face him. Nicholas sat up at once, trying in vain to look as if he had only just nodded off and feeling unpleasantly fuzzy-headed. Resenting all Kate's unvoiced accusations and feeling something like shame at how the day had slipped him by, he scowled unrepentently. Millie, remembering suddenly that she and James had been commandeered to clear up the kitchen and following an instinct to seek moral support from some other party who appeared to be equally out of favour, crawled over towards her father's knees.

Nicholas patted her head briefly and then rubbed his eyes which felt gritty. 'Oh, don't look like that Kate, for God's sake. We're sorry, aren't we Millie, for being such unspeakable slobs. I assume that's why you're looking so appealingly enraged.' He dared a half-smile.

Kate crossed her arms, determined not be weakened by his tactics. After so many years Nicholas had learnt how to be very adept at calming her down. He had that hangdog look on his face now, where his eyes managed to look all mournful and appealing, like a puppy waiting for the scolding to be over. She threw up her arms. 'You're hopeless, the pair of you. I hate being the dragon. It's not fair, Nicholas, you always leave it to me to be cross and boring. The kitchen has become a breeding ground for flies and disease, my son is rupturing his eardrums, while my husband lies in an alcoholic haze, apparently uncaring that his youngest child is acquiring the skills to develop a career as a bookmaker.'

'She might become very wealthy and mollycoddle us in our retirement.'

'But I don't want to make books,' put in Millie, looking worried.

'I give up,' announced Kate wearily, already thinking that it was dull to rant at loved ones for too long. Nicholas came to help her in the kitchen, doing little dance steps to the strains of Millie's piano practice from next door in order to make her smile, and to disguise the fact that inside he felt hopeless and unforgiven.

The next day their spirits had somehow not lifted as far as either of them would have liked, even though the liver had been delicious, even though Nicholas had persuaded Millie and Grace to accompany him on his ritual Sunday morning walk into Elhurst for the papers and then taken the astonishing initiative of cleaning the car. Now the gloom of Sunday evening was upon them all, and somehow very much tied up with Nicholas' angry rummaging in the kitchen drawer. He required scissors to cut out an advert about half-price computer supplies, which he felt was too good an offer to ignore, but which he secretly suspected his meagre literary output did not quite justify.

'Bloody kids,' he said, rifling ineffectually amongst open packets of picture hooks and drawing pins, making the mess immeasurably worse, until Kate could bear it no longer and went to look in Millie's room where she found the scissors together with a brand new roll of Sellotape next to a magazine and a pair of tights under her daughter's bed.

She took them downstairs and held them out to him. As Nicholas reached for them she pulled them away. 'Friends?' she said, her hazel eyes radiant, brimming with one of those unexpected surges of fondness that had nothing to do with prowess in the fields of fathering or table-clearing, but everything to do with why she had agreed to marry him, six months after he'd wandered into the shop where she worked, looking for something to buy for his girlfriend.

'Friends,' he said, with a great sigh, taking her into his arms and crushing the lovely familiar curves, burying his head in her hair and taking deep breaths of the scent of it, as if it was the only kind of air that kept him alive.

4

On Wednesday Kate got up half an hour earlier than usual so that she had time to rinse the grey from her hair and blow-dry it before taking the children to school. Lifting the bedroom curtain carefully, so as not to allow any of the streaming sun to fall anywhere near Nicholas' sleeping face, she allowed herself a few seconds to admire the day, with all its promise of light and warmth. It can't last, all this summer sun, she thought, letting the curtain drop and doing her best to open their bedroom door without it squeaking.

'What time is it?' growled Nicholas from somewhere amongst the bed covers.

'Early,' she whispered, 'go back to sleep.'

She dried her hair on the landing, standing in front of a mirror with Coca-Cola emblems splashed across it, a present from James to Grace the year before, or had it been the other way round? She scowled as a thread of hair caught in the hairbrush, and then allowed herself a humph of satisfaction: the grey bits had come out even more coppery this time, an effect which Kate decided she liked, and which made her think fondly of the far-off days when she had had the time and inclination to mess about with pots of henna and rubber gloves.

'Morning, Mum,' mumbled Grace, appearing from her bedroom and padding through into the bathroom across the landing, idly hoicking up her nightie to scratch her thigh in a way that, given an altogether different audience, might have been deemed highly provocative. Millie appeared next, demanding to have hot air blasted at her curls, whizzing them up into a white frizz, her ears turning pink at the heat. James was the last to emerge, wearing only his pyjama bottoms and moaning loudly about being woken up in a way that reminded Kate, with a lurch of affection, of his father.

'Is that a new dress?' Nicholas asked a little later, in a tone which suggested critical wonderment at the extravagance of such a purchase rather than appreciation of any kind.

'No. It's four years old at least.' Kate turned to check the zip was done up to the top, causing the red cotton panels to flare out like a twirling brolly.

'Well, I've never seen it before,' he remarked, standing behind her and adjusting his tie in the mirror.

'I wore it to that lunch at the Armstrongs' last year – the one when you were so nearly rude about the wine.'

'Ah, did you?' He sounded unconvinced.

Kate completed her outfit by putting on a cream jacket with a round neck and tailored waist, skilfully flattering a figure which, though perfectly respectable, had suffered the inevitable ravages of three pregnancies and an unwaveringly healthy enjoyment of good food.

'Where are you going dressed like that?' asked Nicholas, his eyes wide.

'To an orgy of gorgeous single men.'

'I'm only bloody well asking.'

'No, you're not. Your making a statement of disapproval.'

He threw up his hands at their reflection in the mirror. 'Christ, Kate, don't put words into my mouth.'

'There was a time,' she went on, unable to contain thoughts which she knew could only encourage their conversation to deteriorate further, 'when you would have expressed appreciation at my appearance, pleasure at my ability to raise myself from the quagmire of middle-age and look, however briefly, quite attractive, instead of putting me down and making me feel that it is somehow wrong to dress myself in a way that might, just possibly, with the wind in the right direction and the light in the right place, turn heads.'

Nicholas stood mute and aghast, looking and feeling as wronged as he knew how.

'To answer your question,' she went on, 'I am going – dressed like this, as you so delicately put it' – she pulled out the hem of her skirt and let it fall again, as if in distaste – 'first to take our children to school, then to the supermarket to buy food for our family, then to the station to get on a train and go up to London for an expensive lunch with my brother. I want to look smart, feel cool and have enough space around my midriff to accommodate a fine meal. If you have any alternative suggestions from my wardrobe then I would be happy to consider them.' With that she spun on her heel and marched from the room, maddened that her carefree mood was in tatters.

But once alone in the quietness of the kitchen Kate immediately regretted her outburst, even given what she regarded as justifiable provocation. They had only just smoothed over the last bumpy patch; what had she been thinking of, she scolded herself, as she transferred packets and jars from cupboards to the table, rising to a little taunt like that, a taunt which – if she thought about it logically – was very possibly better than not even having her clothes noticed at all?

When Nicholas introduced his stony face and monosyllabic responses into the subdued mêlée of family breakfast a bit later, Kate did her best to enact a silent charade of regret, touching his arm as she poured the coffee and passing a light hand across the top of his head when she walked past his chair. But Nicholas, suffering with secret shame at the justification of her earlier outburst, resolutely ignored these olive branches, reading them only as signals of pity and a determination to be cheerful. Kate's defiant brightness in the face of absolutely everything was really beginning to get him down.

But Kate was not one for giving up. 'I'm sorry I snapped,' she said, sticking her head in the car window just as he was on the point of what might have felt like an enjoyably dramatic drive-off, without the ritualistic farewell peck from the wife; 'perhaps I should be flattered that after so many centuries my husband is starting to show signs of possessive jealousy.' She kissed his nose.

'I am not jealous, Kate.' His skin tickled from the imprint of her lips.

'No, just cross,' she said with a mock pout, wanting more than anything to get the morning back on track. 'I'll give the dress away – tomorrow – I promise,' she teased, still not satisfied that his mood had lifted, and needing to feel that it had, for the sake of her own peace-loving mind.

'The dress is fine. Let's just leave the whole thing, shall we?' He gently prised her arms from the open car window. 'I'm going to be late and I've got a very busy day.' He granted her a sort of smile before driving off, a weak imitation of the real thing, that nonetheless expressed a kind of regret for the morning's exchanges which Kate chose to find reassuring.

Not even winding back the sun roof and switching on the Radio 4 morning news brought a glimmer of relief to Nicholas' mind. He had slept very badly, his pillows feeling uncomfortably mushy and warm, the creases in the sheet digging into his back like ridges of corrugated iron. Kate's deep, even breathing had only underlined his failure to relax, highlighting the strange sense of panic and irregularity that bubbled deep within the tubes of his own respiratory system. Though he dozed off at times, he had never sunk into anything like the kind of oblivion he craved; his mind flicked awake at the slightest sound or movement, as if vigilant of danger. He had watched through half-closed eyes as Kate drew back the corner of the curtain and smiled at the morning. He had seen the happiness in her face, the look of unbridled optimism for her day, the way she swung the red dress from out of the cupboard, the quiet humming as she slipped it on. And he had felt mocked by such contentment, consumed with a kind of hideous envy. His own day, his own life, sprawled before him, grey and unappealing. How dare she, aged forty-two, with rinse in her hair and wrinkles round her eyes, look so lovely, so utterly at ease with life? While he, the husband, should feel so stiff and old, so uninspired and imperfect. He caught himself remembering with something like nostalgia the distant days when Kate had lain groggily in bed, exhausted after a night up with one of the children, days when gratitude as well as enthusiasm had swept him out of the house and down into the compressed darkness of the London Underground. He had actually felt lucky to be going to work. Did this mean, Nicholas wondered now, his stomach flipping with dismay, that he had found his wife easier to love when she was unhappy?

The car park at Freeman Lyle plc was unnecessarily spacious: needless paddocks of tarmac with fresh painted white lines and low red brick walls marked out at least fifty spaces that were never used. Nicholas pulled into one bearing the label 'DIRECTOR' and switched off the radio. He was ill, he decided, peering in the rearview mirror and cupping his chin in his hand to check on the efficacy of his morning's shave. He put his hand to his forehead in the vague hope of detecting a fever, but his skin felt cool and untroubled. There was nothing worse, he decided, getting out of the car and firing the automatic locking device, than feeling under the weather without any specific symptoms to latch on to. He cleared his throat several times as he strode across the forecourt, imagining the start of a soreness, his mind impervious to the ornate fountains of spouting dolphins, the perfect squares of rainbow coloured flowerbeds, beset by enigmatic loops of sculptured metal which had so impressed him when he first arrived.

'I think I'm going down with something,' he remarked to Janice, his secretary, before entering his third-floor office and flinging himself into the chair by the window, with its dazzling view of acres of rape seed, the yellow burning against a backdrop of flawless blue sky.

The restaurant had a front door with a doorbell and a strutting French waiter who was so much a parody of himself that Kate nearly lapsed into irreverent giggles until she saw that Harry, who was a snob at heart, would mind her misbehaving and possibly even let it ruin their meal.

'For the record, and by that I mean the purposes of my expense sheet,' he said, raising the rim of his glass to his nostrils, 'you're a prospective client – a high-flyer, looking to change careers and make me a bunch of money into the bargain.'

'Hardly,' laughed Kate, lifting her own glass and taking a small sip. 'Your job is immoral,' she declared, as she had many times before.

'Nonsense,' he replied easily, 'we fill a need in the market place. People come to us because they need help, because they are dissatisfied or unhappy—'

'– or greedy, or because you've rung them up on spec and unsettled them with notions about Jaguars and villas and yachts and things.'

Since there was a faint possibility, as they both sensed, that their conversation was in danger of turning serious, they fell upon the menu with exaggerated enthusiasm, though for Kate, studying the dishes was almost as great a pleasure as eating itself. To see what other people had thought of putting together not only filled her with new ideas for her own kitchen, but also left her lamenting the fact that she had to choose just one or two things. On this occasion the menu was so short and refined and she was so unquestionably in the mood for fish, that her task was made relatively easy.

Harry, whose habits seldom varied, went for the only dish offering red meat amongst its conscientiously organic ingredients, while Kate opted for fillets of salmon in an enticing sounding sauce of lime and chives.

'Seriously, Katie,' said Harry in a way he had of suggesting he was picking up an old thread of conversation instead of embarking on a new one, 'don't you wish sometimes that you'd turned yourself into more of a career girl somewhere along the line? Isn't life with old Nicholas and all those infants just a little bit dull?'

'Life with Nicholas is never dull,' she replied with a smile, making Harry wonder, as he often did with her, if there was some secret that this sister of his possessed, some trick to her irrepressible ability to get satisfaction out of the most damnable things. 'And I'm not going to start on about the delights of children; you'd fall asleep, which would be a shame, seeing as you're paying for all this.' She closed her eyes as she swallowed another spoonful of the lobster bisque they had both selected as a starter. 'Hm, if only I could grow shellfish as well as vegetables.'

'Still digging potatoes in your spare time?'

'Yes, and if you start to get rude about my devotion to my garden then I shall start to tease our lovely waiter.' She swallowed more soup, there was a hint of curry in it, or was it tabasco? 'You're to be nice to me, Harry. I sense grumpiness and I can assure you I've had quite enough of that this last week.'

He raised his eyebrows, but she did not elaborate.

'Tell me about Dad and Beth. I could hardly hear anything down that ridiculous toy phone of yours.'

He groaned. 'Same as ever. My golf wasn't bad though. But

can you imagine, taking *her* along too? I didn't say anything of course. I was on my best behaviour – naturally,' he added with a grin.

'I'm relieved to hear it. Beth is all right. I've got used to her. She loves Dad to bits, and that's the main thing.'

Harry rolled his eyes and poured some of the claret he had ordered for his main course into one of the three glasses lined up beside Kate's soup bowl. 'Go on, just try it. It is exquisite. Then I want you to guess the price.'

'Don't be vulgar. I have no intention of guessing the price, though I will give you my unprofessional opinion as to its flavour.' Kate had to suppress real irritation as she raised the crystal glass to her face, the wide balloon of its base resting comfortably in the palm of her hand. It was puzzling, this business of sibling fondness, it went so deep and yet there were so many trying aspects to him, aspects which conveniently melted away when they were apart, but of which she was only too quickly reminded once they got together. Their shared existence in the Pimlico flat had blurred into memories of an idyllic period in her life – freedom in London, enough money to pay the rent and have a little left over for fun, falling in love with Nicholas – when in fact, their three years together had been laced with bickering and stormy disagreements. Harry, in spite of indisputably refined tastes in clothes and food and company, was a domestic slob when it came to daily life. His idea of housework had been to allow their living conditions to deteriorate to a point of unhygienic extremity and then to pay a van load of self-employed women in dungarees vast amounts to apply the snouts of their industrial vacuum cleaners to the cobwebs on the curtains, the scum-coated hairs wound round the plughole and the grit wedged along the creases of the furniture. The smell of their germ-blasting sprays and bleaches would last for days, until it was finally outwitted by the old-man stink of Harry's French cigarettes.

Kate closed her eyes to try and concentrate on the aroma coming from her wine glass. There was a musky flowery smell, with a tang hidden somewhere inside. She took a sip and rolled it round her tongue. The tang came and went, followed by a pleasantly woody aftertaste.

'It seems all right,' was all she remarked, deliberately winding Harry up a bit, since she knew he was looking for exuberance of a more marked kind, 'but I think I'll stick to the white for my fish.'

His handsome face fell, but in a way that only Kate would have noticed. Their conversation then slipped into the inevitable channel of Harry's love-life, or lust-life as Kate teasingly preferred to call it. The theory was, that Harry sought his sister's advice, though in reality, as Kate well knew, he followed instincts of far more primitive origins. Regarding him a little later over a disappointingly soggy chocolate and walnut bavarois, she wondered how long he could go on playing such games, how long his glowing looks would see him through, how long before some kind of disillusionment or fear set in.

'I get bored,' he was saying, 'I always get bored in the end. Why do women cling so?' He shuddered. 'I can't bear being clung on to.'

'What can you expect? You're a bachelor in his prime. You have bagfuls of money, a kinky flat and a fast car. You're the stuff dreams are made of, Harry darling. Women spend their lives fantasising about people like you. So either change your image or shut up and enjoy it.'

He sighed, and signalled for the waiter to fetch him a brandy. Kate, mildly alarmed at the two empty wine bottles before them, refrained from joining him. 'I was hoping for a bit more sympathy,' he admitted ruefully, clasping his hands together on his table mat and bowing his head so that the side panels of his hair flopped down over his temples.

'You know I always tell you everything, Katie,' he added with a spurt of boyish intensity. 'I may be economical with the truth in other areas of my life, but never with you.' He raised his head and looked directly at her, his hard blue eyes shimmering with filial warmth.

'You're getting sentimental, Harry, a sign that you've had too much to drink and that I must go.'

'You'll meet someone one day, I'm sure,' she remarked, once they were outside and strolling towards Victoria, 'someone who, by definition – because she's married or in love with someone else, or held prisoner in some way – you cannot have. You'll love her all right and suffer all the delicious misery that goes with such a state of mind. Your victims succumb too easily, that's their trouble. You should pin a list of rules on your bedroom door, give them an idea of how best to proceed avoiding the pitfalls of dullness and hysteria.'

'It's a bit late for rules in Alicia's case,' he mumbled, frowning at the sky and thrusting his hands into his trouser pockets.

'You mean, it's all gone wrong anyway.' They had reached the crowded portals of Victoria Station and Kate's mind was already upon the unattractive prospect of her homeward journey and the possibility of spicing it up with some Styrofoam coffee and a gossipy magazine.

'I mean she's pregnant and wants to have the thing and screw me for money every week for the rest of my life.' Harry had intended to reveal this disquieting information much earlier on in their meeting and with a far more endearing degree of wit and subtlety, but some kind of fear at how Kate would react had prevented him. She seemed rather acerbic today, not as reassuringly sweet as usual.

'Oh Harry.' Kate stopped walking and looked into his face, hoping to see something other than selfish irritation etched upon it. 'Is that all you can feel about it?'

'At the moment, yes.' He thrust his jaw out at her. 'Alicia has not played fair. She engineered this whole bloody thing, I know she did. She's a scheming bitch.'

'Oh Harry,' Kate said again, very quietly, wanting to take his side but all her instincts pushing her the other way. Hurrying travellers streamed past on all sides, moving round them like water parting at a stone.

'It's true, Kate, I promise. I may be a bad bet, but I do tell my women that – always, right from the start. No false hopes, that's my way. Not raising expectations severely reduces the possibility of disappointments,' he went on, as if reciting something from a manual. 'Alicia knew I wanted nothing long-term,' he punched the palm of one hand with the fist of the other, 'that there were to be no strings attached.'

Kate paused, despairing at her brother's troubling brand of naivety. Or was it naivety, she wondered now, resisting the notion that Harry's attitudes might have evolved into something very much worse, that the core of him represented nothing nobler than disingenuousness, a pure lack of feeling and depth. 'So you think she got pregnant on purpose?' she asked carefully.

'Yup.' He closed his mouth round the word, emphasising the irrefutability of this opinion. His lips, she noticed, were faintly crusted with red from the claret. 'She assured me that there was nothing to worry about,' he went on, 'that it was all under control, that she was on the pill and so on . . . the next thing I know she's asking me what colour to decorate the fucking nursery.' He pushed the hair from his face and smiled at Kate, visibly trying to calm himself. 'I'm only telling you because you are you and it helps. It is, quite blatantly, my problem, and I have every intention of sorting it out.'

'I'm so sorry, Harry,' she murmured, 'what a mess.'

'Would you see Alicia?' he blurted, 'explain what I'm like and so on, how it's all pointless. You're so good at explaining things.'

'You mean, tell her to have an abortion?'

'That sort of thing, yes.' He was looking unattractively eager.

'No, I couldn't do that, Harry,' Kate replied quietly, pressing one hand against the lapel of his suit jacket. 'You shouldn't have asked me. Because although it feels all wrong for you, it might feel right for her.' She was tempted to go on and say a lot of other things, about how little Harry seemed to understand – despite years in their company – of women, how she suspected that decades of easy success and easy living had made him selfish, how she had almost certainly spoiled him all these years, indulging his weaknesses instead of criticising them. But it was too late and perhaps all wrong anyway. Maybe Harry was right and Alicia was a scheming bitch who had planned the whole thing.

After they had said goodbye Kate felt terribly let down. There was an unpleasant drumming inside her head from the wine, and the richness of her dessert had given her chronic indigestion. Since she had just missed a train she decided to touch up her make-up in the Ladies; but having wandered over there found that she did not have the necessary coin to release the lock on the metal turnstile. Not having been in any desperate need until this moment, Kate suddenly found herself hopping from one leg to another, her bladder aching from restraint. A few feet away the toilet assisant mopped casually at some unidentifiable filth on the grey tiled floor, waving the lit stub of a cigarette like a pencil in her free hand, as if to shoo away interruptions. Kate turned in desperation, looking for a friendly, unhurrying face from whom she might beg change.

'Kate Melford!' exclaimed a husky female voice, 'I don't believe it.'

Kate turned, internal problems forgotten, to find herself being warmly greeted by Elizabeth Hale, an old schoolfriend with whom she had kept in touch for years, but hadn't heard from since moving to Elhurst.

'This is too much of a coincidence – I just don't believe it – I was thinking of you only the other day – but how are you, Kate? You look wonderful.'

Elizabeth herself looked much older than seemed fair, Kate thought, although she was extremely well turned out in a style that clearly reflected a serious office life. Her hair, completely grey, was cut into a rather old-fashioned page-boy crop, framing her face in a way that accentuated its length and pallor. She wore a long brown skirt suit, flat black lace-up shoes and a crisp white shirt, with a pretty collar that rose elegantly up her long neck, finishing with a frilly white ruff. She clutched a briefcase under one arm, not of the slim show-off kind, but a bulky old black one with a scuffed gold buckle.

'Have you time for a coffee?'

'I'd love to, but . . .' began Elizabeth.

The two of them stood there, momentarily nonplussed, each wondering whether something more should be made out of this encounter, or whether it should be allowed to pass, as one of those things that happen and get forgotten without being acted upon.

'Give me your address,' urged Elizabeth suddenly, delving in her bag for a pen, 'I knew you were moving and then we moved. How time flies and all that. Isn't it awful to lose track? And I'm up to here,' she touched her temple, 'as always.'

'Still publishing?' asked Kate with an uncharacteristic flicker of envy at the thought of having a real job, instead of being a part-time cook.

Elizabeth nodded, now holding a Biro between clenched teeth and rifling through files for a blank piece of paper.

'Life's hellish really – always on the run – two children showing all the signs of turning into teenage drop-outs – a husband whom I barely see.' Elizabeth scribbled her address and number as she talked. 'I tell you what though, Dotty – Dorothy Smith – do you remember her? – she got in touch with me the other day. She's planning some sort of old school get-together. Could be awful, but you never know. Think about it. I'll be in touch.' And she was gone, leaving Kate feeling somewhat overrun and – having forgotten all about the urges of her bladder – suddenly desperate again to get through the turnstile separating her from the toilets. At which point the cleaner took pity and waved her through a little gate at the side.

'Ten pence to pee – daylight bloody robbery,' she said, her dark face breaking into the broadest of grins, revealing a brilliant set of snow-white teeth and pink gums. 'I'll see you right, sister, don't you worry,' she added, patting Kate on the back and shaking her head with laughter in a way that left Kate wondering suspiciously whether she was party to or victim of the joke.

5

Kate did not get around to telling Nicholas about the complications in her brother's personal life until the morning of their
barbecue lunch, which had begun as a much overdue pay-back
to the Armstrongs and inadvertently grown into something
rather larger and far less likely to succeed. Not only had
Nicholas reacted to a why-do-we-never-see-you tone of voice
from his mother earlier in the week and invited his parents,
but he had also asked Ralph Peckham, an old oil-mining
friend of his who was in the country for just a few days
and who had rung up out of the blue the day before. Kate
was annoyed by these spontaneous invitations, partly because,
in a moment of weakness, she had invited the Sullivans, and
partly because her weekend shopping, cleverly done well in
advance on Thursday morning on the basis of six grown-up
mouths to feed, had been made to look drastically insufficient.

'All I can say is I'm surprised something like this hasn't
happened before,' was Nicholas' response, tossed over one
shoulder while trying to find space in the packed mayhem
of their fridge for three bottles of wine. 'The way Harry lives,
ploughing through women like some kind of crazed bull.' He
stood up, kicked the fridge door closed and dusted his hands
together, as if dismissing the subject.

Kate, having been forced to resort to the expensive but
easy alternative of Mr Edwards' grocery shop yet again, was
unloading the contents of her basket onto the kitchen table,
while a subliminal section of her brain went through the culinary
preparations still required for lunch. Though she was familiar

enough with her brother's shortcomings to see that Nicholas had a point, a reflexive action to do with the illogicality of sibling bonds and the irritations of the morning made her reluctant to agree.

'I might have guessed you'd come up with such a sympathetic response,' she said, inwardly kicking herself for having picked such a bad moment to raise a subject about which she felt a real need to talk.

'Harry does not need sympathy.'

'Maybe not. But it's a horrid situation for anyone to be in.' A lid had come loose on a large pot of double cream, releasing its viscous white contents in a liberal and thorough way throughout the basket and throwing into serious question the possibility of watercress soup as well as fresh garden strawberries for dessert. 'Oh bloody hell.'

'Mother, really,' said James with mock horror at her language, helping himself to a handful of strawberries from the boxful Kate had picked the evening before.

'Help your father, please, James. You can play Boy Scouts together over the barbecue. I shall call Mary and ask her to pick up a pot of cream on her way. Where are Grace and Millie? I could do with some help tidying up.'

'Grace is doing something in the bathroom and Millie is watching.'

'What sort of something?' asked Kate, but then turned on the blender for her soup, drowning out his answer.

'We can't play Boy Scouts, because we are using the other barbecue,' shouted Nicholas

'I didn't know we had another one.' Kate switched the machine off.

'Yes, you did. It lives in the garage and works on gas instead of real fire and my parents gave it to me three years ago and because they are coming we must use it.'

Kate turned her back on her Magimix and crossed her arms. 'I hope you are joking, Nicholas.'

'No, my dear, not for a second.' James, sensing a showdown, backed out of the room.

'Fillet steak, soaked for fourteen hours in a marinade of olive oil, garlic and red wine, will not take kindly to being blasted by a toxic gas flame permanently stuck on maximum. We might as well open a tin of dog's meat right now.'

'Kate,' replied Nicholas wearily, 'you are over-reacting. The gas is not toxic, and there is a panel of knobs marked with encouraging words such as *medium* and *low*.' Bulldog determination had set in as far as the gas barbecue was concerned, a determination that had more to do with guilt about the unforgivable infrequency with which he saw his parents (who only lived in Worthing, a mere thirty-minute drive away), than with any balanced sense of right and wrong. 'If it was Beth and George you would have no qualms about such a small compromise, in the interests of family harmony. In fact I could name several instances . . .'

'Stop, please.' Kate swung back to face her soup which suddenly looked insipid and uninviting, the flecks of green swarming in it like drowning insects. Arguing about their respective families was never a rewarding experience. 'I give in. I don't want to hear about the hateful habits of George and Beth, just as you do not wish me to account for your own confused attitudes towards your family. Charred steak it shall be.' And she turned on the blender to full speed, liberally spattering green droplets across the blue and yellow tiles of her kitchen wall, the side of the fridge and a beloved self-portrait of Millie's from her days at primary school.

Nicholas tramped out to fetch the controversial gift from the back of the garage, eyeing the innocently frothy clouds with suspicion, as if believing that they too would turn against him that day. He was greeted by the sight of his parents' spotless blue Rover nosing its way cautiously between the gateposts of their drive. A jolt of irrational hostility, followed quickly by a surge of guilty affection overtook him. They were precisely three hours early, the silly old duffers. Kate would go mad.

'Mum! Dad!' he called unnecessarily loudly. Dick Latimer, his square black glasses wedged firmly into the gully on the bridge of his nose and sitting very straight behind the wheel, gripping it with both hands, was concentrating too hard on getting parallel with the hedge to acknowledge his son's greeting. Joyce, who never drove herself, fluttered a tentative gloved hand at her son through the car window, as if fearful that a greater show of enthusiasm might in some way detract from the serious business of parking.

Nicholas stood patiently waiting to greet them, feeling strangely separate but well-disposed towards these two frail, but achingly familiar people, now in their late seventies, who, astonishing though it often seemed, had produced and nurtured him for the first eighteen years of his life. His father, though clearly a little stiff from the car, looked robust as ever, his ample girth pressing against the braces of his suit. It was Joyce who caused her son a pang of concern; she seemed so tiny suddenly and so withered that Nicholas instinctively reached out a hand to her elbow as she put two stick legs on the gravel and began to lever herself upright.

'We're a little early, I'm afraid, even though the traffic,' she paused, giving Dick the opportunity to chime in, a duet-like communications system which had grown much more marked in recent years and which irritated Nicholas beyond belief.

'—was bloody awful,' put in Dick, dutifully taking up the theme. 'Summer, tourists and all that. Can't move for cars round us. How are you, Nicholas?' They shook hands. Then James appeared, first smiling and then scowling at the chorus of exclamations about how much he had grown since Easter.

Kate did well with her in-laws, settling Dick in an armchair with the paper and a tankard of beer and directing Joyce to a pile of broad beans and a chopping board. In spite of tensions about families, she was very fond of the two of them, and shared, like Nicholas, an uncomfortable awareness that they seldom got together. It was not purely from laziness or lack of inclination on their part: Joyce and Dick lived in such a tiny house that even they seemed to communicate an understandable reluctance about inviting all the younger Latimers to overpower their sparse spriggy furniture and empty their immaculate larder of its carefully monitored supplies of biscuits and tea-bags. Added to that, the pair of them were usually no good at last-minute invitations, preferring several months' notice for a meeting of any kind, with the firmest commitments about dates and times – a brand of advanced planning at which their son and daughter-in-law had never been very proficient.

With Millie laying cutlery and glasses on the table in the garden and Joyce's arthritic but practised fingers working deftly through the vegetables, Kate's mood began to lift. She was doing a couple of her favourite salads, one with carrots, chicory and raisins in a yoghurty sauce and another with brown rice and fresh herbs. The meal, as it slowly came together, raised her spirits; even the thought of Harry did not seem so awful. He would muddle through somehow, as he usually did, not only surviving, but coming out on top. She grated a small square of Gruyère cheese onto a heap of carrot and raisin, and then stirred in a few generous spoonfuls of mayonnaise and a pot of natural yoghurt. So that just leaves Nicholas to worry about, she thought, idly licking a white blob from her knuckle. It struck her then that her husband had been in a bad mood for as long as she could remember; and that the last few months had been marked by nothing but skirmishes and wobbly truces which seemed to last for no time at all. This, she realised, with a start, instinctively looking round for Nicholas, was something to worry about, if only perhaps because she was beginning to get used to it.

Turning her attention to the French bread, which she began to paste with liberal amounts of mashed garlic and butter and wrap in silver parcels ready for the oven, Kate cast her mind back to previous spells when things had felt so rocky. There had been a bad time when the children were getting her down, making her crabby and crushed with all their demands, particularly the broken nights when James's nightmare phase began and then wouldn't end; then there had been a difficult bit when they first moved to the country and found that, contrary to the optimistic tones of the survey, the house was falling down and they didn't have the money to prop it up. But throughout such episodes there had been an obvious cause for all the friction, something to latch onto and blame, something to talk about and wish away. Whereas now, if there was an identifiable problem, she couldn't put her finger on it.

Perhaps a smoochy dinner would help, Kate thought, pausing for a moment and smiling to herself at the thought; somewhere neutral and new where they could have a proper uninterrupted talk, where Nicholas might own up to whatever it was that was bothering him. It was probably something quite simple and silly, she reassured herself, as she scraped her pretty salads into her best cut-glass bowls; something that just needed proper labelling before it could be treated and persuaded to go away: pressure at work perhaps, she thought hazily, a diagnosis which, while sounding plausible enough, nonetheless did not quite ring true. Nicholas, endearingly in her view, had always had his head in the clouds too much to suffer convincingly from such things.

Kate was wrested back to the present by a glance at the clock and the realisation that Grace still had not emerged from upstairs. 'Where on earth is your sister?' She fired the question at Millie, who was now sitting beside Joyce mutilating shucked beans in an unhelpful kind of way before dropping them from a great height into the awaiting saucepan of cold water.

'She's upstairs doing her hair.'

'What exactly is she doing to it that can possibly have taken since breakfast?'

'It's great actually, Mum, she's using cotton wool and sort of pulling it down like magic.'

This unsatisfactory explanation was all the preparation Kate was to have for turning to find that Grace had transformed her chestnut shoulder length hair into something that appeared to have been streaked with white paint, the sort that would not wash out. Years of experience and memories of her own mother's fruitless outbursts over what she regarded as unsavoury teenage habits, prevented Kate from shrieking, or indeed from saying anything at all.

Grace put both hands to her head, and attempted a smile, though in truth she was in a state of near shock herself. Megan, when recommending the peroxide and cotton wool technique, hadn't warned her quite how startlingly efficient it would be. But having started, one bleached section looked so odd all alone that she had resolutely continued, until only a miserable minority of hairs retained anything like their original hue.

To the intense surprise of all those assembled, it was Joyce who saved the day.

'I always wanted to be blonde,' she said, touching her own wispy purple rinse and patting the space on the kitchen bench beside her as an invitation for her granddaughter to come and sit down. 'Let's have a look then.' Grace walked uncertainly towards her grandmother, not looking at Kate and wringing her hands. 'Hair is the most important thing to a girl, I always say,' clucked Joyce, 'even now, if my hair isn't right, then I'm not right.'

'I suppose I'll get used to it,' murmured Kate, perceiving enough of Grace's own regret to feel something like compassion herself. Her next thought was Nicholas, and the realisation that he had to be warned.

She found him in the garden, setting out chairs and wrestling in vain with the parasol of their garden table, which had a habit of keeling over to one side when confronted by even the flimsiest puff of wind.

'Nicholas, I'm afraid that Grace has bleached her hair completely white.' She rubbed her hands down the front of her apron, though they were perfectly clean and dry. 'It looks quite ghastly, but it's done now and I don't want you to make a thing of it – at least not now because of everyone coming – and perhaps not ever because she clearly hates it and feels awful anyway.'

'White?'

Kate nodded. 'Peroxide.'

Nicholas let go of the umbrella which promptly flopped sideways into its habitual lolling position. 'That's all I needed to hear this morning.' He straightened up and put his hands on his hips, facing Kate aggressively, as if all his anger related directly to her, rather than to the insolent languishing of the garden furniture beside him and the unwelcome news about his daughter. At least that was how it felt to Kate.

'Don't say anything, okay?' she pleaded. 'At least not yet.'

But he just swung his head at her, promising nothing.

The only untroubled aspect of the Latimers' Sunday barbecue was the weather, which simmered stubbornly for them all throughout the afternoon. Kate, who had once believed that, given sufficient quantities of good food and drink, any group of people could be forced to gel into something approaching conviviality, had that theory firmly and finally quashed that day. No one knew anyone well enough to hobble along in conversation for any length of time without eventually requiring the assistance of one of their less than sparkling hosts. The children were of little help: Grace picked at some food and then went upstairs to station herself nearer mirrors and telephones; James hung around for a bit longer before excusing himself on account of a mysterious and unlikely cricket match in the village; and Millie, bored by all the grown-ups, sidled off to watch television, an in-house crime for which both her parents were too preoccupied to volunteer any kind of scolding, either at the time or later.

Although they had never actually met before, the Armstrongs and the Sullivans had heard enough of each to feel mutually discouraged about any prospect of friendship. Victoria Armstrong, who prided herself in being the kind of woman who could wear scarlet lipstick every day and get away with it, could feel only pity for a mouse like Mary Sullivan, with all her faded prettiness and fidgety timidity. As the four of them embarked on a quadrille of handshaking and introductory pleasantries, she eyed Angus with something like curiosity and pity, marvelling that an impressively self-assured, strapping man like him should have ended up with such a frail, sexless thing of a wife.

In recent years Victoria had developed a kind of social double-act with her husband Frank, in which she wittily put him down and took him to task for everything in general, while he offered weak protestations and looked happily despairing. It was quite a good act too, for those first introduced to it, though it palled after a while, as suggestions of other less harmonious themes filtered through.

Victoria was never more vibrant than when in the company of the Latimers, not because she wanted to impress, or because she liked to fluster Nicholas with some flirting, which she did, but because once, a long time ago, she had succumbed to the temptation of confiding in Kate and had felt a need to make up for the weakness ever since.

Victoria's rushed revelations about Frank's affair with a nursery school teacher in Essex – from where they had just moved – had made Kate uncomfortable from the start. While she liked the way women did not shy away from intimacy, compared to men who were so much more inclined to hedge and fence for fear of appearing feeble, Kate could not help feeling that the unveiling of such personal confidences warranted a little longer preparation than the hour or so it took to say hello at the school gates and drink one cup of tea. At the same time she could not help experiencing a shiver of lurid – and slightly self-satisfied – fascination upon hearing a tale of such strife. Nicholas simply would not do such a thing. If he did, it would be the end of them she was sure.

Victoria's subsequent regrets for such a premature outpouring of confidences became apparent the moment Nicholas met Frank and the relationship had to stretch to accommodate four instead of two. The business in Essex was pointedly never referred to again. Though the odd pot of tea was made during term time, the friendship was thereafter pursued along the topical safe-tracks of schools and houses and holidays.

Clad now in psychedelic stretch shorts and a loose black T-shirt, Victoria sprawled on the grass between Nicholas and Ralph Peckham, all thoughts of her husband's indiscretions clearly far from her mind, her red lips hugging one of her white-tipped low-menthol cigarettes, while her eyes widened appreciatively at Ralph's tales of near-death adventures with poisonous snakes and stampeding animals. The children were at her mother's for the weekend and Frank was safely pinioned to a chair at the table, bracketed unhappily between Mary, who could think of nothing to say and Joyce, who felt no need to say anything. Meanwhile Angus, on the other side of her, was regaling Dick with the finer points of a good Spanish grape, unobservant of the fact – so clear to Kate – that his elderly audience wanted nothing more than to be allowed to close his eyes and fall asleep.

'Nicholas,' she called, feeling slightly hysterical and wanting to reassure herself of her one ally in all this madness that they had created, 'could you help a minute?' In fact she had no need of help except of the collapse-in-mutual-horror variety behind the safety of the kitchen door.

But Nicholas was too lost in his own nightmare to enter hers. Ralph was looking sickeningly well, his face smugly tanned and his wavy hair cut in a slick, unruffable shape with only the slightest glimmer of grey above his ears. It was hard to believe, thought Nicholas, studying his friend's self-assurance and well-rehearsed narratives, that here was a man who had moped his way through much of his time at university, struggling with the work and clinging to the coat-tails of people like Nicholas who had a more respectable set of marks and a steadier supply of interesting friends. It made Nicholas wonder what the hell had happened to him since those effortless student days, why he was letting his life drift away in England, not risking anything, not broadening any horizons beyond those offered by an annual cut-price package holiday across the Channel.

'How are Judy and the kids?' he asked, cutting deliberately into one of Ralph's longer stories, wanting to bring him back to earth because he felt so horribly grounded himself.

Ralph's smile never faltered. 'Judy's great. She loves the Middle East – all the servants, the climate – we have a splendid pool in the garden where the boys seem to spend their lives.' He turned to Victoria. 'My wife is the daughter of a colonel,' he said with obvious pride, 'so living abroad is second nature to her.'

'Oh, that's good,' replied Victoria, stubbing out her cigarette on a scuttling ant. 'Mind you, I'd swop Frank's job at the bank and boring old Westbury life for swimming pools and servants any day,' she added, with a slight flutter of her eyelashes, wanting to recharge the conversation, to pull it back from the mundane level of happy families, wanting above all to regain that glimmer of a feeling that Ralph was attracted to her, that he was willing to be pulled back into that conspiratorial fantasy that she now tried to weave with all the married men she fancied.

Kate took a pile of plates out into the kitchen and set them down next to her first-of-the-season strawberries, of which, even though many were no bigger than her thumbnail and some had limey green patches round the stems, she was terribly proud. Mary, after all that, had forgotten the cream, an omission for which she was still apologising some two hours after their arrival. Kate though mildly disappointed, was certain enough of the flavour of her home-grown fruit and the contents of the ice-cream section of her freezer box not to mind unduly. Having taken out a block of vanilla ice-cream and a pot of lemon sorbet, she put the kettle on and began loading crockery into the dishwasher. Beside the kettle the day's post lay still unopened, the envelopes covered in coffee granules and green splashes of soup.

Shuffling through it now, there was one that stood out from the bank statements and direct mail shots since it was addressed to her as Kate Melford, rather than Kate Latimer, in tidy italicised writing that she did not recognise. While the kettle boiled she slid a knife along its sealed edge and pulled out an invitation, filled out in the same perfectly penned style:

Dorothy Gould (nee Smith)
At Home
Reunion Lunch
Thursday 23rd June
12 noon

The address was somewhere in Hampshire, a house with the dubious title of 'Everglades' in a village Kate had never heard of. On the back there was a message in Biro:

'Lizzie mentioned that she had bumped into you. Do hope you can join us. It's girls only – though of course children are welcome too. RSVP asap!'

On impulse, Kate picked up the telephone there and then, dialling the number on the card. Dorothy, whom she recalled as a large matronly girl with hair that reached to her thighs, was not there, but she left a message with a nanny-like sounding person called Drucilla, to the effect that Kate Melford would love to come to the lunch and thank you very much. Nicholas came in just as she put the phone down, closely followed by his mother, tottering under a pagoda of dirty dishes.

'I'll just see to these,' said Joyce, setting them down beside the sink and turning on the hot water tap.

'Leave them, please,' Kate begged, inwardly despairing at the familiar ritual of her mother-in-law tacitly refusing to recognise the superior efficiency of a dishwasher to a bowl of soapy water.

'Could you take the ice-creams out Nicholas – I'll bring the strawberries and the bowls.'

'Who was that on the phone?'

'When? Oh, you mean just now. That was an old schoolfriend
– or rather it wasn't, as she wasn't there. Joyce, please leave
that and come out for some dessert,' she pleaded, 'though I'm
afraid it's strawberries with ice-cream instead of cream, which
isn't exactly as I had planned. Could you bring a couple more
spoons Nicholas, darling?'

'What old schoolfriend?'

'What? Oh, look, I'll tell you later. They'll be thinking we've
abandoned our own party. A tempting thought I must say,' she
added with a giggle, trying to catch Nicholas' eye, but finding
only a turned back and his mother regarding her curiously.

6

Though Kate explained about the phone call later, Nicholas found his thoughts shuffling off in unpleasant – but increasingly familiar – directions to do with how his wife spent her spare time. The result was the burgeoning of a potentially venomous emotion – a hybrid cross of suspicion and jealousy – which sat uneasily next to the healthier loving impulses from which it ultimately derived. If I didn't love her I wouldn't care, he thought bitterly, eyeing Kate through half-closed eyes across a restaurant table later in the week, while she talked at considerable length about their torturous Sunday lunch.

'I thought Angus would never leave. Your poor father, sitting there for all that time, getting such an earful about bouquets and Bordeaux. At one point he actually fell asleep, I'm sure of it, though of course Angus was too full of himself to notice.'

They were having dinner in the new Indian which had opened a few months before in Westbury High Street. Kate was doing what she usually did when her husband chose to remain largely silent, which was to talk too much. She wasn't particularly fond of curry and so had chosen the venue as a kind of unacknowledged treat for Nicholas, a fact which she wasn't going to mention, but which she now could not resist raising, since he seemed so down in the dumps and determined not to enjoy himself.

'I thought you'd appreciate a fiery assault on your palate, while I stand by to put out the flames.'

'Thank you, Kate,' he said stiffly, 'it was a very generous thought to bring me here. Is this to be an annual treat, a cart-the-husband-out-to-keep-him-happy session? Or something more than that?'

Even for Nicholas, who could be brutally acerbic when he wished, these were sharp words, sharper than he intended, though he couldn't muster the energy to apologise.

Kate, deflated and depressed, withdrew. I'm not going to try any more, she thought furiously, we can jolly well sit here in silence. But such a resolution, being so pitted against her nature, could not last for long.

'What is it Nicholas?' she burst out at last, pushing aside a plate of skewered chicken and abandoned fragments of poppadom. 'Is it me? What have I done? It feels like civil war at home at the moment – even the children have noticed.'

Nicholas did not reply.

'Look, there's this old-fashioned approach to a problem of which I'm rather fond; it's called trying to explain what the matter is, thereby giving those involved the best chance of sorting it out. Otherwise known as talking. Call it quaint, but I've seen it work a million times.'

Nicholas, whose meandering suspicions were merely part of a suffocatingly dark frame of mind which he could not understand himself, felt little inclination to invite his energetically cheerful wife to dissect and sort his muddled thoughts into piles that suited and reassured no one but herself.

'There's nothing to explain. I just don't seem to feel wildly communicative at the moment.'

'At the moment? You mean weeks – months – apart from the odd encouraging burst over passing pepper mills and marmalade jars.'

He smiled at her then, his broad mouth curling beautifully and sending shock waves of relief through her, at the rediscovery of this old friend. 'Oh Nicholas,' she whispered, putting her hand on his, 'I do love you.'

'Do you?' The smile wavered.

'Now don't angle for more,' she said, pulling the hand away and trying to tease, anxious to keep open this far more positive vein of communication and, hopefully, develop it into something more permanent than their recent achievements. 'One "I love you" is quite enough for the time being. You might get more later on if you're a good boy and eat up all your supper without exploding.'

Though they managed better after that, with Nicholas visibly relaxing at the excellence of the food and the pleasure of cold beer on a hot throat, a sense of true reconciliation remained elusive. Even the most familiar topics of conversation, the ones they always wheeled out and poked around for a general once-over on the increasingly rare occasions that they dined alone – the children, their parents, his writing – made Nicholas feel like a blind man in a minefield. Wherever his mind turned it perceived nothing but obstacles and problems, an attitude which he would have felt better able to bear – he was sure – if he had felt for one fraction of a second that his wife was experiencing something similar. But Kate, he thought grimly, would always refuse to experience anything of the sort: Kate was a coper, an optimist par excellence, who seemed to grow into each phase of her life with the ease of a blossoming flower.

While Nicholas felt himself slipping back behind clouds of uncertainty, Kate refused to admit to anything but conviction, banging each problem on the head with all the assurance of a hammer to a straight nail: Grace's hair-colour would grow out, James's sullenness would soon pass, Millie wasn't spoilt so much as eccentric, Nicholas' writing was bound to result in success in the end, aging parents were a fact of life and so on, until Nicholas, his plate empty, felt quite stuffed with despair. The only chink in her steel-plated armour of positive thinking, he thought morosely, was over her dear brother Harry, whose dilemmas clearly pained her, but whom, no doubt because she sensed Nicholas' attitude, she now seemed reluctant to discuss.

After offering a pouchful of credit cards Nicholas was forced to resort to the archaic business of writing a cheque, a small irritation which triggered a fresh back-wash of negative thoughts: Why couldn't Kate worry about her husband as much as she did about her brother for a change, he thought stonily, eyeing her over the rim of his spectacles, which had slipped as they always did down the smooth ski-slope of his nose to its very tip? But the faint frown on his wife's face as she cast her eyes over the exuberantly oriental decor of their surroundings was not on account of him, he was sure. Her olive skin glowed with health, her face looked strong and composed; a black silk scarf tied prettily round the thickest part of her hair managed to make her look girlish yet demure, at the same time matching perfectly with her black silk shirt – dotted with brilliant pink flowers – and the velvet leggings that showed the shapely lower part of her legs to excellent effect. She doesn't love me, thought Nicholas, automatically and unwittingly transferring the burden of his own lack of self-esteem to her. She is lying. How can she love me when, compared to her, I am so dowdy, so old, so wrung out.

'Lovely meal,' said Kate on the way home, reaching out to stroke his cheek with the back of her hand.

'Hmm,' he said, sensing only cheerful resolution, a desire for harmony rather than love.

Much later that night Nicholas awoke, drenched in sweat, with a terrible thirst that seemed to run right from the tip of his tongue down into the deepest part of his stomach. Kate was lying on her back, one arm across the soft swell of her chest, the other hanging over the side of the bed, as if poised for a catch. Nicholas, shivering from the cool air on his damp nightclothes, took off his pyjama top and pulled on his dressing gown before quietly leaving the room and tiptoeing downstairs like an intruder.

The fridge hummed gently when he opened it, as if protesting at this unscheduled scrutiny of its innards. He pulled out a pot of mayonnaise, a pack of cheese, a tomato and a carton of orange juice, setting them on the floor beside him like a picnicker. After a few moments, however, he changed his mind, put everything back, extracting nothing but a carton of milk instead. After pouring a generous mugful into a saucepan, he pulled a chair up to the table and began reading one of Grace's magazines. The model on the front had four studs in her nose and matt black lipstick caked onto heart-shaped lips. Headlines boasted a set of intriguing articles inside, including one entitled, 'The Myths Of The Female Orgasm', a topic about which Nicholas felt sufficiently curious to start idly flipping pages.

The thought of sex made him feel guilty. He hadn't laid a finger on Kate in weeks. Having always assumed that couples stopped making love for the simple reason that they had lost interest in each other, Nicholas found his own loss of libido particularly depressing. If only things were so simple. Kate, being Kate, hadn't mentioned it. Bloody typical, he thought, frowning at an unrevealing picture of a man and woman in a limb-hugging clinch; just like Kate to pretend that a floppy goodnight hug would do just as well.

'*The vaginal and clitoral climax* . . .' he read and then stopped, shuddering at the crude terminology, the implication that there were rules and methods, rights and wrongs to it all. He gently closed the magazine and put his head in his hands. Perhaps Kate genuinely didn't miss their sex-life, he thought wretchedly; perhaps she was bored anyway; perhaps . . .

This discouraging chain of thoughts was interrupted by a muffled noise, coming from the hall, or possibly the landing. With one eye on the iron poker that they used to stoke the Aga, Nicholas put his head round the kitchen door and listened, his heart drumming, his mind alert. Another noise, definitely coming from upstairs, drew him further out. Then he smelt a whiff of smoke, which prompted him to move with far greater speed, taking the steps two at a time, up to the first landing where James's and Grace's bedrooms were.

Without any of the hesitation he would have felt during the day, Nicholas opened the door to his son's bedroom. James was sitting cross-legged on the floor beside two lit candles, precariously balanced on books in pools of melted wax, with a cigarette hanging out of the corner of his mouth and his Walkman headphones pressed to his ears. His eyes, which had been closed in order to concentrate better on his music, opened wide at the sight of his father. He took the cigarette from his mouth but did not stub it out in the ash-tray by his knee, a tin lid which had clearly served a similar purpose on many previous occasions.

'James,' Nicholas felt as if he might implode from the sheer effort of controlling his voice, 'I don't know what to say.'

'Then don't say anything,' replied his son with the cool insolence that seemed to invade his expression of even the simplest emotions these days.

'Put that bloody thing out.' Nicholas switched on the light, the crude glare making both of them screw up their eyes. 'And those bloody candles. You'll set the whole house alight.'

James, with studied slowness, pressed his cigarette into the warped, yellowing metal and then wet his finger-tips before squeezing the life out of the candle-flames.

'I suppose you do this every night?'

'No, not usually. Only when I can't sleep.'

'And why can't you sleep?' asked Nicholas tightly, too aware that this was some kind of critical juncture in the business of parenting teenagers to spare a thought for the potentially illuminating parallel offered by his own increasingly frequent bouts of insomnia.

His son shrugged. 'My mind goes crazy sometimes, like it can't stop.'

'And you think inhaling nicotine will calm it down?'

'Something like that.'

He held out his hand, which, to his horror, trembled slightly. 'Give those cigarettes to me, please, and the matches.' It was pointless, he knew, but he felt he had to do something. He pointed at the health warning taking up a good quarter of the packet. 'I don't need to tell you . . .'

'But you used to smoke –' began James.

'That was a very long time ago, when nobody knew any better.'

'And Uncle Harry—'

'Your uncle is hardly a role model for society. Now stop answering back and get into bed. Do I need to say,' he added, uncomfortably aware that he did not sound threatening enough – that he had no resource for appearing threatening at all – 'that I do not wish anything like this to happen again.'

'You mean, you don't want to catch me again.'

'Don't be so bloody cheeky. And you can forget your allowance this month. If this is what you choose to spend your money on, then it's a total waste.'

Despising his lack of inspiration, Nicholas closed the door and traipsed back to the kitchen, thinking miserably that he had lost not only Kate but his children as well.

The milk, left to its own devices for so long, had boiled over, creating a smell far worse than anything generated by James's nocturnal antics. The saucepan, a shiny non-stick one which Kate usually reserved for floury sauces, had a dried brown mess encrusted down its sides and bottom and sizzled violently when Nicholas submerged it in the washing-up bowl.

'Fuck,' he said, letting go of the saucepan handle and seizing clumps of hair in his hands, as if he might tear it out by the roots.

Outside, the first twitter of birds signalled the start of the day, another record-breaking scorcher, by the look of the seamless violet of the sky.

7

After dropping the children at the school gates Kate drove into Elhurst meaning only to fly into the dry cleaners with her red dress, but seeing a parking space outside the new bookshop she found herself slotting into that instead. The peeling paint of what had once been Elhurst's only antiques shop – though now there were two other highly successful competitors – had been replaced by a deep glossy green front, embossed with large gold italics that said: *KINGFISHER BOOKS*. Kate stopped to look in the window, the red dress flying out behind her, its wide panels tagging in the warm wind: all very self-consciously tasteful and cultured, she observed, noting that alongside the books there were a number of carefully selected videos – Beatrix Potter for the children and Shakespeare for the grown-ups – all arranged in neat piles and semicircles on a lush bed of red velvet. In the window on the other side of the door was a large photograph of a local author of whom she had never heard, surrounded by promotional material for his latest detective story.

I'm not in the mood, she thought glumly, turning away. But her eye was caught by a carousel of cards inside. Kate liked buying cards; it gave her an echo of the feeling she got when looking round picture galleries, something she hadn't done for years. Slinging her dress over one arm, she pushed the door open and stepped inside. The place smelt strongly of new carpet mingled with paint gloss. Scores of unsorted books were stacked along several of the shelves. A man in a black polo neck sweater and black jeans was standing halfway up a ladder with his back to her, fixing up a sign that said FICTION A – D.

'Won't be a minute,' he called at once, not turning round.

'Oh don't worry,' Kate replied quickly, 'I'm only looking.' She spun the card stand round, casting her expert eye over the kaleidoscope of cellophane-wrapped pictures. There were a series of pencil sketches of dancers that she quite liked, ballerinas doing up laces and adjusting tutus. Thinking of Millie she picked out the prettiest before turning the stand to study a set of still-life water-colours: apples in bowls, glasses by bottles and jugs of flowers, familiar shapes in startling colours, the everyday made new, she thought with a sigh, feeling suddenly uncontrollably depressed.

Suffering a curry had not changed a thing. Nicholas had hunched over his mug of coffee that morning with a look of such pain on his face that, compelled by an increasingly burdensome need to sort things out, not to have any twists of misunderstanding to darken her day, Kate had felt bound to speak. In spite of every effort to the contrary, a thin vein of impatience now laced her enquiries as to the health of her husband's state of mind, induced by her consistent failure to elicit a satisfactory response.

'Is anything the matter, Nicholas?' she had asked with as much concern as she could muster, feeling like a doctor with a trying patient.

'I got very little sleep,' he growled, staring hard at James, who stared even harder at his bowl of corn pops.

'Perhaps you should take the day off – you do look rather tired,' she added, her tone softening. She was on the point of moving towards him, her hand raised to touch, but he pushed his chair back abruptly, knocking into her knees.

'Don't be ridiculous, Kate, I'm just tired,' he retorted, taking her quite roughly by the arm and propelling her out of the kitchen and into the drawing room, where he told her of James's nocturnal smoking, describing the episode with such over-reactive intensity that Kate found her own responses jumping the other way, out of an instinctive need to redress the balance.

'Yes, well I knew he smoked – his clothes reek of tobacco sometimes.'

'Well thanks for telling me.' Nicholas clapped his hands together and took a step backwards, surveying her with undisguised hostility. 'Thank you indeed for sharing this insignificant information with the father of the errant child.'

'Oh Nicholas, for goodness sake, they're teenagers, this is the kind of thing teenagers do. You did it too, remember?'

'Not till I was considerably older,' he declared, 'and at least to the background of parents who could be bothered to care.'

Kate grew angry then. 'Of course I bloody well care,' she hissed, 'but overreacting to something like this will only alienate him, set him against us so that when some real crisis occurs in his life he will turn away.'

'Real crisis? What are we talking here? An overdose of expensive tablets? Or simply some nasty business with a needle?'

Kate swallowed hard, unable to understand why this small drama, involving the child whom they both loved beyond words, could be turned into such an issue for disagreement. 'It sounds as though you did absolutely the right thing last night, Nicholas. And of course I shall speak to James myself, remind him, with all the vehemence that I possess, that smoking is forbidden at school and at home, and that it would pain me greatly to see him poison his system with nicotine or any other drug. Okay?' She crossed her arms and pursed her lips, daring him to come back with a better reply.

'What does it feel like, Kate,' he said with dreadful solemnity, 'to be the one who is so perfectly under control, the one who does not worry, the one for whom everything is so delightfully manageable and containable, the one who's business it is to be happy?' Though it sounded like a question, Nicholas, upon uttering the last word, turned and left the room, leaving Kate quite shaky at the sharp cut of his delivery, the terrifying sense of intense dislike behind the words. It was altogether new to feel such things from Nicholas.

If he hates me, she thought, spinning the carousel of cards at a speed for which it had not been designed, then there isn't any point to anything.

'I take it you don't think much of my card selection then?'

'Pardon? Oh sorry.' Kate put up a hand to stop the spinning stand. 'No, I do, I think they're lovely – I'm going to buy several.' She pulled out another of the ballerinas and one of a fruit bowl. 'I was miles away, I'm afraid.'

'I could see that,' said the man, walking over to the counter and beginning to sort through a stack of letters. 'I hope you're not going to spend money out of guilt,' he added, looking up from his letters with a half smile that made Kate feel unaccountably foolish.

'Guilt? About what?'

'For being so aggressive with my card holder, of course.'

Kate, nonplussed, began to mumble an apology, but he interrupted.

'Splash out on some books too while you're in the mood. The latest Philip Langton is very good – unputdownable, as they say, if you like that kind of thing, which,' he cocked his dark head at her with unbelievable impudence, 'I suspect you don't.'

Kate, determined not to appear flurried, marched over to the counter and placed her three greetings cards beside a collection pot for cancer research. The man picked them up and examined each one for its price, before punching the numbers into his till. His hair was very dark and long, brushed back off his face and curling at the ends. Though as a rule Kate did not much like long hair on men, associating it with grease and tangle and baldness on top, she found herself conceding that in this particular case it suited the bearer rather well: the hair was indisputably well groomed, but at the same time leant a mysterious, Bohemian air to his appearance, an impression which was none the less effective for being so carefully engineered. One of his ears was pierced, she noticed; she could see the small crack of a hole in the lobe. Elhurst folk wouldn't like earrings in shopkeepers, she thought, unclipping her purse to search for pound coins.

'I usually wear a stud,' he murmured, without looking up from his task of placing the cards in a slim white paper bag, 'a gold one, very small and unobtrusive. Do you think it might frighten the locals?'

Kate, so disarmed at having her thoughts read and unashamedly remarked upon, found herself stammering a convoluted response about not thinking so and not being sure and loving earrings.

She was at the door, longing to be gone, when he said, 'Are you the Kate Latimer who cooks?'

She caught her breath and spun round, her hand still on the door handle. 'How on earth . . . ?'

He patted the side of his nose and grinned, revealing large, but perfectly aligned ivory teeth. Only the incisors protruded slightly, their sharp points lending a wicked slant to even the mildest smile.

Kate experienced mixed sensations of panic and flattery. Though instinct told her the time had come to leave, curiosity prevailed and she remained hovering in the doorway.

'Your friend Mr Edwards pointed you out to me the other day. There's Kate Latimer who cooks, he said, which interested me, as I cook myself – my most favourite hobby, I'd say.'

'Oh really?' A dusty gust of air blew in the door, reminding Kate of an outside world to do with dry cleaners and grumpy husbands.

'My name's Max Urquart,' he said coming forward with his hand extended, as if they had only just met and were standing at a party instead of in a bookshop. 'I hope I haven't appeared rude, only I tend to speak as I think and it puts some people off. I've moved into the old mill house by the river. It's falling down, but very lovely. I was in Suffolk before, but got drummed out by local competition.'

His fingers felt floppy and cool. Kate quickly pulled her hand away. The way Max Urquart had volunteered so much information about himself imposed a sense of obligation that she should do the same, but she resisted, unable to shake off a sense of impropriety about it all.

'Kate Latimer,' she said, though this was clearly a redundant piece of information, and then nearly added, and I'm married, which would have been irredeemably gauche. 'We live near Chivers Farm. I'd better go.' She waved her red dress. 'Dry cleaners next.'

'See you around,' he said casually, before sliding his slim frame behind the cardboard cut-out of Philip Langton and starting to rearrange some of the books.

8 ʃ

When Ralph rang on Thursday to express his thanks for lunch and say goodbye Nicholas rashly offered to take the afternoon off and drive him to the airport. Meeting up this time had been much more unsatisfactory than usual, partly because Ralph had devoted so much of his energies towards impressing Victoria Armstrong, and partly because Nicholas had felt in no mood for their usual bantering exchanges. He was left with the nagging sense of unfinished business and the disheartening realisation that unless they clawed their way back to a certain point this time they might never bother to do anything more than exchange Christmas cards again.

It only remained to inform Janice of this uncharacteristically impetuous change of plan.

'Marketing won't like it,' she said, testily, touching the end of her pencil with the tip of her tongue before drawing a bold line through the various appointments listed for the afternoon.

'Marketing can lump it,' Nicholas retorted, thinking, not for the first time, that there were certain major drawbacks to inheriting a secretary whose time spent working amongst the higher echelons of the company greatly outdid his own.

Janice picked up her large tortoiseshell glasses and slotted them carefully onto her face, mindful of disturbing the sculpted tumble of curls created by her heated rollers the night before. 'I only meant that we have rescheduled your three o'clock slot twice already and the NPD people are keen for the report . . .'

'Thank you, Janice, I am aware of the inconvenience I shall cause.' Nicholas gripped the files under his arm more tightly and withdrew into the sanctity of his own office. Janice was an excellent PA. Everybody said so. After her boss of five years – a doggedly hard-working man called George Marshal – had unexpectedly got the push during a flurry of redundancies earlier in the year Janice had nearly left herself, or so it was rumoured. Nicholas, as he frequently reminded himself, was very lucky to have her at all.

But does she feel lucky to have me? he wondered, leaning his forehead against the stainless glass of his window and staring down into the dazzling pool of yellow below, like a diver gazing from a cliff to the sea. Hidden colours surfaced and shifted as he watched, swallowing his vision, pulling him down into the aching brightness, pressing round him until he could barely breathe. It was hard to raise his head, to wrest himself back to the stuffy shell of the present. As he turned back to his desk he noticed that he had left a visible smudge on the pane, a memento of his hot skin, greasy and blurred, like a botched finger-print.

Tossing a postcard of a cartoon bull slurping from a bottle of wine into his waste-paper basket and beginning a hasty rearrangement of papers into tidy piles, Nicholas allowed his thoughts to focus more tightly on George Marshal. The bull postcard was from him, smugly informing the department of his new life as a restaurateur in southern Spain, telling them that the future couldn't be more promising. So much for the tragedy of redundancy, thought Nicholas with a cynical humph, recalling the hushed horror with which Marshal's enforced retirement had been greeted just a few months before. It all sounded bloody marvellous to him.

Nicholas decided to go home first, so that he could change into something more comfortable and fix himself a sandwich for lunch. As he let himself into the dim quietness of the hall and sidled past the fitness bike, he felt almost like an intruder. It was so unusual to be in the house without Kate there, or one of the children hovering in the background. And having thought this, Nicholas immediately minded that this should be so, that he should feel, even for a second, like a stranger in his own home.

Slinging his jacket over the banister, he made his way upstairs, past the print of Arundel Castle that his parents had given him years before, past the oil-painting of splodgy flowers that Kate so loved, across the landing to the bedroom. Something about the neatness of it, the perfect smoothness of the duvet, the plump rise of the pillows, the poise of all their familiar knick-knacks made him hesitate for an instant, as if wary of imprinting anything of himself upon such an untarnished scene. He sat down on the edge of the bed and pulled off his shoes and socks, letting them fall anyhow, enjoying the feel of some cool air between his toes. He flexed his feet, curling them with prehensile ease into the deep pile of the carpet.

The contents of his side of the wardrobe looked uninviting, his clothes limp and dull. Nicholas rifled disconsolately through the hangers several times before settling for a relatively new pair of black corduroys, which were far too hot for such a day but which most closely attained the smart-but-casual look that he had in mind. To accompany them he selected a plain white cotton shirt with a button-down collar and long sleeves. Aware that he was in a mood to care very much how he looked, Nicholas dared to consider why this might be so. Ralph was one of his oldest friends, one who, as a drinking ally at college, had seen him in indescribable extremes of dishevelment and squalor. How absurd, he told himself, to start minding, at this advanced stage in their relationship, about the impression he created on such a man.

Having changed, Nicholas stood sideways to examine his reflection, sucking in his stomach and pulling out his shirt at the waist so that it billowed more flatteringly round the top of his cords. His bottom looked very big, he decided, patting it hard and tweaking the material on the backs of his trousers. There had been a time, he recalled with a sigh, when his figure could have been categorised as bony, a halcyon, unappreciated era when the unimaginable calories of countless bacon sandwiches and slabs of chocolate were mysteriously and effortlessly absorbed into his body without any side-effects at all. A far cry from the troubles of the last decade, when every spoonful of ice-cream, every cake-crumb and biscuit-nibble seemed to settle in his system with the immovability of lead.

Exercise, a facet of life which had enjoyed a low priority in Nicholas' youth, had now become as unwelcome and boring a preoccupation as the question of how many potatoes found their way onto his plate. The grim truth presented by the bathroom scales had even, in extreme instances, impelled him to resort to the repellent activity of jogging through Elhurst woods, coincidence and sods law ensuring that on each occasion he was forced to wheeze greetings to every hearty walker and dog owner in the village. The exercise bike, sent for from a promising special offer in a Sunday colour supplement, had at first seemed to offer the perfect discreet alternative to this unhappy business of dodging dog muck and waving at people he had no wish to see. But after a few thigh-burning sessions, his enthusiasm – not aided by severe teasing from Kate – had palled. Shaping his legs, he decided, was least of his problems; in fact they represented one of the few parts of his anatomy which were still mercifully presentable.

Some tenuous connection to this ultimately dispiriting study of his figure caused Nicholas to get out his contact lens case from behind the cough medicine in the bathroom cupboard. He did so gingerly, as though confronting an old, unwelcome adversary. He had bought the lenses only a few months before, during a regular check-up for his glasses, after boldly deciding that gold spectacles looked daft, that he no longer relished the faintly scatty, professor-like image which had so attracted him to them in the first place. Soft contact lenses, tinted blue, were much more obviously appealing to a man who, though only forty-six, felt the unspeakable fact of a fiftieth birthday rushing at him with all the speed and finesse of an approaching tornado.

But the contact lenses had failed to meet even the lowest of Nicholas' expectations. After inserting them according to instructions, there ensued a period of intense eye-watering, followed by a stinging irritation that grew steadily worse, pitching towards a feeling akin to that of being forced to stand wide-eyed in a sandstorm. When Nicholas took them back to the optician, it was suggested, with some mirth, that he didn't cry enough, that his lachrymal ducts were too inept to cope with lenses – a diagnosis which Nicholas irrationally chose to find demeaning. He insisted on trying again, begging for a different prescription, a different make of lense, anything to give it a second go. With the replacement pair, the sandstorm effect was less intense, though his eyes still ached in a particularly gritty kind of way if they were worn for any length of time.

Instead of clearing, his reflection in the bathroom mirror blurred. He blinked hard and blew his nose on a square of loo roll. It was just a question of bothering to do it more often, he told himself, as he unwound a spare wad of toilet paper and groped his way out onto the landing. If only Kate was a bit more supportive about such things, he was sure he would be better about sticking to them. But Kate's idea of moral support was simply to say that it didn't matter, that she loved him as he was, that life was too short to torture oneself with lenses and running and resisting puddings. She wore glasses now too – when she remembered to pull them down from the top of her head – for reading and watching television; they made her look deliciously studious, younger if anything, her glassy brown eyes somehow appearing even larger through the slope of the lenses.

After a conscientiously healthy sandwich of brown bread and ham with lots of lettuce and only the thinnest spread of mayonnaise, Nicholas felt justified in taking a couple of chocolate biscuits for the journey, a decision which, due to the extreme temperature of the car, proved less than satisfactory. Instead of making them last, as he had intended, the melting chocolate encouraged eating in a way that was too gooey and rushed to be pleasurable. By the time he turned from Elhurst onto the motorway, his fingers felt unpleasantly sticky on the steering wheel and there was a small brown stain next to a button in the middle of his clean white shirt.

Kate had planned to make a chocolate roulade to take to Dorothy's, but changed her mind at the thought of a two-hour drive across the home counties in a stinking hot car. She made an apple flan instead, perfect layered crescents of fruit on a pastry and cream base with a shiny surface finish of caramelised brown sugar. Dorothy, who had spent a considerable portion of the week baking for her buffet lunch, was mildly put out at being presented with such a gift, seeing at once that it constituted quite a challenge to her own culinary efforts.

'Kate, how exquisite – what a kind thought,' she chimed, while echoes of old school rivalries stirred dimly at the back of her mind. 'And you look just the same,' she exclaimed, standing back to admire Kate's outfit with genuine enthusiasm. The sleeveless cotton shirt hung, cool and loose, over her full beige skirt, looking as though it had been freshly drawn from her wardrobe instead of from a long stint behind the wheel of a hot car. The finishing touch was a long thin piece of fine beige silk which Kate had wound loosely round her neck, its ends trailing back over each shoulder like gossamer wings.

'And so do you,' replied Kate without thinking, when in fact Dorothy looked much scrawnier than she recalled and her hair, though still quite long, now had a fringe, a straggly wispy thing that seemed permanently caught up in her eyelashes and made Kate want to brush it all away.

The car journey had been long enough for Kate to wonder whether she was entirely wise in imagining it might be anything other than disquieting to see so many old and forgotten faces again. Though she had kept in touch with a handful of schoolfriends for several years after leaving, marriage and house-moves had long since cut any remaining ties. There was an aspect of the ease with which she had allowed this to happen that sometimes worried her, since it confirmed a self-sufficiency that she would almost rather not have had. Apart from her family and Nicholas she felt an almost shameful lack of need of other people, a lack which she liked to blame on time and opportunity, and which she covered by befriending people like Mary who were so handy and unthreatening.

Apart from Elizabeth, whom she had seen most recently, Kate found the task of catching up on fifteen or twenty years of news with so many other people almost too daunting to be bothered with it. After relating an unsatisfactorily shallow-sounding potted history of herself to a couple of people, she sank back into a listening role instead, finding that it took only a couple of questions to encourage the most interesting revelations. Though what in fact struck her most keenly was how little they had all changed. A couple of marriages had floundered, several of their parents had died, someone had lost a brother to a religious sect, but other than that it seemed to her that they were all striding on through the middle years of their lives, hauling husbands and children in their wake, accepting the limitations and options of whatever circumstances prevailed without any fuss at all. Though she felt there was something to admire in this, it depressed her too. Sitting in a deep armchair on her own for a few minutes, stirring cream into her coffee, Kate felt something like a presentiment for the future, a fear of what there was to come, of what suffering must surely await them all.

'Glad you came?' Elizabeth, stirring her own coffee, came to perch on the wide leather arm of Kate's hideaway.

'I think so. But it is strange – I feel as if I know everyone and yet I don't.'

Elizabeth laughed. 'I know what you mean. The only person I see anything of these days is Charlotte Jewel over there – mainly because she lives near me and her husband edits books, so there's an extra link. Friendship is the most haphazard of things.'

'Yes, I suppose it is.' Kate ran her finger-tip round the rim of her empty cup. 'I feel I should be rushing round taking down phone numbers,' she paused, 'but I don't think I shall – it will only make me feel guilty about not calling and not arranging to meet – apart from you,' she added quickly, realising that she was in danger of sounding rude. 'It's just that I find there isn't the time these days – what with one's family and everything.'

'You've no need to tell me,' agreed Elizabeth who then looked at her watch and swore. 'I've simply got to go. An afternoon off – interviewing Scandinavian au-pairs.' She scowled. 'A twenty-minute chat on the phone during which one is supposed to be able to decide who won't resort to physcial violence while supervising homework, cooking fish-fingers and moping about the lack of a social life. Charlie and I simply can't bear the ones that hover round the kitchen, chain-drinking coffee and missing boyfriends. Still, mustn't complain, I suppose – our last girl was marvellous.' With that Elizabeth downed the last of her coffee and stood up, looking round for some convenient niche on which to deposit her cup. 'By the way, your apple tart was absolutely delicious. There's not a crumb left, had you noticed?'

Kate blushed and muttered a thank you.

'I don't suppose you've ever thought about doing something in that line?' Elizabeth slung her bag over her shoulder, clearly in a hurry, but standing determinedly before Kate now that the idea had taken hold.

'I do a bit of cooking locally – I don't enjoy it much, to be honest. I like cooking for Nicholas and me – making up things – not having to fill out orders.'

'No, I didn't mean that. I meant writing your recipes down, getting some kind of book together. We publish a couple of cookery books – you wouldn't believe how popular they can be, especially if there's a health or slimming angle.' She handed Kate a business card. 'It's worth thinking about.'

Kate stood up, took the card and kissed Elizabeth on the cheek. 'It's a fine idea, but I'm certain I haven't got the time or the self-discipline for something like that. And I could hardly advocate slimming,' she added laughing openly, quite at ease with the comfortable curves of her figure, knowing that they had surprisingly little to do with how attractive she felt or appeared.

'You could try a kitchen garden approach,' called Elizabeth over her shoulder, as she headed off in search of their hostess, 'from garden to cooking pots – home-grown greens – that kind of thing.'

Kate shook her head, smiling at such an improbable idea. She was on the point of making her farewells when Charlotte Jewel approached to say that a group of them were going on a walk and did she want to come too. Though reservations flooded her mind, Kate found herself accepting, saying that a walk was just what she needed after such a lavish lunch. Behind them various infants were being rounded up and two dogs, let out from a long spell in a closed room, were yelping with anticipation, their claws scratching and sliding on the polished parquet of Dorothy's hall floor.

'We'll walk to the White Horse,' called Dorothy, raising a walking-stick and speaking as if she were addressing an army corps. 'And I mean the one on the hillside, not the pub down the road.' The assembled party laughed good-naturedly, nudging each other and exchanging looks at the ridiculous thought of a group of women going drinking on a Thursday afternoon. Kate's weak smile went undetected. She felt faintly nauseous, hating the feeling of being part of a chattering female gang, wondering at herself for not having escaped like Elizabeth, for having felt obliged to conform, when not conforming was one of the most pleasurable aspects of growing up.

9

Harry strode into the airport departure hall with his hands in the trouser pockets of his suit. The front of his double-breasted jacket hung open, revealing the pink and purple zigzags of his silk tie, carefully coordinated with the shimmer of pink in his shirt and the perfectly folded silk handkerchief in his breast pocket. He walked with a slight swagger, whistling, looking about him with bright intelligent eyes, a man ready to take on the world. It was typical of Harry that, despite the potentially stressful purpose of his visit to the airport, he nonetheless had the gall to appear so totally casual and collected. Some fifty thousand pounds teetered on the success of his errand – a last-ditch attempt to persuade an extremely senior executive target called Warner, to change his mind about a job offer. Harry's company had identified an excellent post for the man, but one which after much chest-beating and for a series of convoluted, unconvincing reasons he had ultimately chosen to reject. If Harry could persuade Mr Warner to change his mind and take the job, twenty-five per cent of the salary would be his, a highly satisfactory contribution to the prospect of an already bulging annual bonus. It was the sort of challenge Harry relished: backs-to-the-wall time, with everything to play for and everything to lose.

Manoeuvring Mr Warner also constituted a welcome alternative to wrestling with the problem of an increasingly troublesome Alicia. At the memory of their most recent lunch Harry clenched his hands into fists in his pockets. None of his slick negotiating methods were helping him there. He had more hope of sending a client to Mars, he thought grimly, digging his nails into the flesh of his palms, than of persuading his lover to do anything against her will.

Whereas Mr Warner's dilemmas were part of a reassuringly familiar scenario – old loyalties to his current employer, fear of unnecessary risk, the temptation to play things safe – the arena in which he found himself confronting Alicia was unchartered territory, hazardous emotional stuff at which he was no good at all. Even offering her a two-week cruise in the Caribbean to recover from the trauma of an abortion had caused her to do nothing more encouraging than wave a forkful of spinach leaves in his face and shake her pretty blonde head in despair. She wanted the baby, she said, and that was that, whether Harry was interested or not. She would make no demands, she said, beyond the most basic monthly allowance. Harry's handsome jaw tensed just thinking about it. Women who promised not to make any demands were, in his wide experience, the ones guaranteed to make claims of the most intrusive kind. He ground his teeth. A baby was such a disturbingly vivid notion, a growing noisy thing that would no doubt make demands of its own, something with the capacity to mess his life up for good.

As the leather soles of his suede brogues clipped softly across the expanse of polished linoleum, Harry channelled his mind towards the more soothing prospect of a drink. He quickened his pace, his long arms swinging loosely at his sides. He would play it by ear as usual, he decided, softly softly, the kid-glove approach. There was over an hour until the flight, ample time to make his case.

On reaching the door to the first-class departure lounge Harry paused for a moment to run his hands back through his glossy head of hair and to do up the buttons of his jacket. With a last pat to his pockets he entered and made straight for the corner section of comfortable chairs, where a respectable, dark-haired man in his late forties sat, an open briefcase on his knee and what looked like a glass of mineral water at his side.

'Mr Warner,' said Harry, extending his hand well in advance of arriving beside his client, 'how good of you to see me, when I know you are so pushed for time. If, as I understand, it's Riyadh you're going to, you'll be needing a drink. Scotch on the rocks was your tipple, wasn't it, American style with a glassful of ice?

I'll join you.' He signalled to the waiter, noticing with a start as he did so that his brother-in-law was seated in the corner with a sun-tanned man whom he did not recognise.

Nicholas was sitting with his back to the door, his third gin and tonic in hand, listening attentively to Ralph's vivid account of job prospects in Dubai, the suitcases of money that could be made there by any businessman with a bit of flair and enough common sense to play the game according to Middle Eastern rules. They were directly below the blissful cool of an air-conditioning vent. Having arrived feeling hot and cross, Nicholas was now lolling comfortably in the curving soft leather of his chair, picking at the salty remains of what had once been a full bowl of mixed nuts, nodding his head sagely whenever Ralph paused. He had no intention of going to Dubai; but it was nice to pretend that he could, to imagine for a brief spell that such glamorous options – an existence involving Range Rovers and swimming pools – really were open to him, that his life was not, after all, a spiralling sealed capsule of inevitable conclusions.

'A marketing man came out just the other month,' Ralph was saying,' can't remember where the hell from now – but he seems a good sort. A bit younger than you maybe – stunning wife and a small baby – I think he's going to do very well. Got that look about him, if you know what I mean.'

Nicholas nodded, a thread of gloom snaking its way through the solace woven by gin and nuts.

'You ought to come out and stay – you, Kate and the children,' Being sensitive enough to recognise that for whatever reasons Nicholas was not on top form, Ralph's face lit up with an enthusiasm fuelled by a genuine desire to help. It never occurred to him that his own fresh-faced buoyancy, together with the indisputably expensive cut of his flawless buckskin jacket and the youthful, flattering cut of his white jeans had been significant contributory factors to Nicholas' underlying state of mind. 'It would give you an idea of what it's like over there. I could introduce you to a few people, check out the options and so forth.'

Nicholas leant forward, rolling his glass between both palms. 'That's very kind, Ralph, and I would love to take you up on it, but,' he paused, 'it's Kate, you see. I'm afraid she wouldn't warm to the idea – can't bear to be too far away from England – bit of a home-girl and all that.' He smiled and sat back, relieved to have diverted a potential collision with reality so deftly.

'Everything's all right in that department, is it Nick?' asked Ralph smoothly, crunching an ice-cube between his teeth and casting his friend a look that suggested it was time to talk frankly.

'You mean Kate?' Nicholas pressed the tip of his forefinger down onto the last salty crumbs in the nut bowl and then placed it on his tongue. All his instincts jangled in alarm at the thought of talking about Kate. It was bad enough feeling the need to confide in anyone about anything, let alone when the worries were so confused, so horribly related to the belittling business of not being happy with himself. The thought that Kate no longer loved him, no longer needed him, sat like a stone in his heart.

Ralph, moving towards very different conclusions, remarked that all marriages ran into problems at some stage, hinting with a clumsiness bordering on enthusiasm that he had strayed from the bumpy track of marital fidelity himself from time to time. While a small, ignoble part of him relished this excuse to point out the continuing health and success of his sexual appetites, his primary aim was in fact to make Nicholas feel more at ease with similar temptations, to say, man-to-man as it were, this was how things were, this was what life was like, and that none of it need involve guilt or a sense of failure about loving one's family. But since the focus of Nicholas' concerns was quite the opposite of what Ralph imagined, these half confessions were quite wasted on him.

'The writing is not going well,' declared Nicholas abruptly, wishing that this truthful statement about his feeble literary struggles could in fact account for his state of mind. 'I'm working on a play – quite a complicated plot—'

'Nicholas, I thought it was you.' Harry was standing beside him, appearing taller than usual and looking infuriatingly pleased with himself. Nicholas stood up so quickly that he was almost overcome by a spell of dizziness that induced a momentary but dismaying temptation to place a hand on his brother-in-law's pin-striped arm in order to steady himself.

'Ralph, this is Harry Melford, Kate's brother. He plies a

deathly trade in the city, hunting heads and offering them up for sale.'

'A headhunter? Good man.' Ralph shook Harry's hand. 'Which firm? I used Coopers when I made my last move – very fine operators – I've got no complaints at all.'

'Coopers are amongst the best,' conceded Harry, taking a seat beside Ralph and drawing deeply on a freshly lit cigarette. Mr Warner, whom he had successfully talked round after just thirty-six minutes, was a non-smoker of the most vehement kind. It had taken considerable powers of self-control to refrain from lighting up, especially after the celebratory turning point in their conversation when Harry realised he had won him round.

The convective powers of the air-conditioner seemed ingeniously designed to convey the smoke from Harry's lips on a curving but deadly accurate course into Nicholas' eyes. In consequence, his lenses, about which he had temporarily forgotten, now began to make their presence felt with all the subtlety and comfort of jagged glass.

'Excuse me a minute,' he said, blinking hard, 'I shan't be a moment.' Ralph and Harry, chasing a conversational hare about mutual acquaintances in the city, glanced up only briefly, allowing Nicholas to scuttle off to the Gents without having to explain his problem.

Appalled at the blood-shot spectacle of his eyes, he clumsily squeezed and prised the lenses out, sacrificing all finesse to the cause of expediency, before folding them carefully into a clean corner of his handkerchief. The relief of having his eyeballs unmolested was intense. He splashed water onto his face and dabbed himself dry with a large piece of curiously water-resistant paper. Thankfully he had a spare pair of glasses in the car; they were old, the prescription years out of date, but they had served on many an occasion before. Suddenly, he wanted nothing more than to get home, to put his arms round Kate and to feel – even if he could not quite believe – that everything was all right, that everything would be all right in time. He hurried back to the table and said his farewells, shaking hands with a heartiness that reflected his keenness to be gone rather than any regret at having to say goodbye.

10

Mary sat in one of their three blue velvet, high-backed armchairs with a magazine on her lap and a cushion wedged behind her back in a vain attempt to ease the premenstrual ache in the lower part of her spine. Three aspirin and still it persisted.

She fingered the small gold crucifix round her neck as she read, her eyes merely skimming over the glossy columns of words, registering little more than the black fuzz of print and coloured blur of the accompanying illustrations. The article was about kitchens: grease-resistant curtains and non-scratch sink units, hand-painted tiles, soundless waste disposal systems and invisible swing-bins. Drudgery made beautiful, thought Mary, bringing her eyes sufficiently into focus to admire the gleaming example of an interior which had clearly never seen the imprint of a human hand or foot beyond those involved in the production of the photograph.

She relaxed her eyes again, while her finger-tips felt their way round the bobbled edge of the crucifix, counting each one as they might a rosary. There were forty-five in all, tiny bubbles of gold. Next she counted the sides of the cross. There were twelve of these, a number with enough biblical connotations for Mary to feel a faint thrill, as though she had stumbled across a fact of more than geometric significance. She would have liked to have expressed this thought, to extract it from the labyrinthine channels of her mind and see how it sounded, but only Angus was there, sitting across the room from her with his customary glass of red wine in one hand and the *Telegraph* crossword in the other. Since the thought was whimsical and, worse still, connected to religion in some way, she knew that it would have been not only pointless, but positively disruptive to mention it to her husband. Angus thought God a waste of time and made no pretence otherwise. I'll write it down, she thought, so I won't forget.

Mary's lack of interest in her reading material stemmed from a concealed desire to watch the television. There was a programme she had been looking forward to all week, about people who claimed to have been abducted by aliens; the television guide had promised graphic accounts of their experiences, together with intriguing evidence of implantations into the victims via their tummy-buttons. Mary had marvelled at her luck that such a thing should be scheduled for Thursday, the one night of the week when Angus – if he wasn't travelling – played bridge in Westbury.

'Know any rivers begining with *a*?'

'Amazon?'

'No, it's got nine letters. *A* something something something *p* something *l* something something. At least I think it's a river,' he muttered, squinting at the paper.

'A shame about your bridge game,' said Mary quietly, closing her magazine and looking round for her embroidery. She was working on an elaborate cushion cover of the alphabet, in which each letter was entwined with dense, vine-like flowers of finger-aching detail and depth.

'Bloody nuisance.' Angus, who liked the timing of his daily and weekly events to occur with the precision and certainty akin to that provided by his Rolex watch, slapped the paper on his knee with irritation. 'I spoke to Roger only yesterday to confirm. And I'll be away next week myself in France.'

'Oh really?' Mary's heart skipped a beat. 'You didn't tell me.'

'Yes I bloody well did. A mind like a sieve, that's your trouble.'

These harmonious exchanges were interrupted by the telephone.

'If it's Roger, tell him it's too bloody late, I'm not coming now,' barked Angus, assuming correctly that his wife would answer the phone. He turned his head back to the crossword, tapping the paper with the end of his pen, all the while listening hard to what was being said through the open door behind him.

Nicholas, given his reason for calling, was relieved that Mary rather than Angus answered the phone.

'No, Nicholas, I haven't seen her all day. In fact,' she went on, 'I haven't seen her since Monday afternoon when she and Millie came by for a cup of tea.'

'Fine, fine, I just thought I'd ask,' replied Nicholas, glancing at the kitchen clock for the hundredth time and wishing he hadn't bothered. Having received no useful information as to where Kate might be at seven o'clock on a Thursday evening he was anxious to end the conversation as quickly as possible. But Mary was all breathless concern.

'Oh goodness, I do hope she's all right.'

'Yes, yes, it's nothing, I'm sure. Probably got held up in traffic.'

'But it's so late—'

'Yes, Mary, thank you so much. Better stop now in case she's trying to get through herself.'

'Heavens yes, I hadn't thought of that. Do call back if there's anything—'

'Will do. Okay. 'Bye then.'

Nicholas put the phone down with unnecessary force. Where the bloody hell was Kate? He had raced back from the airport, driving far too fast, all in a fluster about seeing her, only to find Millie and James on their own, feasting on tinned baked beans and jaffa cakes in front of the television. Their own lack of concern had merely served to fuel his.

'She said she might be late and we were to fend for ourselves,' said James, not taking his eyes from the screen.

'And where's Grace?'

James shrugged.

'At Megan's, I think,' said Millie, 'that's where she usually is.' She made a face. 'Megan's got three holes in each ear and one in her *nose* – a real diamond, she says, but I don't believe her.' She nibbled a portion of the chocolate layer off her jaffa cake and began licking the jam underneath. 'Imagine blowing your nose with that thing in it – how all the . . .'

'That's quite enough thank you, Millie,' put in her father hastily, in no mood for the predictable thematic development of such a notion.

He returned to the kitchen where, in a spurt of self-righteous fervour, he began washing up all items within lunging distance of the sink, irrespective of whether they were dirty or could have been slotted into the dishwasher instead.

Kate got back some twenty minutes later, by which time Grace too had appeared and Nicholas had worked himself up into a frenzy of displeasure that had developed far beyond any rational or affectionate grounds for concern.

'Sorry I'm a bit late,' was all she said, kissing the side of his cheek and dumping her handbag on the kitchen table. 'I expect everyone's starving. I've got an egg flan in here somewhere' – she began shifting things authoritatively round the freezer – 'we can have that with some salad and cheese.'

'I don't know how you dare.'

'I beg your pardon?' She stood up, nothing but amazement on her face, clutching the flan in both hands, her fingers sticking to the frozen metal of the dish.

'I've been worried to death – I even phoned Mary. I came home especially early to see you. I wanted . . .'

'Wanted what?' She was still standing with the dish in her hands, her fingers quite numb.

'Oh never mind.' He pulled a chair out from the table and sat down. What had he wanted exactly? It was hard to remember, beyond a fuzzy need for reassurance.

Kate walked slowly over to the oven, placed the flan on a shelf and turned the dial before speaking again. 'Nicholas, I told you – I had that reunion thing today. It was in Hampshire. I meant to leave after lunch, but didn't quite manage to. We went on a short walk which turned into a really long one. We had a cream tea in a tourist rip-off tea shoppe. By the time we got back it was gone five. I have driven very fast to get home.'

'Well you can have the pleasure of phoning Mary to explain that you have not, after all, been mugged or concertinaed into a pulp by a multiple collision on the motorway but that you were simply too busy enjoying yourself to bother about your family.' He stood up and turned his back on her, ramming his hands into his pockets.

'I just don't believe this,' said Kate, her voice breathless with exasperation. To think she had been looking forward to seeing him, to making him laugh about some of the awful bits of the day, to test him out on Elizabeth's idea of a cookery book. 'For your information I did not enjoy myself that much and I tried to phone from a garage, but it was engaged.'

'There was a time,' he began, his voice low, 'when I could count on you.'

She spun round. 'That's not fair, it's just not fair. You're trying to make me feel guilty and I won't have it. How many times have meetings and train cancellations and goodness knows what made you late? Your unreliable wife has done all right then, hasn't she, keeping meals warm and not complaining? I tried to ring,' her voice trembled. 'If you must know it wasn't much fun at all and it was miles to drive.' She started plucking at lettuce leaves, but then threw them all into the sink and went to the door. 'I never thought you were selfish, Nicholas, but something seems to be making you so.' She spoke very quietly, with her back to him. 'You seem to hate me at the moment and I can't quite work out why. If you know why, I would most appreciate being told.' She raised her shoulders and dropped them again in a great sigh. 'I'm going to see the children and put a jumper on.'

'Be a love and do my feet,' said Angus a little later on that evening, throwing his head back against the white linen square on the back of his chair and closing his eyes. Running one's own business was so relentless, he found, so utterly unstoppable. 'I'm going to give it all up and retire soon,' he murmured, as Mary approached his chair, carrying a small plastic bottle and a hand towel.

'You know I think you should,' she said quietly, 'we could easily afford to.'

'Ha! I like that. If only you knew, my dear, if only you knew.'

Mary knelt down in front of him and began undoing the laces of his shoes.

'We've got more than we know what to do with already.' She picked at a knot in one of his laces, using the ends of her nails, appearing to concentrate very hard when in fact all her thoughts were directed towards their conversation. It wasn't often she could speak so openly to Angus without getting him cross. Only when she did his feet, or rubbed oil into the hairy folds of his back, could she ever venture such bold thoughts. He was always pliant then, massageable, like the mounds of warm skin beneath her hands.

'If only you were right, my little Mary,' he said gruffly, reaching forward to pat the top of her ashen blonde head. 'It would be nice not to have to worry about money.' He sighed and closed his eyes again. She was peeling his socks off now, holding each foot in turn by the heel, before placing it gently down on the towel folded across her knees.

Mary began with her thumbs, working them in small circular motions over the ball of his foot and steadily down to the arch and hard flat of the heel. Angus' feet were oddly soft and pink for such a large man, apart from two knobbly corns on both of his little toes. He liked her to rub those too, using a dab of the white cream, working round and down with the flat of her thumb.

'Oh but we do have enough dear,' she said, pausing before daring to go on. 'I sometimes think we have too much already, that . . .'

'And you'd like to give it away to starving black babies, I know, I know.' His voice sounded almost fond. 'While we live on bread and soup for the rest of our lives, I suppose.'

Mary began now to work on each toe individually, pulling and kneading with just the balance of gentleness and firmness that she knew he loved. 'Of course not, Angus. You know I enjoy our creature comforts as much as you.'

'Do you, my little one, do you really?' He smiled at her with such tenderness that Mary felt drawn to look up, acknowledging the treat with a gratitude tinged with the regret that such warmth could not more easily and more frequently be hers, that she had to wait for it like a powerless child, that she had to miss it so. She smiled and lowered her eyes back to her task, her hair falling over the velvet barrier of her hairband, its thin ends tickling her pale cheeks. It was nice to feel small and loved. It was how she had felt from the first with Angus, how she had once expected to be allowed to feel forever, before life got complicated and overbearing. Using the palm of her hands and a blob of cream she began to massage the top of his foot, pushing up to the anklebone in skilful strong motions that made him catch his breath from pure pleasure. Angus had always had sensitive feet. Sometimes she thought it was the most sensitive thing about him.

'But I would like to give a little to St Cuthbert's special appeal,' she said, almost whispering the request, having waited to time it so exactly, slipping it in between the smooth movements of her hands, making it easy for him to say yes. 'They're collecting for Bosnia – there's going to be a convoy of lorries. Medical supplies and clothes and toys for children.' Though her voice rushed a little bit once she started, the slow sure work of her hands never faltered.

Angus kept his eyes closed, feeling indulged and indulgent, as she had meant him to.

'Will a hundred pounds keep my little bird happy? Would that make her sing?'

'Thank you, Angus,' she said humbly. 'A hundred pounds would be wonderful. You are such a good man,' she added, bending low to kiss the arch of his foot.

11

Feeling that all other courses of action had failed, Kate, in danger of revealing the extent of her impatience with the situation, began endeavouring to ignore the fact that her husband seemed to have set his heart on being unhappy. It was only a phase, she told herself, something which had to be gone through, like James's bed-wetting and Millie's fear of clowns. After an initial period of difficulty (it was hard to ignore the impulse, the reflex-action of wanting to sort Nicholas out), she found that it was undeniably refreshing to separate herself in this way; it made her feel altogether lighter, less burdened by problems that she could not understand. Though she attended to all the usual domestic details of their life with her customary care, Kate was dimly aware that – with the back-up of an emotion that she would have described as confidence rather than complacency – she had to some degree stepped out of the framework of their marriage, left it hanging apart but within reach, waiting until such a time as they both felt able to breathe life into it again.

Fortunately, there was a lot for her to be getting on with in the meantime: costumes to make for Grace's play, churches to visit for a project of Millie's and, since James was now an established member of St Alberry's first eleven, twice-weekly cricket matches to watch. As if this was not enough Kate, if ever she found herself unoccupied and alone, had started, very tentatively, to collate a few recipes, using a typewriter that had once belonged to her mother, settling self-consciously down at the kitchen table with a mug of tea and her glasses perched high on the bridge of her nose, sheafs of grease-stained papers about her and the Tippex bottle at the ready. It felt more silly than real, as if she was acting out some sad fantasy of a frustrated housewife; so she mentioned it to no one, stowing her papers away in a bottom drawer in the kitchen and wedging the typewriter back into its dusty corner behind the curtain in the study after each session.

Nicholas, recognising the distancing shift in attitude from his wife, chose to feel abandoned. Suspicions hardened into beliefs. If Kate did not already have a lover, then, he believed, she must be actively searching for one. It was just a question of time. The world, which for almost two decades had been a comfortably homogeneous blur, now presented itself as an increasingly threatening landscape of sexual predators. That there was as yet no identifiable person or behavioural pattern on which to pin these dark thoughts only served to make him feel more hopeless.

Perhaps a private eye is the answer, he thought miserably, as he stood shaving, on the morning of St Alberry's sports day, when his relentless depression was being irritatingly accentuated by nervousness at the approaching challenge of the fathers and sons cricket match.

Having cut himself twice, once on the slight cleft in his chin and once right in the middle of his upper lip, Nicholas decided to examine the blade of his razor. He had only put it in the day before, so it was puzzling that it should feel so blunt. Upon removing it under a running tap, a small clog of hair fell out and whirled down the basin. Attempts to extrapolate some samples for further examination resulted only in the removal of a curious web of sodden cotton threads from the bowels of the plug-hole. Irritated and a little repelled, he rinsed the blade thoroughly, clicked it back into his razor and made a cautious assault on the left side of his face, where the shaving foam was beginning to flake off from having been so long unattended. Though better, the blade still cut a sluggish swathe across the contours of his lower face, making his skin feel bumpy and sliceable.

The door opened and Grace came in. Ignoring her father, she began rummaging in the bathroom cabinet on the wall behind him and fiddling with handfuls of her hair. Even after several weeks, Nicholas found his daughter's self-inflicted coiffure hard to accept; it was almost worse now that dark roots had started showing through along the line of her parting, reminding him of those tired child-women he saw in shopping precincts, pushing buggies full of papery-faced toddlers sucking grimy dummies and munching crisps. Feeling riled, but knowing that he had probably communicated his opinions on the subject of Grace's hair with too much intensity already, Nicholas chose another tack for venting his feelings, one that was easy to hand and very much in the forefront of his mind.

'I don't suppose you would know anything about my razor being quite unusable this morning, young lady?'

'No, Dad, I wouldn't.' Grace, who was playing in the mothers and daughters tennis match with Kate, was now standing on tiptoe beside Nicholas, competing with his shoulders for some space in the mirror while she clipped her fringe out of her eyes. Though at a stage in life when it was unacceptable to appear sporty to any degree, Grace was in fact rather competent when it came to tennis. Her steady strokes had qualified her to reserve for the first team a couple of times that term and, though she would not have admitted it to Megan for anything, she was secretly rather pleased at having been selected for the sports day tournament. If chosen, one had to play, so there was no face lost there.

'Well, Mum doesn't use my razor.'

'And neither do I,' she retorted, tugging at her pony-tail and sticking her chin out. 'Honestly, Dad, you blame me for everything, these days. It's not fair.'

Nicholas rinsed his face and patted it dry with a towel. 'And who else can I blame in this instance?'

'Try Millie.'

'Millie?' Nicholas was aghast.

'You've got foam on your ears,' was all she remarked, apparently unmoved by her father's expression and wanting to leave the bathroom in order to search for James. He had a tennis racket which was much weightier and more powerful than her own, but which she suspected would only be made available to her if she could come up with a substantial barter in return. Remembering a cassette which she knew he badly liked but couldn't yet afford, and which she was prepared to lend him for a day or two, Grace started confidently down the stairs.

'Grace?' Nicholas came out to stand on the landing, a fleck

of foam still cresting the tip of his right ear and a towel slung around his shoulders. 'Were you serious about Millie?'

'Get real, Dad,' came the withering reply, barely interrupting her passage down the stairs – taken two steps at a time, the white pony-tail swinging jauntily behind.

'Get real,' murmured Nicholas to himself, going across to the closed door of Millie's bedroom, where the sight of a sign saying 'No Grown-ups Allowed' stuck on with aging Sellotape beneath a lopsided smiley face that she had drawn herself, made his heart lurch. She was still so young. He knocked gently and opened the door.

Millie was practising the moves for the gym routine her class were putting on later that afternoon. When her father came in she was up on the ball of one foot, holding onto the wardrobe door for support and raising the other leg fast and hard towards her chest. Having done this twice she then leapt forwards and rolled into a summersault, ending up with her feet crashing down against her bookcase.

'Ow,' she said crossly, sitting up and rubbing her heel. 'My legs are too long. Why are you dressed in those old clothes?'

Nicholas who was feeling sufficiently self-conscious about the straining seams of his cricket flannels not to require wisecracks from his daughter, threatened her with a teasing swipe of his towel. 'Grace seems to think you might have taken to shaving.'

Millie straightened her back and looked haughtily at him. 'Body hair is horrid. Ask Mum and Gracie.'

'Yes, well, Mum and Grace do not use my razor and leave it unrinsed on the edge of the basin.'

'Oh, sorry,' her defiant little face fell. 'Only I just wanted my legs to be all nice for the show today.' She came and stood before him with a bowed head, absently winding her twiggy fingers in the belt loops of his trousers. 'Sorry, Daddy, I won't do it again.'

'That's all right then,' he growled, feeling won over and defeated. 'And no more shaving, eh?' He took her chin in his hand and raised her face to look at his. 'There's plenty of time for all that later on. You're lovely as you are, little mouse, remember that.'

She grinned and poked her finger into his tummy. 'And so are you.'

A lump ballooned in his throat. Millie was about the only one he could be sure of these days.

'You're a pumpkin,' he said, to cover the moment, ruffling her hair with the flat of his hand. She skipped away to the mirror to brush it back into place, sticking her tongue out with concentration from the effort of trying to master control over the silvery yellow ringlets, ringlets which, for the last five years or so, had seemed nothing but a liability but which she was just beginning to regard as something of a potential asset.

Downstairs Kate was preparing a picnic while a man on the radio lectured her on the crisis of European food mountains. Since her father and Beth were coming down for the occasion and Harry too – he had invited himself during the course of an impromptu phone call a couple of days before – she felt bound to prepare something a little beyond the level of cheese sandwiches and hard-boiled eggs. Though a couple of cookbooks lay on the table, she was in fact doing her usual thing of thinking and making things up as she went along, combining ingredients in her head on the basis of what was in the fridge and easy to put together. Some frozen chicken livers lay defrosting in the bottom of a saucepan, in preparation for blending into a pâté with a few fresh herbs, cream and sherry. On a piece of kitchen paper sat a heap of crispy fried bacon, left to cool before being added to a salad of broad beans, French beans, feta cheese, chives and sliced mushrooms. Kate was rather pleased with this salad and had already made a mental note to add it to her pile of contenders for the book: it used several things from the garden and would look pretty too, with all those greens and creams together. She had prepared a spicy vinaigrette dressing in an old marmalade jar to serve along with it.

'Are we ready?' Nicholas asked, though it was plain to see that they were not.

'There's hours yet. Could you carve the turkey into manageable chunks – I thought it would make a change from chicken – I cooked it in a bit of French mustard – it's come out rather well.'

Kate turned her back on him, chivvying along the liver with a wooden spoon and humming quietly to the familiar tune which she couldn't quite place but which was mercifully bringing the food mountain man's drone to a close.

Having decided that she would prefer to change into her sporting gear in some dark corner of the school cloakroom when necessity dictated, Kate was wearing a sun-dress of peachy brown and white with a pair of low-heeled, white leather shoes. It was a sun-dress which, though quite matronly at the front, revealed considerable quantities of her smooth honey-skinned back when viewed from behind; a fact which her apron happily did nothing to conceal and which made Nicholas long to reach out and trace a finger down the firm line of her spine, to create those small shivers of pleasure which he loved and of which he had never grown tired. Christ, it was a long time since they had made love. Weeks. Maybe even months. He tried not to think about it, distracting himself by picking at the tempting pile of fried bacon beside the stove.

Kate held out the carving knife for him to take. 'Please could you do the turkey?' she asked, fearful for the supply of such a key ingredient to her precious salad and wanting to stop him picking at the bacon without actually saying so – avoiding confrontation being an integral aspect of her new approach to the challenge of Dealing With Nicholas.

'You look very nice,' he said, the remark grinding out of him as it did these days, sparks flying from the strain of trying to sound normal.

'There'll be lots of hats and things. I thought I'd better make an effort.'

'Do you think I should change then?' He looked genuinely dismayed.

'You'll be playing for most of the afternoon – it would be pointless to go in anything smarter. Honestly, you're fine as you are, darling,' she added, since his expression had not changed. She patted his arm very lightly – patronisingly, as Nicholas felt – before returning to her task of loading up the picnic hamper – a battered but noble wickerwork affair which Harry had given them as a wedding present.

*   *   *

Kate was right about the hats. Even Beth was wearing one – wide-brimmed red straw, to match her lipstick and shoes.

'I love all this stuff,' she said, after kissing each member of her husband's family and waving her bangled arms expansively at the school grounds and milling groups, 'all this English business of tea and cricket.'

'It's lunch and cricket,' Millie corrected her, 'and tennis and my gym display.'

'Oh I know, honey, I know,' agreed Beth quickly, 'and I'm not going to miss one bit of it.'

They had arranged to meet outside the main entrance to the school at twelve o clock, but Kate, spotting her father and Beth two cars ahead of them as they drove into the grand sweep of St Alberry's drive had, with a considerable amount of horn-beeping and waving, managed to synchronise parking arrangements so that they were next to each other. Being reasonably early, they were directed by a series of officious sixth-formers with red flags and walkie-talkies onto an attractive knoll under two large oak trees, right beside the cricket boundary.

'Been practising your spin, eh Nicholas?' joked George, patting the pockets of his smart, gold-buttoned navy blazer, at ease with the appealing prospect of a snoozy day under his panama hat, full of his daughter's lovely food and some fine wine.

'I'm more of a batsman these days, George.' Nicholas used a smile to cover the fact that the prospect of his own afternoon could not have been less relaxing. To his troubled and blinkered eyes all the other fathers wandering around in whites looked obscenely young and fit – apart from one obviously rotund figure for whom he found himself nurturing irrational surges of goodwill.

'Who's that chap over there?' he had asked James, pointing as discreetly as he could, 'the rather large one with a cap on?'

'That's Hegarty's dad,' James had replied. 'He's useless.'

Since everyone proclaimed themselves to be ravenous and the cricket match was due to start at one o'clock, Kate volunteered to go in search of Harry while the others laid out the rugs and started eating.

It was the finest of summer days, as bright and fresh as only England could manage, the sky as crisp as a laundered tablecloth.

Kate, feeling cool and good in her dress, walked with a lilt to her stride, swinging her arms loosely and looking keenly about her, enjoying the spectacle of families en masse. Though St Alberry's had begun life, some two hundred years earlier, as an exclusive private boarding school for girls, it had long since been forced, for financial reasons, to open its doors to day children of both sexes at considerably lower rates. So there was an interesting cross-section of people to study, ranging from the champagne-out-of the-back-of-the-four-wheel-drive variety, to those equally happy with a warm beer leaning on the bonnet of the car. Kate, taking it all in, wondered quite where she and Nicholas fitted in, managing the fees, but only just, drinking white wine out of plastic beakers and gnawing on poultry bones. She nodded at several people that she knew, enjoying the feeling of belonging, of having some kind of niche, however dull and middle-class in origin.

As she was making her way back round to the front of the school, along a narrow tarmac path that ran past the tennis courts, she heard her name called, but on turning round saw no one that she recognised.

'Up here,' called the voice again.

It was the bookshop man, Max whatever he was, waving from a window.

'Oh, hello,' she said, a little too quietly, since it felt unseemly to holler up when she hardly knew him and people were streaming by on every side staring at her.

'Stay there,' he shouted, and disappeared.

Kate hovered self-consciously near a wall until he emerged from a side door, still in the black jeans but wearing a black T-shirt this time instead of a polo-neck. A gold stud glinted in his ear-lobe. His hair, which looked wavier than before, was pinned back into a gleaming pony-tail.

'I didn't know you had a child at the school,' she said, realising as she spoke that she did not even know if he was married, though she had assumed he was.

He laughed, opening his mouth wide enough to reveal a glimmer of gold amongst some back molars. 'I don't have a child at all – far too irresponsible for all that sort of thing. Though I did try for a while,' he added, with a gleam in his eye, 'with a partner who has wisely now gone her own way.'

'Oh, really,' she said, thinking that 'partner' meant he was not married and that the conversation was in danger of feeling inappropriate again, as it had done in the shop. He's dangerous, she thought suddenly, with a little thrill that made her suck on her cheeks to stop a nervous smile from forming. 'So what are you doing here, if you don't mind me asking?'

'I've got a book stall set up in the hall – good of them to let me – helps with sales and publicity and so on. Come by and have a look. You never know, you might want to buy something this time.'

'I bought something last time,' she replied archly. She looked at her watch, 'I might drop by later on but I've got to find my brother now. He'll be late as usual, I expect.'

'Where's he supposed to be?' Max asked, looking about them, as if there was some possibility that he could help in the search.

'Under the clock at the front. I'm on my way there now. Don't let me keep you from your books.'

'I wouldn't dream of it,' he said, giving her a quick nod and disappearing through a swing door.

Kate continued on her way, aware that she had a funny feeling in her stomach that had no business being there, aware too that the very possibility of such a feeling had quite a lot do with Nicholas' recent behaviour. Perhaps he really doesn't love me any more, she thought, as she scurried across the flagstones of the school forecourt, her dress blowing round her knees, her heart quickening at the way her mind was working.

12

Harry was late because Alicia had been creating problems. Having initially invited himself down to the sports day as a pretext for getting away from the threat of an entire weekend being devoted to an analysis of their situation, he had found himself agreeing to let his lover come too. None of which would have happened if he hadn't succumbed completely to the lethal effects of two martini cocktails, followed by a bottle of Volnay and several hours' uninhibited viewing of Alicia's stockinged legs. Remarkable from any angle, she had chosen to spend a good part of the 'frank discussion' for which she had negotiated hard, uncrossing and crossing these prize assets on his sofa, granting Harry tantalising glimpses of suspenders and pearly thigh and generally stirring some very fond memories indeed.

She had played her cards well that night – to a tee in fact, Harry thought miserably, as he thrashed amongst the rumpled bed-covers the next morning, trying to find a position that would go some way towards relieving the ache in his head. Alicia, of course, hadn't drunk a thing. 'This is just so lovely,' she had kept on saying, taking minute sips of her sparkling mineral water and nailing him with her baby-blue eyes, 'talking and being friends. It's all I want, you know, Harry, to be friends.'

And Harry, being the fool that he knew he was, allowed himself to slip from an original position of steely resistance, into an alcoholic state of amiability and irrepressible lust. Drink had never been a problem for him in that regard.

The only vaguely positive aspect to the day that he could think of now was that Kate might take pity on him and have a quiet word with Alicia. At least, it was to this tenuous hope that Harry clung as he edged his Porsche through the congested exodus of London weekend traffic, his face ashen, his bloodied eyes shielded from the gaze of his lover and the glare of daylight by the darkest of his various pairs of sunglasses.

Alicia sat in silence beside him, looking lovely and very unpregnant in a pale pink suit, the skirt of which barely reached the middle of her thighs. Every so often she checked her reflection in the small mirror of the sun-guard above her, pressing her pink lips together and nudging the blonde frame of her hair. Meeting Harry's family was a big step, a very big step, especially the sister, to whom she knew he was very attached. If I can make her like me too, she thought, then anything could happen. Which led her on to fill the prolonged silence of their journey with secret hopes for her child and its father, of whom she was extraordinarily fond and who, one day, she hoped to understand.

Kate could see at once that Harry was hung-over. As a man who had always prided himself on an immaculate exterior, the lank flop of his hair and the pallor of his cheeks, so stark against the black lenses of his designer glasses, told her all that she needed to know.

She tapped him on the shoulder, ignoring the tall blonde woman standing next to him whom she assumed was also waiting to meet up with relatives.

'How bad is it, Harry, on a scale of one to ten I mean?'

He scowled, as she stood on tiptoes to kiss his cheek.

'I'd put it quite near the ten mark myself, judging from your face. Does it hurt to smile, or simply when you breathe?' Kate laughed, linking her arm through his and starting to lead him away. 'What you need, Harry my love, is a drink.'

'You are absolutely right there, Katie,' he said, his voice hoarse, 'but first,' he stopped walking and turned round. 'First I must introduce you to Alicia, who has chosen – incredible though this may seem – to spend the day with me and my enchanting relatives.'

'Alicia . . . oh, but how do you do – you're more than welcome of course.' Kate would have been happy to restrict their greeting to the safe informality of a nod, but Alicia, anxious to start a relationship which she intended to value on the right footing, eagerly extended her right arm. As they shook hands Kate, impressed by the cool firmness of Alicia's grip, could not help wondering how very short and dowdy she must seem, beside such a swaying willow of a woman, with her chic silky hair and glassy blue eyes.

'I can't tell you how pleased I am to meet you,' bubbled Alicia.

'And I, you,' murmured Kate, inwardly cursing Harry for having complicated the day by bringing her.

It's hard to believe she's pregnant though, she thought, as the three of them made their way towards the car, exchanging small talk about the weather and the various sporting challenges that awaited all members of the Latimer family. It occurred to her then that an arrangement might already have been reached, that the baby had been terminated and the two of them happily reunited in non-parental bliss. She looked hard at Harry's face for a clue. But Harry was shuffling along with his hands in his pockets, his shaded eyes firmly on the ground, giving nothing away beyond the fact that he had a monumental headache.

It may have been the split in the crotch of Nicholas' trousers that caused him to drop the catch, a gaping hole of a thing – four inches long at least – which had been acquired during the opening minutes of the game, when he unwisely dared to imitate a bit of impressive leg-stretching being undertaken by a strapping fielder to his left. The knowledge of the split was certainly a burden, not just because it would have been unsightly to reveal any of the unsporty red spots on his boxer shorts, so tightly packed within, but also because it would provide overriding and highly public suggestions of a weight problem. Before a split, such trousers could merely have been described as snug. After a split there was no escaping the fact that they were too small.

The catch was the sort that confident, ego-surging fielders dream of – a high peach of a shot, sailing smoothly through the air in an arc clearly destined to terminate very close to the region of Nicholas' terrified cupped hands. But at the last minute the ball seemed to dip a little, falling short of where Nicholas had estimated it might land, so that catching it cleanly would have required an impromptu lunge forward, a small feat of acrobatics which just did not feel easy with air blowing up the seat of his pants and the fear of how to land on forty-six-year-old elbows without smashing them to bits. The combined result of all these factors was a sort of stumble forwards, while the ball bounced off his knuckles and onto the grass at his feet, and then, in the most humiliating of finales, trickled between his legs before rolling cockily on towards the boundary.

He saved the four – just – and threw it in well, practically all the way back to the bowler, but it was too late by then. James, who was sitting in the pavilion waiting to come in, looked to Nicholas as if he was hanging his head in shame at such geriatric antics from his father. He edged further back towards the outer markers of the field, wishing he could walk off altogether. To feel shame for himself was bad enough. To feel it on behalf of his son, in front of such a host of athletic veterans, was intolerable. Even the useless Hegarty, stationed behind the wicket, was performing with some panache, sticking out his large behind and bending with remarkable flexibility to await each delivery, getting his gloved hands behind the fastest of balls without so much as a flinch.

Instead of joining everyone for the sit-down tea in the pavilion Nicholas trudged over to the car, ostensibly to retrieve his batting gloves from the boot, but actually in the hope of finding some inspirational solution to the problem of his trousers.

Beth clapped and shouted 'bravo' as he approached.

His father-in-law, more attuned to the nuances of the game, tipped up the brim of his hat and offered a milder commendation, before adding, 'Strong sun out there – hard to keep an eye on a ball.'

'The sun's fine,' said Nicholas, not wanting sympathy from George or anyone else, though in fact he had a hell of a headache from standing in its glare for so long without a hat. Harry had arrived, he noticed; he was lying fast asleep under a nearby tree, watched over by a strikingly pretty woman with a short skirt and eye-catchingly long legs. Nicholas smiled at her, half-hearted combinations of hatred and admiration for his brother-in-law pumping his heart. Harry would never turn into a middle-aged old fool with insomnia, an indifferent wife and bursting seams, he thought miserably.

'Hey, Dad, you've got a hole in your trousers,' exclaimed Grace. From where she was lying, flat on her back on the rug amongst the debris of the picnic, she did indeed have a very clear view of Nicholas' sartorial problems.

'I know, thank you, Grace,' he hissed. 'Where's your mother?'

'Changing. We're on in ten minutes.'

'I'm going to watch them instead of you,' said Millie from behind a book. 'Cricket is deadly boring.'

Spotting Kate, now attired in a becoming pair of white Bermuda shorts and a long white T-shirt, heading their way, Nicholas set off to corner her about the possibility of a safety-pin, hurrying as best he could with his thighs pinned together.

'Are you all right,' she said, laughing, 'you're walking in the most peculiar way.' She hadn't seen the dropped catch, having spent most of the cricket match chatting to Beth, looking round only when a pattering of clapping hands told her that something significant had happened.

'Isn't this fun? I thought James batted wonderfully – twenty-five is most respectable.'

'It was twenty-eight.'

'Twenty-eight – sorry,' she corrected herself curtly, marvelling at Nicholas' capacity for ill-humour in the face of absolutely everything. 'Shouldn't you be eating tea with your team-mates?'

But when Nicholas confided his problem she took pity at once, knowing him well enough to see that he was seriously embarrassed. After discreetly performing the miracle of unearthing no less than three safety-pins from the bottom of her spacious handbag, she skilfully applied all of them to the offending area, undertaking the delicate operation behind the screen of an open car door, so that Nicholas might emerge with both pride and trousers more or less back intact.

'Thanks, Kate,' he said quietly when she had finished. 'And I'm sorry . . .'

She waited for him to go on, eager for some light at long last to be cast on what was happening to them, on the acrimony and impatience that seemed to have taken root in his system, especially as regards her. 'Yes?' she said, very gently, lifting his hand between both of hers.

'I know I'm being . . . it's just that I feel so . . .' he gripped her fingers, 'so hopeless.'

The last word came out as such a mumble that Kate wasn't sure if he had said 'helpless' or 'legless'. She was on the verge of clarifying the point when James came running over, out of breath, his fringe damp and clinging to his forehead.

'Come on, Dad – you're missing the tea – everyone's there.'

Nicholas released himself from the grip of Kate's hands and followed his son back across the dry grass towards the pavilion, the long shadows of the trees falling across their path like giant hands.

'Bad luck about the catch,' said James after a couple of minutes, 'I hate those really high ones when there's so much time to think about it. They're the hardest of all, don't you think?'

Nicholas could only nod, deeply touched by such adult reassurance from his son, but despairing that he should feel the need to give it.

13

To the surprise of all they had quite a party afterwards. As things turned out, there was rather a lot to celebrate: Kate and Grace reached the semi-finals, Millie got a gold star for her gymnastics, James got three wickets and a catch, while Nicholas, much to his own astonishment and that of his team-mates, scored eighty-five not out. The fathers won in consequence and Nicholas was declared man of the match.

It was nothing less than joy that he felt as Kate drove them home afterwards, the children giggling and singing in the back, playing semaphore games with George and Beth who were in convoy behind and – which presented more of a challenge – with Harry and Alicia who, being last in line, only came into view when they pulled out to overtake, their efforts constantly thwarted by the broken but persistent thread of oncoming coastal traffic. Nicholas sat with the miniature silver trophy with which he had been presented wedged between his thighs, his little fingers hooked into its tiny handles. Life could be so beautifully surprising, he thought, relishing this rare mood of celebration, the tingling echo of a feeling that, for once, he had been a hero.

After a long sleep and a plastic cup or two of wine Harry had begun to come round, emerging from his hangover like an insect from a chrysalis. Alicia too had spent a considerable portion of the afternoon asleep, her head in the crook of his arm and her famous limbs curled guilelessly up under her. Though she was fortunate enough not to feel sick, a weighty tiredness had wrapped itself about her from the very outset of her pregnancy, only days after the Sunday evening when she had lied to herself about her cycle, overcome by something like impatient curiosity and an overwhelmingly erotic sense of power over Harry who had been too far gone to stop at anything. Conception had seemed such a small possibility at the time, such a tiny spy-hole of a risk, that even now she could not quite believe the train of events that had been set in motion. She was thirty-seven; having devoted all of her sexually active life to the business of not bearing children, there was something of a relief in the unthinkable at last having happened, at going with the natural flow for once, especially since her chances of doing so – if she were to believe her magazine articles – had been narrowing by the month.

'I'll drive back,' she promised Harry, having boldly accepted Kate's invitation to supper on behalf of both of them. 'You enjoy yourself,' she added, meaning of course that he could drink and not worry.

Harry felt trapped but weak. The thought of London was not enticing on such a balmy night; far more fun to decamp back at Kate's for some good food and old-fashioned family jollity.

'You win,' he said wearily to Alicia, once his sister was out of earshot, 'but you'll be bored, I warn you. Her children can be fiendish and Beth's so exhaustingly American no one knows how Dad puts up with her.'

'I think Beth is very nice,' Alicia had replied, since she had exchanged more words with her than anyone else, even if it had only been on the subject of property prices in London, a subject upon which Alicia, who had inherited her own Knightsbridge flat from an uncle, was in no position to comment with any authority.

Beth, having recently succeeded in persuading George to consider buying a place in London, was in a phase of quizzing everyone she met about property – or real estate, as she still insisted on calling it. Now that George was at last fully retired, with the time and money to enjoy such an investment, she found herself thinking longingly of elegant, high-ceilinged flats – in Victoria somewhere, or perhaps St John's Wood, near one of London's stunning parks and all those enticing shops and theatres and restaurants. Though she loved the Oxfordshire countryside, she found herself, after several years of it, in danger of getting just the tiniest bit bored with village life. Once the novelties of having creamy milk delivered to her doorstep and driving down roads that appeared designed for nothing wider than a bicycle had worn thin, she found herself making frequent trips into nearby towns, as if drawn to the reassuring bustle of urban life. A weekend residence in London – to turn the conventional aspirations of many of her recently acquired compatriots on its head – seemed the most perfect solution.

'Just imagine, George,' she sighed, as he concentrated on keeping a respectable distance from Kate and Nicholas' bumper, 'all those plays we could see, all those art galleries—'

He cut her short. 'Beth dear, I am not going to start being a tourist in my own land thank you very much.' He patted her knee. 'Now I've said I'll think about it. Maybe get a pied-à-terre in the docklands – something like that – where property's very cheap.'

Beth didn't like the sound of the docklands. She pictured brown mudflats and stifling one-bedroomed apartments. Such images, aside from being unalluring in themselves, brought to mind uncomfortable recollections of the tenement block in the grey industrial suburbs of Baltimore, where she had been forced to surive for several years after the car insurance husband had left. She put her hand on George's thigh, pressing her fingers into the blue cotton of his flannels. 'Any old place, so long as it's pretty,' she cooed, while inwardly resolving to be more patient. Her dear sweet Englishman was going to need a little more working on, she could see.

They went straight out into the enclosed tranquillity of Kate and Nicholas' garden, taking cushions and blankets with them to make up for the sparse supply of chairs. The grass, which Kate had watered in spite of the threat of a hose-pipe ban, appeared luminescent in the failing light, its glossy blades shimmering like the fibres of a nylon carpet. Though the wisteria had lost its flowers, white and pink roses were in bloom along the walls on every side, their velvet heads and glimmering green leaves ranged round the borders of the lawn like intricate embroidery on a delicate handkerchief.

'It's beautiful,' breathed Beth, looking round in awe, the thought of London properties for once far from her mind.

James brought out his ghetto-blaster, playing something monotonous but soothing, and placed it in the centre of the lawn. Though most of the grown-ups were cronies, it felt good to have a glass of wine in his hand, to be able to slurp it freely knowing that on this night at least he was not going to be watched over or ordered up to bed. He eyed Harry's packet of cigarettes longingly; a smoke would have been the most perfect finishing touch.

Kate, who felt guilty about not talking to Alicia, asked her if she could lend a hand in the kitchen. Her languor throughout the day, the heavy dreamy look in her eyes told her as clearly as anything could that the pregnancy was still very much an issue, that the baby lived on.

'I thought I'd just put everything from the fridge onto the table and let people help themselves. Perhaps you could cut some bread – put it in that basket there – there's some herb butter somewhere which might go nicely.'

Alicia, now that she had Harry's sister to herself, felt inordinately shy. Knowing, because Harry had told her, that Kate knew about their rather intimate dilemma, did not make matters any easier. Kate, her head focused with unnecessary intensity on the inside of her fridge, felt the same, and would have given anything at that moment to have been as ignorant as Beth, so that she could chat happily about trite things like house prices without appearing anything other than sociably polite. Knowing about the pregnancy introduced the most uncomfortable obligation to discuss it.

'I wish the inside of my fridge contained stuff like this,' said Alicia admiringly, as Kate produced an assortment of half-eaten salads, cheeses and pies. 'Frozen meals are my thing, I'm afraid – I'm quite hopeless in the cooking department.'

'I have to confess to a great love of anything to do with food. Terribly sexist of me, I expect, but there we are.' Kate peeled cellophane off various bowls, laying it carefully in a corner by the bread bin for use later on. 'If ever poor Nicholas dares to try and help I end up tearing my hair out and begging him to leave. I'm the most unforgivable tyrant when it comes to the kitchen.'

Alicia laughed politely. 'Well, if the picnic was anything to go by, then I shouldn't think Nicholas minds too much.' She had finished her allotted task and was standing before Kate with a basketful of rather unevenly sliced bread. 'Do you think Harry will ever change his mind?' she asked quietly, unable to maintain their pretence any longer.

Kate caught her breath and stopped fiddling with jars and spoons. 'I really don't know.' She shook her head, unable to hold Alicia's imploring stare, torn between wanting to reassure her and a fearful knowledge of quite how self-centred her brother could be. 'You're not at all as I imagined,' she ventured, noting that Alicia's looks, though well cared for, were enviably natural, that though she now had only the faintest trace of make-up round her eyes and a smudge of pink left on her lips she still looked quite lovely.

'I'm not the obviously maternal type, I know, which is probably why I've never settled down with a husband and babies. But now that it's happened,' Alicia let out a long sigh and began tearing at a bread-crust, 'I just want it so badly . . .'

Kate began to say something, but Alicia hadn't finished.

'Since I'm nearly thirty-eight, time is not exactly on my side. So I will go ahead anyway, you see, with or without Harry. It's not marriage that I'm after, just a sense of commitment – and love, I suppose – for the baby I mean, not me. I don't really need any money either, though of course I think Harry should help out a little.' She put the bread-basket down. 'Though I guess what I'd really like is for us to try being together properly, just for a bit – people say that babies can be very unifying, don't they?'

Kate couldn't help smiling, recollections of sleepless nights, interrupted love-making and grumpy mornings filling her mind. 'They do say that, though I assure you the opposite is equally true.' I can't begin to tell this woman what to do, she thought, with something like relief, it has nothing to do with me. But by the same token she felt it impossible to put any pressure on Harry either. 'You must do what feels right, Alicia, that's all I can say. As for Harry,' she crossed her arms, 'he's very good deep inside, but I'm afraid he's been rather spoilt all his life and won't be very good at letting all of that go. I'm sure he'll help out with money and so on,' she paused, 'but as for the rest, I really have no idea how he'll react. I shouldn't think he does either.'

'Come along, you two,' bellowed Nicholas from the doorway, 'this is no time for gadding in kitchens. It's practically pitch black out there – we need candles to eat by, candles to dance by.' He waltzed over to Kate and swung her round the kitchen table, slopping his wine a little as they went, singing something that resembled The Blue Danube but in a throaty Elvis-like warble. Alicia clapped her hands and laughed at the pair of them, her faith in the possibility of cohabiting bliss thoroughly recharged.

Nicholas slipped his hand up under Kate's T-shirt and ran his finger under her bra strap. 'We will make love tonight,' he whispered in his best Russian accent, blowing warm air into her ear.

'Shh,' she said, rubbing the tickle from her ear and glancing apologetically at Alicia. Though more than happy to receive Nicholas' attentions, she wished it could have been without the obvious aid of so much wine. 'Steady on,' she whispered back, 'or we won't be making anything.'

Outside, Grace and James were lying either side of their uncle Harry on the largest of the rugs, taking surreptitious drags of his cigarettes when they thought no one was looking. Between puffs Harry was telling them a lewd but quite witty joke about three nuns and a sock factory.

Millie meanwhile was doing a re-run of her gymnastic display for her grandparents, complete with a running commentary from the games mistress, whose toothy grimace and barking voice she imitated with merciless attention to detail.

'She's destined for the stage, that one,' remarked her grandfather a little later, when they had all heaped food onto their plates and were enjoying a candle-lit picnic in the garden. 'Another artist in the family, eh Kate?'

'Who's the first artist then?' enquired Alicia, hugging her goose-pimpled arms and wishing they could all retreat inside.

'Why Nicholas of course,' boomed George. 'He's had a play on the radio – I'm surprised Harry didn't mention it.'

'Not a play, George,' corrected Nicholas, happy to grab the chance of mentioning his one literary achievement to a fresh audience. He turned to Alicia. 'It was just a short story,' he said with careful nonchalance. 'They read it out on Radio 4, oh a couple of years ago now. I'm working on a play at the moment, but of course it's a rather bigger project.'

'How wonderful.' Alicia's admiration was undisguised and most satisfactory. 'When on earth do you find the time to do it?'

Nicholas, his mind scanning the countless evenings and weekends of failed good intentions, avoided Kate's eye as he answered. 'Saturdays usually – Sundays too if there's nothing much in the papers and the children aren't on the rampage.' He filled his wine glass and offered some to Alicia who shook her head. 'It's an uphill struggle all the way, of course.' I'll write tomorrow, he thought suddenly, his heart surging with such enthusiasm and self-belief that he was almost tempted to slip away to his study there and then.

Millie, fighting sleepiness, danced over and hung on her father's arm, begging to be allowed to have a sip of wine. Nicholas indulgently poured her her very own glassful and watched with twinkling eyes as she took a great gulp.

'Great,' she spluttered, accompanying the opinion with so much nose puckering and coughing that it was all the grown-ups could do not to laugh out loud. Millie, sensing that she was in danger of being mocked, gripped her glass more tightly and set off towards the threesome still sprawling on the rug.

'Oh God, we'll all have headaches tomorrow,' said Kate, surveying the party with a happy sigh. 'There's loads more food inside if anyone's got room.' Having topped up her own wine glass, she sat back down next to her father, stretching out her legs and arms with a wide yawn. 'All that tennis has finished me off, I'm afraid, though I let Grace do all the running – mostly chasing the shots I missed.'

'Nonsense, Kate.' Her father patted her knee. 'You're a fine tennis player.'

'Thanks, Dad,' she said dreamily, closing her eyes.

'Do you think I could possibly borrow a jumper or a sweatshirt or something?' asked Alicia shyly, 'this silly suit is really not the thing for the evening.'

'I'll get you one,' replied Nicholas at once. He was beginning to feel rather sorry for the woman, since Harry, with his usual élan, seemed to be ignoring her completely. 'Any particular colour?' he joked, before going inside.

Alicia shot him a tight, grateful smile, her skin now looking stretched and thin, the outline of her lips showing faint traces of blue.

Nicholas was upstairs rifling through the big bottom drawer of the chest of drawers when the phone rang. He ignored the first few rings while he continued his search, only picking up the receiver beside the bed when he had found what he was looking for, a blue cashmere polo-neck that his sister Alison had given him for Christmas the previous year, still in its see-thru plastic bag. Nicholas hated polo-necks. He hated the way the wool tickled his chin, the decapitated look they gave a head, as if it was being served up on a hairy plate.

'Nicholas, it's Alison.'

'Alison – this really is extraordinary – you won't believe it but I'm standing here holding the jumper you gave me, the blue one – last Christmas, do you remember?'

There was a long pause. 'Alison? Are you still there? I said, I'm holding that jumper you gave me; the one—' He raised his voice still further, 'Alison, are you still there?'

'Oh God, Nick, don't say you don't know.'

'Don't know what?'

The mini-vacuums of silence, due to the entirely natural phenomena of time-differences between global zones, exacerbated the stilted feel to this exchange, at the same time lending a snapshot, jigsaw sense of a picture forming with tantalising slowness, a picture full of an urgency that Nicholas could sense, but not yet understand.

'Don't know what?' he repeated.

'About Dad.'

'Dad?' Nicholas' mind struggled with the absurd notion that his antipodean sister should know anything about their father that he did not. 'What about him?'

'He's . . . he's had a heart attack.'

'When, for Christ's sake?' Nicholas stood up, heedless of the cashmere jumper which, still in its wrapping, slipped from his knees to the floor. 'How the hell do you—?'

Once the urgency took hold it was even more impossible to converse smoothly with the interruptive seconds coming in between. Their jerky sentences kept overlapping, each one starting as the other did, and then stopping and starting again, like an ill-tuned radio.

Kate, who had come up in the interests of Alicia's by now audibly chattering teeth, stood frozen in the doorway behind, listening to Nicholas' end of the conversation, the hairs on her neck standing stiff and straight. There was a crisis, she could see at once, from the way Nicholas was crouching over the phone, from the atmosphere in the room, the sense of an awful discovery.

'Mum phoned about an hour ago – just before the ambulance arrived – she seemed to think—'

'Why the hell didn't she phone me?' He was seized by a tremendous anger.

'I don't know,' Alison was sobbing now, 'perhaps she tried, she didn't say.' There was a long silence. 'I don't think he's going to make it, Nick.'

'Where are they? Which hospital?'

'St Richards.' She sounded suddenly more composed, soothed perhaps by the practicalities the situation presented. 'I've been on the phone about flights. Keith will stay here with the children. I'll let you know when I'm arriving.'

'But Alison – are you sure? I mean people have heart attacks all the time – it could be—'

'Nick,' she cut in, 'Mum wasn't even sure he was still breathing.'

After Nicholas had put the phone down and seen Kate standing there, he said nothing, felt nothing. She came across the room towards him and put her arms around his waist, very loosely, resting the side of her head against his chest. She could feel the thud of his heart, smell the faint odour of stale sweat through his shirt.

'Oh Nicholas,' she said.

He stood limp and unresponsive.

'Shall I call the hospital?'

'No, no I'll do it,' he murmured, pushing her away absently, his eyes unblinking and unfocused. 'You go downstairs. Get rid of them all.'

Obediently she dropped her arms and turned to leave. Nicholas did not move, not until she was almost on the landing. 'Kate, why didn't she call me? Why did she tell Alison first?' This fact, above all others seemed to stick in his mind as the least digestible, the most hurtful.

'She probably did try,' said Kate gently, 'but we were out, remember? We've only been back an hour or so. Of course she tried to ring you first.'

'I suppose she must have,' he muttered, sitting back down on the bed and cradling the telephone in his lap. Kate went downstairs to break the news. Everybody left at once, subdued by shock, murmuring sympathies and offers of help.

Talk about bad timing, Kate couldn't help thinking bitterly, as she cleared up later on. Though Grace had shut herself in her room, Millie and James came to help, fetching and stacking things from the garden with a respectful silence, still more in awe of what such a turn of events meant for their parents, rather than feeling anything as direct as sorrow for themselves.

Memories of her mother's death, the carefully buried casket of sorrow, spilled open inside Kate's head, taking her back to the timeless pain of watching someone wither and die, all the jolly bravery, the helplessness. It was too horrible to think of Nicholas and Joyce having to go through the same thing with Dick, the cycle of hope and despair, of guilty longing for it all to end.

She was on the point of going upstairs when Nicholas came into the kitchen, his face pinched, his eyes dark and staring.

'He's dead,' he said, 'I'm going to the hospital.' And he was gone, before any of them could say anything coherent. Millie flung herself, sobbing, into Kate's arms, while James quickly left the room, a drying-up cloth still over one shoulder.

14

What baffled Nicholas was that he minded so much and in such a complicated way. It was as if his father's death turned a key in his mind, opening a forgotten door upon feelings which he had assumed were safely stowed away for good – unfulfilled yearnings and fears from his childhood, anxieties which he never would have credited with any relevance for his adult state of mind. Though there had never been great domestic dramas between him and his parents (he sometimes thought it would have been more fruitful if there had), neither had there existed anything like, say, the intimacy that Kate enjoyed with George, a teasing affection which Nicholas had come to see as the unique privilege of fathers and daughters, something which he hoped, one day, to manage with Grace – if she ever came through the alarmingly egocentric business of being a teenager – and which, he prayed he would never lose with Millie. With James, it was already different, depressing signs that history was in danger of repeating itself, that in a few years his own son would withdraw into the false security of adult life, as he had done, leaving his father with nothing but handshakes and the gruffest, surface-scraping exchanges about things that really mattered.

It struck Nicholas as something of a con trick that years of maintaining such an uncluttered and distant relationship with his father should turn out to be no guarantee against pain upon his death, that the loss of a man whom he seldom saw and whose post-war attitudes and blinkered views had never failed to grate when he was alive, should have the capacity to cut so deeply.

All of which was rather hard to explain to Kate, who,

catapulted back into a painful re-run of her mother's death, seemed incapable of appreciating that such losses needed to be endured in different ways. Clearly frustrated by Nicholas' grim-faced silence, she all but commanded him to break down, lacing her entreaties with what were intended as reassuring comparisons about her own experience of bereavement, but which only served to harden his resolve to suffer as he chose. While recognising with some small, helpless part of his mind that such stoicism could seriously threaten the already crumbling walls of his marriage, Nicholas simply could not bring himself to erupt in an emotional explosion solely for the gratification of his wife. You do not have the monopoly on how to grieve, Kate Latimer, he thought, but did not say, because even given the selfishness of self-pity and mourning, he knew that she had instincts of her own to follow and that saying such things would hurt her very deeply. As a result, Kate developed her own somewhat ungenerous set of theories about her husband's grieving state of mind, based on the assumption that he was – understandably – worried about Joyce and that, beneath all that, there lurked lorry loads of guilt about never having made enough of an effort to see or understand Dick when he was alive.

Greeting his glowing, big-boned sister was a great help to Nicholas, partly because it brought so much obvious comfort to his mother and partly because it granted him an echo of a sense of their old sibling infrastructure in which she had always been the one to take responsibility and control. He drove Joyce to the airport to pick Alison up, after which the three of them motored back south to his parents' small terraced house in Worthing, where they sought solace in the time-honoured British tradition of tea.

Set several layers of streets back from the seaside, but still within shouting distance of seagulls and promenades, the house in Barnet Street was part of a location that had been attracting retired couples for decades. A fact which did nothing to prevent Nicholas' shudder on noticing that the big double-fronted Victorian building on the corner of their street had a sign he hadn't noticed before saying, *Heathcote Lodge: Hospice For The Elderly*. To his relief, neither his sister nor mother remarked upon it, leaving him to wonder alone about what Joyce's long-term future might hold and whether 'hospice' implied bed-pans and terminal disease. Several inmates were to be seen sitting happily enough on a bench in a wide slant of sun on the front lawn, sticks and walkers close to hand, blankets spread across their bony knees as protection against the warm, buffeting breeze.

Alison and Joyce, sitting on the back seat, had talked quietly all the way back from the airport, making Nicholas feel like something of a chauffeur, curious, but wary of appearing so. It was wonderfully soothing to have Alison there, so tanned and blooming, so self-assured as always. The relaxed outdoor life in Australia had suited her right from the start, when she arrived with one suitcase and a certificate of nursing as her only passport to a job. The intended year away had turned into two and then five and then ten. Her patently happy marriage into a big family had, as they all knew, set the seal on her absence for good.

In addition to his gratitude at having her there, however, Nicholas could not help thinking how unfair it was that she should be the one who would be flitting back across the globe, leaving him, so ill-equipped, to cope with picking up the pieces alone. Joyce and Dick, though they had been part of a generation whose priority from a pitiably early age had been to put by an adequate nest-egg for their retirement, were not handsomely well off. Financial constraints meant that their trips to Melbourne over the years had been few and far between, as had Alison's to England, for similar reasons. Now that Dick was gone, Joyce was going to be wholly dependent on him for solace and emotional support. Nicholas dug his finger-nails into the steering wheel at the thought of it, the disturbing image of the doddery folk on the lawn still large in his mind.

They ate fruit cake with their tea, Joyce's home-made family favourite, with a brown sugar coating and a dense filling that was moist and crumbly all at the same time. Nicholas broke off bite-sized pieces with his fingers, holding his head well over the plate so as not to spill any onto his mother's immaculate carpets; with his mind's eye he caught a sudden glimpse of his father doing the same thing, over so many teas, eating in that careful way he had, pressing every last crumb off his plate with his finger-tips, not wasting an ounce. Cake clogged Nicholas' throat, its bits of fruit as dry and indigestible as unswallowed pills.

'You will come and stay with us, Mother, won't you?' he declared, gulping hard on clods of cake. 'Kate and I would love to have you – you know that.'

Alison give him a grand smile, showing off her mess of teeth, which for some peculiar reason perhaps connected to the exuberance of her character, the irrepressibility of her confidence, did nothing to detract from her attractiveness.

Joyce nodded at him, her dry delta of a mouth twitching. 'My father was eighty-nine when he died,' she said sadly, 'Dick was only seventy-six. Seventy-six is not such a great age for a man.'

'No, Mum, it isn't,' put in Alison, who was sitting beside her on the sofa. She reached out and took Joyce's hand, stroking the liver-spotted knuckles and knobbly fingers as she might caress the hand of a distraught child. Alison with her nurse's hat on, thought Nicholas watching her gratefully – calming and in charge. 'But think how much worse it would have been,' his sister went on firmly, 'if Dad had suffered for any longer, been ill and stuck in bed or something. He would have hated that – and so would you.'

'I'll be next, I suppose,' said Joyce, her hand lifeless in Alison's, her mind bent on navigating its own treacherous course.

'Now don't talk like that, I won't have it,' scolded her daughter, shooting Nicholas a look that urged him to join in with some reprimand to back her up.

Nicholas tried his best to think of something to say, but nothing convincing came to mind. She might well be next, if the rest of them were allowed to see things through to their natural end. Though seventy-six didn't seem so very old, he agreed with her there. As each decade cruised by, he found his preconceptions about what constituted old age being reshuffled dramatically.

'I'll wash up,' he announced, standing up abruptly, scattering cake crumbs from amongst the creases of his trousers.

Joyce, gesturing at a modest mantelpiece of flowery, gold-embossed cards offering *Sympathy* and *Deepest Regret*, pulled herself to her feet, using the arm of the sofa with visible effort, saying that she really ought to write some replies. She went upstairs to do this, which puzzled Nicholas since the desk lived in the sitting room, slotted into the inglenook to the left of the coal-gas fire. Perhaps she wants us to go, he thought with a jolt, perhaps she wants to be able to cry alone. She hadn't shed a tear since it happened, at least not in front of him.

'Mum's coping very well, don't you think?' remarked Alison, as the two of them washed and dried up saucers and teaspoons, placing them back in cupboards and drawers in a way that neither would have dreamt of doing in their own homes.

'Is she?'

'Well,' Alison pushed a clump of greying brown hair, coarsened by too much sun, back from her face, 'she hasn't broken down or anything. In fact, she seems very calm.'

'I thought that wasn't supposed to be a good thing,' said Nicholas gloomily, putting away the washing-up liquid in the cupboard under the sink and patting the jay cloth into a tidy shape. 'Nearly fifty years of marriage – I can't imagine – it must feel like losing a leg or something.' He pulled out a chair and slumped into it. 'I feel so much worse than I expected – I mean, we weren't exactly close, Dad and I – but somehow—' He broke off, as unwilling as ever to embark upon an expression of the curious tangle of reactions inside his head. 'How are you anyway? How are things down under?'

'They're great,' Alison answered quietly, 'I love it.' She rested her chin in her hands and stared at Nicholas with her wide blue eyes, now set amongst scores of tiny lines, but still as bold and bright as when she was a little girl. 'Oh Nicko,' she sighed, 'I'm so sorry that I've got to go back and leave all this to you. I do feel bad, you know, I really do. I can stay until the middle of next week and then . . . but we'll do our best to make it back over Christmas . . .' Her voice tailed off and she reached out to pat his arm. 'You look shot to pieces. I should go home now. Mum will be fine with me.'

'And after you've gone,' he said cruelly, 'will she be fine then?'

'Yes.' Her stare was unflinching. 'For the time being.' She placed her hands in front of her on the table, pressing the palms flat against each other, as if she was saying a prayer rather than making a statement. 'She's in good health and tough as anything underneath. Besides, she's got friends round here . . .'

'Who?'

She threw up her hands. 'Hell, I don't know, but look at all those cards.'

Nicholas shook his head doubtfully. 'I just can't bear to think of her alone,' he said, his voice throaty with concern.

Alison stood up and went to the door to listen for a moment. All was quiet apart from the ticking of the clock in the hall, a fine cedarwood grandfather which had belonged to an aunt of Joyce's and which Dick Latimer had wound every Sunday evening of his life with a small metal key that lived in the pot by the telephone.

'Look here.' Alison turned to face him, her hands flicking up to her head where they expertly scraped the hair back off her face, looping it into a loose knot that sat on her crown. 'It'll be us one day. We wouldn't want our kids to go into a panic about us, when the time comes, would we?'

Nicholas tried and failed to imagine his offspring as middle-aged grown-ups with children and mortgages of their own. 'I suppose not,' he sighed, getting up and putting on the jumper which was slung round his waist. 'I'll see you on Friday then.'

'Sure. We'll all feel better when the funeral is over.' She came over and gave him a slightly awkward peck on the cheek before suddenly flinging her arms round him, burying her head in his shoulder. 'Oh shit,' she said, pulling away and sniffing noisily, 'this is so bloody awful.'

'Yes, isn't it.' He kept his arm across her shoulders and squeezed hard. 'Are you sure you don't want me to stay a bit longer?'

'No, no, you go on home. Kate'll be wondering where you are.' She blew her nose loudly into a scraggy piece of tissue that she had extracted from the back pocket of her jeans. 'How is Kate anyway?'

'Oh Kate's fine, just fine.'

He called goodbye up the stairs on his way out, but there was no reply.

'I expect she's fallen asleep,' said Alison, yawning herself, 'she must be exhausted.'

On the doorstep Nicholas paused, car keys in hand. 'Do you think – I mean, do you want to see the body?'

Alison put one hand to her neck, as if instinctively seeking to protect her own life. 'No, I don't think so,' she whispered, shaking her head slowly.

'It's all right – I mean, he looks okay – quite peaceful.'

'I'm sure he does,' she put in quickly, 'it's just that I don't think I could bear it.' She tried one of her wide smiles, but her bottom lip trembled visibly. Nicholas kissed her on the cheek and left, thinking, not for the first time that week, that grieving was the loneliest of things, that, when it came down to it, there was absolutely nothing that one human being could do for another to make it any better.

On the way home he found himself pulling into a service station, ostensibly to get some petrol, though the dial registered a quarter of a tank and what he really sought was a breathing space. Adjacent to the petrol forecourt was an eating hut, a caricature of a Swiss chalet, its roof sporting giant cut-outs of hamburgers with legs and pizzas wearing hats. '*Eat your heart out*', said the sign above the door as Nicholas pushed his way in, making him even more aware that the emptiness inside had nothing to do with hunger or thirst.

He ordered a cup of tea, causing a frisson of impatience from the waitress, who stuck her pencil behind one ear and adjusted the angle of her green cardboard hat.

'You're supposed to eat if you sit here,' she said, flicking a cloth at the salt and pepper cellars and repositioning the menu.

'I don't want to eat.'

'If you don't eat, you're supposed to sit over there.' She indicated a cordoned-off area near a vat of orange juice and a sign for the toilets. The place was virtually empty, injecting a futility into her statement of which she herself could not fail to be aware.

Nicholas sat tight.

'Please yourself,' she said, tucking her cloth into the belt of her green dress, her voice the texture of cold steel. 'One cup of tea then.'

Nicholas was for a moment tempted to tell her that his father had just died, to use the information as a way of extracting courtesy if nothing else. In his dreams he talked to people about it all the time, tapping strangers on the shoulder, warning them not to be fooled as he had been, not to imagine that just because they didn't care now they wouldn't feel anything when the foreseeable end finally became real.

The only people Nicholas had told – colleagues at work in order to explain his need for some time off – had shuffled quickly from expressions of sympathy to enquiries as to Dick Latimer's age. On hearing that he was well over seventy they had shaken their heads sagely, as if to say it was what one had to expect, implying that such inevitability should somehow make it easier to bear, less shocking. Which to Nicholas was missing the point. If Dick had been ninety-two it would have felt the same, he was sure.

The little tab for the lid of his milk carton had broken off, making access to the contents quite a challenge. Nicholas stabbed the metallic covering with his thumb nail and clumsily tipped it in, spilling several precious drops onto the saucer. The tea looked brown and thin, like poor man's soup. It smelt faintly of cabbage, but tasted inoffensive enough. He burnt his lips on the first sip, bringing tears to his eyes. Blinking them away, he looked out of the window beside him, towards the unpromising view of the petrol station and motorway beyond. It was nearly dark now, dark enough for a blurred reflection of himself to be visible in the glass. He looked old and alone. There was no barrier now between him and his own death, no ceiling of protection. He was no longer a father's son. Nicholas blinked hard, but his vision would not clear.

With leaden legs, he crossed the room to phone Kate, wanting yet dreading the ring of concern in her voice, the unspoken, suffocating invitation for him to talk about his feelings, to be weepy and womanly about it all.

'Nicholas – where are you? I phoned Alison – I was worried.'

'Yes, yes – I stopped for petrol – I'll be home soon.'

'Are you all right?'

'Yes. A bit tired – lots of driving. Be home shortly. Don't bother about supper. I'm not very hungry.'

15

'I've been praying for you,' said Mary, when she bumped into Kate in Elhurst during the week after the funeral.

'Thank you,' said Kate, mildly alarmed at the thought of Mary kneeling on one of St Cuthbert's thin felt hassocks on their behalf.

'How is Nicholas?' Mary lowered her voice, her pale face ablaze with empathy.

'Nicholas is . . .' Kate faltered. She did not know how Nicholas was. She was beginning to think she did not know Nicholas. 'He's finding it hard,' she admitted eventually, 'very hard. It came as quite a shock.'

'Oh dear,' sighed Mary, unsure what to say next, half her mind still on the unsettling fact that she had spent a good thirty minutes in the new bookshop when five was all she had needed. She had gone in to pick up the book she had ordered for Angus' birthday, a glossy tome on South American wines, filled with breathtaking pictures of mountainous vineyards and toiling peasants in multi-coloured ponchos with crumpled bowler hats on their heads and black-eyed babies strapped to their backs. The man called Max had recommended it to her, when she had confessed to not knowing what on earth to get, disclosing the small, disloyal secret that buying presents for her husband was always a trial, since he was a hard man to please and hated anything that wasn't truly useful. Max, having heard of Angus' business, had suggested the wine book at once, pointing it out to her in a catalogue, reading aloud the snippets of reviews printed underneath, slowing down over key words like 'incisive' and 'comprehensive', making her feel as if he understood exactly how important it was to get the present right, to give Angus something that would make him proud of her.

'If your husband sells to small-fry like me, I'd be very interested,' he had said just now, wrapping the book for her, folding the corners crisply and tightly with his slim fingers, strands of dark hair falling in his eyes. 'I've quite a weakness for wine,' he laughed, handing her the parcel, 'though I'd only be able to afford a case or two.'

'Oh I'm sure Angus would be more than happy – I'll tell him, shall I?'

'If you would mention it, Mary, I'd be most grateful,' he said, dropping her name gently into the sentence, smiling at her in that open way which had set her heart fluttering shamefully from the first.

'What do you think of the new bookshop?' she asked Kate now, doing her best to sound critically disinterested.

Kate, who was in a daze that morning, reeling from a series of bad nights coupled with the overpowering sense that Nicholas was slipping away from her, pulling himself down to a level where he knew she could not follow, where he did not want her, blinked at Mary and muttered that the new bookshop seemed fine.

'Well, I hope Nicholas feels better soon,' said Mary, sensing that she was being dismissed and puzzling sadly over the mysterious distance which suddenly seemed to have opened up between her and Kate Latimer. Once upon a time it would have been unusual for a week to go by without them getting together under some pretext or other. Now she perceived a coolness blowing through Kate's attitude towards her, a preoccupation which deliberately shut her out. Since Mary inclined towards the belief that her own life was considerably lacking in substance when compared to those of other, infinitely more sparkling people around her, it seemed only natural that Kate, having had time to be her friend for a while, should now have to move on to more important things. So she tightened the knot of her headscarf and said goodbye, pushing disappointment to the back of her mind. Though it would have been nice, she thought wistfully, turning back with a last little wave, to tell Kate about the wine book, and about the flower arranging class run by the tiny Chinese lady in Westbury who served homemade sesame sticks and salty dips for her students to pick at, while her short, deft fingers worked on the most magical displays.

After the heatwave of early summer, the July weather was up to its old tricks. Kate found that whatever she put on in the morning felt either insufficient or excessive by lunchtime. Walking quickly now down the street towards the post office, she hunched her shoulders against the whipping breeze, hugging her basket to her and looking longingly at the sky for some sign that the clouds would relent and let a torchlight or two of warmth through the grey. The day had not begun well: she had to wrest herself from the deepest of sleeps, a warm, soundless cavern into which she had finally – thankfully – sunk in the small hours, worn out from countless games of yank-the-duvet with an equally restless Nicholas. Bleary-eyed, she had pulled on the flimsy skirt and shirt which lay on her chair from the day before – a muggy airless day that had forced her to change out of trousers after lunch – not even bothering to lift a corner of the curtain for an inkling of the cooler temperatures that lay in store. Having deposited the children at the school gates – only ten minutes late after speeding, grim and silent, through the countryside – she had been seriously tempted to climb back into bed and pretend the day had never started. But the sight of the manuscript beside the kettle in the kitchen pulled her up short, reminding her of how maddened she was by Nicholas, hardening her resolve to make one thing at least work in her life if everything else was so hell bent on falling apart.

Having kept the recipe book such a secret, even after Elizabeth had seen a few extracts and been so encouraging, Kate had experienced no small degree of excitement about finally breaking the news of its existence to her husband.

'Well done, Kate,' was all he had said, flicking briefly through the pile of papers, patting her on the back and then announcing that he was going to be late for work. Though a part of her argued fiercely that it had been both naive and selfish to expect anything more, that in Nicholas' current state of mind even winning the National Lottery might have elicited only the tamest whimper of jubilation, Kate could not suppress her disappointment at such an outrageously low-key response. To think that she might have stumbled upon something worthwhile that she could do, something which earned a little money and which she enjoyed, some reward for having survived the tough transition from being a full-time mother of infants to a part-time slave of teenagers was nothing short of revelationary. How dare Nicholas behave as if she'd done nothing more than blow her nose? Even when she went on to tell him about the photographs, how they were threatening to come down and take snapshots of her vegetable garden in order to build up the whole angle of it being a Good Life kind of cookery book, a DIY manual for aspiring, health-conscious gardeners with a few homegrown tomatoes and green beans in the fridge – as Elizabeth so glibly put it – even then Nicholas had said 'wonderful' in a flat kind of way, pulled on his jacket and picked up his briefcase as if it was a morning like any other. If it hadn't been for the children, who went in for far more gratifying expostulations of praise and amazement, Kate might have burst into tears.

The post office was right at the end of Elhurst High Street, the last of the shops before Havers Bridge and the countryside beyond. Inside, there was a long queue, only one window being open. Kate nodded at a few familiar faces before deciding to return when the place was emptier. On impulse, she turned left out of the building, away from the town, making her way along the narrow, cobbled pavement towards the river. It was even colder now, the wind whirling down the lane towards her, pressing her thin skirt against her legs and raising the hairs on her arms in paltry defence against the elements. For July this was arctic, even by English standards.

Beside the bridge a stony track led down to the towpath, a sandy sinuous route, popular with joggers and dog-walkers, that wound all the way through Westbury and on to the coast. Kate walked as far as the nearest of several benches and sat down facing the water, holding her basket with both hands on her lap, the big brown envelope addressed to Elizabeth sticking out awkwardly to one side. The river looked greeny black and uninviting. A child had drowned here once, she remembered, an accident on a family barge holiday. The little boy had slipped in without a sound apparently, without so much as a splash; it had been several minutes before the parents even realised he was missing. Kate shivered and pulled out a piece of paper at random from her envelope. Elizabeth had asked to see the whole thing, encouraging Kate to add more comments of her own at the head of each recipe, to give more of an intimate feel to the book, she said, to set up a closer relationship with the reader. Kate worried whether her efforts would come up to scratch.

Bean and Feta Salad

Broad beans make a wonderful base for a salad, especially if they are fresh from the garden and boiled for only a couple of minutes so that they retain all their flavour and texture. The mushrooms too, must be fried in sizzling butter for only a minute or two and then drained at once and spread out, so as to prevent them cooking any further in their own steam.

The colours of this salad are especially attractive and a variety of dressings go equally well with it. (See dressing section in Chapter 8.)

After starting to check her list of ingredients for spelling mistakes, Kate suddenly gave up, shoving the paper roughly back down amongst the rest, feeling thoroughly despondent about the whole thing. Nicholas' lack of enthusiasm blocked any possibility of her savouring her achievements alone. No amount of putting on a brave face could prevent her from caring what he thought, from seeing what he felt and being affected by it. Nothing she had tried seemed to work. He didn't want to talk to her, he didn't want to be comforted by her, he didn't want to make love to her. And, while her rational self rapidly swooped down with reassurances that this last matter was entirely Nicholas' doing, that their non-existent sex-life had nothing to do with any failing on her part, she could not quite feel it that way, not deep down. She was fed up with trying not to mind or seem hurt, when she minded dreadfully. Leaning back and staring up at the dense dance of jostling leaves overhead, she set about working out just exactly how long it was since she and Nicholas had made love. It was frightening not even to know, to have given up counting the weeks. There had been long spells before, a few weeks of not touching, icy patches which had melted, once the argument had been settled or grown irrelevant with time. Kate marvelled at people who claimed to embark on passionate reconciliations in the bedroom. Nicholas and her were not like that, never had been. They made love when they were happy with each other, when things were good, never as part of moves in a peace initiative.

Reluctantly, Kate forced herself to think back, holding her breath as she made the calculations. Nearly five months. Could it really be so long? Could it really be that mid-February had seen their last embrace, on the evening when she had prepared – of all things – a Valentine's meal – just for a laugh – fillet steak with cream and mushrooms, a cheesecake in the shape of a heart, tinned raspberries tumbling over its lush sides in cascades of crimson. Even a red rose in a vase in the centre of the table.

'So you're trying to win my heart,' he had joked, pretending to play hard to get, telling her with his eyes that he wouldn't be hard to get at all, that he was already hers, that beneath all the relentless, compromising hassle of family life he still loved her with a passion, a passion that he would prove later that night, pulling her into the well-known shape of his arms, taking his time, giving and receiving pleasure with the gentle skill and generosity that were the untrumpeted rewards of sleeping with the same person for over twenty years.

Instead of tears, Kate vented her self-pity through an anger that made her push her basket aside and start pacing the towpath, enraged at her own helplessness, at how things could have slipped so absolutely from her control in such a short space of time. She cursed Dick Latimer for the timing of his death. With all the triumphs and innocent fun of St Alberry's sports day to give them a boost, that evening had seen the emergence of a tentative hope that Nicholas had turned whatever corner it was in his mind that he needed to turn, that they were almost through the bad patch. It would have been hard to imagine that things could deteriorate still further, that the death of his father, instead of drawing them closer, should fall like an axe between them, cutting Nicholas off more sharply than ever.

Max Urquart caught sight of Kate as he crossed the bridge, on his way home for lunch. Usually he took a sandwich into the shop but that morning he had overslept, barely having time for a cup of coffee before he ran out of the door.

He paused, leaning his elbows on the cold stone, watching her clasp her arms and stamp her feet on the grassy verge of the river. Though she kept brushing it from her eyes the wind slung her hair back and forth across her face, revealing ripples of silver amongst its dark roots. That she was cold and upset he did not doubt for a second; his only hesitance was over whether to intervene. Thanks to the rushing of the water and the rustling agitation of the fierce wind in the trees, she clearly had not yet noticed him. Max was hungry. The thought of a fresh crusty sandwich and perhaps a glass of wine was enticing. He turned to walk on, then slapped the palm of one hand hard on the stone and started back to join the track that led down to the towpath. He didn't want to yell a greeting from the bridge; it might make her think he had been spying on her.

'Hello there,' he called as he neared the bench. He kicked a loose stone with the tip of one black suede shoe, and casually slipped his hands into the hip-pockets of his faded, perfectly pressed, blue jeans.

Kate, caught completely off guard, grabbed her basket and walked stoutly towards him. 'There was such a queue in the post office,' she gabbled, wondering why it should feel so unseemly to be found alone by a river, 'I thought I'd have a stroll – go back when all the pensioners have collected their cheques.'

'But it's lunchtime now,' he said, 'everything is closed.'

'Oh damn – I mean – how stupid of me.' She looked at her watch. It was already several minutes past one o'clock. 'We've lived in the country for years and I still expect every shop to stay open all day every day. Wednesday half-closing catches me every time.'

'It's Thursday,' he said, suppressing a smile.

'See what I mean?' She laughed in spite of herself and together they made their way back up to the road.

'Why not have lunch with me?' he asked suddenly, his voice matter-of-fact, as if he genuinely believed there to be nothing remotely inappropriate in the suggestion. 'My place is just down there.' He gestured over the bridge, though Kate knew very well where the old mill house was. 'It would kill time until the shops are open again, save you driving back in later.'

She looked round, unable, in spite of his nonchalance, to stop herself minding if they were seen. Then she thought, why the bloody hell not? and nodded her head. 'That would be nice – but are you sure? I mean – haven't you got work to do or something?' She gripped her basket, feeling frumpy and self-conscious.

'Nope.' He shook his head firmly. 'It would be a pleasure.'

So Kate went to have a Camembert and tomato sandwich with Max Urquart, seen by none save Mary, who drove by just as they were turning the bend of the short, woody drive that led up to his front door. 'The Mill House,' she said aloud, reading the freshly painted sign, that's where he lives; then she saw the bookshop man and Kate walking close together, too absorbed in conversation to bother with turning round and noticing who might be at the wheel of the red car passing behind.

16

Nicholas, having asked his secretary to fetch him some sand-wiches for a working lunch at his desk, closed his door and leant back against it with relief. Janice, watching the movements of his shadow through the glass panels of the door, assumed an expression of something like concern. It was ages since her boss had eaten in the staff dining room, an establishment that welcomed secretaries and board directors alike, its kitchens famous amongst several companies for their quality and range of food. Janice herself had already decided, while fetching Nicholas' sandwiches, to throw caution to the wind and go for the pasta dish that day, a thick creamy looking lasagna, dribbling with cheese and meat juices and smelling like heaven. She'd have Diet Coke instead of the real thing for a change, she told herself, to make up for the extra calories.

Before going back down to the dining room she tapped on the dappled glass section of Nicholas' door, using the clicky tips of her impressive finger-nails.

'Yes?' he called, sliding his newspaper into a drawer and reaching for a document from his in-tray.

Janice's manicured triangle of a face appeared round the door, her blue-laquered eyes looking slightly startled without the protection of her large spectacles. Though she saw very poorly without them, vanity still dictated that glasses were donned solely for the otherwise impossible tasks of typing, driving and watching the telly. She squinted at Nicholas, trying to sharpen up his edges: 'Are you sure you wouldn't like me to get you anything else? They've some lovely puddings today. Apple crumble? A scoop of orange sorbet?'

Nicholas shook his head. 'Thanks, but no.'

Janice refused to give up, spurred on by a host of homespun beliefs to do with appetites and healthy states of mind. Though no one talked about Mr Latimer's father dying, they all guessed that it must still be very much on his mind, from the way he looked, the sad hang of his eyes which, given all the laugh-lines, looked especially neglected somehow.

'How about an apple then? I'll bring it back up with me, if you like.'

Nicholas sighed, acknowledging defeat and recognising that in her own oblique way Janice was trying to help. 'An apple sounds good. Thank you, Janice. Could you close the door behind you?'

She shut it quietly and set off in the direction of the lifts, congratulating herself on a job well done. Nicholas Latimer had mellowed quite a bit recently, she thought, nothing like the arrogant swank he was when she first started working for him.

Nicholas pulled the pink tail of a small prawn that was poking out from between the crusts of his wholemeal bap and thought about the burden of expectation that life should be happy. From where did such expectations originate? How much easier and more sensible to labour under the supposition that the world was nothing but a vehicle for misery and disappointment; how much brighter then would shine the moments of relief.

He placed the prawn in his mouth and chewed slowly. Eating felt like nothing more than habit these days, a necessary ritual, like pouring petrol into a car. The prawn tasted faintly metallic. With a sigh he pushed the plate to one side and shook his newspaper out in front of him, trying and failing to lose himself in the stories of the day, stories which he had already heard on the Nine o'Clock News the night before and on the radio on the way to work. Nothing new had happened, nothing had progressed or changed; it all seemed stale and pointless; fragile peace agreements, poverty and death. Abandoning the paper, he picked up his bap and went to stand beside his wide glass windows, watching a silver pinprick of an aeroplane weave its way in and out of clouds, leaving a trail of flimsy grey smoke in its wake.

Nicholas had registered his uninspired applause of Kate's

recent achievements and her subsequent disappointment with all the helpless detachment of an audience watching a bad play. Unhappiness was numbing his senses, freezing his emotions into thoughts, cardboard cut-out expressions, behind which there prowled only fear. The pernicious gloom which had snaked its way into his life during the past few months, the sense of loss and futility, looked, with hindsight, to be part of a presentiment of Dick's death. Unlike Kate, who unravelled life's threads for inspection as her way of mastering them, Nicholas had long since given up any attempt to understand what was happening to him; identifying the myriad threads of failure and misery which had brought him to the present moment would, he was sure, do nothing to loosen their stranglehold upon his life. A drowning man does not seek to comprehend the elements that are destroying him.

He had lost a father. And, he was almost certain, he had lost a wife. The secret development of the recipe book only served to confirm the terrifying notion that Kate had for some time been intent upon developing a life without him that, soon, she would have no need of him at all, that she would finally spurn all his hopelessly unadorable ways for good. There was an ironic balance to it all, he felt, a sinister logic, that one life should fall apart just as the other was coming so beautifully together.

He tipped the remaining half of his by now unacceptably soggy prawn mayonnaise lunch into the bin and turned back to his desk, sliding the phone out from under the newspaper and staring hard at the panel of numbers. He was on the point of picking up the receiver when a small headline in the newspaper, which he had abandoned at the weekly science page, edged into the tramlines of his vision. *Apoptosis*, it said, *The Body's Self-Destruct Mechanism*.

Expecting – and wanting – to feed his mood, Nicholas read on.

'Every cell in the body is programmed to die. While as individuals we cling doggedly to life, our cells kill themselves with abandon – hundreds of millions every hour. The process, known as apoptosis, is not as purely destructive as it sounds; some parts of our body are sculpted by cell death. Our hands, for example, start out as

spade-like structures and the fingers emerge as the cells between them die . . .'

Nicholas gripped the paper, reading and re-reading the article, clinging to the metaphorical dribble of comfort that it seemed to offer, its little promise of life through death. Then he tore it out very carefully and placed it in the bottom right-hand drawer of his desk, under a pile of brown envelopes. The morsel of reassurance it had provided was, he knew, a measure of his hopelessness, and not something to which he would have easily confessed.

The telephone beckoned once again. He did not want to call his mother, but felt he should. The avalanche of sorrow that had overwhelmed him in the days immediately following his father's death had now fused with his melancholia about life in general. In some ways he missed the sting of that initial grief, the rawness of it all, the way it felt so true. He was left with a fat blur of worry – about himself, about Kate, about his mother.

'Hello, Mum, it's me. How are you?'

There was a small intake of breath before she spoke. 'Not so good today, I'm afraid. Still, it's early days yet, isn't it?'

'A shame Alison couldn't have stayed a week or two longer . . .'

'Yes, that would have been nice. Not to worry. She said they might come over at Christmas – did she tell you?'

'Yes, she did mention something about that. But then hopefully you'll get out there some time next year.'

'I hope so,' she said, her voice sounding brittle.

Nicholas couldn't bear it. 'Look, Mum, Kate and I were talking and – well – we think you should come and live with us for a while.'

'Oh no, I couldn't possibly – it wouldn't be right – you two have got your own lives to lead.'

'Of course it would be right. For heaven's sake, what are families for? Honestly, Mum, I mean it. For now it would be the best thing possible – for all of us. Do you think Kate and I like the thought of you struggling along alone?'

'Well, I don't know . . . really, Nicholas, I don't know if it would be for the best.' Joyce looked round her spotless hall, her eyes instinctively seeking and immediately missing the sight of Dick's hat on the near peg of the hatstand, ready to grab on his way out for their morning walk. An old coat of his had lain folded in a bag by the door for four days. She couldn't decide whether to give it away or have it dry-cleaned. It was a drab old grey thing from way back, with fraying cuffs and bare patches on the elbows. She couldn't decide about anything very much, she found, not even what to eat or which programmes to watch on the telly. 'You say you've talked to Kate about it already?'

'Absolutely.' Nicholas closed his mind upon the lie. It was a necessary lie, he told himself, made in the best possible cause. 'I'll talk to her again tonight and call you back tomorrow.' As he put down the phone, he realised that he felt excited. At last he was doing something helpful, something that felt good and right and unselfish. Of course it wasn't ideal to have one's mother living under the same roof, but it was by far the best solution for the moment, he told himself, since it would stop him worrying at the same time as giving Joyce some company other than the television, some reason to get out of bed in the mornings and keep on living. And of course it would keep Kate busier at home. This last thought merely fluttered in the back of his mind, a feathered whisper of an idea which he knew better than to analyse too deeply. There were good reasons aplenty for doing what he was doing, without having to examine subterranean motives like that.

On the way home from work that evening, he stopped in a lay-by and bought Kate twelve yellow roses from an old lady with tatty knuckle-length gloves and an unlit brown cheroot glued into one corner of her mouth. Upon request she handed him a leaky Biro and a slightly grubby piece of white card on which he wrote, *Congratulations Darling Kate – or should I call you Delia?'*

Although Kate had never been there, she had heard a lot about the Mill House, since its previous owners but one had turned out to be money-laundering crooks. It had caused quite a scandal in Elhurst at the time, allowing the locals to swop I-always-thought-so stories for months after the inhabitants had been carted off for suspended sentences and long retirements in the more temperate climes of Southern Europe. After that the place had been bought by a fat American with a pretty young English wife who was rumoured to have been a model, but who so seldom set foot in the town that many of the residents, feeling in some way cheated, started rumours of a crippling disease. Whether sick, or simply shy, the young wife's retiring nature clearly bore little relation to marital bliss, since barely a year after moving in, when thousands of pounds (or so it was said) had been spent fighting battalions of worms, beetles and several rare species of mould, the young wife moved out, hotly pursued by her American spouse. The house had stood empty for several months, until Max Urquart moved in.

Even before she had passed through from the dome-ceilinged hall into the oak-panelled sitting room, three of its walls lined with bookshelves from top to bottom, it struck Kate that to have bought such a place and a bookshop would have required sums of money of which she and Nicholas would only ever dream.

'Wow,' she said, her eyes quickly taking in the striking features of the room, and coming to rest on a set of carved panels on either side of a black cast iron mouth of a fireplace. 'What are those, saints or something?'

'The apostles. Originally lifted from a church in Ireland. Do you like them?'

She cocked her head. 'I think so. Though they look rather censorial. I should feel I was being watched and disapproved of. Did you put them in?'

'Yes, they are one of the largest of the items to make their way over from Suffolk. We had one of those documented agreements, my partner and I, or perhaps I should say disagreements.' He chuckled quietly, before adding, 'She was rather wealthy and, as things turned out, absurdly generous too.'

Kate, though intensely curious to find out more, thought it would be impolite. 'Could I have a quick look round? Would you mind?'

'Be my guest,' he said with a mock half-bow. 'Would you like a guided tour or shall I fix some lunch?'

'Lunch? Oh . . . perhaps just a sandwich . . .'

'That's all you're getting,' he laughed, leaving her alone in the sitting room.

By the time she had explored the rest of the house, silently marvelling at the cleverly created sense of light and space, the high ceilings and countless odd-shaped windows, each decorated with different borders of coloured glass, Max had prepared two fat French bread sandwiches, which he had placed on the table together with fluted glasses of lemony wine, a bowl of green salad, gleaming with dressing and flecked with granules of fresh pepper. He laid a fork beside each plate for the salad, together with a starchy damask napkin.

'Next time you come to eat at my house,' he said, pulling out a chair for Kate, and speaking as if the possibility of a subsequent meal together was not in question, 'I shall prepare something a little more refined, I promise. As I told you, cooking is my most favourite hobby.' He raised his glass at her before tipping it carefully towards the smiling curve of his mouth. He studied the colour of the wine appreciatively. 'Though I make such statements with due wariness, knowing myself to be in the presence of a true expert.'

'Oh don't be silly.' She blushed, trying to take an elegant bite through the wide crusts, causing soft cheese and tomato pips to bulge out on all sides.

'What does your husband do?' he asked suddenly, prompting her to swallow a large lump of food that really needed more chewing.

'Nicholas? He . . . he's in research – a director at Freeman Lyle – have you heard of it?'

Max shook his head, drawing her attention to the glint of his single earring, on this occasion a thin silver ring which made her think of pirates. She wondered how old he was. It was hard to tell, since his whole style, the long hair and casual clothes, was one that she associated very much with a person younger than herself; yet his face possessed enough signs of wear and tear for him to have been in his forties, like her.

'Does he like it, this research job?'

'Why do you ask that?'

He shrugged. 'I don't know, I suppose because I should hate it so.'

Kate paused, wanting to be fair to Nicholas, yet some wicked part of her urging her to side with the man opposite. 'I think he likes the security of it,' she said carefully, 'the way it supports us all.' Seeing a computer installed on a wide table down at the far end of his kitchen, set in a small bay window with a view of the river, prompted her to go on in some detail about Nicholas' writing success and then, far more dismissively, to mention her own recent efforts to get into print.

'That's what I need to do at the post office,' she added timidly, 'post my recipes off to my friend to see if her publishers are really interested. It'll probably come to nothing in the end.'

Max was effusive in his admiration, immediately running out of the room and fetching her basket from the hall so that she could show him some of her work.

He studied a page or two intently, rubbing his chin and frowning. 'You know what you need,' he commented, looking up at last.

'What's that?' asked Kate a little curtly, unable to stop herself from bristling at such candour, steeling herself for criticism of some kind.

'A computer. It would just look that much smarter – more professional. And you could iron out these typos in a couple of seconds.'

'Typos?' She snatched the papers from his hands and scrutinised the pages. She had checked each of them for mistakes countless times.

'I believe *stirred* has two *rs* not one. Or are you using the Anglo-Saxon spelling of the word?' His arms were crossed and he was leaning back in his chair, laughing at her.

'Damn,' she said, 'I wanted to get them off today . . .'

'Use my machine,' he offered, 'you'll have the afternoon to yourself. I'll switch you on before I go – show you how to use the word processing bit – and then switch you off when I get back.' He clicked his fingers. 'Couldn't be easier.'

Kate eyed the sleek silhouette of his computer longingly, thinking hard, fighting with herself over whether to accept. It was such a simple offer, so straightforward, and yet . . . If he really is being straight with me, she thought, then it might be all right to agree to such a thing. Was he flirting with her? Under the guise of lifting her glass, she risked looking straight at him. His Adam's apple moved vigorously as he chewed and swallowed. His eyes were intent upon another page from her envelope, apparently absorbed by the contents. It was impossible to tell what he was thinking. He wasn't her kind of man. Not even in her mildly wild youth had she ever gone out with someone from such a mould, someone who gave such a good impression of being daringly self-contained, someone who clearly cocked a snook at social conventions yet somehow continued to exist on the fringes of them. There was something of the artist to him, something decidely Bohemian . . . he looked up and she dropped her eyes at once.

'Well now,' he said, his voice teasing, as if he had somehow followed her line of thinking, 'have you decided?'

'Nicholas works on a computer,' she said weakly, 'perhaps I'll ask him to give me a hand.'

'I'm surprised he hasn't offered already,' Max said quietly. 'Are you sure you won't let me give you a quick tutorial? Then you can startle your man with your skill.'

Kate, suspecting that there was nothing Nicholas would hate more at that moment than to be startled by her skill, politely refused and got up to go. He followed her through into the hall, applying no more pressure for her to stay, but his silence somehow making her feel the need to justify her reactions a little further.

'Small country towns are funny places,' she began, 'people draw conclusions about things . . .'

'You mean someone might think we had been making passionate love on my hearthrug if they knew you had been here?' He kept his eyes fixed very firmly on her, enjoying the flush of colour in her cheeks.

'Something like that, yes.'

'Don't worry, Kate.' He pressed his finger to his lips, 'I shan't say a word.'

'Right then,' she replied, unhappily thinking that secrecy was as bad as suspicion, that pretending they hadn't met was almost as bad as admitting they had. 'Though I'll probably mention it to Nicholas,' she added airily. 'I usually tell him what I've been up to.'

The conversation lingered on, as farewell conversations in doorways have a tendency to do.

'Will he mind?' enquired Max, leaning one arm against the frame of the open door.

'Oh heavens no – I mean – I shouldn't think so. You see,' Kate swung her basket and looked down the leafy glade of his driveway, noting with a small part of her mind how many different greens there were amongst the mass of leaves. 'Actually, his father has just died and he's sort of distracted. Very unhappy, in fact. I can't get through to him at all. He's really not very interested in anything at the moment – except being miserable.'

It was as if, having got as far as the safety of the exit, with the end of their meeting so firmly in sight, some guard within her slipped.

'Poor Kate,' said Max, reaching out to stroke her cheek, a reaction which took her so much by surprise that she did not think to brush the hand away and which was closely followed – sympathy often having such unwelcome side-effects – by the most horrible urge to cry.

'Oh no, not poor me, poor Nicholas,' she said quickly, forcing her voice under control and keeping her eyes fixed upon the stone under her feet, counting the number of steps down to the gravel – one, two, three, four – driving her mind back against the emotional hiccough which was in danger of overcoming her completely.

'I should like you to feel that you can come and talk to me whenever you want, whenever you need to,' he said gently. 'My life is very simple at the moment, so I've plenty of time and room for someone like you.'

'Well, thank you,' she said hastily, brushing a troublesome tear from the side of her nose and starting down the steps. 'That's very kind, Max.'

'Good luck with the computing,' he called as she set off down the driveway, acutely aware of his eyes on her back, willing herself to make it to the bend without turning round.

As Kate walked back over the bridge and down Elhurst High Street, grateful to encounter nothing except a bouncing labrador and a white-faced woman with a pram, her heart continued pumping at twice its normal speed. While feeling as though she had made some kind of daring escape, she also could not resist imagining what life might have been like if she had embarked upon the adult section of it with someone like Max Urquart instead of Nicholas. Would being with such a man have made her more interesting, she wondered, less obsessed with domestic order and tidy emotions? Kate allowed her mind to drift further down the same avenue, thinking how buried bits of her might have developed, how the peaks and troughs of the last twenty years would have taken place over such vastly different terrain.

17

Sitting on the bus, Grace was aware of the silky lycra of the black body-vest against her skin, bunched up inside her school shirt, exactly where she had stuffed it inside the shop, first undoing her top three buttons so as to make the transition easier. It had been in a sale bin just inside the main entrance to the store, a messy jumble of half-price items, on special offer for the crime of being out of fashion or shop-soiled. That made it not nearly so bad, Megan had whispered, when Grace began to have doubts at the last minute, the palms of her hands turning clammy at the sight of the weasly-faced man in uniform, opening doors for grannies and mums with prams.

'A decent bust at last,' she had joked afterwards, patting the bulk filling out her school blazer, her heart soaring with relief that it was all over, that she hadn't chickened out.

This delicate bubble of euphoria burst the moment she arrived home. There it was, depressingly unchanged – a red-bricked, cliché of a cottage, with twee roses curling round the door, white shutters and flowery curtains, oozing an impression of family domesticity that was totally false. Feeling as though she had been away for years, that criminality had aged and transformed her, Grace experienced a numbing anti-climax at the sight of it, together with an almost physical revulsion at the thought of going in. Nothing felt right at home at the moment. It hadn't done for months.

To make matters worse, her father drove into the front drive just behind her, honking his horn and waving, goofily pleased at seeing her there. Grace cringed, as if an audience of people like Megan – who prided herself on having a father who worked nights and who had the decency to ignore his daughter except for dolling out wads of money – were lined along their driveway wall watching her.

She lifted a half-hearted hand in return, before quickly crossing her arms to camouflage the inexplicable increase in her chest size.

'Good day, darling?' called Nicholas, slamming the car door shut and striding over to her, his round face eager for a kiss. Grace lifted her cheek to receive his greeting with hasty reluctance, offering nothing in return. Her father had a bunch of roses in his hand and looked nauseatingly pleased with himself. He held them out for her to sniff. 'What do you think? Not bad, eh? A surprise for Mum.'

'Well, I didn't think they were for me,' she retorted, quickening her pace so that she could push open the front door ahead of him and race up to her room without being accosted by any other members of the family.

Once the door was safely locked behind her, Grace pulled out the lycra top and held it up to admire. It was a size twelve, too big really, with her measly height and silly little hillocks for breasts. Megan's bust was a thirty-six already. She had a proper cleavage too, not the puny channel created by underwire bras and tight cups that Grace relied on. After a few moments she knelt down and buried the black top amongst the jumpers in the bottom of her chest of drawers. She would never use it. Taking it was one thing; but wearing it would have taken another sort of courage entirely.

Downstairs Kate was busy preparing a complicated midweek meal, stirring a sauce that refused to thicken and keeping half an eye on a pastry crust which was browning in the oven. She knew herself well enough to recognise that all this industry was to do with how she had spent her day. Where some people ate Mars bars and bowls of cereal to combat confusion or unhappiness, Kate had always taken refuge in cooking. Appetite had nothing to do with it, eating being for her a celebratory thing, never an act of consolation.

Nicholas came in with his yellow roses just as she was struggling with the lid of her bayleaf jar, which had aways had a tendency to stick but which she kept because it was very old and had a pretty engraving on the side. At the sight of the flowers her mouth dropped open in an expression of silent surprise which remained for two seconds at least, while her hands stayed frozen round the lid of the jar.

'Well,' she said at last, quickly removing the sauce from the heat, setting down her bay leaves and rubbing her hands on her apron. 'What are these in aid of?'

'Nothing in particular,' he replied, smiling sheepishly, pleased at her amazement, but worried about what he had to say next. 'Though, if I'm honest, they are a bit of a sweetener.'

'A sweetener?' She took the flowers and kissed him lightly on the lips. 'Whatever for?'

Nicholas took a deep breath and shuffled his feet, placing them hip-width apart as if to steady himself for a fight. 'I want you to do your best not to be cross.'

'I don't like the sound of this,' she said, frowning and sitting down. 'Do I need a strong drink or something?'

'You might.' He remained standing, hands in pockets, puffing out his cheeks, looking at her from under his eyelids. 'The fact is, I have invited my mother to come and stay for a bit.'

Kate was actually quite relieved. After such a build-up and given the state of things between them, she had been expecting something far more dreadful. 'And how long is a bit?'

Nicholas drew in his breath. 'I'm not sure . . . I thought we might see how things went.' He went over to stand behind her, placing his hands on her shoulders and rubbing his fingers soothingly into the muscles at the base of her neck. 'When I rang today she sounded so low, so . . . so bewildered . . . I couldn't help myself – the invitation just sort of slipped out. I'm sorry – for not speaking to you first – but I do think it might be the right thing to do, for the time being anyway.'

Kate reached up and put her hand on one of his. That she could manage to be so impassive about such a mythical horror as a mother-in-law coming to live under the same roof was due to a complicated mixture of things, not the least of them being the sheer pleasure of having Nicholas wheedling so sweetly, making her feel needed, and just a little bit powerful, it being such a very long time since she had felt such things. Then there was her guilt too, the aftertaste of her meeting with Max Urquart which, as she had known full well at the time, she wouldn't dream of mentioning to Nicholas. Agreeing to take Joyce in felt, at that moment, like atonement, poetic justice, albeit for a sin which had never quite taken place.

'Katie, you're a marvel.' Nicholas bent down and put his arms around her. 'You know,' he said, kissing the top of her head, 'I really thought you might mind. I really thought I might have a bit of a tussle on my hands.'

'Hence the roses?' she said teasingly, closing her eyes with relief. How good it felt to be close again.

'I never was the subtle kind.' He blew very softly into her ear, his warm breath sending shivers down the back of her neck.

'You're telling me.' She gently eased his arms apart and stood up. 'I have a lumpy sauce to contend with and also' – she smoothed her hair – 'a favour to ask in return.'

Nicholas raised his eyebrows. 'Go on.'

'Please could you teach me how to use your computer – just the most basic things – so that I can type up and print out my recipes.' She added a dollop of cream to her sauce and stirred furiously. 'It struck me today just how horribly amateur my efforts look – wobbly letters and Tippex plastered all over the place. And,' she paused, to dip her finger in the mixture which was now swelling beautifully, thick and silky as custard, 'isn't there something called a spell-check I could use – I'm just so hopeless at spotting my own mistakes?'

Nicholas whistled, feigning awe at her computer-speak. 'It doesn't sound like you'll need much help from me.'

'Seriously, darling. Please will you help?'

'How can I not, Kate, how can I not?' He came up behind her and put his arms round her waist, slipping his hands into the wide front pockets of her apron. 'We can start right now, if you like,' he murmured, wondering if he would be able to smell another man in her skin, shameful but powerless before his own jealousy, hating its incoherence and confusion, the unrelenting concentration of its potency.

'Stop, that tickles.'

Behind them Grace, who had entered the kitchen in search of food, turned and crept away. Parents were so horribly confusing: all cold silences one minute and nauseous petting the next.

Megan said she had once walked in on her parents when they were making love, describing in detail their exact positions on the bed, how her father had looked over his shoulder at her, his face red and sweaty. Grace had been extra careful about going into Nicholas and Kate's room ever since, though she found it hard to believe that they hadn't got bored of each other's flabby bodies long ago. The very thought of her parents being anything like lustful with each other was somehow ludicrous and, if she really thought about it, a little disgusting. Sex should be the preserve of the young, Grace believed, like nude sun-bathing and tight shorts. She would have been appalled to know that between showing her mother which keys to press on the computer keyboard Nicholas untucked Kate's shirt from her skirt and massaged his hands across the smooth pastures of her back until they made contact with, and expertly unclipped, the fastening on her bra strap. By the time Kate's tutorial was over she was in no state to concentrate on anything very much, except how to get upstairs to bed without the children wondering why their mother was half-dressed.

'It's lucky Millie's sleeping over with a friend,' she whispered, as the two of them tiptoed past closed doors like burglars, clutching garments and shoes, heading for the more accommodating location of their own bed.

Even James was surprised when he went down for a drink later on to find his mother's manuscript all over the place and at least four sinkfuls of washing up strewn across the table and worktops.

'The lazy sods,' he muttered, rinsing a dirty glass for himself under the tap and taking a can of Coke from the bottom shelf of the fridge.

18

As Alicia's stomach swelled, so did Harry's desire to spend weekends out of town. Having never considered himself the running-away type, he now found himself spending a considerable portion of his time attempting to do just that. Though he recalled well-publicised cases of brave men in liberated countries like Sweden going to court about rights to force girlfriends to have abortions, he knew that he was not the sort of chap who – either mentally or financially – could ever weather such an ordeal himself. Besides, Alicia would win. It was almost sinister how the woman had changed, metamorphosed from an unassuming sugar-drop of a thing into a prepossessing, daunting female, capable of the most disarmingly articulate diatribes on The Situation and Harry's choice of roles within it. While seldom coming to his flat, Alicia had developed the subtle art of being a constant and penetrating presence within the telecommunications infrastructure that governed and connected all parts of Harry's life: honey-voiced messages on the answering-machine, notelets dropped through the letter-box, faxes at work. It was like a one-sided war, yet with peace as its theme. For never at any time did Alicia get tough or specific, nor even too cloying and lovey. Her messages, sweetly delivered, were always casual and reasonable in tone, telling him things which he thought he didn't want to know but which were somehow interesting nonetheless: that the scan was okay, though the heartbeat a trifle fast; that her weight had gone up by two kilos in one week; that she couldn't face cabbage but adored lemons; that if it was a girl she thought maybe Laura, and Toby for a boy; that a trust for the school fees might be wise, though didn't he agree that boarding school was out of the question until twelve at the earliest. Harry had no choice but to receive these communications with a heavy, helpless heart, wishing he could turn the clock back, wishing he could banish the flickers of involvement which such matters managed to ignite in his unwilling mind. There was no getting away from it, ever: A bloody baby. His bloody baby. And barring accidents, his toddler and teenager too. The idea appalled him, but so did the thought of mishaps along the way.

Since his weekdays were invariably busy, it was at weekends that Harry felt most vulnerable. Each ring of the phone set his brain buzzing with apprehension, burdening him with the unwelcome sense of obligation to account for his time, making him feel he should shore his life up with barriers against the possibility of meeting Alicia. Quite unaccountably, pregnancy had not succeeded in making her any less attractive to him. Since Harry had never reacted to the sight of waddling mothers-to-be with anything beyond pity for their husbands, this unshiftable lust came as something of a shock. If anything he wanted Alicia more than before. Her breasts were so magnificently full, so delicately etched with the fine baby-blue lines of risen veins, the nipples so teasingly bulbous and red. Her whole body seemed to have taken on a statuesque voluptuousness that made him want to bury himself in it, to lie against the huge curves and sink into their warmth. Believing such disturbing urges to be unnatural, Harry's first instinct was to avoid them, the most secure course of action being to absent himself entirely.

Apart from Beth and George, in whose company he found himself flagging quickly, all of Harry's other obvious bolt-holes contained serious drawbacks in the form of infants and animals, neither of which held much appeal for him since, like his sister, he sneezed badly in the presence of even the sleekest pet, and, given his present circumstances, he had no desire to be reminded of the unremittingly distasteful activities of the younger generation. Faced with such dead ends, and having given the matter careful consideration, Harry found himself picking up the reins of a friendship with an ex-colleague called Rupert Kershaw, who was actually a bit of a rough diamond for Harry's tastes but who, due to some highly dubious off-shore deals in his spare time, had retired from the lucrative challenges of outplacement to live in considerable style in a ten-bedroomed mock Tudor mansion on the outskirts of Dorking. His back garden consisted of a fine row of stables and several acres of fields, in which – under the guidance of an equestrian expert – he had taken to housing race horses, a species of animal which, so long as a handkerchief was kept within proximity to his nose, caused Harry barely a sniffle. The most attractive thing about Rupert Kershaw, besides his opulent lifestyle, was that he was divorced and – for the time being at least – without domestic dependants of any kind, furry or otherwise.

Rupert, who had come to the conclusion that the most rewarding aspect of luxurious acquisitions was the opportunity to show them off to other people, was more than happy to invite Harry Melford down for what turned out to be the first of several exhausting bachelor weekends. They slept, ate and drank a good deal, rising after midday and spending the afternoons at the races or on the golf course. Though Harry did his best to enjoy such pastimes to the full, the shadow of Alicia's impressive silhouette would cast itself across his mind at the most inopportune moments, clouding his day with repetitive preoccupations about what lay in store. Rupert, in whom he eventually confided the most obvious points of The Situation was generous and forthright with his advice.

'Pay the girl a fat cheque and start screwing someone else – with precautions,' he bellowed, wagging his finger in a manner suggestive of rich personal experience in such matters. 'It's her bloody funeral mate, I can tell you. Kids are trouble, believe me. Leave her to it and good riddance. Get your lawyer to draw up the documents – make it all legal – and pay her off. She'll be a millstone round your neck forever otherwise – use the kid to screw you later on, I shouldn't wonder. These Child Support Agency people make the Spanish Inquisition look like Noddy and Big Ears.' He chuckled at his own wit, leaving Harry to ruminate unhappily beside him.

They were ensconced in Rupert's deep leather armchairs late on a Saturday night, smoking fat cigars and swilling whisky. 'Did it on purpose, did she?'

'I don't know, maybe.' Harry sighed, abandoning his cigar,

which had gone out for the fifth time, to an enormous trough of an ash tray which sat on the footstool between them. His head ached. 'I think I might drive over to see my sister tomorrow, if that's okay with you.'

Rupert shrugged. Harry was no fun when he was feeling morose. 'Suit yourself. I've Grey Lady running tomorrow – so I'll be tied up with that. Sure you don't want to come?'

'No, thanks.' Harry, patting his trouser pocket to check that his lifeline of nicotine was to hand, pulled himself out of the chair and announced that he was going to bed.

'Can I take a bet for you?' Rupert winked. 'She's looking pretty – and the odds are marvellous.'

'No, thanks, Rupert, not this time.' Though Harry's smile was faintly apologetic, it had no reason to be. He had lost more money by placing faith in Rupert's horses than he cared to think about.

Any vague hopes Harry nurtured of a quiet word with Kate the following day were quashed almost immediately upon his arrival. Indeed, if a crystal ball could have granted even so much as a fragmented glimpse of the scenes taking place in the Latimer household as he made his way there, Harry would have made a considerable detour to avoid it.

The first shock was Joyce, who opened the door to him, looking so much older than he remembered, a wrinkled shrew of a thing, all blinking eyes and fidgets. Though Kate had mentioned Nicholas' astonishingly altruistic intentions towards his mother, Harry – given all the other, more pressing matters on his mind – had temporarily forgotten all about it. Knowing Kate to be a determined, sensible creature, he had never really expected her to allow such a thing to happen. So it was uncomfortably startling to find Joyce on the doorstep, drowning in a navy-striped butcher's apron of Kate's, her pink twisted fingers dripping with washing-up water.

'Oh,' she said, looking terribly flustered, 'Kate didn't mention . . .'

'Hello, Mrs Latimer.' Harry, never sure about kissing or handshaking such indirectly acquired relatives, eyed her wet hands and opted for a peck on the cheek. Her skin felt powdery soft and smelt of lavender. 'Kate couldn't have mentioned it because Kate didn't know. I was just passing . . .'

'Who is it?' called Kate, coming down the stairs, her arms full of clothes, her face looking tense and flushed. The summer holidays were in full swing, the children, lunging between boredom and exhilaration, argued fiercely over everything; Nicholas, meanwhile, had wriggled back inside his spiky shell, leaving Kate to feel that apart from domestic order of the most superficial kind, family life had veered right off course again.

'Harry – what a surprise,' she said, her voice flat. 'Come in. We've had lunch, but there's loads left over. No one was hungry – I suppose because it's so hot again.' Harry eased his tall frame between the exercise bike and Joyce – who seemed determined to let him pass before moving herself – and gave his sister a hug, washing and all, before following her into the kitchen, where she began loading and unloading various household appliances, slamming cupboard doors and drawers between sentences.

'A bit of a busy time, as you can probably see. All three children are off tomorrow, thank God. It's the summer holidays, Harry,' she said impatiently, exasperated by his blank expression, 'all parents do their best to get rid of their children for at least some of the time otherwise we all go mad. Coffee?' She put the kettle on without waiting for his answer and started looking round for a teaspoon. 'I hate chaos,' she muttered, frowning. 'Aha!' She scooped a spoon out from under a tea towel and waved it at him. 'You'll have to settle for instant I'm afraid, I'm in no mood for fiddling with the percolator. Besides, I think we're out of filters.' Joyce came in while she talked, taking up a position in front of the sink and starting to scrub away at something which never emerged from the water and which Harry eventually decided must be the washing-up bowl itself.

Kate, unaffected by the presence of her mother-in-law to a degree which her brother at first found admirable but then suspected might be downright insulting, continued with her commentary on the state of family life.

'It's rather a stroke of genius to have got them all going away together, though of course I'm paying for it now, finding enough clean things to put in their suitcases. Millie appears to own the grand total of three socks – all different colours.'

Fighting, with only modest success, to suppress a series of eye-watering yawns, Harry leant back against the hard cross bars of the kitchen bench, thinking how uncomfortable it was and wishing he hadn't come. His head, though not exactly aching, seemed to be placing undue strain upon the muscles of his neck. Rupert and he had lunched as well as dined the day before – two bottles of wine and roast pheasant at his local pub, resulting in quite the slowest and loopiest eighteen holes that Harry had managed for a long time.

'James is off on a cricket tour to Devon and Cornwall,' Kate was saying, 'Millie is going to stay with a friend on the Isle of Wight and Grace, much to her disgust, is going to stay with a family in Montpellier to brush up for her French oral.' She placed a steaming mug of coffee in front of him and then started surrounding it with tottering piles of underpants and socks.

'Where's Nicholas?'

Kate looked round, as if she too would have been glad of an answer. 'In his study, I expect. He's spending a lot of time in there at the moment. I'll give him a shout.'

'Don't worry – if he's working – I don't mind.'

Nicholas, who had heard the arrival of a car, followed by the unmistakable, rather nasal voice of his brother-in-law, decided that he had every right – seeing as it was only Harry who had presumably come to see Kate and not him – to finish his paragraph. He had abandoned the play and was now working on a bitingly satirical story about a man whose father suddenly dies, leaving the only son with the dilemma of what to do about his mother. It made a welcome change to feel strongly enough about something for sentences to form in little runs instead of one faltering word at a time. It also gave him a good excuse to get away from the unforeseeably irritating presence of his mother.

Exuberance at having persuaded all parties concerned of the positive aspects of grandma coming to stay had been short-lived. As sole creator of the situation, Nicholas was painfully aware that he was not best placed to start criticising it. Kate's initial acquiescence, the night of the giggling computer tutorial, which was followed by their first love-making in months, had been followed by the sort of let-down which only too often accompanies a blast of reality. An immediate regeneration of trust and understanding was simply not to be. While Nicholas hid behind a walled silence of anxious and somewhat guilty second-thoughts, Kate resignedly cleared out the poky spare room, where her sewing machine lived, together with a pile of mending that had sat there so long that some property tycoon of a spider had created a gossamer metropolis, connecting a ripped dressing gown of James's to the saucer of a pot-plant on the window-sill. After managing a marathon of perfect humour and non-stop smiling for the first week of Joyce's arrival, Kate had since slumped into a hearty see-how-well-I am-coping attitude, which made Nicholas less rather than more inclined towards empathy and which precluded all possibilities of mutually supportive discussion.

It might have been better, Nicholas told himself, if his mother had shown a little more gratitude, instead of standing mutely by, watching him load up her two suitcases and knitting bag as if he was nothing more than a cab driver. Though it was unrealistic to expect anything approaching wild enthusiasm from a person whose emotions, for as long as he could remember, had always been held on the tightest of reins, Nicholas couldn't help continuing to hope for appreciation of a more visible kind – a gleam of pleasure maybe, some detectable hint that she was thankful. Anyone could see what lengths had been taken to make her little room look welcoming – the basin glistened, a vase of pink and yellow flowers bobbed prettily on the small table beside the open window, the freshly washed curtains stirred on the faint summer breeze – but Joyce had simply sat on the bed and patted the counterpane, looking as if none of it meant anything to her, as if she wasn't really seeing it all. She didn't even comment on the portable television, which they had hired specially and which took up most of the space on top of the chest of drawers right opposite the bed, so that she could watch it lying down if she wanted to.

'We thought you might like a telly to yourself,' Nicholas couldn't resist saying, tapping the top of it and pressing all the buttons, as if she simply needed proof that it worked in order to light the missing spark in her eyes.

'Though of course you're welcome to use the main one whenever you want as well,' put in Kate quickly, worrying that Joyce might interpret the presence of the mini telly as a sign that they wanted her to leave them alone. Which they did of course, but not all the time.

During the intervening weeks the well of Nicholas' compassion, so easy to feel when its object had been at a safe distance, had all but run dry. While Kate maintained an infuriatingly good show, Nicholas found that he could only muster the shortest bursts of sweetness and patience, the effort of even these paltry offerings often leaving him shaking with frustration at his mother's ways, her silence, her complete lack of response.

Almost worse than specific irritations themselves, Nicholas found, was the uncomfortable sense of having an audience in the house, of having space filled that he was used to having empty. It was unrelenting: Joyce was always there, helping Kate in the kitchen, not intruding in any audible sense, but making him feel that he had somehow lost his place in the house. Even when she wasn't there, even when she took herself off to watch telly or potter in her room, the threat of her reappearance remained, the hovering, grating possibility of yet another timid offer of unwanted tea or help which, with the cruel illogicality of such things, only seemed to highlight every other tension in Nicholas and Kate's lives. As for any twisted notions about the presence of Joyce tying Kate more to hearth and home, Nicholas almost laughed when he thought of them. If anything Kate seemed even busier than before, even more unreachable.

Joyce, terrified of being a burden, went to great lengths to earn her keep, helping out in every menial way she could, unwittingly causing fresh ripples of domestic unease every day. The bathroom and loo were two of her favourite targets for improvement, usually through the liberal use of pungent aerosols which made Kate's eyes stream and which reminded Nicholas of gruelling product-testing sessions during the early stages of his career, when he would come home with his clothes reeking of chemically sweet fragrances, most of them far too sickly ever to advance out of the confines of a test-tube. Pomanders and mini sacks of herbs started appearing in niches all over the house, tucked into drawer corners and slung round coat hangers, emanating fragrances that lingered in Nicholas' clothes long after he had left the house, shadowing his movements like bad thoughts.

Laundry too was a field in which Joyce felt she had a valuable role to play: the result being that Nicholas' socks were frequently to be found wedged in beside his handkerchiefs instead of in the organised jumble of the belt and braces drawer below; his shirts, rather than being hung loosely, were buttoned onto their hangers, adding precious seconds to his hasty morning ablutions, forcing his unwilling, sleepy fingers to grapple with the hurdle of additional buttonholes. After a while, even his underpants began to appear in tiny, regimented piles, each pair folded and pressed to the size of a small handkerchief – an unnecessary, intimate attention which made Nicholas' flesh creep, fuelling the harrowing sensation that the minutest details of his life were being tampered with in the most obtrusive way.

All attempts to penetrate Kate's high-voltage, multilateral, I'm-not-going-to-let-this-get-me-down defence systems met with little reward. Joyce needed to be kept busy, she said, her voice coated with irreproachable tones of uncrackable neutrality, and if that meant flat socks, life-threatening air fresheners and tooth mugs which kept disappearing into the dishwasher, then so be it. As far as Kate was concerned, control over the purchasing and preparation of food was her main priority. So long as she could keep Joyce at bay on that score – which she had, after a sticky incident or two concerning boiled instead of steamed marrow and an assault on the skins of some lovely chubby-stemmed button mushrooms – she felt able to rise above the rest. It was a question of keeping her eye on the ball, she told herself, keeping control over the things that mattered most to her, until – although she couldn't quite imagine how – the situation resolved itself.

Some twenty minutes into Harry's ill-timed visit, Nicholas' paragraph was interrupted by a timid knock on the door. 'Nicholas?' came the muffled voice of his mother, 'can I come in a minute?'

'Yes,' he replied between clenched teeth, beginning to press the buttons to save his work and close the machine down.

'Sorry, dear, it's just that Kate's brother Harry has arrived – he's having a coffee in the kitchen—'

'Oh really? Well I'd better rush out and say hello then, hadn't I?'

If she heard the sarcasm in his voice she had the grace to make no acknowledgement of it. Instead, she began fussing round his desk, putting papers in piles and flicking at specks of dust.

'Just leave everything, could you, Mum?' he said tightly. 'If you tidy in here I'll never find anything again.'

A hurt look passed across her face, immediately making Nicholas feel awful, and even more so when she explained that she was looking for a copy of Kate's book, a freshly printed version having been run off by Nicholas' computer and subsequently approved by a cookery editor.

'Kate asked me to bring it through, so she can show Harry.'

'Oh I see.' He joined in the search, suppressing the urge to have a moan about how his wife's papers seemed to take up more space than his own these days, how sitting down to write took twice as long as it used to because he had to burrow through heaps of her stuff before he could get to the keyboard.

'So exciting,' his mother was saying, 'to think that Katherine is going to be in print. She says some television people are coming to take pictures this week—'

'Not television people, Mum, some photographers who specialise in leeks and tomatoes,' corrected Nicholas, hating himself for minding so much, for feeling so pathetically threatened by the thought of Kate being surrounded by tousled, tight-jeaned men with cameras – all those smooth-talking media types who used kisses instead of handshakes and had relationships instead of marriages.

While perceptive enough to recognise the element of irony in his wife becoming an author – albeit of a list of recipes – in just a few months, when he had spent years trying and failing to be a part-time artist in his own right, it wasn't jealousy for the book upon which Nicholas' heart alighted so much as for the opening doors that went with it, the new world that was unfurling before her. That Kate herself seemed to be taking it all so very much in her stride, complaining about the idea of cameras in her kitchen, quite convinced that any work of hers which made it in to print would soon end up propping open the doors of second-hand bookshops, did little to reassure her husband. Nicholas was beginning to believe that such displays of nonchalance were nothing more than that – a front, to hide her relish, the excitement of new horizons, the prospect of escape . . .

'Is this it?' Joyce held up a fat red file that had been hidden under a dictionary with an empty mug on top of it.

'I believe so,' said Nicholas, his tone softening at the sight of his mother's gnarled fingers, the way she had to use the palms of her hands to hold the file. 'Everything all right, is it, Mum?' he asked quickly.

'Oh yes,' she said, patting the stiff wisps of her purple-tinted perm and leading the way out of the study, Kate's work pressed to her chest.

In the kitchen Millie was asking her uncle to explain exactly why some ferries sank and what her chances were of arriving on the Isle of Wight without plumbing the murky depths of the Solent.

'Not that I'd mind drowning,' she added dreamily, cupping her face in her hands with her elbows resting on the table, 'they say your whole life flashes before you, like the fastest of films.'

'I'm not sure I'd like to see a film of my life, thank you,' remarked Harry, before noticing Nicholas in the doorway and getting up to reach across the table and shake his hand. 'The muse is with you, I gather,' he announced, sitting back down.

'Yes, sorry I didn't emerge sooner,' drawled Nicholas, determined not to be roused at the dig in Harry's tone, 'but I was having a little spurt.'

'What are you working on exactly?'

'Oh, just a little story about a family – nothing much.'

Harry raised his eyebrows. 'Have you read it, Kate?'

Kate, heading upstairs with basket of freshly laundered towels, shook her head. 'I haven't been allowed to.'

'Nonsense,' called out Nicholas crossly, 'you haven't asked. There's no secrecy,' he said, turning his attention back to his brother-in-law.

'Can I read it then?' asked Millie at once, sitting on the table and starting to peel the last banana from the fruit bowl.

'You'd find it very very boring, my love,' said Nicholas, ruffling her hair.

'Can I read it?' said Joyce from behind the door, where she was arranging the folds of Kate's apron so that it hung nicely from its hook, hiding the gash in the door where somebody had once done something unspeakable with a hammer.

'I think I had better concentrate on finishing the damn thing,' replied Nicholas evasively, his heart quickening at the thought of how Joyce might react to his blue-rinse protagonist with a penchant for floral aerosols.

His mother, behaving as if she had never raised the question, then proceeded to ask each one of them in turn whether they wanted a cup of tea. Everyone said no except Harry, whose stomach was suddenly roaring with hunger and who had spotted a rather fine-looking fruit cake sitting on a plate on top of the fridge.

19

'So what do you think about having Grandma to live with us?'

Millie ran her stick along the fencing beside them, making the wire vibrate like an instrument. 'Dunno, really. It's okay, I suppose.' They were strolling along a narrow path between the largest of the two fields that backed onto their house, Nicholas having used his daughter's impending departure as a way of escape, on the pretext for a last walk together. 'Though I'd prefer a dog,' she added, making her father erupt in laughter and reach out to hug her bony shoulders.

'Grandma would like that,' he said, wiping his eyes, still chuckling. 'Swop her for a dog.'

'I'm serious,' said Millie, hurling her stick into the field, trotting to keep up with his long strides. 'Everyone in the world has a dog except us.'

'That is a slight exaggeration, my love,' said Nicholas, smiling. 'Dogs are harder work than grannies,' he went on, thinking to himself that this might not in fact be the case. 'They need walking twice a day, crates of expensive horse-meat and armies of people to look after them when you go away. Besides which your mother would never stop sneezing.'

Millie sighed deeply and tugged at the sleeves of her top so that they hung several inches over her hands; it was a favourite faded pink sweatshirt that had once belonged to Grace and whose shape had already been stretched two sizes at least through countless subjections to the vagaries of the washing machine. 'It's not fair. Why does our Mum have to be the only one in the world who's allergic.'

'She's not. Uncle Harry is too. It runs in the family. And you're jolly lucky it hasn't been passed on to you.'

At this timely moment they encountered a dog coming the other way, a giant collie of a thing, who bounced gleefully at Millie, putting his paws in her hands and planting generous licks on her chin.

'Monty! Down!' shouted its owner, jogging to catch up with her exuberant hound. 'He's quite harmless – sorry,' she said breathlessly, seizing the dog by the collar and pulling it off Millie.

'It's not a problem, I assure you,' laughed Nicholas, as Millie carried on stroking and petting the animal, making gurgly, crooning noises with the back of her throat.

'Thank God for that,' said the woman, smiling for the first time, her big mouth looking almost shy of its size. 'Some people mind dreadfully. You just can't tell these days. Could get sued for assault by a friendly dog, I shouldn't wonder.' She was wearing faded jeans that were torn at the knee – clearly as a result of overuse, as opposed to the scissor slits that sometimes appeared in the knees of Grace's trousers – tucked into black riding boots that looked scuffed and muddy. The jeans were tight too, Nicholas couldn't help noticing, perhaps even a little too tight, outlining impressively wide thighs and hips, together with the sort of bottom that he rather ungenerously associated with horsewomen. 'We don't usually walk round here, do we Monty? We've been having tea with a friend.' She clapped her hands. 'Let's go now, Monty; come on, boy. 'Bye,' she added, smiling again, her tanned, faintly leathery-looking face creasing dramatically round the eyes and nose.

'What a lovely dog,' said Millie, swooning for a moment before tugging on Nicholas' arm and shouting, 'Race you to the top.' The pathway widened as the gradient of the hill increased, leading up to a clump of trees and a trig point that overlooked Elhurst valley and its network of fields and curling black roads.

Nicholas groaned, reluctantly breaking into a jog, knowing that the days when he could beat even the youngest of his children had long since passed him by.

'Come on, Dad,' she yelled over her shoulder, 'you're not even trying.'

He put some effort in then, feeling the muscles in his thighs stiffen at the sudden demands being made upon them, while his lungs pushed against his rib cage as if indignant at having to vacuum up such unaccustomed gusts of air. Having made up some ground, and with a handful of the baggy sweatshirt just inches from his fingers, Millie put on a final spurt, accelerating out of reach, shrieking in delight at the chase having been so keenly fought. They collapsed, wheezing, at the top, leaning up against the warm stone of the trig point and laughing between gasps.

'Not bad, Dad, not bad.'

'I'm an old man,' said Nicholas, patting his pounding heart and wiping his forehead on his sleeve.

'Not as old as Grandma though,' said Millie quickly, feeling a twist of panic at the recollection of her grandfather and the thought of who might be the next one to die.

'Has Mummy said anything to you about Grandma?' asked Nicholas slyly, still fighting for breath but unable to resist the opportunity of a little family detective work.

Millie, unsuspecting, tugged at tufts of grass and moss and shook her head. 'Not really. Grandma is always helping in the kitchen and stuff, washing up and all those boring things. Mum must like that, mustn't she?'

'I suppose she must. But then Mum is always happy about everything, isn't she?' he went on carefully.

'Oh yes. Mum's brilliant. I wonder if I'll feel homesick on the Isle of Wight. Do you think I will?'

'Not for a moment, love. You'll be fine. It'll be us that miss you.'

She snorted in disbelief and got to her feet. 'I don't suppose you want to race back, do you?' she enquired, balancing on one leg and eyeing the slumped figure of her father with some concern.

'I don't think I do, thank you,' he replied, holding out his hands for her to help pull him to his feet.

'She hates how the Westbury people do her hair,' remarked Millie, as they approached the final bend in the back lane that skirted Chivers Farm.

'Who does?'

'Grandma. She told me the other day that it was much better at Snips in Worthing – that they got the colour right there. Will she live with us forever now,' she asked suddenly, 'until she dies?'

'Oh I shouldn't think so,' Nicholas replied uneasily, his mind still marvelling slightly at the fact that his mother should have confided in Millie about something as personal and adult as a hair-do.

'What'll happen then?'

'We'll see how things go,' he said, trying to sound breezy when the idea of the future – not just Joyce's, but his as well – filled him with hazy dread. 'We had to take her in, you know, Millie – I mean family is family and all that – it was the least we could do.'

His daughter shrugged. 'I'm just not sure she's very happy.'

'Well, no – of course she misses your grandfather—'

'I didn't mean that. I mean that I don't think she likes living with us very much.'

This unexpected and rather intriguing opinion was interrupted by the slowing down of a car behind them which, as they stood on the grass verge to allow it to overtake turned out to contain Mary Sullivan. In spite of reservations on both sides, a sense of social duty prevailed. Mary wound down her window to answer questions about the health of Angus and the wine-trade before replying in kind.

While the grown-ups talked Millie pressed her face against the window and peered in to the back of the car, the interior of which was spotless – quite unlike their own with its used tissues, discarded magazines and broken pencils. Her eye was caught by a pair of large black binoculars on the back seat.

'Oh, can I have a go?' she interrupted, already opening the rear door to reach inside.

'Careful, please,' begged Mary, looking flustered. 'They belong to Angus. He doesn't know I'm using them actually,' she added, her pale face ripe with the guilt of such a crime. 'He's in Portugal on business, you see.'

'A spot of secret ornithology on the side, eh Mary?' joked Nicholas, his mind more on the sudden darkness pulling round them and the fact that he had promised Kate he would get Millie back in time for an early night.

'They give me a headache,' said Millie, squinting at Nicholas.

'It's too dark and you probably need to adjust the focus. And we haven't got time.' With a stern look he lifted the binoculars from Millie's neck and gently replaced them on the back seat, before slamming the door shut. 'Spotted anything unusual then?' he asked, not because he was really interested, but because it was a last something to say before excusing themselves.

'Oh here and there,' Mary replied tightly, releasing the hand-brake in preparation to move away.

''Bye then,' called Nicholas, waving her off with false cheer, his other hand firmly on Millie, whose jigging toes were dangerously near the wheels of the car.

Once round the bend Mary drove quite fast, her mind flitting between worries about the binoculars – how she would have to polish them ever so carefully with Angus' special little square of non-scratch cloth, before restoring them to their padded silk womb of a case – and about Nicholas, whose crinkly-eyed mockery made her afraid.

Though it has all been in the interests of some harmless detective work, she reassured herself, lifting her foot off the accelerator so that the speedometer needle swung back to a less unsettling number – and in an area in which Nicholas himself had the most vested of interests.

But, as she motored slowly home, Mary could not quite rationalise all her guilt away. For it had been undeniably nice to watch Max Urquart through the powerful lenses, to see him so close to and yet so unaware, lying in a hammock, as he had been that afternoon, all that sleek hair in a pony-tail, his shirt off, displaying a great mat of black hair from his neck to the waistband of his shorts, his expression inscrutable behind the double protection of reflector sunglasses and an open book. How could one not be fascinated by such a man, especially if one knew – or suspected to the point of knowing – that he was having an affair with a friend, and a married friend at that?

Encouraged by Kate earlier in the year, Nicholas had booked two weeks' holiday to coincide with the children's various summer excursions, the idea at the time being the highly attractive prospect of the two of them enjoying a little undisturbed time alone. For reasons to do with a massive roof leak the previous winter and three lots of school fees, there was no question of going to France that year, though they were still considering a late – and wholly unexpected – invitation to spend a week in Devon with Victoria and Frank Armstrong, who had rented a large farmhouse for the summer and now seemed to be wondering what to do with it. While both Nicholas and Kate had the sense to be wary of such an offer from people with whom they had never been exactly intimate, the maddeningly silent, sink-scrubbing presence of Nicholas' mother made the idea of getting away increasingly attractive. Yet Joyce was also the principal reason for hesitating, since the invitation did not extend to mothers-in-law and would certainly not have been as appealing if it did. The thought of leaving her (like the thought of a domestic pet, thought Nicholas ruefully, remembering his conversation with Millie) was complicated.

In the meantime there was the business of photographing Kate behind baskets of strawberries and courgettes to be endured. On the day when the camera crew were due to arrive Kate got up before dawn in order to have herself and her kitchen ready for the invasion. She had stayed up late the night before too, polishing surfaces and the glowing skins of her freshly picked produce with the same duster, to the accompaniment of unhelpful comments from Nicholas, who was being despatched to Worthing with his mother for the day and who – though he could see the sense of it – was struggling to accept the prospect gracefully.

'Elizabeth says they'll turn the place upside down,' said Kate, not for the first time, 'wires and lights all over the place – you'll hate it.'

'I don't mind going or staying,' said Joyce, carefully swallowing one of the tinned grapefruit segments which she liked for breakfast, together with a modest bowl of the bran cereal which made Nicholas think of animal droppings and which Millie refreshingly referred to as Grandma's brown worms.

'Kate wants us out of the way, Mum, hadn't you noticed?'

Kate shot him a look, but Joyce, nodding her head and smiling blandly, said again, 'I don't mind going or staying.'

After only a nibble of her toast, Kate left the table and started fussing round the kitchen, not unlike her mother-in-law, thought Nicholas with some despair, moving things that did not need moving, marking time. After some consideration, she had chosen to wear a blue, sleeveless cotton dress which she had bought on holiday in France the year before; casual but smart, it had a flatteringly low twenties-style waist with the most delicate silky pink trim round the neck and shoulders. On her feet she wore low-heeled blue leather shoes, her favourites, which she had had to polish hard to hide the scuffs. Her hair, freshly washed that morning, shone in the sunlight that was already streaming in from the garden. Rather than using the hair-drier, she had let it dry unaided, the result being that it hung naturally loose and full, as Nicholas loved it best. Watching her, wiping cupboard doors that already shone, bending down to pick invisible grains of food off the spotless floor, tresses of copper-tinted hair falling elegantly across her carefully made-up face – blue round the eyes, pink round the lips to match the trim of her dress – it seemed to Nicholas that there was now no question that she moved in a world of her own, that she was already happy without him.

In spite of the constraining effect of his mother's presence, he grappled daily with the temptation to confront Kate on the matter of this treacherous independence, to challenge her with accusations as to what else it entailed, who the new focus of her life might be, who could be responsible for her sickening happiness, such inner radiance and self-belief; knowing that, he, Nicholas, with all his pathetic self-doubts, his moping, his clear lack of achievement and prospects, could never have been the architect of such a blossoming state of mind himself. But all confrontations continued to take place only within the vast, echoing confines of his head: elaborate fantasies about private detectives with bulging grey files and smudged, sexually incriminating photographs danced on the fringes of Nicholas' mind, teasing and cruel, filling him with too much fear ever to find the courage to haul such fictions into the spotlight of reality. Suspicion, though corrosive and painful, at least allowed for the accommodation of hope, however weedy and deluding that hope might be. Whereas the confirmation of a suspicion, as Nicholas knew all too well, would blast every atom of hope out of existence, calling for the kinds of action and follow-up of which he felt quite incapable.

Meeting the crew, who looked as though their collective ages would be less than his own, and who burst in with cheeky remarks about coffee and bacon sandwiches, nicking notches of paint off doorways and walls with protruding bits of metal and sharp-edged boxes, did nothing to relieve Nicholas' general anxiety. The cast of characters was even worse than he had imagined: apart from a woman in red flared trousers and a clinging ribbed white T-shirt, with a pencil stuck behind one ear and a cigarette behind the other, they were all men. The one in charge, who had a spruce head of densely streaked blonde hair and a smile that clicked into place with suspicious ease, made Nicholas especially uncomfortable. He introduced himself as Jake, extending a dead fish of a handshake, a wet limp offering which felt like an insult.

'It will be just fine,' drawled Jake, the moment Kate confessed to being worried, his voice laced with a designer-trace of an American accent, his arm insouciantly reaching out to touch her naked shoulder, making Nicholas want to lunge between them, ranting uncouthly about feelings to do with wives, even ones who had abdicated from their marriages.

Instead, he pressed his lips together hard and clung to the inner lining of his pockets with the intensity of a man gripping a cliff-edge.

'Shall we go then?' he said at last, turning to his mother, who was looking wide-eyed at all the bustle.

'Elizabeth said she would try and get down later,' put in Kate weakly, clasping her hands, feeling quite out of her depth. The men and the girl in red trousers buzzed about them, talking about light-readings and reflectors, looking for wall-sockets and pushing open windows.

'I'll leave you in this gentleman's capable hands,' said Nicholas dryly, nodding at the back view of Jake's impressive coiffure and taking hold of Joyce's knobbly elbow in order to steer her towards the front door.

'What a lot of fuss,' his mother remarked, as she pulled out unnecessary quantities of seat belt and then struggled to feed it back again.

'What a lot of fuss indeed,' agreed her son grimly, slotting the belt in its buckle for her before nosing out of the drive and turning for the coast.

They were driving along a precinct of shops parallel to Worthing's main high street, having negotiated no less than twelve roundabouts (Nicholas counted) and eight sets of traffic lights – all on red – when Joyce asked if he would stop the car. Somewhat irked, he pulled over onto a yellow line and enquired rather brusquely if she felt sick. Their journey had been undertaken in silence, aided by a radio programme on the plight of the homeless.

'I just want to pop in and see if they can fit me in.'

Nicholas craned his neck out of the window and scowled. Worthing on a summer's day was not the most appealing prospect. 'Pop in where?'

'Snips,' she retorted, as if her own son should have been blessed with sufficient powers of telepathy to have worked this out for himself. 'It's just across the way.' She unclipped her belt and began trying to open the door with the knob for winding down the window.

'I thought we were going to Barnet Street to get some of your things,' he said testily, folding his arms and watching her grapple ineffectually with handles from out of the corner of his eye. 'You didn't say anything about going anywhere else.'

Joyce put both hands on the top of her handbag, a large blue leather one which Dick had given her one birthday many years before, and gripped it hard. 'I want to go to Snips,' she said, not looking at her son, but staring, unblinking, at the windscreen. 'I want to have my hair done.'

'Fine. Okay. No problem. I just wish you had mentioned this before. We could have made an appointment or whatever. They might be too busy.' Alarmed by some indefinable aspect of his mother's behaviour, an aspect which he could not immediately decide was something to be pitied or feared, Nicholas switched on his hazard lights and got out of the car to help her across the road, raising his free hand imperiously at the nearest of the crawling cars. 'Thank you, Nicholas,' she said, patting his arm when they reached the other side, 'you are always very kind.'

Knowing this to be a statement of blatant untruth Nicholas was tempted for a second to deny it outright, to present her with the bald facts of his selfishness, his resentment at having to deal with her, the insidious intrusion of her presence in his ailing marriage.

'Nonsense,' he mumbled, before pushing open the door into the hairdresser's, which jangled like an ice-cream van, welcoming them with a blast of synthetically warm air that blew into their eyes and up their nostrils.

Nicholas hovered beside a pile of magazines and a wig display while Joyce approached the counter.

'Joyce – how lovely to see you,' exclaimed a carrot-headed girl with a broom. 'Look, Tracy – it's Joyce come by to see us. How are you keeping, love? You look well. It's been a while.'

His mother said something inaudible at which the other women smiled and nodded. Nicholas, feeling superfluous and disliking the aromatic greenhouse heat of the place, played with a small cutting of hair under his shoe, pushing it back and forth across a smudge in the linoleum until the hairs were scattered about him like scratches on the floor.

'You must be Joyce's son. How do you do.' A large lady with a squashed face and black hair piled in jagged tresses on top of her head stood before him with her hand held out; there were fat dimples between each knuckle, like kneaded dough. 'We have missed her,' she said with a cluck of her tongue, turning to smile again at his mother, who was now following the orange-haired girl towards a row of basins at the back of the salon. 'We'll do her now, seeing as she's come in so special. I'd give us an hour if you can – there's such a queue for the driers. Who'd have thought it on a Tuesday?'

Who'd have thought it indeed, echoed Nicholas to himself, while shaking the sausage fingers and assuring their awesomely proportioned owner that one hour was no problem at all, that he would return promptly to pick up his charge.

Once outside he was at rather a loss as to what to do. Finding a parking space would probably take an hour, he thought gloomily, as he stepped boldly out into the jam of traffic, daring a lime green Volkswagen to run him down. After a few minutes of driving past spaces that filled as he approached or emptied just after he had driven by, Nicholas decided to resort to the sanctity of his parents' house in Barnet Street, where there was at least off-street parking and the possibility of coffee. Some idle channel-surfing on the radio then reminded him that it was the fifth day of a salvageable Test match, thereby affording the prospect of a more indulgent morning than he could ever have dared to hope for. Indeed, so distracted was Nicholas by the thought of the tranquil fifty minutes or so that might now lie ahead, that he almost forgot to brake at a zebra crossing, coming to a noisy stop just a couple of feet away from a straw-haired woman with a prancing collie. As she turned to cast a contemptuous look at the perpetrator of the screeching tyres, tossing her hair angrily over one shoulder, Nicholas recognised the woman as being the owner of the dog who had licked Millie's freckled cheeks with such enthusiasm a couple of days before. Since his window was wound right down and a stream of pedestrians were still crossing behind her, he had plenty of time to stick his head out and express apologies.

'I'm so sorry – I was miles away – dog's all right, I hope,' he called.

After a moment's frown, her face broke into a smile, the wide mouth revealing very large but well-formed teeth.

'Oh hello,' she called back, waving from the safety of the pavement.

There was a solid line of cars behind Nicholas and no obvious space to pull over. The cricket match, a mug of coffee – maybe even a biscuit if he was lucky – beckoned. Yet there was something about this coincidence which made him want to prolong it; something inextricably tied to all the confused unhappiness of the last few months, the sense of being so miserably adrift, of being bounced and bruised along by a life which had lost all sense of identity and hope. In the face of such chaos, encountering the same friendly-faced woman and hound for a second time in as many days, felt alluringly like fate, like something that – at long last – was meant to be, and which, by virtue of that fact, was therefore wholly permissible.

'Hang on!' he called, motioning at the woman to follow his car, which he turned down the nearest side road and brought to a halt with its two near-side wheels right up on the high pavement, so that any impatient motorists to his rear – his own steering-wheel thumping impatience forgotten in an instant – might pass with ease.

At first he thought she had ignored him. But after a couple of moments her head appeared at the window of the passenger seat. Nicholas reached over to wind it down, wondering what on earth he was going to say.

'Are you lost?' she asked, squatting down to his level, looking more puzzled than anything else.

'Er . . . yes, sort of . . . trying to park – it's hell, isn't it?' As if in verification of this only partially honest statement, a very large lorry now turned into the street behind him, its fat wheels hissing on the hot road. The driver, neatly framed in Nicholas' rearview mirror, stuck his middle finger rudely in the air and began mouthing vigorously at the audacity of selecting such an inappropriate parking place.

'Well you can't stay here,' said the woman with a smile. Some of her dry sandy hair had blown across her mouth and stuck to one corner of it, making Nicholas want to brush it away, not out of any desire to caress her face, but because it was mildly annoying, like a label sticking out of a jumper or a speck of spinach between front teeth. She was not his kind of woman at all – far too thick-set and wide, the kind of shape which he had always found implicitly threatening, since it smacked of a brand of hearty robustness which he had never been able to consider wholly feminine. But in spite of these physical attributes, this woman did not strike Nicholas as hearty in the least, her voice being soft and tentative and there being an appealing timidity in her eyes which made him feel bold.

The lorry driver began sounding his horn, looking round for understanding and approval from passers-by at the unforgivable folly of the driver blocking his way.

Nicholas was on the point of giving up and driving off when the woman put her hands to her ears and shouted that she knew where he could park, if he would like her to show him the way.

'Yes, please,' he shouted back, pressing the door handle down so she could get in. The lorry driver, perceiving that some progress was being made, deigned to take his hand off the horn.

'Christ, that's better. Now, where to?' Nicholas accelerated off the pavement, bumping down onto the road at such speed that something under the car scraped horribly on the concrete. The dog, which had jumped onto the back seat, began snuffling round Nicholas' right ear, fighting for a share of the warm air drifting in through his open window. His breath smelt fishy and hot.

'Monty, do please sit down,' said the woman, but not very fiercely, leaving the collie to feel quite free to continue resting his damp lower jaw on Nicholas' shoulder, his tongue lolling to one side like a slab of raw meat. 'Left here,' she instructed, giving Nicholas so little warning that he had to swerve sharply to comply with the command, causing Monty's dribbling mouth to lurch with unpleasant force against his cheek and giving the lorry driver a pretext for one last long blast on his horn.

'God, some people,' she remarked, shaking her head. 'Right at the lights, then third left and you're on Galpins Road where there's a Harvester pub with an enormous car park round the back. I always use it when I need to shop and so on.'

'Perhaps we could have a drink there?' suggested Nicholas, feeling adolescently gauche and wishing he had the courage to butt Monty's head hard against the side of the car.

'Sorry, it's no dogs allowed in there,' she said, not sounding sorry at all. 'Monty goes mad in cars. He would destroy everything if we left him.'

'Oh dear. Well that rather puts the lid on it, doesn't it? But thank you anyway for showing me where to park. Very useful indeed,' stammered Nicholas, as he drove into a small alleyway that led past the side of the pub, 'I shall remember this next time.'

'But we could walk along the front if you like – grab a coffee or something.'

Having not till now detected any enthusiasm on her part to draw out their acquaintance further than was strictly necessary, Nicholas was momentarily taken aback.

'Well, fine, let's do that then,' he replied after a quick glance at his watch. 'I hope you aren't too many miles away from where you wanted to be,' he added, as Monty scrabbled across the gear stick and began scratching at the window for release.

'Oh no, not at all. I come here because Monty likes the beach. And also I had a broken watch to collect – but it wasn't ready. I live in Hougham, which only has a village post office, so Worthing's my nearest town for everything else.'

Nicholas got out of the car and stretched with unnecessary exaggeration. 'A walk would be nice,' he said, endeavouring to sound casual. 'I've got forty minutes or so till I have to rescue my mother from under a hair-drier.' As the words came out he caught himself wishing that he had offered a rather more glamorous scenario of commitments. The mention of a mother seemed somehow deflating.

But his companion was impressed. 'Gosh, how kind for a grown-up son to be taking his Mum to the hairdresser.'

'Oh, I'm not kind at all,' he replied quickly, 'it's just that she's living with us at the moment – my father died a couple of months ago and—'

'Oh no. I am so very sorry.' They were walking parallel to the sea, along a broad but crowded pavement whose side-wall was broken at regular intervals by stairways leading down to the pebbled beach. She stopped and touched his arm, staring into his face as she spoke, clearly wanting to seem sincere. 'And you've taken your mother in – I think that's wonderful. It just doesn't happen enough these days. When you think how that kind of behaviour used to be the norm – using granny as a baby-sitter and so on. I think it's lovely.'

Nicholas blushed, casting his mind over the sober reality of having his mother as a house-guest, how much it differed from the image she was painting, how the only good thing about it was that Joyce's presence provided a deflective shield for the unmentioned crisis between him and Kate. 'It's not that easy,' he admitted, following her down a flight of steps to the beach. But the strong on-shore breeze blew his words away.

'There you are, my boy,' she said, crouching down to unclip Monty's lead. The two of them stood and watched as the dog raced eagerly towards the flat glints of muddy water.

'He loves it best when the tide's out,' she said, squinting into the sun, one hand raised to her forehead to take away the worst of the glare.

Nicholas coughed. 'Hey look, I don't even know your name.'

'Joanna – Joanna Wyrall,' she said at once, turning and holding out her hand. Her arm was deeply tanned, he noticed, covered in glossy fair hairs; the hand he gripped was large and dry-skinned, a working hand, more than a match for any man's.

'And I'm Nicholas Latimer,' he replied, the spectre of school-boy awkwardness rising to haunt him again, as colour rushed to his cheeks and a false tinniness invaded his words. She wore wedding rings, he noticed, a thin gold band next to a cluster of sapphires and diamonds, clinging to her fourth finger like a jewelled insect.

They occupied a table in the first of the beach-side restaurants that they encountered, an impersonal linoleum-floored place that smelt strongly of fried onions.

After requesting two coffees, Joanna ordered herself a slice of pizza. An odd thing to eat with a mid-morning coffee, Nicholas couldn't help thinking, as he eyed the lank strings of cheese dangling over the sides of the plate, the pink squirls of anchovy, the blackened slivers of pepper and mushroom, all shiny with oil. But he liked women who ate, women with appetites. It was one of the many things that had first attracted him to Kate, the way she loved food, consuming it with unabashed pleasure, easily favouring such gratifications above traditional female concerns about waistlines. Kate ate, without shame, whenever she was hungry. The result, curiously perhaps, was that, though wholesome and beautifully rounded, her body had never been reduced to the belittling business of a weight problem – not even when the children were small, when Nicholas found himself drawn by invisible, magnetic force towards the tea table, where he plundered mouthfuls of half-chewed sausage and cold fish finger, invariably soggy with spilt juice or tomato sauce. In addition to which, Kate, in all the twenty-odd years that he had known her, had maintained the infuriating ability to stop eating at the precise moment when she was full, sometimes – incredibly – with a forkful of food halfway to her mouth, regardless of whatever other uneaten delights lay scattered about her plate.

The manner in which Joanna's wide mouth closed greedily around her thick slab of pizza suggested a history of rather less control where food was concerned. Nicholas, enjoying watching her, tried not to stare.

'Henry doesn't allow pizza at home,' she confessed at length, seeking to clear a crumb from her upper lip with her tongue, 'he's a bit a of a snob when it comes to food. Hates the Americans,' she added, as if this explained everything. 'So Monty and I sneak out for treats sometimes, don't we, Monty?' She kicked the dog gently with her toe, causing a couple of thumps from his bedraggled tail.

'My wife's rather a good cook,' said Nicholas, feeling obliged to balance out the topical turn of the conversation with some contribution of his own. 'She's got a book coming out soon – full of healthy recipes – spinach quiche and rhubarb soufflé – all that sort of thing.'

Joanna rolled her eyes in admiration. 'That's amazing – a book – you must be incredibly proud.'

She licked the grease from her fingers and looked round for a napkin.

'Yes, I suppose I am,' he said, handing her a small papery rectangle which had been pinned under her plate. 'Of course I am,' he added more firmly, guilty that his first acknowledgement must have sounded so woefully half-hearted. Kate's achievments were granted a second or two of respectful silence before he found himself spilling out the story of his own paltry success on the radio. It felt more and more like a party-piece these days, an anecdotal thing that he produced whenever he felt the need to be interesting. It was such an unspeakably long time since it had happened.

But Joanna was enthralled. 'You're joking. That's incredible – I mean, I listen to Radio 4 all the time – I've got radios all over the place – in the bathroom, kitchen, stables – I must have heard your story – what was it about again?'

Encouraged, Nicholas bothered with a more detailed account of his narrative than he had managed for a long time, thinking as he did so, that it really hadn't been a bad idea, that he had probably captured the character of the lonely old man rather well.

'I'm sure I remember it,' she squealed. 'Was there a little boy?'

'A little girl,' he corrected, willing her to remember something definitive, wanting to believe that he had met a face from the blur of his one-time anonymous audience – wanting to believe it with as much intensity as Joanna wanted to believe that she was conversing with a genuine author of something she had heard. They struggled on for a few moments more.

'Oh, but I'm sure it's the one I'm thinking of,' she exclaimed finally, after a silence fraught with the possibility of mutual disappointment and frustration. 'It sounds so similar.' She pushed her empty plate and cup to one side and leant forward on her hands so that her breasts appeared to rest along the wall of her arms. She wore a blue denim shirt, unbuttoned just to the point where the widest V of her cleavage was visible. There was a thin gold chain round her neck, from which dangled a tiny gold charm of the letter J, resting in the deep nook formed by the strikingly protuberant edges of her collar bone. 'So what are you working on now? Do you do much research? Gosh, I just don't know how you people do it – thriller writers and such, who travel to exotic places and read up manuals on how the inside of a bomb looks.'

Nicholas thought of his abandoned play about an unhappy middle-aged man and his new short story about a tiresome grandmother. 'Research?' he coughed. 'I should do more of it – I only wish I could – but there's so little time – trying to write and hold down a fulltime job, you know, it's . . .'

'A miracle you get anything done at all,' she finished for him, her face glowing with admiration.

'I'm just so thrilled to have met a writer,' she said, 'really, it means a lot to me.'

Nicholas squirmed and fiddled with his watch strap, covered with the confused pleasure of receiving a compliment that was not remotely deserved. In such a frame of mind, it was a few seconds before he registered the time staring up at him from his wrist. 'Bloody hell. I've got to go.' He pushed back his chair and looked about him, anxiously trying to catch the unseeing eyes of the one solitary waiter attending the tables. It was almost lunchtime now, and the place was twice as full as when they had entered.

'Bloody hell,' said Nicholas again, looking at his watch in despair and starting to pull change out of his trouser pocket.

'Don't worry about that.' She put a restraining hand on his arm. 'Please, let me pay. I'd like to, really.'

'No, I couldn't possibly,' he began.

'You can pay next time,' she interrupted, delivering something of a sly look from under her sandy eyelashes, but speaking very quietly, perhaps in case it suited him better not to hear.

'Next time? Oh, I – well, I suppose that might be possible,' he faltered.

'Won't your mother need her hair doing again?' She was teasing him now, having seen enough reluctant enthusiam in his stammers to decide that he was tussling with his conscience rather than any lack of appeal her suggestion held.

'Here.' She quickly scribbled her name and number on the back of the napkin, the Biro working faintly over the greasy bits where she had wiped her mouth. 'Just in case.' She stuffed the napkin in the breast pocket of his shirt, an action which was done hastily but which nevertheless felt a little thrilling, like the cool, large hand on his bare arm a few minutes before. Nicholas patted the pocket, unsure quite what to say, his mind already focusing on the more pressing business of navigating his way back to the hairdresser's.

'Call after eleven – I'm always riding before then.'

'Right. Well then.' He rubbed his hands together, before quickly extending one out to her. She shook it firmly, half her face at least taken up with smile. It really was one hell of a mouth, thought Nicholas, as he smiled back, sure that he would never see her again, sure that such things were not for him, that he simply wasn't the sort to follow up such invitations. Coincidences were one thing, he told himself, as he sprinted along the front and cut up in the direction of the car park, but arranging a rendezvous on purpose was in a league quite beyond his reach.

Before starting the engine, he took the napkin from his pocket and studied it hard, willing himself to tear it in little pieces and throw it away. Instead his mind took a fictional detour of its own, leading him down avenues to do with glamorous spies memorising vital codes and swallowing the evidence. The napkin looked indigestible. And though the name Joanna Wyrall was firmly inscribed across his brain, the numbers, when he closed his eyes, would not form. He screwed the paper into a ball, then carefully unfolded it again, tearing off the section that had the numbers on it and folding it very very small, until it was no more than a pellet of a thing, of the kind James had once used as ammunition for his catapult. This he placed in the very bottom of his glasses case, his spare pair, that lived in the car.

With this task done he drove away feeling safe; as safe as the smoker who has given up, but who knows where a cigarette is, just in case he needs it, should the unthinkable emergency arise.

21

Kate did not like the man called Jake. He reminded her of an American boyfriend from her teens, a sixth-former with springy hair and Donny Osmond teeth. Though he had to be credited as the first male to make her realise that the business of sticking tongues in mouths could be erotic as well as slimy and uncomfortable, he had quickly ruined it all by spouting reams of unintelligible Spanish poetry between embraces, and glancing with more tenderness at his reflection in the mirror behind than at Kate herself. Vanity was not a quality that Kate had ever admired in men. Though she would not have dreamed of mentioning it at the time, Nicholas' outrageous lack of dress sense when they first met, the way his hair blew up into odd shapes that he did not bother to rearrange, the holes in the elbows of his stringy jumpers, were all things that had endeared him to her greatly. Nor did the decision to accept his proposal of marriage constitute anything like a crusade to chisel her husband into a more socially conforming shape. He had slowly done that himself – sometimes, in Kate's soppier moments, when she remembered the red corduroys and yellow shirts, to her regret – being forced into it by a growing self-consciousness that had burgeoned on its own, a reluctant awareness of the more superficial expectations that went hand in hand with promotions at work, the lamentable fact that spotty ties and double-breasted suits could be helpful aids in the slippery scramble up the proverbial ladder.

Jake Harcourt paraded his self-awareness like a badge of merit, as if the immaculate state of his billowing silk shirt and artfully streaked hair were visible proof of the infallibility of his work. He wore pointed suede ankle boots with metal heel and toe caps that clicked noisily on the tiles of Kate's kitchen floor, jarring against her nerves as he strutted between lights and wires, fiddling with props and screens, not getting anything done.

The first whirr and click of the camera was something of a relief. Kate posed, her face a stiff mask of cheerfulness, sitting in an apron at her table, behind precarious pyramids of asparagus and strawberries, a polished tomato in one hand, a glass of white wine in the other. But it soon became apparent that her prized vegetables were posing something of a problem to the artistic sensibilities of the director. They'd do what they could, sighed Jake, looking disconsolately at his preparatory Polaroid snaps, but a re-shoot in a studio with plastic models of food was almost certainly on the cards. Kate, incredulous, summoned enough courage to argue politely that such methods would betray the whole point of her book, pointing out that home-grown produce, like most living things, did not emerge in perfect circles or oblongs, but suffered the natural inconvenience of bumps and blemishes. All of which caused Jake Harcourt, as he stroked the cultivated crop of bristle on his cheeks, to embark on an impassioned diatribe about the role of art in creating a semblance of reality, the tricks that had to be played, the needs of the marketplace and other concepts which made Kate's mind reel with despair. The crew, meanwhile, lit up cigarettes and lolled around the kitchen watching their leader perform with expressionless faces. When he had finished, Kate, with trembling fingers, made herself a coffee that she did not want, while Jake punched numbers on his mobile phone – clipped into the belt of his jeans like a fancy buckle – and began a series of lengthy calls to London, discussing the problems posed by pear-shaped tomatoes, and many other things besides.

When Nicholas phoned from the hairdresser's to say that he would be a while yet since they still hadn't been to the house and were about to go out for a bite of lunch, Kate longed to tell him of the farce going on about her. But since she was speaking from the kitchen, surrounded by the visibly deflated members of Jake's team, now quietly discussing their love-lives as opposed to faulty light-meters, a lifetime's training in civility constrained her. Besides which Nicholas had sounded rushed and preoccupied, not remotely in the mood for being sympathetic.

Instead she told him that progress was slow and that she was thinking of going out to lunch herself, perhaps with Mary, whom she hadn't seen properly for weeks. Having put the phone down, she dialled the Sullivans' number at once, only to be greeted by a recording of Mary's voice, sounding warbly and self-conscious, saying that she would be glad to take a message after the tone.

'It's Kate, just calling for a chat,' she said weakly, before retreating upstairs to comb her hair and have a think. Her face, usually cool and dry, was noticeably sticky and moist from its brief spell under the hot glare of the artificial lights, especially across her forehead and round her nose. Taking a yellow tissue from the box beside her bed, she pressed it to her face, closing her eyes and breathing deeply. Nothing was as she wanted it to be at the moment. Nothing was working out. In a mood fast approaching desperation she then tried phoning Harry, but his secretary said he had gone to lunch with a client and wouldn't be back for two hours at least. Finally, she tried Elizabeth, letting the phone ring at least twenty times before slamming the receiver down, grabbing her handbag from where it was slung over the back of her bedroom chair and marching down the stairs. She took her car keys from the hall table and dropped them into her bag.

The crew were sitting on the doorstep and in the doors of their van, the sleeves of their T-shirts rolled up to their shoulders to catch the sun, eating doughnuts and sandwiches from white cardboard boxes. The girl was perched decorously on top of Nicholas' exercise bike, which had been parked out on the gravel in order to increase the width of the thoroughfare through to the kitchen.

'Can't get hold of anybody helpful at the present moment in time,' drawled Jake, patting his telephone, the first hint of an apology threatening to cloud his handsome face.

'Neither can I,' she said curtly.

'But we'll keep on trying – see if there's anything else they want us to do down here – otherwise we'll reschedule a date in town. We've got all the shots of the dishes to do anyway,' he added, observing from Kate's expression that she was seriously agitated, 'it's not like we ever had a hope of wrapping the whole thing up today.'

Though it was almost certainly pointless saying anything, she was unable to restrain herself.

'It seems to me,' she said, tossing her head defiantly, daring them to mock her, 'that this whole exercise has been something of a shambles. I suspect a lot of money has been wasted. I'm only glad it is not mine. If Elizabeth calls, could you tell her that I want to speak to her urgently? Thank you.' And with that she strode out of the drive, having at the last moment decided that what she needed was fresh air.

'Excuse me – when will you be back?' called the girl in the flared trousers, cycling slowly, her legs only just reaching the pedals, which had been adjusted for Nicholas.

'Shortly,' she retorted, turning back with a brief grimace of a smile.

As she walked along the edge of the road, stepping carefully round the boggy edges of the grass and the remains of what had, a couple of days before, been continual lines of deep puddles, she found herself wishing more than anything that she had not banished Nicholas to Worthing for the day. It would have been good to have some moral support in the face of the studied nonchalance and barely veiled condescension to which she had been subjected. Nicholas would have spoken his mind, she was sure, stuck up for her far better than she could herself. After all I'm merely a woman who cooks, she thought petulantly, side-stepping a puddle only to find herself landing right in the middle of another one; I am not intellectual or artistic, she said out loud, looking down to study the specks of mud on her bare white shins.

'Shit,' she said, more loudly still, not on account of her legs, but because her beloved soft leather shoes had acquired a dark black water-line round their edges and were looking far worse than when she had set about polishing them the day before. In retrospect, all her excitement about the book seemed naive beyond belief; a thought which led her on to speculate with uncharacteristic gloom about how so many things in life which seemed to beckon with the promise of glamour or fulfilment only turned into the bitterest anti-climaxes. To be offered the possibility of being paid for her ideas about preparing food, such a simple instinctive process for her, had seemed, at the time, like something irrefutably good. Now, not only because of the failure of the morning but because of Nicholas' unforgivably lukewarm attitude to it all, she was beginning to wish none of it had ever happened, that she had never gone to the reunion and allowed herself to be egged on by Elizabeth. There was no happiness or satisfaction to be had out of any of it that she could see.

Having got as far as a field in which four boys were playing football in nothing but shorts and Wellingtons, their T-shirts having been assigned to the more important role of goal markers, Kate stopped and leant on the gate to watch them, thinking of when James had been so stick-limbed and pot-bellied. It made her nostalgic for a moment to watch the little lads, who could not have been more than five or six years old, to see all that unrestrained eagerness, to remember a time when all the crossed wires at home had been visible ones. There was so much silence and sulking between all of them these days, she thought, turning away from the gate with a sigh, resolving – by no means for the first time – to try and make things better, not to use the irritation of Joyce as a pretext for not coping with anything else.

In spite of the miserable state of her shoes, Kate found herself walking back with quite a bounce to her stride; with her head high and her arms swinging loosely, she acknowledged the swaying branches of the high trees on either side of her like waves of encouragement, as if they were sweeping her back home with fresh energy and inspiration. The recent rains had sharpened the green edges of summer, so that the jumble of leaves overhead gleamed with a new richness and depth. So much colour, she thought to herself, arching her back to look upwards, forcing herself to notice it all, to see with new eyes.

It was quite a surprise to find that the van had gone. The only evidence of her visitors was a few cigarette ends squashed into the thin layer of gravel directly before the front door. Even the exercise bike had been put back inside. Though Kate was by no means sad to see the back of them, she did find herself marvelling at the fact that while it had taken the best part of two hours to unload and set up their equipment, the reverse process had been achieved in less than half the time. She looked in her bag for her doorkeys, brushing irritably at her hair, which, when left to its own devices, without any discipline from the hair-drier, fell forwards all the time, getting in her eyes. Once the bag had been checked several times, she instinctively patted the sides of her dress, the places where jacket pockets would have been had she worn a jacket. It took time to accept the cruel blow that, after all her rallying optimism and resolve, she now had to face the fact that she had been foolish enough to embark on her walk without taking the keys to the house. Unwilling to surrender to her predicament, she made her way round the house, trying every window and door, incredulous that Jake and his crew should have been so fastidious about locking everything up again. When these last endeavours had proved fruitless, she stood in the middle of her driveway and screamed 'fucking hell' at the cornflower blue of the sky, tears of frustration stinging her eyes. An old man on a bike, cycling within earshot at the critical moment, cast her a curious glance over the wall of the drive, nearly losing his balance in the process, before standing on his pedals and disappearing round the corner at a discernibly increased speed.

It was just a question of killing time until Nicholas returned, Kate reasoned with herself, willing good sense to prevail where hysteria threatened. Apprehensively, she slotted the car key into the ignition; given the pattern of her day so far, it seemed almost logical that the engine should fail. But the motor kicked into life without a murmur; and with this small release of tension came the realisation that she was hungry. It was two o'clock already and she hadn't eaten more than a bite of toast all day.

Elhurst was so quiet that she was able to park along one of the rare sections of pavement not protected by a yellow line. Taking her time, she strolled down past the gleaming black front door of The Badger pub and a boarded-up window which had once been a butcher's, until she came to Mr Edwards' grocery shop. Having intended to treat herself to a packet of flapjacks and some fruit, she suddenly recalled having seen Mrs Edwards on occasions selling freshly made sandwiches from a hatch window at the back of the shop. Though the flap was closed, Kate knocked gently on the wood. Mrs Edwards, her cheeks veiny-pink and her corkscrew fuzz of grey hair bobbing indignantly, stuck her head out of the hatch with undisguised reluctance. She was in the middle of eating her own lunch, a pasty full of meat and veg from a batch she'd made the night before. Kate could see it half eaten on a plate in the background, beside a small portable television and a large mug with a faded picture of Lady Di and Prince Charles on the side.

'Oh don't worry,' she began.

But the moment Mrs Edwards saw that the intruder was Kate Latimer her face creased into a welcoming smile.

'I'm locked out,' confessed Kate. 'My husband will be back any minute, but I haven't had any lunch. I know it's late,' she faltered.

'Say no more my dear.' Mrs Edwards wiped her mouth with the back of her hand and listed what she had to offer. 'No ham or beef left, but I can do you egg mayonnaise on granary – or there's Cheddar and pickle if you'd prefer.'

'The egg mayonnaise sounds lovely. Thank you so much.'

Kate had already taken two mouthfuls before she left the shop. Though the mayonnaise tasted suspiciously like salad cream, the bread was soft and fresh. Chewing a little self-consciously, she continued walking down the street, waving through the window at Mrs Prowser seated, as always, behind the sewing machine in the dry cleaners, before coming to a stop in front of the bookshop.

22

Having used the time it took to finish her sandwich to muster the courage to go in, Kate was somewhat disappointed to find that instead of Max Urquart, a middle-aged woman in a green cardigan and long tartan skirt was manning the till. She was tapping a pencil nervously against a pad on her knee and frowning.

After a few minutes of time-wasting over the central display of the latest hardback releases, Kate dared to approach the counter.

'Is Max – I mean Mr, er – is he not in at the moment?' Her eyes kept darting to the door at the back of the shop, from where she expected the proprietor to emerge at any instant. She did not want to be caught asking after him. Exactly why she wanted to see him was not something Kate felt very keen to analyse, beyond the easily acceptable fact that she needed to kill time until Nicholas returned home with a key to their front door. Beyond that lay the disquieting sense that her desire to talk to the owner of the bookshop was more than tenuously connected to the frustrations of her morning, or perhaps, more disquieting still, to the frustrations of her life in general. It was almost like needing a pick-me-up, a tonic for disappointment, a few soothing strokes to a tattered ego.

'Are you a friend of Mr Urquart's?' said the woman eagerly, slipping off her stool and clasping her pad to her breast. Kate took a step backwards, murmuring, 'No not really', as if she had been accused of something far graver than friendship; but the woman, happily oblivious to Kate's confusions, continued with her assumptions regardless. 'Oh I'm so glad. The thing is,

Mr Urquart said that if the large brown envelope came I was to deliver it in my lunch-hour. Normally I wouldn't mind at all – all part of the job and so on and I know where he lives because he explained exactly – but then it turns out that the patisserie doing my son's birthday cake – he's twelve and I'd ordered an entire football pitch with goal posts and everything – looked smashing in the picture – but now they say they can't do it in time and I had to rush off and see if I could find another caterer – sort something else out. I had no luck at all, so I'm just ringing round now, to see what I can fix. Twenty hungry boys and no cake.' She grinned meekly. 'My fault, of course, for leaving everything to the last minute. So if you could take this to Mr Urquart for me, I'd be so thankful. I only temp now and then – I'm not even desperate for the cash at the moment – but when the agency called up yesterday morning they said that I was absolutely the only one for the job – an old trick I know, but I fell for it anyhow. And I do think it's important to keep one's hand in, though secretarial is usually my thing, not running shops single-handed. Still, it's been nice and quiet, apart from the last hour yesterday when the till jammed and I had five people all waiting to pay.'

'Is Mr Urquart ill then?' cut in Kate a little desperately, since the woman's thread of conversation seemed endless.

'Oh, he looked terrible yesterday. Yellowy cheeks and all green round the eyes. Just how my Stanley looks when he's not well – though getting *him* to take a day off is another matter entirely. Anyone would think doctors were there to make you feel worse from the way he goes on.'

'Where is this envelope?' enquired Kate politely, now mastering the art of beginning her own sentence before the woman had quite come to the end of her own.

'Here we are. No idea what it is, mind you. Only I did promise, seeing as he was so insistent, that I would drop it by in my lunch-hour. If it hadn't been for—'

'Yes, I quite see – very difficult for you. It will be no trouble.' Kate took the envelope which was fat and heavy. 'I can take it to him right now.'

'Well that's one of my prayers answered for the day.' She smiled, her whole body seeming to relax as she did so. 'Funny if you think about it: there I was, just thinking what I need is a friend of Mr Urquart's to walk into the shop and help me out – and here you are.' She clapped her hands. 'Do you know him very well then?' she asked.

'Oh not at all,' replied Kate hastily, 'just a passing acquaintance really, nothing more.' She tweaked the corners of the envelope with the tips of her fingers.

'He's a dark horse by all accounts,' the woman went on, leaning both elbows on the counter, all panic about birthdays apparently forgotten, her eyes dreamy with gossip. 'Jenny Fletcher, who works at the bank, says he's got the most awful money problems, yet he lives like a lord. Apparently there was some funny business before too.'

Kate, against her better instincts, was intrigued. 'What sort of funny business?'

'Oh, it's only talk mind you, but they say he's got something of a wild past. He ran a shop on the east coast – East Anglia somewhere – but went bust. Too much partying by all accounts. Had a big house there too – always full of crazy types from London, living it up with – well, you know the kind of thing. He was virtually bankrupt they say, until some lady bailed him out. Titled apparently – the honourable Samantha or Matilda or something.' She lowered her voice. 'They say he's a kept man.'

'Do they? Well I've seen no evidence of it.'

The woman, put out by such an unexpectedly curt response to these pleasantly digestible tidbits, pulled out a phone book from under the counter and began thumbing through it busily. 'I suppose I might find something under *Caterers*,' she muttered, casting Kate a disparaging look and licking her fingers between flicking pages.

'Good luck,' Kate offered by way of a parting comment, suppressing the urge to volunteer her own services. The last thing you need is a bloody football cake, she told herself as she pulled the door of the shop closed behind her, while an obstinate part of her brain toyed with the enticing challenge of edible goal posts and corner flags, fluffy butter-icing turf and crisp white pitch-lines.

The Mill House looked shuttered and silent, its curtains tightly drawn, its grey brick walls seeming to accept the flattering attentions of the afternoon sunshine with reluctant gloom. Kate hesitated for a couple of minutes before lifting the heavy black iron door knocker and bringing it down with a sharp rap. It was a lion's mouth, the jaws permanently open, the teeth black and sharp. Her stomach fluttered nervously while she awaited a response. Maybe he was asleep. Maybe he hadn't heard. Catching a glimpse of herself in a glass panel of the door, she tried to flatten some of the wild bounce from her hair, wishing she had thought to run a comb through it before getting out of the car.

She was on the point – infused with a curious mixture of relief and disappointment – of giving up and leaving, when a faint shuffling could be heard on the other side of the door, followed by the noise of metal bolts being drawn and keys turned. The door swung slowly open, revealing a waxy-faced Max Urquart in a red towelling dressing gown that reached only to his knees, and with some strange looking thickly knitted socks on his feet. The pallor of his face was heightened by the dark mask of unshaven hair across his cheeks and round his mouth. When he spoke his breath smelt faintly of honey.

'Kate, thank God it's you and not that dreadful woman.' He seemed disconcertingly unsurprised to see her.

'I'm playing postman,' said Kate brightly, stepping into the icy cool of the domed hall, anxious to establish at once – if only for herself – the pretext for her visit.

'Yes, thanks. Come in.' The door banged shut behind her. 'Come and have a coffee or something. I'm not contagious.'

'You don't look very well,' she faltered, following behind, noting that his curly dark hair was falling out of its pony-tail, and staring again at the curious socks.

'Yesterday I thought I was dying. But today I think it's food poisoning.' He managed a grey-lipped smile. 'Oysters.' He made a face. 'Serves me right.' He filled the kettle with water and put several spoonfuls of ground coffee from a gold foil packet into the bottom of a glass jug.

'Really? And why is that?' Kate put the envelope down on the kitchen table, silently marvelling at how clean and ordered the house looked. In her experience men, if left entirely to their own devices, were incapable of keeping houses in such conditions, especially not if they were trailing round in dressing gowns feeling sorry for themselves.

Max turned and leant against his fridge, tipping his head back and closing his eyes. 'That coffee smells good. I must be getting better,' he remarked with a smile, his eyes still closed. His lashes looked very long and dark, as dark as the glossy brush-strokes of his eyebrows. The skin underneath was not green, as the lady in the shop had described, but violet blue, making him look very vulnerable. Kate pulled her eyes away and began fiddling with a strand of hair by her ear, coiling it round and round her middle finger.

'I took my ex-lover out to dinner – champagne, oysters, the works – something I swore I'd never do.' He sighed, pushing his hands into the pockets of his robe, causing it to fall open a few inches more than it was already, revealing quantities of the dark hair that Mary had so admired through Angus' binoculars. 'But then it's curious what money can make people do.'

'You need money?' Kate frowned, inwardly giving him a plus-point for honesty and then checking herself for thinking along such lines.

'Yes, boring isn't it?' he replied, yawning. 'However much I have, it never seems to be enough. I blame my other half entirely. During our time together we were hardly disciplined about such things.' He chuckled to himself. Though the switch on the kettle had long since popped out, he had done nothing about it, leaving Kate to wonder whether she should not after all respond to her better instincts and leave altogether.

He started to yawn again, but stopped halfway through, gently hitting the side of his head with the palm of his hand. 'Oh Christ, coffee – sorry.'

Kate stood up. 'I really think I'd better go. You're not well . . . I only came to deliver your mail.'

Ignoring this remark entirely, he began loading a tray with mugs, milk and sugar, before filling the coffee jug with boiling water and stirring its frothy contents with a long silver spoon. He lifted the tray and turned to face her. 'Let's go in the garden, shall we? If you wouldn't mind opening that door – the lock's a bit stiff, you have to turn the key very slowly – sneak up on it –

no, slower than that – and pull it out slightly as you turn. That's it. Christ, what a glorious day.'

The garden of the Mill House was a rambling delight of overgrown paths and snickets that led down to the riverside, where a majestic weeping willow curved graciously over the water, poised with balletic melodrama, the fingers of its long green leaves trailing elegantly amongst the reeds below. A deck chair had been placed in the shade of the willow, beside a low wooden table and a small bench. A few feet away a hammock swung lazily between the branches of two sturdy young beech trees, with a towel folded at one end of it, as if for a pillow, and a pair of cracked leather sandals neatly positioned beneath, like slippers under a bed.

'Welcome to my camp,' he said, placing the tray carefully on the table and stretching his arms up towards the glowing blue of the sky. 'There's nothing to beat an English summer's day, don't you think?'

She shook her head, looking round admiringly at the graceful limbs of the trees and the shimmering water. 'It's lovely,' she said quietly, entwining her fingers together behind her back, and making more of a show of inspecting the hammock than was really necessary. What on earth am I doing here? she thought. I must be mad, quite mad. She pulled at the side of the hammock, making it sway.

'Try it out,' he said, from somwhere very close behind her.

'Oh no, I'd fall asleep,' she lied, walking quickly towards the water's edge, not turning to look at him for fear of finding that his face was only inches from hers.

They met again, a few moments later, on either side of the reassuring solidity of the table. Kate stood, holding her mug of coffee between two hands, while Max lolled on the bench, looking much more himself, his eyes focused with unnerving intensity on her face.

'Thank you very much for coming by,' he said casually, fishing a small insect from out of his mug with his little finger. 'The envelope you delivered contains stuff from my lawyer. All about money.' He made a face. 'Letitia and I once drew up one of those cohabiting settlements – a sort of prenuptial agreement but without the nuptials.' He smiled tightly and briefly, his eyes unmoving, suggesting in that one facial reflex a whole history of failure and disappointment. 'Her idea at the time, I may say. But in my present predicament I find myself driven to investigating whether the thing could be regarded as valid. All very distasteful, I'm afraid, but there we are. Money is distasteful, full stop. I hope they're paying you potfuls for your book, by the way.'

'Oh no, barely anything really,' she murmured. 'It's all a bit of a mess actually.' She put down her mug and began tugging idly at the long green tresses of the willow branch nearest her. 'I feel quite a fool for having imagined that any of it might be fun.' And she found herself telling him all about the fiasco of the photographic session that morning, how pointless and contrived it all seemed, how it had put her off caring whether her recipes were ever published or not.

'I'm luckier than I thought,' he said, when she had finished. 'If you hadn't lost your temper with those cameramen you wouldn't be here at all.'

'I did not lose my temper,' she replied hotly, the colour rushing to her face.

'You have the most beautiful eyes,' he said, studying her through half-closed lids and smiling at her confusion. 'They are so dark and yet so full of light, especially when you're cross.'

'I am not cross.'

'What then? Embarrassed? Because I have paid you a compliment?'

'Maybe.' She crossed her arms and moved further away from the table, further away from him.

'I only said what I thought,' he went on. 'I could say a lot of other things too. I could say that I am particularly fond of your hair, the way it curls under on one side but not the other; that I like your hands, so small and strong. The colour of your skin draws me too . . . and your breasts . . .'

'Stop,' Kate almost shrieked, putting her hands to her mouth in horror.

He was still sitting on the bench, watching her, a devilish smile on his face. 'True thoughts are the only ones worth mentioning. All the other stuff is a waste of time. The world would be so much more interesting if everyone spoke their mind more often, don't you think? I find you extremely attractive, Kate, a piece of information which I hardly think you should feign to find so shocking.' He cocked his head at her, trying to force her eyes to meet his. 'Come on now. And you are attracted to me too. Aren't you? Why are you here otherwise, eh? What the fuck are you doing here if you're not?'

'I don't know,' she said in a small voice, her hands still at her mouth, as if they might afford her some protection held that way. 'I don't know what I am doing here. I must go. I—'

'Now don't rush off like a scared rabbit.' He reached out a hand towards her. 'Come and sit down. Here,' he patted the seat of the bench, 'beside me. Come and have a proper talk. I won't grope you, I promise, much as I would like to. Not a stroke of a breast, not a whiff of a kiss. I'm ill, remember? Not really in the mood for sex, not yet anyway,' he added wickedly.

'You're playing games with me,' she said, not moving.

He nodded. 'Yes, yes I am. As you have been with me.'

'No.'

'Yes. Admit it. We've both been playing games, Kate. The question is, where do we take it from here?'

She took a step, almost tottering, towards the table, leaning on it as if for support.

'There are several possible scenarios,' he went on matter-of-factly. 'We could have sex – now if you like – on the grass under the willow there. I can assure you, it's the most comfortable of love-nests . . . Oh Kate, for God's sake come and sit down. We're only talking. It's a new game called Telling The Truth. All those pheromones whizzing round us, racy heartbeats, little patters of expectation and uncertainty. Personally I can only take so much of that kind of thing. Then I boil over with a need to know where it's all going.'

Feeling dazed, she went obediently to sit down next to him, on the very edge of the bench, keeping her eyes fixed upon the verdant clumps of grass at her feet, the velvet cushions of moss in between.

'I'm not sure I'm up to this,' she began, 'I really didn't expect . . . I think I should go home . . .'

'A fat lot of good that would do. We'd be back to square one the next time, with all these unmentionable things still unmentioned.' He placed his arm across her back, making her hunch and tense her shoulders. 'Relax,' he said softly, 'it's just an arm. If we're not going to be lovers then friends would be nice.'

'It's not possible,' she whispered, but letting her shoulders relent a little under the pressure of his arm.

'You're probably right.' He took the arm away. 'Look, speaking for myself, I'd be happy with some lustful romping under the willow – three times a week, maybe four. You are extremely attractive, Kate, more so than I think you realise, which – of course – is probably at the heart of it all. But anyway – where was I? – ah yes.' He patted his bare knees, 'As I was saying, what I can't bear is all this frigging around, not knowing if it's on the cards or not.' He paused, 'I fear it's up to you, my dear.' He brushed back a handful of her hair so that he could see her face better. 'Cheer up. We're discussing something potentially rather pleasant.'

'It's not pleasant,' she burst out, 'it's awful – I feel awful – I don't know what's going on, or what I'm doing – I don't know anything. I suppose I've been flirting with you and I shouldn't have and I don't know when or why I started and I wish it would all just stop and everything could go back to normal.'

'What's normal?' he enquired gently.

'At home.' She swallowed the lump in her throat. 'Nicholas has been miserable for so long I think he's forgotten what it feels like to be happy. He seems to blame me for everything, as if it's my fault he can't write anything and his father died and his bloody mother has come to live with us and spray her fucking air sprays all over the fucking place. And the bloody recipe book is just one more thing to worry about, one more thing to go wrong. And my brother's in a mess and seems to think that I can sort it all out, as if I've got some magic wand to wave all over the place and find answers where there aren't any.' Tears came into her eyes as she talked, but she was too far gone to let them stop her now. 'And if you're so keen on the truth then yes, of course I think you are attractive, though it's probably just what you seem to represent that makes it all seem so alluring, because you've got no boring ties like spouses or children, because you rule your own life without having to bother the whole bloody time about how everyone else is, whether they are happy and if not, why not and wonder whether it's your fault and whether you could or should do anything to make it better.'

'Whoa there, hang on a minute. You were doing pretty well, apart from that middle bit.'

'I'm just making even more of an idiot of myself now,' she mumbled, biting her lip.

'Not quite.' He took one of her hands and held it loosely between his own, tracing the lines on her palm with his fingers. 'But you have got some of it wrong. I don't embody half the things you seem to think I do. I'd have thought it quite obvious that the reason I live alone is because I have made such a balls-up of trying anything else. I can't even look after myself, let alone anyone else.'

'But you always look as though everything is so beautifully under control.' She gestured through the trees at the house, 'Everything looks so lovely, so in place.'

He laughed loudly at that. 'So I'm good at being tidy and buying expensive furnishings. I can assure you it's no recipe for lasting happiness. I am penniless, in debt to a woman whom I no longer love, but whom, if all legal approaches fail, I may well have to woo again in order to pay my bills. I'm a shameful bastard and that's the truth.' If his facial expression was ever teetering on the brink of communicating self-disgust, he quickly hid it under a roguish smile. 'And I feel it's only fair to warn you,' he went on, shifting closer to her, 'that I've changed my mind. I am in the mood for sex after all.'

Kate edged away from him, pressing her knees together and hugging herself with her arms.

'Okay, okay, I can take a hint,' he said, reaching for his mug and shrugging his shoulders.

'I'm sorry, but I just can't,' she said quietly. 'I'm afraid I've been looking for some kind of consolation . . . sort of teasing myself with ideas . . . about you . . . little fantasies—'

'Tell me more,' he interrupted, putting his hand on her knee. 'This sounds wonderfully promising.'

'—but it wouldn't help at all in the long run.'

'What about the short run then?'

She smiled, surprised and relieved to find that in so candidly discussing the undercurrents that had surged between them –

wresting all the innuendo out into the open – they had somehow defused them, made them less overpowering. She was almost tempted to thank him.

'You and me . . . it would be unwise,' she replied, still smiling. 'I'm far too sensible at heart.'

'And Nicholas keeps you happy in bed, does he?'

She found the audacity of the question shocking, even given the outspoken nature of all that had gone before.

'Yes,' she said, after the slightest hesitation, 'we've always been rather proficient in that area – though we are somewhat out of practice these days.'

'Shame,' he commented, loading their empty mugs back onto the tray and tightening the cord round his waist. 'He must be a bloody fool.'

They had reached the kitchen door when he said, 'There remains the question of what to do about Mary.'

'Mary?'

'Mary Sullivan. She thinks we're having an affair.'

'Don't be ridiculous.'

'She's been watching me,' Max said laconically, running a finger under the sealed flap of the envelope from his lawyer and starting to scan the contents, a deep frown settling across his forehead.

'Watching you?' Kate was incredulous. 'That's absurd.'

'I couldn't agree more. But I'm afraid she was watching the two of us just now.'

Kate's instinct was to look out of the window, as if Mary's pale face might be peering in at them at that very instant. 'How do you know? Whatever for?'

He shrugged. 'I was rather hoping you could shed some light on the matter.' He fell silent again, pensively rubbing the dark stubble on his chin with his finger-tips while he studied her. Something about the intensity of his gaze made Kate, for the first time that afternoon, feel slightly afraid. 'She's got that frustrated look about her,' he went on, his voice cold and hard, 'sort of pinched round the mouth, tight and miserable, like old virgins. Perhaps she gets some kind of voyeuristic pleasure out of it.'

'Really – I hardly think . . .' Kate was shocked, both by the cruelty of the idea and by the stony nonchalance with which it was expressed.

'She uses binoculars,' he continued. 'I've seen her on the river bank, on the other side, dodging behind bushes and things.'

'I've never heard of anything so ridiculous.' Kate picked up her bag, wishing she could feel as dismissively incredulous as she sounded.

'I couldn't agree more. Are you off then?' He came up to her and kissed her on the forehead, cupping the sides of her face gently in his hands. 'I don't suppose you'll be back.'

She shook her head.

He sighed. 'I didn't think so. It was a risk I had to take.'

She turned to go.

'Tell me one thing, Kate. If I had played it any differently, been less forthright, let things drag on a bit, do you think I would have stood more of a chance?'

'I don't know,' she said absently, her mind still wrestling with the image of their tête-à-tête by the river, how it would have appeared to even the most impartial observer. 'God, I do hope you're wrong about Mary. It would be awful if she thought anything.'

'Don't you worry,' he said, patting her arm, 'I'll take care of Mary. She won't be a bother, you'll see.' He rubbed his hands together, throwing back his head with a harsh laugh, showing the gold fillings in his back teeth. 'You never know, I might even enjoy it.'

'You're always to be nice to Mary,' said Kate anxiously, 'she has a lot to put up with. Angus is a beast.'

'A beast, eh? Poor little Mary. Though, in my opinion, people generally get what they want in life – or what they deserve, at any rate.' He was on the point of closing the door when he added, 'And you be nice to Nicholas, for that matter. If you're not going to succumb to the lascivious charms of a scoundrel like me, then the least you can do is sort things out with your husband. I'd feel much better about my rejection if you did.' He pulled a face of exaggerated suffering.

'Goodbye, Max. See you around.'

'That rather depends on you,' he said quietly, before disappearing back behind his big front door.

23

As the afternoon wore on, the heat gathered intensity, pressing round houses and cars and people like clingfilm. Kate, who stopped in at the bookshop on her way back through Elhurst to commit herself to making a football pitch out of sponge and icing for the following afternoon, felt the surge of almost euphoric relief, which had overcome her on leaving Max Urquart's, being quickly superseded by a piercing headache. Release of tension, she told herself, as she huddled in a pitiful square of shade to the left of her front door and sucked on a squashed, ineffectual-looking Disprin, whose square of metallic covering, yellow with age, she had unearthed from a deep, dark gritty corner of her handbag. She tried hard not to look at her watch, determined not to staunch the flow of contrition and optimism with impatience that Nicholas and Joyce still should not have returned. They would be home soon. Meanwhile there was a lot to think about: she had been to the brink of infidelity with someone whom Nicholas did not even know existed – she still trembled to think of it. It seemed nothing short of miraculous that she should have been able – been allowed – to pull back just in time. There was some kind of marital guardian angel watching over her, she decided, someone who had granted her a second chance. Now it was up to her to make the most of it, to cut through all the claptrap of the last few months and set things truly right again. Though a part of Kate felt almost unfashionable to be so shaken by what had happened, adultery being a common enough theme in every corner of the globe, she found it impossible to downplay the sense that she had come very close to ruining her life completely. Any notion that her marriage could withstand the shock-waves of a sexual liaison with a third party was unthinkable. It would have changed everything forever, whether Nicholas found out or not. Making love to Max Urquart would have been the end of them. Swallowing the last powdery grain of her tablet, Kate breathed deeply and closed her eyes. If only being flirted with wasn't such a treat – such a rare occurrence for married mums of over forty; I'll have to flirt with Nicholas instead, she thought dreamily, the challenge of such an idea beginning to mingle with half-formed plans for dyeing desiccated coconut a turf-green and moulding marzipan into the perfect round of a football.

Nicholas, sitting opposite Joyce in the dining section of a large pub on the outskirts of Worthing, placed a piece of overdone steak in his mouth and wondered how his mother could look so cool and papery-skinned. His own face felt doughy and moist. The temperature in the packed dining room seemed to have risen steadily since their arrival, the initial relief of being released from the cauldron of the car having rapidly been replaced by this more gradual but equally unpleasant sense of over-heating. The arrival of food did little to ease Nicholas' discomfort; steam wafted up from amongst an unpromising heap of flabby green beans, while the steak looked dark and cracked with age and over-cooking. Even the chips appeared saggy and despairing, as if they had merely lain in a bath of cold oil, instead of being tossed in the gunshot heat with which Kate tackled any deep-frying. The thought of Kate gave him a jolt, first of guilt, which he thrust to one side, and then of something like anger.

'So clever of Kate,' Joyce was saying, chewing with slow precise movements, as if fearful of swallowing her teeth, 'to get her cooking ideas accepted by those publishers.' She had chosen Dover sole with new potatoes and salad; her plate was a sea of suspiciously bright yellow melted butter, but she appeared not to mind, dabbing at dribbles in the corners of her mouth with her napkin between dainty forkfuls of food, all the while emitting murmurings of appreciation. She had suggested the venue herself, much to her son's amazement, disclosing that it had been a favourite place of his father's, and navigating them through the turgid seaside traffic with impressive, unflurried ease.

Nicholas, too preoccupied with his own thoughts to notice that his mother was happy, bristled at this all too frequently repeated comment upon his wife's success.

'Yes, marvellous. Kate is marvellous.' He could feel his shirt sticking unpleasantly to his back; a single cold trickle of sweat snaked its way down from one armpit, coming to a halt somewhere around the tyre of his waistline. Though he had chewed the piece of meat in his mouth at least a thousand times – little bits of it were now lodged between the uneven ridges of his back molars – it was still showing not the slightest sign of being ready for digestion. Nicholas thought hard about extracting it by hand, of placing it with as much delicacy and discretion as he could beside the dry crust of bread on his side plate; but instead he chewed on, fearful of upsetting his mother, whose eyes, though she spoke little, looked bright and observant. It would have been impossible to jettison a masticated lump without being noticed. A trip to the toilet though an option that he considered, was rejected on the basis that it could only solve one mouthful at a time.

'Lovely,' said Joyce quietly, pressing her lips together and tidily laying down her knife and fork while she paused for a sip of water. Her son had suggested wine, but she wouldn't hear of such a thing; it gave her migraine, she said and he had the driving to think of. With some regret, Nicholas had asked for orange squash, a liquid accompaniment that was doing nothing to enhance the flavours or texture of his meal.

'Funny, really,' Joyce continued, now using her napkin to wipe away a blob of the buttery oil which had found its way onto the table beside her glass, 'when you think how much you wanted to break into the world of the media.' She enunciated this last phrase a little self-consciously, since it was one that Dick had coined, and used quite frequently with reference to their son's recent mysterious preoccupation with writing stories. As parents they both felt – and had occasionally said – that Nicholas should concentrate on one career only, instead of being distracted by artistic whims. Commitment brings success, Dick used to say, one of numerous adages on the subject of Nicholas' working life which had caused his son exasperation whenever they were expressed and which now seemed to echo across the table through the ever loyal tones of his mother. It made Nicholas both sad and furious to feel the presence of his father so acutely.

'Yes, isn't it funny – deeply ironical, in fact – that my wife should have succeeded so effortlessly where I have failed?'

'Don't be silly, Nick,' scolded Joyce, detecting petulance in his voice and secretly thinking how little men ever really grew up. 'You've done jolly well.'

The encounter with Joanna Wyrall had actually left Nicholas feeling quite light-headed, not unlike the effect of a slug of alcohol on an empty stomach. On getting back to the hair-dresser's – only ten minutes late – he had clucked admiringly at Joyce's violet-tinted bee-hive hairdo and then gallantly offered her an arm as they left, much to the cooing and appreciative elbow-nudging of the fat lady and her ginger-headed assistant.

Now, as the realities of his imperfect life pressed about him once more, the recollection of Joanna Wyrall's eager, weathered face, instead of being a source of guilty concern, began to burn more brightly in his heart. It felt good to have a secret, especially one that was mildly wicked. While the meat in his mouth turned cold and stringy with chewing, Nicholas, switching off from his mother, allowed himself to dwell on this thought a little longer: apart from the odd erotic dream about film actresses (he had a favourite where Michele Pfeiffer starred in one of his screenplays) and the occasional borrowing of Kate's embroidery scissors for snipping the hairs in his ears and nostrils, it struck him now that there was nothing that his wife did not know about him. Nicholas scowled and swallowed hard, forcing the cluster of chewed gristle down his throat in the same fashion with which he had once despatched braised meat at school. There was no inner sanctum to his life, he thought bitterly, no real retreat, nothing that was entirely his, nothing that Kate didn't know about or the children didn't meddle with. Apart, that is, from the phone number, that very very small paper pellet, screwed up in its deep, safe hiding place in the glove compartment of the car.

'Nice steak?' enquired Joyce, with a critical glance at his full plate.

He nodded, but then owned up to a lack of appetite.

'You'll regret it later on,' she warned, another old echo from the past, from high teas when Alison would scrape her plate clean and gloat at her little brother's famous reluctance to consume food at meal times.

For a couple more minutes Nicholas ploughed on, reacting to the motherly chiding with some kind of absurd Pavlovian obedience. But then he thought to hell with it and roughly pushed his knife and fork together, right on top of a discarded stack of leathery meat and a beached seaweed heap of flaccid vegetables.

Joyce pursed her lips and fidgeted with the gold clip on her handbag. The waste these days, she thought, with a mind-caste set irrevocably by a society that had known and never quite recovered from the hardships of ration books.

After Joyce had returned from the Ladies, her lips freshly reddened and her hair patted high, Nicholas ordered them both a coffee before excusing himself on similar grounds. The men's toilets were on the other side of the pub, next to the telephones and a back door onto the car park, a coincidence which sparked an idea in Nicholas' troubled mind, a lit fuse of a thought that refused to fizzle out. Having relieved himself, he washed his hands quickly, shaking them dry in the air as he made his way out into the car park in order to retrieve the scrap of napkin from the bottom of his glasses case. He could feel the heat rising from the ground as he walked swiftly across the soft tarmac, its springiness seeming to spur him on, to make him feel more justified and daring. Once back in the dimly lit corridor that housed the telephones, he sifted through the change in his pocket with trembling hands, his heart thudding.

Joanna answered almost at once, after only two rings, giving the reassuring impression that she had been expecting the call.

'Joanna speaking,' she said, her voice sounding much lower than he had remembered it.

'Joanna, it's Nicholas. We – er – we met this morning . . .'

'Nicholas – how lovely of you to phone so quickly.'

His mind, scouring her words for hidden meanings, latched onto this response as the most encouraging of green lights.

'I just wondered – well, the fact is I'm on holiday for the next couple of weeks, so I just thought that . . . well . . . we could perhaps meet for another coffee or something – that is if you still wanted to. My mother likes shopping in Worthing,' he gabbled, panicking a little at her silence, 'so, as you might imagine . . .'

'Of course,' she put in, bailing him out from a sentence that was going nowhere at all. 'How about tomorrow afternoon? As I explained, I have the horses to exercise in the morning, then I'm meeting a friend for lunch, so the afternoon would suit me best.'

'You sound terribly busy,' he stammered, thrown by the prospect of meeting so petrifyingly soon, 'perhaps another day would be better.'

'Oh no, not at all. I love being busy. I'll have to walk Monty anyway. We could meet on the sea front, by the steps where we were this morning.'

Though the thought of having the drooling hound as chaperone held little appeal, the flashing digits on the box warned Nicholas that he had only two pence worth of conversation remaining. 'That sounds fine.' He thought of Kate. 'If something comes up – if I can't make it for any reason . . .'

'I'll give you ten minutes and then not worry.'

She sounded so noncommittal he was almost offended.

'Right you are. Oh, hang on, what time?'

'Shall we say three pm?'

'Sounds good to me. 'Bye then.' With a jerking hand he replaced the receiver and wended his way back through the crowded main bar to where Joyce was sitting, unnaturally upright and alert, her handbag on her knees, her napkin folded, her coffee cup pointedly empty.

'You took your time.'

'Sorry.' Nicholas downed his own coffee, which was barely tepid, in two gulps. 'I'll just settle up.'

'It's all right, I've already done it.'

'Mum – really – this was my treat.'

She smiled and leant forward to pat his hand. 'Fiddlesticks. I've had a lovely time – all thanks to you. Both you and Kate have been so kind . . .'

'Don't be silly,' he cut in, shamed by her gratitude. He stood back to let her go first and then reached over the top of her head to push open the heavy door. 'If you'd like to pop back for some shopping or something – tomorrow for instance – I'd be more than happy – seeing as I'm on holiday and everything.'

'Oh no, that's very sweet dear, but not tomorrow thank you. Later in the week perhaps . . . yes, maybe later in the week.'

24

By the time Nicholas and his mother returned from their adventures on the coast, Kate was weighing up the costs and advantages of hurling a brick through one of her own front windows. As if to highlight her predicament the telephone had rung twice, each time the caller holding on for twenty rings while she tugged hopelessly at the front door and shouted profanities through the letter-box.

'Where on earth have you been?' she said, smiling tightly and blinking as she stepped out of her cage of shade into the glare of the sun.

'We've had such a lovely lunch,' said Joyce gaily, leaving Nicholas to comment on the fact that Kate appeared to be marooned on her own doorstep.

'It was all the most ghastly muddle, from start to finish,' she blurted. 'That lot achieved absolutely nothing this morning and then had the check to sneak off while I was out on a walk trying to collect my wits. Would you believe I got back to find the place deserted? To cap it all I had left my keys inside so I've had hours to kill on my own, waiting for you to get back.'

'Poor Kate,' said Nicholas, kissing her cheek, while needling suspicions sprang to life about the vehemence of her protestations, her obvious eagerness to make him believe she had suffered rather than enjoyed her day.

'So they took some flashy pictures of you and your gooseberries, did they?' he remarked airily, as he unlocked the front door and let them all into the enveloping cool of the house.

'Nicholas, you're not listening,' insisted Kate, fighting exasperation at his aloof, unsympathetic response. 'It was a farce,

I tell you, they did nothing that we can use and want to set the whole thing up again in some London studio with plastic models instead of the real thing.'

'That might be interesting,' he murmured, flicking through the morning's post. 'Will they make a plastic model of the cook too?'

'Oh Nicholas, be nice to me, please – I've had such a horrid day.'

'The price of fame,' he said lightly, neither resisting nor fully accepting the arms that she put around his waist, staring down at the soft white skin of her parting while she pressed one side of her face hard against his chest. 'And how did you spend your time of banishment then? You had your car, didn't you?'

She pulled away, sweeping the hair back from her eyes and reaching past him for the kettle.

'Oh yes, I had the car.' She had to raise her voice over the sound of running tap-water. 'I grabbed a sandwich from the grocer's and dawdled round the bookshop, where I somehow got committed to making a football birthday cake for twenty boys. An Arsenal fan apparently, or was it Manchester? Damn.' She stopped, kettle in hand, her mind a blank. 'Oh God, I'll have to ring and check – I said I'd write it round the side.' She frowned. 'How could I not remember something like that? It must be the heat or something . . . I hope to goodness it's cooler in Devon.'

'About Devon,' he began, before noticing that Kate had sat down and was shaking her head. 'What's up?'

She clasped and unclasped her hands. 'Well, we're sort of committed now.'

'What do you mean "committed"? You make it sound like a process that has occurred all by itself.'

'Oh Nicholas, please don't be cross. The Armstrongs rang this morning, in the middle of all the mayhem, and it seemed so rude of us not to have responded definitely after all this time – they asked us so long ago – that I just felt I had to say something one way or the other and so I said yes, but just for a long weekend. We need a break, don't we?' she added weakly, cruelly aware of the great gulf between her intentions about getting along better with Nicholas and the reality of making those intentions come true.

'This is my summer holiday,' he said, his voice deathly quiet, 'the only two-week stretch I get off a year. I had hoped to do some work at my computer, to get down to some writing maybe – make the most of some proper peace and quiet without the children – that kind of thing. Unlike you, most of my time tends to be rather heavily accounted for. So don't pretend to be surprised that the idea of gorging ourselves on cream teas and glugging cheap wine with the bloody Armstrongs does not fill me with joy.'

'Well,' she countered, indignation rising in her throat, 'you should have ruled it out right away then, instead of saying that it might be fun. We'd left the invitation open for so long I just felt I had to accept.' She stood up, close to tears. 'I'm sorry. I should have asked you. I'm sorry.'

At which point Joyce came in and started clattering round with cups and saucers and tea-bags, while her son and daughter-in-law looked on in silence.

Harry lay in bed with only a sheet pulled up over him, clutching his small shaving mirror in one hand and a thermometer in the other. According to the reading on the thermometer he was dead, a fact which he realised might have had something to do with the hot whisky and lemon which he had drunk some ten minutes before but which nonetheless added to his sense of desolation. The mirror, referred to at frequent intervals, confirmed his worst thoughts. Only the most deadly of viruses could reduce his usually effortlessly radiant looks to such rubble: the two days of stubble on his cheeks contributed dramatically to the effect of physical decline, as did the fact that he had not washed his hair for three days, an uncharacteristic act of neglect which caused it to hang in distressingly greasy strips around his ears and eyes. Saying 'ah' at his reflection several times had revealed little of the condition of his throat, though it felt inflamed and pustuled beyond repair.

Unfortunately for Harry, the receptionist who answered his croaky plea for help to the surgery had manifestly not shared his concern. A home visit was not granted except in the most exceptional circumstances, she had explained, sounding distant and unconcerned. Only by showing the most exhausting persistence was Harry eventually rewarded by having his call grudgingly put through to a nurse. The soft Scottish voice that came on the line was unmistakably male, a small twist to the morning's events which threw Harry – who believed nursing, like au-pairing and shorthand, to be intrinsically female activities – off balance, adding to his sense that the world in general was growing increasingly hostile. Having recovered his equilibrium, he nonetheless proceeded to itemise his symptoms in graphic detail, sparing the Scotsman nothing in his account of the wracking fever, the sodden bedclothes, the raging thirst and bursting head. While managing to communicate more sympathy than the receptionist, the nurse had coolly responded with a short lecture on the prevalence of viral summer flus in London and the inabilities of the doctors to do anything about them. If Mr Melford wished to make an appointment, that was fine, otherwise, he explained in lilting tones, the best counter-measures were probably lots of rest and two paracetamol tablets every four hours. Harry, certain that such prognosis and treatment did not begin to do justice to the ferocity of his condition, had hung up in a huff.

He blew his nose hard, making an impressive trumpeting noise, but producing little of satisfaction in the tissue and causing the throbs in his head to double in both speed and intensity. A disconsolate glance in the mirror revealed that his nose was beginning to show signs of abuse; the end looked raw and pink; little white bits of dry skin had formed round the edges of his nostrils and along the rim of his upper lip.

'Oh bloody hell,' he groaned, yanking another tissue from the box beside him and endeavouring yet again to clear his head with a violent blow. On examining the tissue afterwards, he experienced a small stab of self-justification on identifying a speck of blood amongst the paltry smear of phlegm. As he looked, another drop of blood fell and then another, until a crimson tulip of a patch had formed on the snowy whiteness of his man-size tissue.

Harry tipped his head back and swallowed hard, tears of self-pity welling up in his eyes. He had never been any good with blood. Its warm, metallic taste on the back of his throat disgusted as much as it alarmed him. He had an abhorrence of being ill, let alone of being ill without anyone to ply him with sympathy and pat cool fingers to his forehead. On every other occasion in his life that he had been forced to stay home from work, there had been a girlfriend to call, one who had gladly dropped everything in order to be of service, to have the rare chance to fuss and mollycoddle so elusive a lover. He sighed deeply, keeping his mouth wide open and pinching the bridge of his nose between finger and thumb, while with the other hand he pressed the tissue hard up against the leaking nostril. As the unpleasant trickle of blood continued at the back of his mouth, solace presented itself in the form of a fuzzy line-up of some of his most favourite conquests: Lucy, the part-time model and secretary; Henrietta, the stockbroker who liked to eat four cream eggs in one sitting; Claire, the tiny shop assistant with magnificent breasts and miniature feet, Rosie, who arranged flowers for weddings and liked sex after breakfast. Since Alicia it had all gone to pot, he thought grimly, sticking a tentative finger up his nose to see if he had successfully staunched the flow. Since Alicia, his filofax of female phone numbers had been pitifully neglected – not a single new one put in that year, in fact. Dealing with Alicia was so exhausting, a roller-coaster ride from the start, time-consuming and utterly dispiriting.

The worst of it now was that – without any warning at all – Alicia had apparently given up on him entirely, a relatively recent and wholly unexpected development to which Harry was still trying to adjust. The daily barrage of notelets, faxes and messages had simply stopped. He had no idea where she was or what she was doing, her own answering machine having long since run out of tape, and there never being anyone to answer the buzzer to her block of flats. In spite of Harry's campaign to avoid Alicia at weekends by escaping to the country, – and his careful weekly diet (whenever he could muster the discipline for such physical self-restraint) of brief, or at least infrequent meetings with her, he nonetheless felt at liberty to be quite outraged by this sudden and totally unannounced withdrawal of attentions. Besides which, it seemed the cruellest of ironies that she should have chosen to disappear just days before he needed her most. If she only knew how terribly ill he was, she would come running to his side – the swell of her belly permitting – he was sure, ready with that soothing creamy voice of hers and a vanity case crammed with all sorts of unpronounceable herbal remedies to help him sleep and clear the vile clogs in his head.

Finding himself so cross, bereft and dangerously feverish, Harry had even considered calling his stepmother, Beth, to see if, between her manic bouts of London house-hunting, she could drop by with a few provisions and a dose of sympathy. But then he remembered that she and his father had recently left for a cruise of the Greek Islands, three weeks of undiluted indolence of which they both claimed to be badly in need but which Harry sceptically regarded as one of the numerous breakaway milestones that such active retired couples needed in order to get themselves from one end of the year to the other without going completely mad. Inactivity scared Harry more than anything, time to think being for him – with so much that he preferred not to think about – the most disquieting time of all. Indeed, it was one of the chief drawbacks of being confined to his bed, without even the energy to read a paper (there were several days' worth piled on his door mat), that his mind had all the time in the world to run wild with uncomfortable conjectures about things like Alicia and all the messy business of the baby.

There was nothing for it, he concluded, the nose-bleed having run its course, but to call Kate, ever his last resort in times of greatest need. The one thing about his sister was that she was always there, always organised and reliable, he thought fondly, as he reached for the phone and dialled her number, unable to prevent himself from rather relishing the prospect of croaking into a sympathetic ear about his woes. Dear, sweet Kate, he thought, resting his head back amongst his pillows and closing his eyes while the phone rang.

After a discouragingly protracted length of time, Nicholas answered, the impatience in his voice betraying the fact that their telephone had done nothing but ring all afternoon and that all of the calls had been for Kate, who was now elbow-deep in a large bowl of green buttery sludge, making faces at him that she didn't want to talk. She had already had several exchanges with Elizabeth Hale, who had been suitably apologetic about

Jake and his crew, but who had nonetheless rung her back to try and persuade her that a studio shoot was going to be necessary, whether they used plastic food or not. Kate, rapidly losing conviction about the strength of her arguments, had asked for time to think. There had followed an interlude of twenty minutes or so, during which she tried to elicit Nicholas' opinions on the matter, only to find that, probably because he was still cross about the Armstrongs, he was, frustratingly, not prepared to voice firm views either way.

'Let them handle it as they think best – after all they've been doing this kind of thing for years,' he said at length, patently dismissing the matter. In truth, Nicholas was mostly preoccupied with thoughts about Joanna Wyrall and whether he really wanted to see her again. Logistically, it was going to be tricky, too tricky probably to bother with, since his mother had no wish to return to Worthing the next day and now Kate had rashly committed them to three days in Devon at the end of the week. Though doubts had assailed his mind ever since leaving the pub, not being able to keep his tryst was making him feel more and more as if he would have liked to. As did Kate's infuriating rushing between the telephone and the oven from where perfect oblongs of golden cake kept emerging as if by magic. She really doesn't see me any more, he thought bitterly, watching her whirl between cupboards, her apron strings flying; she's only pretending to be in a tizz, when in fact she's loving every minute of it.

'She's a bit tied up right now, Harry – I'll see if she can drag herself to the phone.' Nicholas held out the receiver, his hand cupped over the mouthpiece. 'It's Harry. He sounds unwell and wants to talk to you.'

'What sort of unwell?' Kate asked at once, wiping her hands on a cloth, concern flooding her face.

'Snotty,' remarked Nicholas with brutal succinctness. 'Says he's been off sick for two days.'

'Two days?' Kate, looking appalled, took the receiver from her husband and settled herself in a chair in a way that suggested she was fully prepared to spend quite some time there.

'Harry, whatever's the matter?'

'I don't know, Katie.' He was pleased to hear his voice sounded gratifyingly throaty. 'They say it's probably a virus, though to be honest I haven't had the strength to to get to the doctor's.'

'Poor Harry. Can't they send someone round?'

'Tried that. Too busy, probably not within their budget capabilities.'

'You do sound jolly rough.'

Nicholas, pouring himself a glass of wine from an open bottle in the door of the fridge, signalled at Kate to ask if she wanted a drink as well. She batted him away with her hand, as if trying to swat a bothersome insect, he observed bitterly, as if he was of no greater consequence than one of the sleepy fat wasps that had started drifting into the kitchen from an as yet unidentified nest under the back guttering. Having taken a generous swig, he topped his glass right up to the rim and pulled out a bag of peanuts from the cupboard above his head.

'Supper's in twenty minutes,' she declared, breaking off from her conversation and casting a critical eye at his salty snack. 'I defrosted some lasagna – and garlic bread too.'

'I am hungry now,' he grunted, clenching the packet of peanuts in his teeth so as to free one hand to open the kitchen door and escape.

Kate shrugged and returned her attentions to her brother. 'Have you taken your temperature?'

'105 and climbing.'

'Harry – my God—'

'But I had a hot drink a bit before,' he felt bound to add, though not without a twinge of regret at having to dilute the drama of his predicament.

Thank goodness for that.' Kate eyed her unfinished cake on the side across the room. The coconut butter mixture had come out a beautiful livid green – an unarguably fine shade for a football pitch. 'Look, Harry, we haven't eaten and I've got a monster of a cake to make for a ten-year-old Arsenal fan . . . is there anyone who could pop round to check up on you?' She paused, before daring to be more specific. 'Like Alicia for instance?'

'That's out of the question, I'm afraid,' he replied. There followed a dramatic pause. 'She's done a runner. Not a word to me. Just disappeared into thin air. So you see,' he paused again, 'I'm completely alone.'

'Oh Harry, you poor love.' Kate was torn between doling out more sympathy and getting back to her baking. 'Though I must say, I'm surprised at Alicia . . .'

'I say, dearest Kate, you couldn't see your way to coming up here, could you?' he interrupted. 'Feed me grapes for a while – cheer me up.'

'Harry, I don't think so, though – hang on – I could do with seeing my publishers.' Her mind flicked through the logistics of getting up to London for the day. After all, they weren't going to Devon until the end of the week and it wasn't as if she had the children to worry about. Nicholas returned to refill his glass just as she was outlining the finishing touches to her plan. She would take the train up to visit Harry the following day, she promised, stay the night in his flat and then see Elizabeth and her editor the next morning, en route back to the country.

Nicholas raised his eyebrows at Kate before tipping out the last couple of inches of wine from the bottle. So I can meet Joanna after all, he thought, his stomach leap-frogging with excitement, then curdling with uncertainty at the idea.

'I thought you'd be pleased,' Kate said a few hours later, when they were both getting ready for bed. 'It means twenty-four hours of quiet – time to yourself – to work or whatever.' She pulled back the duvet and got into bed, puffing up the pillows behind her so that she could sit up and fiddle with the alarm clock. 'I'm going to have to finish icing that thing in the morning – I just hope the goal posts haven't sagged.' She set the clock to one side and folded her hands on top of the bedclothes, saying nothing more while Nicholas undressed, but thinking fondly that she wouldn't swop him for all the Max Urquarts in the world, that even given all the awfulness of recent months, he was still the only man whose socks she would ever truly not mind washing, the only man whose heavy stomach she would ever like to feel pressed up against her own.

'I am pleased,' declared Nicholas, when in fact he wasn't quite sure what he felt. It was irritating that Kate should be prepared to drop everything to run to the bedside of her malingering, self-centred brother; but at the same time the thought of being able to keep his rendezvous in Worthing was undeniably thrilling. Not so much because he longed to see Joanna again, but because it made him feel faintly powerful, an emotion which had not featured in his life, in any context, for what felt like years.

When Kate rolled over in the dark and began stroking his chest, Nicholas responded with baffled reluctance; while his body welcomed her embrace with a hunger that had always felt like an addiction, his mind ricocheted between fresh bouts of anxiety at the thought of meeting Joanna and confused suspicions as to Kate's motives for suddenly being so attentive.

A book fell unnoticed from amongst the covers of their bed and landed with a thud on the floor. The noise made Joyce sit up in her cubby-hole of a room below, interrupting her prayerful whispering to Dick, the nightly ritual which helped ease the emptiness enough for her to sleep. She strained her ears to listen, but heard nothing more.

Afterwards Kate's eyes fell closed at once, leaving her husband to nurse dark, glowering thoughts, like a miser with a hoard of unusable gold; thoughts that left all guilty apprehension about the next afternoon far behind, as they sped down fresh, treacherous roads to do with the unlikelihood of sick brothers and publishers really being the justification for a night away from home. Away from him. In the light of such notions, the fact that they had made love began to seem like an act of deceit rather than bonding.

If only I didn't care, he thought miserably, folding his arms across his chest and continuing to brood, his body stiff and troubled, his eyes fixed on the crack of landing light, its slit of warmth offering no solace for the torture in his head.

25

Mary was working on her needlepoint when Max's car pulled up on the gravel drive outside her front door. Though embroidery was a reward that she usually reserved for the evenings, Mary had decided to break the habit of a lifetime and treat herself that day. Like reading a novel, it felt unforgivably indulgent to be doing such a thing in broad daylight, all on her own, with nothing but the silence of the wringing heat to keep her company. While better than doing nothing at all, it warned her – as if she needed any reminding – that she had somehow slipped into a new and desperate phase of life, a phase that seemed to involve nothing but a relentless and debilitating struggle to fill her time.

Not seeing Kate was one of the things that appeared to have taken an absurdly large toll on Mary's sense of being busy. Although she missed their tea and chats dreadfully, a small part of her could not help but be grateful as well: how awkward it would be to see Kate now, knowing what she knew; how impossible to meet the gaze of those steady brown eyes and pretend that nothing had changed. Though would the eyes have seemed so steady now, Mary wondered, with the secret of Max Urquart buried inside?

In addition to which, it felt to Mary as though Angus had been away all year, the balance of his trips having truly shifted to the point where it now seemed as if the time he spent at home was being sandwiched between excursions abroad. It was a wine society do this time, some claret guild or other was treating all its members to five days of feasting and wine-supping somewhere near Avignon. Mary didn't even know exactly where, a puzzling oversight which she told herself was tied up with Angus' toing and froing from London the week before, rather than with any failure on her part to enquire. She cast her mind back to the few days of flurry before Angus left, the pleasant bustle of taking suits and ties to the dry cleaners, sorting out the right shirts and cufflinks, making sure he had a fresh tube of toothpaste and enough floss, the unwaxed kind that he preferred. Angus liked to floss at least twice a day and sometimes after lunch as well. His gums gleamed.

'But I must have asked,' she murmured to herself, genuinely unsure, her needle with its blue silk thread poised for the next stitch. 'Perhaps he told me and I didn't listen.' The thought, though unconsoling, reassured her enough to continue with her stitching. She was now working on a complicated design of exotic flowers, whose brilliant colours ran into each other at the edges, so that she had to strain her eyes to make out when one shade began and another one ended. She had pushed the armchair over towards the biggest of the sitting-room windows, so as to make the most of the ebullience of natural light outside. Sitting in the garden itself, an idea which had originally held considerable appeal, had quickly proved impractical: even on a deck-chair in the shade of the beech tree, she felt as though she was being gently poached; her fingers slipped unpleasantly on the needle, while the thread began to look limp and bedraggled from all the extra tugging.

The unexpected jangle of the doorbell made Mary jump with such energy that the needle slipped and pierced her middle finger. A ruby bauble of blood surfaced immediately. She stared at it for a moment, before placing the finger in her mouth and rising slowly from her chair, her mind casting round dimly for who could be at the door other than a postman. For Mary's days had reached such a pitch of emptiness, that she felt as if she knew every possibility contained within them. Now that the flower-arranging course had ended, she had no reason – apart from shopping and dry cleaning – to leave the house. When Angus' taxi had arrived to take him to the airport, shortly after dawn on Monday morning, Mary had for a second entertained the wild notion of flinging herself upon him, begging him not to go. Though common sense prevailed in the end. Poor Angus would have been so shocked – so appalled probably – to realise that his wife, in spite of all her churches and charities, could have been lonely. He liked to cultivate an image of Mary as a tidy, sweet, scrubbed mouse of a spouse, whose daily troubles were incapable of fluttering beyond preoccupations to do with flowers and recipes, shared with other like-minded women over pots of herbal tea and homemade biscuits. Mary herself would have loved to play such a role, to be a conforming member of local society; though women's groups of all kinds certainly thrived in the environs of Elhurst and she had for many years forced herself to hover on the edges of them, she had recently grown too shy, too unsure of herself, even to keep up the pretence of holding her own in such circles, which, contrary to the opinions of people like her husband, could be battle zones of the most ferocious kind.

When Mary opened the door to find the figure of Max Urquart leaning up against the archway of their porch, nonchalantly chewing a long piece of grass and wearing a baseball cap backwards on his head, she almost fainted.

'Hello, Mary,' he said, chewing slowly and blinking with lazy confidence, 'may I come in?'

'Mr Urquart – what a surprise – of course.' She pulled the door wider and motioned for him to enter. He looked very hot, she noticed, his dark black hair sticking in flat curls to his forehead where the rim of his cap had pressed against them. 'Would you like something to drink?' she enquired hesitantly, wholly unsure as to how to react to such an unexpected visit.

'A quadruple Scotch on the rocks would be nice.'

'Oh – well – I'll see—'

'Don't worry – just teasing,' he said, smiling at her from under the dark shelf of his eyebrows. 'I'll have something fizzy and cold, if you've got it – a Coke or a lemonade.' He wiped his forehead with the back of his cap. 'Christ, it's steaming out there.'

'Oh dear, I don't have any of those things,' Mary said a few moments later, staring disconsolately into her fridge, which, containing only pots of salad and yoghurt, bore all the hallmarks of Angus' absence.

Max stuck his tongue out and pretended to pant like a dog. 'Water,' he gasped, 'anything.'

'I've got fizzy water,' she exclaimed, her face lighting up, 'would that do?'

'Perfect.' He shot her another smile, an open charming one this time, and pulled out a stool for himself. Like every other surface in the kitchen, the top of the stool and the bar-top upon which Max now placed his elbows sparkled with disturbing cleanliness, a gleaming showroom of a place that looked quite unsuited for human habitation.

'Tell me, Mary,' he said, having drained the entire contents of his glass while she looked on in silence, 'are you lonely?'

Her mouth dropped open. She wrung her hands. 'Really . . . I . . . what a question. Sometimes . . . isn't everybody?' She straightened herself, dropping her arms and beginning, unconsciously, to clench and unclench her fists. 'What exactly . . . are you here about the book . . . ?'

'Your book on country flowers, you mean?'

'Yes – yes, the flower book.' She brushed an imaginary crumb off the surface nearest to her and then inspected the palm of her hand. 'Is it ready for me to collect?'

'No, no, another two weeks yet, I'm afraid.' He did not take his eyes off her as he talked. Mary squirmed under the unaccustomed glare of such scrutiny.

'It's my lunch hour. I've come by for a chat. Is there any more of that water? It really hit the spot.' He rubbed his left hand appreciatively across his stomach, ruffling up the edge of his T-shirt and revealing a glimpse of dark stomach.

Mary looked away. 'More water,' she murmured, taking his glass and returning to the fridge in a trance of uneasy confusion. On reaching inside for the bottle, his empty glass somehow slipped from her other hand, landing with a crash on her tiled floor, whose immaculate squares looked as carefully attended as the segments of a patchwork quilt. Shards of glass went spinning in all directions, while Mary froze in shock and Max watched her with curiosity. It wasn't going to be quite as much fun as he had thought. There was no sexiness to her, not the remotest sense of how to play the game, not like Kate Latimer, whose escape – untouched – from his house still baffled him. It was so unlike him to offer a way out like that, to take pity when conquest was so close at hand. As for Mary, it would be like seducing a dying fish, he thought glumly, watching her tight white face twitch in horror at the mess at her feet.

'Where do you keep your brooms and brushes?' he asked, leaping off his stool and making a big show of tiptoeing round the broken pieces, rising high on the balls of his black trainers.

'Over there.' Mary, who was now crouching down and gingerly picking up the largest of the fragments by hand, pointed to a tall thin cupboard next to the utility room door. 'Thank you so much . . . so careless of me . . . my hand just slipped.' Her hair had fallen out of its tidy, bobbed shape, curtaining off her face as she bent over the floor, hiding the extent of her distress. Though Max was being perfectly helpful and polite – unlike Angus who would have shouted at her clumsiness – Mary's painfully raw sensibilities detected the disdain behind his handsome smile. It was the thought of such scorn that she minded more than anything. She liked Max Urquart a lot – not in the everyday sense of liking, but in the irrational, euphoric sense of filmstar adulation. He was like a Tom Cruise or a Mel Gibson, someone whose life she could only gawp at, someone whom she could never really affect or get to know, beyond the most meagre exchanges. To find such a creature in her house, while not exactly a dream come true, had a dreamlike, surreal quality to it. And now, to have shattered all that, to have shown herself up as faltering and inept, made her want to weep with despair.

She couldn't wait for him to leave. But, even after the glass had been swept up, the broom and dustpan replaced, he lingered on, picking up and examining her collection of miniature cottages on the window sill, and stroking the leaves of her pot-plants with his long fingers.

'Too much water,' he said quietly, when he got to the cyclamen, which looked droopy and doomed.

'Mr Urquart . . .' she began, trying to summon the courage to ask him quite what he was doing, what he wanted. 'I'm afraid I've got to go out in a minute . . . lots to do . . .'

'Why have you been spying on me, Mary?' he asked, keeping his back to her, one finger lingering on the silky-haired leaf of an African violet.

'I don't know what you mean . . .'

'Oh yes you do.' He turned round slowly and shook a scolding index finger at her. 'You've been very naughty, Mary Sullivan. You've been looking at me through your binoculars – from the other side of the river.'

'I – watch – birds—' she faltered.

He merely raised his eyebrows, leaning back against the sink, clearly in no hurry to get through the showdown.

'Was it sex you wanted?' he enquired next, as if responding to something as commonplace as the request for a book. Then he put his hand to the top of his flies and began pulling down the zip.

Mary, horror-stricken, let out a small scream.

With one hand he undid the top button of his trousers, all the while pinning her with his black eyes. 'It's okay, Mary,' he said nonchalantly, 'it's okay to want sex with people. It's quite normal in fact.' He raised his voice just a notch, like a note going up one place in a scale.

'What is not quite so socially acceptable is ogling people through binoculars. Do what you like with me in your dreams, Mary Sullivan – rape, anal sex, teasing seductions – feel free to help yourself. But if you want something for real, then have the grace to ask next time. Plain speaking is something I value rather highly.' He started to pull his trousers down and then stopped abruptly. 'Here or upstairs? I've got fifteen minutes, so let's not hang around.'

Mary began to cry.

'Oh dear, have I got it wrong then?' He hoicked his trousers back up to his waist, but made no move to do them back up again.

Mary closed her eyes, while the tears rolled down her cheeks, wetting her fingers where they gripped her face, her nails making small deep lines, like cuts, where they dug into her skin.

'Do you mean you only wanted to look, but not to touch? Is that it?' His voice was very quiet now. 'Well, that's not allowed, I'm afraid – not in my book anyway.'

Mary tried to mouth something, but no sound came out.

'Do you want a screw, Mary? Do you?' Before she could think to move, he strode across the floor and pressed himself up against her, pulling her so hard towards him that she could feel his hip-bones thrusting into her waist. Her whole body shook. 'I'm willing to oblige, you see, now that it's all out in the open, as it were.'

She shook her head, still unable to speak, her hands now on her ears, her eyes screwed shut, as if trying to block him out.

He let go suddenly and quickly zipped up his trousers. 'Well, I'm glad we've sorted that out then,' he said, switching to a jaunty let's-be-done-with-it attitude and looking at his watch. 'Heavens, time to go. The way things are going I won't be running the shop much longer, I'm sorry to say. I'll give you a phone when that flower book comes in, shall I? Don't worry, I'll see myself out.' He picked up his cap from beside the sink and disappeared through the kitchen door into the hall; but a few moments later he was back. 'No more bird-watching, eh? Oh, and by the way, Kate Latimer and I – contrary to how it might appear to prying eyes – have never had an affair. More's the pity, I say.'

Mary remained standing in the middle of the kitchen floor for several minutes after the front door had slammed shut and the sound of his car engine had receded into the distance. Then, leaning first on the wall and then on the banisters for support, she made her way slowly upstairs. Every part of her trembled from a combination of terror and relief. She had thought he was going to rape her. Worst of all, she had felt as though she deserved it.

Once inside her bedroom she found herself collapsing down on all fours, dragging herself towards her bed as if the wounds she felt inside were real. There was a jug of water and a glass on her bedside table. She took a sip and then opened the small cupboard door below, where her cap lived in a round red box, beside a tube of spermicide cream and a bottle of tablets. The tablets were sleeping pills which she used when Angus was away: one a night, just to help her drift off, through that bad patch of racing fears and mangled thoughts, when each creak of the house sounded like the tread of a predatory foot, when each rustle of the beech boughs grated on her nerves like tinfoil on teeth. Angus won't like it of course, she thought, as she wrestled weakly with the cap, which had always seemed designed to be as impregnable for adults as children. She tipped the contents of the brown plastic bottle into the palm of her hand. Seven tablets. A measly seven. It wouldn't be enough. Pulling herself up with the aid of the bed, she staggered into their ensuite bathroom and roughly pulled open the doors of the pine wall cabinet. 'Paracetamol,' she whispered, now coming out of her daze, her eyes scanning the shelves, 'that'll do the trick.' Packets and bottles fell into the basin below as she searched. In her clumsy anxiety the sleeping tablets slipped from her hand; two of them managed to stick fast to the wet edge of the basin, but the remaining five rolled down the plug hole. Only when she had examined every packet of ointment, cough mixture and cream did Mary accept defeat. There had been some paracetamol she was sure – there always was, because of her headaches. Angus must have taken them with him, she concluded wretchedly, to help him combat the effects of wine. If he had been drinking heavily he liked to take two or three tablets – along with a pint of water – before going to bed. It meant he never got hangovers, or so he liked to boast.

To have reached the point of wanting to end your life only to find that you do not have the only imaginable wherewithal to do it struck Mary as the nadir of failure. She perched on the side of the bath, staring hopelessly at the ransacked cabinet and the mess in the basin below and cried silently, letting her tears fall and her nose run unattended.

When the crying had stopped, she got to her feet, her face still puffy and wet, and began, very slowly and methodically, to restore order, wiping each bottle with the cleaning cloth that she kept wedged behind the basin pipes and replacing it carefully to its rightful place in the cupboard. Once the cabinet was back to normal, she blew her nose several times on the cloth before dropping it in the waste bin beside the toilet.

The man at the fruit stall had a disconcertingly lopsided stare, as if one eyeball had rolled slightly out of place. Kate tried to concentrate on the good eye, which was friendly and focused on her, as opposed to the glassy pupil fixed on something near her left ear. Though the grapes looked too tight-skinned and bright, as if they had been harvested some weeks before their prime, she felt bound to buy some, since Harry, who had sounded so very much in need of cheering up, had mentioned them specifically. She bought some peaches as well and three bananas for good measure, though, as she walked away clutching her purchases, she was assailed by a vague recollection of Harry and bananas having parted company some years back.

Fulham, with its heavily congested streets and over-priced corner shops, was not Kate's favourite part of London, though Harry's flat lay in a pleasant enough patch, being at the heart of a residential sector of impressive Regency houses, whose crumbling exteriors had been painstakingly restored and repainted a few years before he moved in. Each building had its own elaborate portico and accompanying set of steps, lined with lacy black railings up to wide double front doors. Going on the size of her brother's accommodation, which was a third-floor flat with vast rooms and high ceilings, Kate doubted very much whether any of the others remained as private houses, even given the smattering of sports cars and four-wheel-drive vehicles slotted into the residents' parking areas in the street outside.

A couple of minutes after she had pressed the button labelled *H G Melford*, Harry responded with a welcoming grunt into the voice-box and an electronic buzzing that released the lock on the door downstairs. Kate pushed it open with difficulty, shivering at the stark drop in temperature, the echoing, marbled foyer making her think, as always, of churches and crypts.

Harry left the door open and scampered back to bed, anxious to create the most extreme impression of sickness that he could, especially since he was feeling much better that day, a fact which he intended to keep from his sister and which he suspected bore direct relation to the amount of unmentionable green fluid now flowing quite liberally from his nose and being hacked up from his chest. A cold really was the most disgusting thing, he mused, pulling his tartan-patterned duvet up to his chin and trying out a cough to see if there was a cough to be had. How exactly did it originate, he wondered, as he lay back to wait for Kate; how was all the green gunk created? Where did it come from and why?

'Harry, you poor old thing.'

'Hello, Katie,' he said meekly. 'Not on top form, I'm afraid.'

'I won't kiss you.'

'Wouldn't hear of it. Journey and everything okay?'

'Fine, thanks. Though London in a heatwave is even less attractive than usual.' She couldn't help noticing that the room smelt – an unpleasant mixture of stale air, body odour and eucalyptus – which no amount of window-opening on such a muggy day was going to do anything about. She opened a window wider anyway – it could do no harm – and dangled her bunch of grapes at him. 'Just as sir ordered.'

'Katie, you're a marvel,' he sighed happily, feeling even better.

'I'll just go and give them a rinse. I got some other fruit too,' she called from the kitchen, 'I wasn't sure whether you'd have anything . . .' she broke off mid-sentence, having seen from one glance into Harry's cadaverous fridge-freezer that there was nothing to eat beyond a badly assaulted half pound of butter and one very grey-looking sausage roll.

'Harry, love, your kitchen is a wasteland,' she scolded, on returning with a battered metal colander in which the grapes now sat, their pert shapes glistening with beads of water.

'I haven't exactly felt like eating,' he croaked, tossing a grape in the air and catching it neatly in his mouth.

'No, no, of course not,' she murmured, smiling at his antics, echoes of happy childhood times coming at her with a force that threatened to get unhealthily nostalgic. 'Poor old Harry,' she said gently, coming over to him and patting his pillows and straightening his duvet.

He snuggled his head backwards, like an animal rubbing itself in summer grass, warming, as always, to the incomparably soothing effect of female attention.

'I could change your sheets, if you like . . .' she looked round uncertainly, 'that is if you have any spares.'

Harry pointed silently to a large tea chest at the foot of the bed, in which all his spare linen was housed, mostly in a jumble of unwrapped starchy parcels from the dry cleaners – an establishment upon whose services he relied more heavily than any of the ten programmes offered by his sleek German washing machine. Buried deep amongst towels and table-cloths, Kate discovered a set of satiny blue-black bed linen, comprising a double sheet, a duvet and two pillow cases, with the initials *HM* embroidered in loopy gold thread on the corners. She couldn't resist making a face, but Harry's eyes were closed.

'Would you be up to eating anything tonight?' she enquired, with a half-smile at his pitiful state.

'There's a marvellous new shop two blocks away,' he replied at once, sitting up and blowing his nose between sentences. 'Open all hours. It's called Luigi and Bendini – has the most beautiful fresh pasta and ready-made sauces and exotic fruits and every kind of ice-cream flavour you can think of. It's based on a chain of upmarket delis in New York – barrows of coffee beans and dried apricots – you know the kind of thing.'

'From that I take it you could force some food down,' she remarked dryly, crossing her arms and cocking her head at him with mock severity. 'I must say you've got a bit of a starved vulture-look about you.' She placed a cool hand on his cheek, stroking its rough surface fondly for a second. 'I'll buy some pasta and rustle up a sauce. If you're an especially good boy you can have ice-cream for afters.'

'Christ, Nicholas is lucky,' murmured Harry with a deep sigh, stretching his arms luxuriously above his head. 'Every chap needs a spot of mothering now and then. If only Alicia . . .' He stopped short, midway through his stretch, letting his arms fall back on top of the covers and suddenly looking truly exhausted and miserable.

'Yes,' said Kate soothingly, starting to strip the bed and nudging him to decamp to the armchair in the corner, 'I was going to ask you about Alicia.'

'Nothing to say,' he pouted, pulling the duvet round his shoulders like a great padded cloak and obediently shuffling over to the chair. Without its tartan wrapping Harry's bed looked very shabby indeed; yellowy patches and unseemly brown splodges covered its once creamy surface like a smudgy map of the world. 'She doesn't even know I'm ill. She took off just before – God knows where – left no note, no message – nothing. How do you like that?'

Kate pursed her lips, tugging with unnecessary vigour at the corners of the sheet and punching the pillows so hard that quantities of dust and feather fragments billowed up in the still air and seemed to hang there, as if riveted in space by the slants of afternoon sun. Her eyes suddenly began to stream and she sneezed hard, five times in a row – dry reactive explosions that did nothing to ease the itch in her nose. 'I expect she feels rejected,' she wheezed, finishing attending to the bed as quickly as she could, sensing, from years of experience with such episodes, that another equally ferocious bout was lurking just around the corner.

'Rejected?' Harry snorted, having expected more of a sympathetic response and finding himself irrationally irritated by Kate's sudden round of gunshot sneezing. 'There's only one party with any right to feel rejected at the moment,' he huffed, climbing back into bed and holding the corners of the duvet while Kate slipped on the dark satiny cover, marvelling to herself how anyone could sleep in such a grim shroud. But I've come to be nice, she warned herself, not to be riled by Harryisms. Though the sneezing had mercifully stopped, her eyes and nose were running badly. After trumpeting several times into a tissue extracted from one of several boxes scattered round the bedroom, Kate took a deep breath.

'I'll nip off to do a bit of shopping then. Is there anything else in particular that sir requires?'

'A dirty mag or two would be nice.' He grinned wickedly. 'It's so dull in bed alone.'

'You'll be lucky,' she replied laughing, looking round for her handbag. 'I was thinking more in the line of aspirin or *The Economist*.'

Harry scowled and shook his head. 'I've got a week's papers to catch up on, thanks.'

When Kate got back Harry appeared to be dozing, though the television was on, a giant beast of a screen which lived on an imposing plinth in the top corner of his bedroom, the effect being – for Kate anyway – rather sinister, as if it was a machine designed for watching, rather than being watched itself.

While she sliced vegetables in the quiet of her brother's palatial but sorely neglected kitchen, Kate found her mind creeping back for a reappraisal of Harry's remarks about Nicholas, how lucky he was to have such a mothering wife. For, as she realised with something of a start, it was rather a long time since she could be said to have done any such thing. Kate caught herself recalling the last time Nicholas had declared himself unwell – several weeks before – when he had taken the day off work complaining of a bad throat and head. She had been irked by his presence in the house, all the clumsy huffing and puffing for sympathy, the unsubtle mantle of self-pity that seemed to go with the peculiarly male territory of being incapacitated by everyday illnesses. Nicholas had wanted to be mothered then all right, but she simply hadn't been able to summon the patience to oblige, not even for one day, she scolded herself, now judging the episode with a perspicacity of hindsight that suggested she had probably been rather mean. Such a memory, when viewed in the light of this trip up to London to minister to her brother – albeit on the back of a meeting with Elizabeth the next day – caused Kate to feel the stirrings of something like guilt. So much so, that after washing the smell of onions and garlic from her hands, she telephoned home. Having got her opening sentence all worked out it was something of a disappointment – not to say a surprise – to find that Nicholas was not there. Joyce, sounding sleepy and subdued, as if she had been woken from a nap, said that Nicholas had gone shopping after lunch and that in the meantime there had been a phone call from someone called

Mary Sullivan. Recoiling at the thought of having to face Mary, Kate repeated some needless instructions about dinner – which sat in various foil-covered dishes 'beside the stove – and then rang off feeling somewhat cheated and let down. Shopping for what? Nicholas never went shopping – not unless he absolutely had to, like on the afternoon before her birthday, or in the two hours before the shops shut on Christmas Eve.

They dined on the bed, side by side, with trays on their laps. Harry ate greedily, spilling dribbles of the creamy vegetable sauce onto the front of his Noël Coward style dressing gown and gushing expansively – between mouthfuls – about the excellence of his sister's cooking. Kate, feeling somewhat subdued, ate with less enthusiasm, unable to taste the flavours she knew were there, because she was thinking too hard about other things. The television, which offered them a choice between various quiz shows and a film on parasitical molluscs, was an unwelcome distraction, though Harry insisted it should remain on, in case something good came on he said, as if they had not the wherewithal – half a rain forest's worth – to check on such a thing. By way of a concession, he turned the volume right down, so that a quiet droning – not properly intelligible, but loud enough to encourage an attempt at comprehension – continued as a maddening background to their discussions.

Harry liked noise, Kate remembered, as she sat chewing beside him, trying to contain her annoyance, while a series of ancient quarrels came to mind from their flat-sharing days, when Harry had blasted her eardrums with a succession of machines, sometimes individually, sometimes all at the same time. The image of her brother jigging in headphones, while his thumbs worked the buttons of a hand-sized video game in his lap and his eyes flicked to and from a live television screen was not one of Kate's most endearing memories of their time together. He was scared of silence, she had once accused him, scared of what it might bring, a potentially penetrating comment which had been greeted at the time with a derisive snort and a V sign.

'So Alicia's gone,' she remarked, laying her tray to one side and steeling herself to cling on to some vestige of the goodwill with which she had embarked on the visit.

'What I want to know, Katie,' he said, not at first appearing to pick up the thread of her remark, 'is how the hell one can be sure – you know – about marriage and so on?'

'Marriage?'

'Take you and Nicholas, for example.' He wiped his middle finger round the rim of his plate and licked off the very last of his sauce, regarding his empty dish with evident regret. 'At what point did you know that he was the one for you? There must have been something that made you certain. You were so bloody sure – I remember – the pair of you charging round so bloody smug and full of beans. It was clear nothing in the world would make you change your minds.'

Managing to forget the television for a moment, Kate cast her mind back the quarter of a century or so since Nicholas' courtship of her, if it could be described in such terms. What she remembered best was feeling instantly comfortable with him, and completely in league, as if they two alone – out of the entire population of London – were privy to the secret of how best to take on the world. They had regarded other people – couples especially – with something like pity, sure that they were ill-matched and unhappy, sure that no other pair could have as much fun in bed, or laugh at the only things worth laughing at, or care for the only things worth caring about . . . 'It was so terribly arrogant,' she murmured.

'What was that?' barked Harry, having been momentarily distracted by some fast-speed photography of a maggot inserting itself into something resembling the inside of a bicycle tyre. He took aim with one of several consoles on the bedside table and turned the volume down two notches. 'You see, the thing is, Alicia irritates the hell out of me sometimes, and of course there's the business of the baby – which was not exactly part of my game-plan – and yet . . . yet the devil of it is I seem to be missing her. Does that mean it's the real thing, for God's sake? I certainly can't remember missing anyone quite like this before, not apart from, you know . . . the sex side of things.'

'So you've been expecting a blinding flash of light, have you, Harry, a revelation of some kind – angels, music and a lifetime guarantee?'

'Of course I bloody haven't. And don't be so sarky. I'm asking for some sisterly advice here, in case you haven't noticed.'

'I'm sorry,' she said gently, touching his arm, 'I know you are. I'm sorry for being foul. It's just that . . . you always seem to assume that Nicholas and I have some kind of unshatterable concrete edifice of a marriage – dull and grey maybe, but bound to last.'

'Well, you're still pretty thick the two of you, after all this time . . .'

'Yes, but – well I suppose what I'm trying to say – I wish you'd turn that bloody thing off – is that it's not remotely easy and that the only thing that really keeps it going sometimes is the wanting to keep it going. There's a sort of belief, a faith in it all being worthwhile, that you cling on to when . . .' her voice tailed off, the analysis given for Harry doubling her sense of the crisis grinding on at home.

'I say, are you all right?' Kate, though not exactly crying, was gulping hard. She nodded vigorously, biting her bottom lip, not trusting herself to speak.

Harry tactfully left the bedroom to get them both some ice-cream. Mint with chocolate shavings. He couldn't have chosen better himself.

'Sorry about that,' said Kate meekly when he returned with two full bowls, teaspoons sticking out of the clods of ice-cream like silver flags, 'but the fact is Nicholas has been behaving rather oddly for quite a while now – things have been quite tense, in fact.'

'I suppose what with his father kicking the bucket . . .' offered Harry cheerfully, before cramming his mouth with dessert, making his eyes water from the shock of the cold on his teeth.

'Yes,' Kate murmured, 'that certainly made things worse. And I'm not sure I was any real help to him. With Mum I just wanted to cry and talk to everyone about it all the time, but Nicholas seemed so infuriatingly bent on coping alone. He just went into himself – and seems to have stayed there,' she muttered. She turned back to her brother. 'Were you like that? I can't really remember.'

'Yes, I suppose I was.' Harry licked the back of his spoon thoughtfully. 'It is best just to press on after these things,' he said matter-of-factly, breaking his wedges of ice-cream up into small green glaciers with the tip of his spoon, 'that's all there is to do in the end. Anyway, I'm sorry to hear that you're having a bit of trouble . . .'

'Oh no, we're fine really – deep down – where it counts,' she added decisively. 'It's just been a difficult summer, what with one thing and another.'

'Having the Granny can't help,' said Harry, his attention now being drawn by the intriguing reproductive antics of what appeared to be two obese caterpillars.

'No,' said Kate firmly, not wanting to get onto the subject of Joyce. 'God, I can't eat another mouthful.' She put her bowl on the tray beside her, from where Harry quickly retrieved it, tucking into her portion with relish. 'But to go back to Alicia . . . now that she appears to have gone you'd quite like to have her back, is that it?'

He shook his head vehemently. 'No. I mean, I don't bloody well know. I just can't see myself being good at fatherhood, fidelity and all that stuff.'

'The thing is to take it one day at a time,' advised Kate, 'don't worry about the future so much. I expect she'll come back. Then just go gently. Follow your instincts. See what happens.'

'And it sounds like you should do the same,' he laughed, turning up the volume of the television, since writhing molluscs had been replaced by the opening credits to one of his favourite programmes – a comedy about a decrepit cricket team, whose members spent more time drooling over the cream teas and vital statistics of their captain's curvaceous blonde wife than they did playing the game.

He always was inclined to be a bit morose, old Nicholas,' he added, half turning his head towards her and raising his voice against the rapid dialogue and canned laughter now emanating from the telly; 'likes to bear the weight of the world on his shoulders, your husband – sometimes rather indulgently, if I may say so – I expect he'll perk up soon enough. I don't see how he couldn't with such a perfect wife to turn to.' He planted a dry peck of a kiss on Kate's cheek and settled back happily amongst his pillows, his mind clearly having switched with insulting ease from the inherently dramatic theme of their discussions to the altogether less challenging subjects on the screen.

Kate, depressed and unreassured by such snippets of brotherly wisdom, retreated with their trays into the kitchen.

27

As the morning wore on Nicholas had begun to feel slightly sick at the prospect of what he might be about to do. Taking refuge in his study, he stared blankly at his computer screen, his mind lurching between the hope that there was nothing untoward in making a secret friend of a horsey woman with a dribbling hound and the fear that he had embarked upon an irrevocable course of action for which he was neither ready nor convinced. Any notion that his expectations of Joanna Wyrall did not extend beyond the boundaries of platonic friendship had been seriously undermined by the length of time he had spent in the bathroom that morning, checking his face for blemishes likes some kind of paranoid teenager, and splashing mugfuls of water on his hair in an attempt to stop it sticking up quite so much at the front.

An unprecedented dilemma over what to wear provided further evidence that a subterranean part of Nicholas' psyche was entertaining grave and guileful possibilities about the meeting that lay ahead. Underpants, usually pulled with sleep-gummed, unseeing eyes from Joyce's tidy stack in the top left-hand drawer of the chest of drawers, were, on this particular morning, surreptitiously selected with the greatest care. The shiny yellow and black ones saying *TIGER*, for instance, which Kate had put in his stocking the year before and which in fact fitted rather snugly, were rejected that morning, as were several other less dashing articles, because they had holes along the seams. The winning contenders were some light blue boxer shorts which, though by no means Nicholas' favourite or most comfortable pair, seemed in the end to offer the best combination of aesthetics and practicalities. So as not to arouse Kate's suspicions, he then lay on the bed pretending to read the paper while his mind worked upon the further challenge of what to wear over the boxers. If Joyce hadn't been there it wouldn't have mattered of course. He could have pulled on any old thing and changed later. But with the paranoia of the true guilty party, Nicholas was not prepared to take any chances. By the time he had scanned the headlines several times over, his feverish mind had settled on a much loved short-sleeved stripy shirt and a pair of cream cotton trousers which tended to pinch at the waist, but which he hoped embodied all the cool summery nonchalance that he aimed to borrow for the occasion.

Kate, busy with last-minute touches to her football cake – a culinary triumph, Nicholas had to admit – and packing an overnight bag for London, was too preoccupied to notice any unusual fastidiousness in her husband's morning ablutions. She smelt of jasmine, he noticed, when she offered her cheek up for a virginal kiss, the passion of the night before clearly having been overriden by a more immediate concern not to have her lipstick smudged.

'Kate . . .' he said, grabbing one of her hands as she turned to go.

'Yes?' She looked at her watch. 'Darling, I'm so late. I've got to drop this thing off and get to the station for the twenty past. If I miss that I'll have to wait another hour.' She pulled her fingers free and bent down to pick up the cake from the hall table. 'Be a love and open the door, could you?'

'Give my regards to Harry,' he said gravely, before standing back to watch her drive away.

The first thing Nicholas noticed was that there was no sign of the dog, an omission which in his hypersensitive state, struck him as being of potentially awesome significance. The second thing was that Joanna's blue eyes looked much darker and more alluring than he remembered, an effect which his new friend had deliberately achieved by the liberal application of a kohl pencil along both the outer and inner rims of her eyelids. It was a trick Joanna had learnt as a teenager and one that she now reserved for all occasions when she felt a particular need to impress.

'Hello,' she said, coming immediately to stand very close to him, so close that he feared she might 'smell the beer on his breath, a quick half pint sipped in the dingy back bar of the Harvester pub, to quell the most appalling attack of last-minute nerves and to kill some of the fifty-five minutes that he had in hand.

'Hi.' Nicholas lifted his arm and did a small twirling wave with his right hand, a gawky, needless gesture which he regretted at once. 'What have you done with Mucky then?' He pretended to scan the horizon for the dog.

'Monty,' she said, with just a trace of tension in her voice, 'is meeting his girlfriend today. I'm trying to breed him. He has such a stunning pedigree it would be a crime not to.'

'Quite,' responded Nicholas, thrusting his hands – which now appeared to be flapping uselessly in the tugging onshore breeze – deep into his pockets and trying to wrest his mind from the hazardous course of drawing parallels between the actions of dog and mistress.

'You seem a bit . . . on edge. Are you all right?'

'Rather,' he reassured her, with a vehemence he did not feel. 'Shall we walk?'

They had gone a few yards when she suddenly linked her arm through his and led him across the road, away from the beach.

'This is my car,' she declared, 'I thought we might go for a drive. It's got air-conditioning,' she added, perhaps discouraged by the expression of unrestrained doubt that clouded his face. 'Much nicer than frying out here.' The car, which looked to Nicholas as if it had been designed for luxury safaris in the tropics rather than shopping trips to the English coast, towered above them, regally poised on bulging wheels, its silver flanks glinting in the sun. 'Get in,' she commanded, before skipping round to the driver's side. Sitting inside such a monstrous vehicle struck Nicholas as being not entirely dissimilar from the sensation of riding on the top of a double-decker bus. He strapped himself in, all the while trying to keep his eyes from roaming towards the lacy designs pressing through the flimsy cotton of her tight pink T-shirt.

'My place or yours,' she said, laughing, before starting up the engine and steering easily out of her parking space. Much to Nicholas' immediate relief she did not seem to expect an answer.

As they drove along Joanna seemed content to talk about herself, showing none of the reserve or awkwardness that Nicholas would have felt if called upon to describe his own family circumstances. After a mercifully short, introductory narrative about the various personalities of her favourite horses, she moved on to more personal topics, though without any faltering in tone.

'I married an American naval officer when I was nineteen – met him on a trip to Disney World, of all things. Complete cock-up the whole thing. We lasted three and a half years in the end. He wanted ten brats and it turned out that I couldn't have any. I had a sort of breakdown. Well over it now. There was a bad patch – rather a long one – until good old Henry rides up on his white charger and offers me a way out. He's always preferred horses to children anyway, so that's all right.'

Since Joanna's tone during this account of her adult life was light almost to the point of being dismissive, Nicholas was uncertain as to whether to offer condolences of any kind. He was still pondering the matter when she suddenly pulled into a layby, switched off the engine and leaned across him, pressing her pillar-box mouth hungrily down upon his. For a second their teeth clashed, bone on bone, alien and uncomfortable

'There', she said, pulling back after a few moments, 'at least we've got that over with. The first kiss is always the worst, don't you think? It sort of hangs there, needing to be done.' She turned the engine back on and accelerated furiously onto the road. 'Nearly there now.'

'Where?' asked Nicholas faintly, his lips still vibrating not altogether pleasantly from the recent assault.

'Great Croft. My place.' At that moment she turned hard left and Nicholas found himself confronted by a large brown board, pinned to a post beside a five-bar metal gate. GREAT CROFT STUD, he read, his brain – as if in a state of deep shock – working slowly over the painted white letters. Meanwhile Joanna had leapt nimbly out of the car to open the gate. 'Your turn when we're through,' she said, panting slightly, once she had clambered back into her seat. Nicholas did as he was told, wondering as he clanged the heavy metal gate shut behind them whether he wanted – whether he could – turn back now.

'Your husband . . .' He cleared his throat and started again. 'Your husband is at work, I take it?'

She cast him a knowing look out of the corner of her eye and made a tut-tutting noise with her tongue.

'Henry – since you ask – is in Ireland looking at stallions. And where's yours?'

'My . . . ?'

'Wife. Where's your wife?'

Nicholas had an irrational urge to lie and say that Kate was at home, expecting him any minute. He was not enjoying the sense of being so absolutely out of control of events, of not having a clue what might happen next. Joanna, in contrast, appeared to be burgeoning with more confidence as each moment passed. She was now telling him about Henry's business, what a fine eye for horse flesh he had, how this was the overriding thing that had attracted her to him in the first place, how some of his horses were now being ridden by the best equestrians in the country, winning trophies at every turn.

The road up to the house was bumpy, full of deep, dry trenches and potholes. Even in their safari vehicle, the two of them swayed side to side, lurching dramatically as they advanced.

When Kate stepped out of Harry's building on the following morning she was confronted by a tall, blonde, heavily pregnant woman in a billowing yellow silk dress, who was making her way slowly up the steps, clinging onto the railings, her face tensed with obvious strain.

'Alicia,' Kate exclaimed at once, hurrying down to put a supporting hand to her elbow.

'Oh – it's Kate – oh thank you.' She seemed to be breathing with considerable difficulty. 'I'm not blooming any more,' she said, pausing to pat her ballooning stomach, 'I'm expiring. It's so hot, isn't it?' Having reached the top of the steps she turned and leant her back up against the front door, smiling as she inhaled a deep gulp of air. 'I've been in Scotland with my parents. It's so fresh up there. I needed some time to think – you know, about Harry and everything.' She threw up her hands. 'It's hopeless, you see, I'm mad about him and that's that. I've come to tell him – to try and explain that without him it will all be meaningless for me – I've tried being brave – for months and months – and it just doesn't work.'

Kate's first instinct was to nod in acquiescence and turn away. It was their mess not hers, in spite of Harry's earlier attempts to solicit her active involvement in the most distasteful way. Besides which, during the course of her short stay, she had found herself growing increasingly frustrated by her brother, by his inability to listen to more than two words in a row, his absolute refusal to sustain a serious discussion about anything. Though he was clearly very much on the mend, he was still languishing in his kingsize bed, filling it with crumbs and blobs of marmalade and coughing violently for her benefit whenever she came into the room.

In consequence, they had parted on rather cool terms, Kate feeling that he had not shown nearly enough gratitude for her visit, and Harry thinking that unless one offered help with goodwill there was little point in offering it at all. It had been grand to see Kate at first, but things had tailed off badly after supper, the turning point apparently being when the telephone went on the blink, doing its usual trick of emitting an engaged tone to put you off the track. It was quite late by then and Kate had stomped off clutching sheets and blankets for the bed in the spare room, saying goodnight over her shoulder in the most hostile way, as if it was his fault that she couldn't phone home.

Kate was on the point of hurrying off down the steps when something made her stop, some instinct tied to the gush of compassion she felt – a singularly female gush – at the sight of Alicia fanning her soft pink face ineffectually with one hand, while the other rested on the swell of her belly. 'I tried to call last night,' Alicia continued, now studying herself in the mirror of a powder compact, 'but couldn't get through. So I rang the office this morning only to find he's been off sick all week, poor love.' She put the powder compact back into a yellow leather handbag and pulled out a small bottle of eau de cologne. 'So you've been visiting him – how kind of you, Kate. Is he very unwell?' Her eyes, now full of concern, did not blink as she fired small jets of scent behind each ear.

Kate, thinking of the relish with which Harry had launched himself at a full tray of breakfast, shook her head. 'He's much, much better.'

'But still off work . . . thank goodness I arrived in time to be of some help.' She reached her hand out towards the panel of names and bell-buttons for the occupants of the building.

'Alicia . . .' Kate took a step forward. 'Do you have time for . . . for a quick chat? No, don't ring Harry quite yet.' She had to grip her arm quite hard to stop her from pressing the button. 'I'd like to talk to you first, if I may.'

'What about?' said Alicia, her eyes full of surprise and mild irritation at being prevented from carrying out her intentions.

'Harry,' replied Kate firmly, leading the way down the steps.

They found a bench under the shade of two pretty silver birch trees in a small park that acted as the centrepiece of a square nearby.

'Forgive me for appearing so presumptuous,' Kate began, 'but I suppose I do know Harry quite well and on that basis – and given that I know there have been various . . . hiccoughs between you two along the way – I thought I might just say a word or two.'

Alicia sat in silence beside her; if she felt any resentment at Kate's by now obvious intention to intervene with some of her own views, her face, unsmiling but impassive, showed no signs of it

'It's just that – well actually Harry has been missing you like hell – he told me so. Though you may not have planned it that way, your going off to Scotland like that really seems to have shaken him up. What I'm trying to say is that it would not perhaps be the wisest move to go throwing yourself into his arms declaring undying love.'

'Why not?' Alicia was genuinely puzzled. 'Especially if he's missed me so.' She couldn't resist a small smile of pleasure at the thought.

'Because then he'd know immediately that he had you again and would probably cool off as a result.' Kate wondered if it was having such undeniably stunning looks that had allowed her brother's girlfriend to grow up to be quite so guileless and uncalculating. 'Seeing as you know how he's been feeling – since we had the luck to bump into each other – it might be better to hold back a bit, play things a little more coolly. Tell him where you've been, that you're back and so on, but hold on to all the other stuff for a while . . . I suppose what I'm trying to say is, let him come to you, let him do the running for a change.'

'I say,' Alicia's eyes had grown wide at the thought of such deviousness, 'that's an idea.' But then her face fell. 'I'm no good at hiding my feelings though, especially not at the moment.' She stared at her stomach morosely, tracing a line with one finger from the middle of her breast bone down to the place where Kate imagined her tummy button must lie, or at least what remained of it. 'I'll make a hash of it, I know I will.'

'I'm sure you won't. Just let him tell you how much he's

missed you first – you just might find it changes things completely – adjusts the balance, so to speak. Harry is a love but,' she paused, leaning back in the bench and putting her arm along the back of it, 'he's also an arrogant sod. It'll be good for him not to be able to take you for granted for once – make him think a bit more clearly about what he really wants . . . it might help work things out for the two of you – and the baby.'

Alicia turned to face her, her eyes brimming with tears. 'You're so kind . . . thank you so much . . .'

'Well I'm probably just being an interfering old fool—'

'No, no not at all. It's just wonderful that you care so much.' A clean hanky extracted from the yellow bag was carefully dabbed round the eyes before she startled Kate by holding out her hand for a formal shake. 'I'll go home then,' she said, now smiling broadly, 'and take it from there.'

'Good luck. When's it due, by the way?'

'September the thirtieth – a Libran,' she announced happily, before swinging the strap of her bag over her shoulder and striding off in a way that struck Kate as almost miraculously elegant, given her size and condition.

Having summoned the nerve and energy to offer such advice, Kate felt rather pleased with herself, but her self-satisfaction did not last long. After Alicia had gone she sat back down on the bench with a sigh. The prospect of meeting Elizabeth and her team did nothing to lighten her frame of mind; she was in no mood to be forthright and forceful about anything; she would cave in to everything – she knew she would – because she was timid and ignorant and because they were paying.

But it was to the continuing worry of Nicholas that her mind kept reverting. While easily able to see how the embers of her brother's affair might most effectively be fanned, Kate remained more uncertain than ever as to how to apply such principles in her own case. Feeling guilty was a new and even more confusing aspect of the equation, having until now assumed that the problems were all of Nicholas' making, that she was not in any way culpable herself. Had she been neglectful after all? Kate made her way slowly towards the iron gates of the little park with the sneaking thought that she probably had, that even before all the recent distractions in her life she had almost certainly fallen into the trap of taking the basics for granted, forgetting that they had to be attended to, maintained at regular intervals, like the inside of an engine.

At the top of the steps down to the Underground, her musings shifted back to the night, a couple of days before, when they had made love, of how – through the curtains of pleasure – she had sensed that Nicholas was holding back, as if a part of him which had always been there for her was sinking out of her grasp. Getting the two of them back on track was going to be a lot harder than sorting out Harry and Alicia, she concluded with a sigh; her brother and his lover still had so many possibilities before them, while for her and Nicholas it was like trying to wrest something from the past, a lost tune, a tune so sweet, so nearly recalled, and yet not there.

29

On the day the Latimers left for Devon the weather broke. It started as they were loading the car, a few fat droplets on their bare arms, oozing like sweat from cracks in the muddy sky, until, as if overcome by the effort and weight of such suppression, the full torrent broke free. Borne on a lancing wind, rain-arrows hurled themselves at the crouching defences of the South Downs with all the ferocity of an advancing army. Scurrying to and from the car, with coats pulled up over their heads, slamming doors and offering hasty farewells to Joyce, Kate felt the drumming downpour as nothing more than an extension of her husband's displeasure, a phenomenon against which her powerlessness was beginning to make her quite afraid.

Nicholas drove steadily, silent and frowning, while Kate studied the map, suggesting routes in what seemed to him to be uncharacteristically forced and sugary tones. He could sense her guilt in every false poise, in every breath; it trailed her like a shadow. 'I've missed you,' she had said in the most un-Kate-like way when she got back from London, clinging to him like a piece of wreckage, her whole body smelling strange and flowery. There were more hugs to follow, embraces that made him stiffen because they were so unfamiliar, because they came from a Kate whom he no longer knew, one who now spoke to him as she might a stranger, one who seemed to be parading in the role of wife, overacting the part. Harry had been hateful, she declared, so ardently that Nicholas, though he longed to believe her, could not manage it. She would have to spend quite a bit of time preparing food in some studios in Battersea she then said, slipping this piece of information to him like a note under a door, all cowardly and sly.

Nicholas, wondering who her lover was, whether it could possibly be the creepy Jake, gripped the steering wheel hard, scowling at the feverish jerks of the windscreen wipers, beating across the screen like stricken wings, never quite keeping up, never doing enough to make the picture clear. The countryside, drenched and grey, seemed to shrink from this sudden onslaught from the sky; cows and sheep stood in dejected clusters under trees, heads bowed against the elements.

'It might be better further west,' she said brightly.

'I thought you wanted it cooler.'

'Yes, sweetheart, I did, but a tornado was not quite what I had in mind.'

Nicholas humphed and started trying to tune the radio to something other than a barking fizz, taking his eyes off the road for far longer periods than he knew he should, relishing Kate's unvoiced alarm, the way she sank more deeply into her seat and struggled not to complain.

Having located a radio station that was playing a vaguely familiar tune, Nicholas tapped his fingers in time to the music, wishing he could jig his thoughts into something as harmonious. To think he had been naive enough to imagine that having his mother to stay might bring the family closer together. How wonderfully absurd. How desperately had all desperate remedies failed, he thought, his face darkening at the recollection of the existence of Joanna Wyrall.

Instead of providing comfort, Joanna had demanded it, in bucketfuls. It was as if Nicholas had muttered some mysterious password during their hurried love-making, a password that allowed her to pour out, with no inhibition whatsoever, more troubles than he could have imagined her experiencing in a lifetime. Henry hadn't made love to her for two years, she sobbed, minutes after she had pinched fistfuls of his skin in her big hands, clutching at him in fearful – and painful – displays of violent pleasure that made Nicholas wince out loud. She longed for children, she moaned, in spite of Henry's indifference, in spite of what she had said before.

Nicholas opened his mouth to offer condolences. But there was more.

Henry had a woman in Ireland, and one in Paris too. She was so lonely she drank herself to sleep each night; she didn't love Henry, but was terrifed of growing old on her own. She was abhorrently fat and unattractive.

Such a catalogue of woes, given Joanna's earlier, appealingly unemotional revelations about her life, coupled with his impression of her as a mature, cheerful sort, was bad enough in itself. What was far worse was the expectation – apparently generated by their antics on the sofa – that Nicholas should now take the mantle of responsibility for these woes upon himself, that he should, during the course of the last half-hour, have acquired a sense of duty about helping to put them right.

'Of course you're not fat,' he had offered weakly, aware, even in his own confused emotional state, that it would have been catastrophically unacceptable to confess that he was far too preoccupied with the myriad failings of his own life to muster any heartfelt sympathy for anyone else's, that he had almost certainly stumbled into this sexual liaison out of disappointment rather than any impulse of romantic or honourable design. 'You are most attractive, Joanna.'

'The most attractive woman you've ever met?'

'Er . . . I should think so, yes.'

'You don't mean it, I can tell,' she sniffled, burrowing her wet nose in his neck.

'Now don't be silly,' he muttered, doing his best to sound tender, thinking all the while that the image of this woman inside his head had been nothing but that, an image, and that making things up about other people was a dangerous way of filling in the blanks.

It had all begun in a dark corner of a long line of stables. 'Tell me you want me – tell me, tell me,' she had murmured, pressing herself against him, tugging at his earlobe between two moist and agile lips and feeling for the buttons on his shirt. Nicholas, who had somewhat naively assumed that nothing so overtly physical would be on the cards until her guided tour of the house and grounds encountered something resembling a bedroom, had been caught badly off-guard. It didn't help that at the time of this impulsive embrace they were standing with unsettling proximity to a steaming beast with a white blaze on its forehead and a crazed look in its eye; it was dancing on its back legs, like a boxer limbering up for a fight, bouncing closer to Nicholas' toes with every jig.

'Yes, yes, of course,' Nicholas had whispered, looking round anxiously both on account of the horse and the fear of eyeballing one of the many green-booted, androgynous stable-hands whom they had passed on their way there, lugging metal buckets and barrows of straw. Having successfully disentangled himself, he managed to stay that way until Joanna served them with cappuccinos and wedges of toffee cake in the kitchen. Perhaps spurred on by the creamy smoothness of his coffee, the gooey sweetness of the cake, not to mention vivid flashes of Kate having a high time without him, Nicholas – with considerable aid from a most willing accomplice – quite suddenly found that he had crossed the flimsy threshold between restraint and surrender. After bowling along a hallway or two, staggering against walls and doors, they found their way into what looked like a children's sitting room, where they tripped over bean-bags towards the relative comfort of a small sofa.

Contrary to fictional representations of such scenes, the reality felt rushed and uncomfortable. Nicholas, severely hampered by being only partially undressed, remained constantly aware of the dangerous narrowness of their chosen bed. Nor did he glean any additional excitement from the sensation of embracing a woman whom he barely knew. Joanna felt startlingly broad and hard across the back; instead of softening in his embrace as Kate always seemed to do, shrinking into him, these unfamiliar shoulder blades jutted out in a way that felt almost hostile, while the bits in between felt full of muscle and sinew – all tense and unyielding.

Beside him in the car Kate sneezed violently, several times in a row. 'A dog—' she gasped, between two more sneezes, 'I can smell – a dog.'

It was a chance to be honest. Yes, he could have said, yes, there was – there is – a dog, with a needy, straw-haired, broad-backed mistress who, for some unfathomable reason, has selected me – plain, boring old Nicholas – to soothe the troubled waters of her life. No, I do not love her, no, I do not find her attractive in any violently irresistible sense, but having her there and interested has made me feel that I am redressing the balance somehow, making up just a little for the fact that you have left me, the fact that you appear to have resigned from our marriage. I have screwed her twice now and may even do so again. The first time was rather awkward – you know how these things are – the sofa was very lumpy and small and my mind was racing to interruptive matters like whether the door handle was turning and what would happen if I farted or slipped three inches to the left and fell shattering my pelvis on the parquet floor. The second time – yesterday, to be precise – was marginally more relaxed, since I took the liberty of using the spare key to Barnet Road, so we were at least on a bed – the spare bed of course – and even had time for a quick cup of tea afterwards, along with a stale digestive biscuit that I found in the cupboard, in that old green and cream tin, the one which, long ago, had toffees in it. A gift from us to my parents one Christmas, do you remember? Joanna is not as good a lover as you, not by any means; she's greedy and hasty – not my type at all really – but there we are. Funny old business, life, isn't it?

'Nicholas? Are you listening? I said I think a dog has been in the car. I can smell it.' She sniffed several times before blowing her nose.

'A dog?' He sniffed too, detecting clearly the lingering aromatic delights of Monty's wet breath and fur. 'Don't be silly – can't smell a thing.'

'Well, something's making me sneeze.'

'Perhaps it's the pollen count.'

At which comment they both turned to look out of their respective side-windows, as if pollen was something that could be glimpsed if stared for hard enough through rain-dribbles and steamy panes.

Victoria and Frank Armstrong fell upon their guests with a desperate glee, suggestive of certain marital misunderstandings of their own. Carrying a large, vibrantly coloured golfing umbrella, Victoria was the first to appear, springing towards them in a short mac and flip-flops, showing off crimson toe-nails and tanned legs. 'How lovely that you're here,' she shouted, skipping round puddles, muddy smuts smearing her ankles and feet. This started yesterday. We can't get it to stop. Hoped you two were going to bring some sunshine. How are you both? Lovely – come on in. Here, Nicholas, huddle under this with me. Let's leave the others to get soaked, shall we?'

Frank, who wore nothing but a floppy canvas hat by way of protection against the intemperate weather, hollered an equally energetic but more concise set of greetings, before seizing a bag from Kate's hand and ushering her inside.

The farmhouse, which was of grey brick, with a red tiled roof from which there now poured rows of small water-spouts, looked imposingly large. Kate made her way round the side, dodging roof dribbles and cascades from leaking gutters, following Victoria and Nicholas past several tumbledown out-houses to a side door at the back which led straight into a stone-floored kitchen, decorated with brasses along its beams and sporting shelf-loads of gleaming saucepans and crockery. The air felt chilly and damp.

'The front door's stuck – from all the rain, I expect,' said Victoria shaking out the brolly. 'Come on, Kate, let me show you to your quarters; we've put you in what we call the green room – there are so many – I think this place could sleep twenty if it had to – because it's got its own basin and a nice view of the sea – except at the moment of course. Can't get the heating to work, I'm afraid, but we've found two hot water bottles in the cellar – rather a triumph – so we shouldn't be quite so cold tonight. Who'd have thought it in August? It was baking last week when the children were here. Heavenly to be without them, don't you think? Ours are on a week's sailing course run by the school. We did wonder whether it was safe – what with all those teenagers tipping out of canoes and drowning last year – but then, as I said to Frank, if you don't take risks, you don't do anything. We're just as likely to be blown away by a serial killer or gassed in our sleep, as they are to die at the hands of some incompetent sailing instructor.' Kate, not called upon to say anything herself, followed Victoria back down the stairs, past a line of hunting prints and several oils of the sea.

'Do you miss yours?' Victoria enquired, as they entered the sitting room where Nicholas and Frank were standing with bottles of beer, admiring a glass case of guns that hung above the fireplace.

'I haven't really had time, to be honest,' Kate replied, thinking it was going to be even worse than she had thought, her eyes flicking over to Nicholas who was nodding sagely at Frank, in the way that he did when he was being deeply polite.

'Do we miss what?' asked Nicholas, seizing eagerly upon a pause in his host's lecture on firearms.

'Your children.'

'I miss them like hell, actually,' announced Nicholas, causing a fractional pause of surprise followed by uncertain laughs all round. 'Children are so wonderfully honest, don't you think?' he kept his eyes from Kate. 'If they're pissed off they communicate it with no trouble at all; likewise if they're happy, or think – for a few fleeting moments – that they love you, then you generally get the picture.'

'Christ, ours are as sly as foxes,' laughed Frank, 'never know what the hell they're up to.'

'Nicholas is thinking mainly of Millie, I suspect,' put in Kate quietly. 'Our Millie is very straight. All storms and sunshine. Not much in between.' At the mention of storms, the four of them found their eyes drawn to the wall of vast windows behind them, beyond which, somewhere behind the sodden barbecue and brimming birdbath, lay the beach and the sea, now an indistinct grey mass shrouded in cloud and rain.

Victoria rubbed her hands together briskly and made stagy shivering sounds with her teeth. 'Come on, Frank, do something useful like light the fire, can't you? And how come only the boys get offered drinks? Girls get thirsty too, you know.'

'If you're cold, why don't you change into something a little warmer, dear?' responded Frank with a tight-lipped smile, before turning to offer Kate a drink.

Victoria, unwilling to admit that the reason behind her skimpy attire was to show off the full extent of her suntan – acquired through a painstaking and sometimes uncomfortable commitment to sunshine and oily moisturisers the previous week – knelt down in front of the fire and began riddling inexpertly through the ashes with one of the many irons leaning up against the hearth. A particularly racy gust of wind chose that moment to force its way down the chimney, causing a shower of grey and black to fly up against Victoria's spotless white shirt, neatly tied at the midriff to expose the flawless brown of her stomach and lower back. 'Bloody hell, now I will have to change,' she wailed, sitting back on her heels and surveying her sooty front with dismay.

Everybody's mood lightened considerably over dinner, aided by several preprandial drinks and two bottles of cheap Spanish wine to wash down a rather chewy, but nonetheless quite tasty spaghetti bolognaise. Even Nicholas found his spirits lifting, thanks in part to the shameless attentions of his hostess. Victoria's behaviour, which might have been categorised in the most unfavourable terms in the sober light of an ordinary day, struck him as quite acceptable in the draughty candlelit dining room, where alcohol felt like the only reliable sandbag against disappointment.

'. . . All I mean,' Victoria was saying, gesturing with her glass at Nicholas, 'is that Nick has one of those faces that speak directly to a woman.' She swung her glass one time too many, spilling a few drops of wine which immediately sank into the dry wood of the dining table, leaving a neat chain of plum-coloured stains. The four of them, seated opposite each other in the middle of the long table, looked almost as if they had squashed together to keep warm, huddling between the vast expanses of empty wood on either side of their place mats. 'Nicholas' face has a kind of specially sensitive and sensuous—'

'Good alliteration,' interjected Nicholas, who, as ever, inclined to something of a literary mood once a certain quantity of drink was inside him. 'Specially sensitive and sensuous – very good.'

'May I remind you, Victoria,' put in Kate, who was feeling sleepy and hoping very much that nobody planned on doing the washing-up before bedtime, 'that this is my husband.'

'Lucky old you.' Victoria pressed her lips together and blew Nicholas a kiss across the table, at the same time kicking off one of her flip-flops and working a set of painted toes up the shin of his left leg. 'I'm only being appreciative from a distance. Aren't I, Nicko?'

'Behave, Victoria,' said Frank lazily, topping up his own glass and staring in surprise at how rapidly the second bottle had emptied itself.

'I'm for bed,' said Kate, standing up and yawning.

'So am I,' murmured Victoria, her eyes pinned on Nicholas, who looked away, smiling and blushing.

'Are you coming, Nicholas?' asked Kate in a small voice.

Nicholas did not really want to go to bed, though a sensible, sober part of him suspected that he probably should. What he did not like was Kate summoning him, like some kind of obedient hound, just because she had had enough frivolity for one evening.

'In a minute,' he replied, without looking her way, not wanting to see the bristling displeasure which he assumed would be his reward.

Though Nicholas, now feeling no pain whatsoever, felt as though he could have stayed up partying all night, the carousing of the remaining threesome was brought to an abrupt end by Frank's inability to produce another bottle of wine and Victoria's sudden decline into such floppy-headed sleepiness that she required her husband's assistance to make it up the stairs.

When Nicholas entered the bedroom, rubbing his forehead where he had knocked it on no less than three of the low beams slung across the doorways of the house, he found Kate apparently wide-awake, lying on her back with her hands behind her head staring at the ceiling.

'God, didn't Victoria make an idiot of herself.'

'Not really, no.' Nicholas folded his clothes with tipsy finicality, making a neat pile on a rather fine rosewood chair next to his bedside table, before going across to the basin to do his teeth.

'Oh, come on. She was being totally ... I mean, all that double-entendre stuff across the table. Rather pathetic really.'

'You mean she was flirting with me?'

'Yes, she certainly was – Christ, I don't know how Frank puts up with it.'

'Perhaps he loves her.'

'Perhaps. Though you may recall ...'

'... that Frank had an affair – yes I do recall that very well, thank you – I had a sort of feeling you would bring that up. It doesn't necessarily mean he doesn't love his wife.' He spat twice into the basin and rinsed his mouth, using his hand to cup the water to his lips. It tasted unpleasantly cold, and looked faintly brown. 'Though the real point here surely is that you seem to think it absurd that another woman should find your husband attractive.'

Kate raised her eyebrows and blew out her cheeks. 'Oh, don't be ridiculous, Nicholas.' She turned on her side, determined not to fall into the trap of a silly argument, knowing they were both too drunk to talk sensibly.

'Whereas I know that truckloads of men find my wife irresist-ible – and I'm not supposed to give the matter a second thought,' he continued, convinced now that he was being more rational and clear-headed than he had for months. 'What a sorry state of affairs.'

'I never said—' Kate began, but then stopped short. 'Oh forget it. You'll probably not even remember this conversation in the morning.' She wrenched a generous section of the bedclothes over to her side and rolled away from him. 'We'll all have headaches and feel sheepish and regretful.'

Nicholas turned out the light and lay blinking in the dark. His feet seemed to have solidified into two numb lumps, quite weightless with cold. He turned on his side and watched Kate, sleeping as always on her back, her chest rising and falling very gently with each breath, her hair curling into the soft bend of her neck. Not being loved by this woman felt like the loneliest thing in the world. He had always imagined – and now he wished – that her infidelity would have engendered hate, or coldness at the very least. Something simple and certain.

Tentatively he placed one cold toe up against her leg, enjoying the small beam of warmth that radiated from it. Moving slowly, he gradually began to press more of his foot up against the lovely furnace of the leg, feeling the blood starting to move deliciously round his icy toes. But she suddenly jerked it away from him, a sudden spasm of retraction suggestive of pain.

Somewhere outside something screeched. Dimly, he could hear the sea tossing on the dark shore. Nicholas pulled his knees up to his chest and massaged his toes with his hands. Thinking of Joanna did no good at all. Not because he felt guilty – it was almost too meaningless for that – but because she offered no consolation of any kind, a fact which only sharpened his unhappiness. Joanna had only happened because of Kate.

He tried to think what he should do, daring himself to confront Kate with his suspicions, to imagine the unimaginable – the next step – separation, divorce . . . But his mind, as if in protest at such unpalatable thoughts, chose that moment to rest, allowing his eyes to fall shut at last, while his hands still clung on to his feet.

30

Joyce decided to clean the house as her parting gift. It took a long time because, while giving the impression of being quite organised, every room was in fact filled with a dismaying number of unsorted piles of one kind or another: books, scraps of home-work, magazines, old newspapers (which Kate kept for recycling) were stacked in numerous corners of the ground floor, together with various plastic bags whose contents offered up dispiriting items like muddy studded boots, a swimming costume, a pair of ballet shoes, or simply a receipt that looked too important to throw away. There was so much to go through and tidy that Joyce did not in fact commence the cleaning side of things until well into the afternoon of the day on which she had originally hoped to leave. She had to phone the taxi company and ask them to pick her up at lunchtime the next day instead. She wanted time to do a good job because it seemed the best – the only – way of saying a proper thank you.

After waging war on every surface in sight – even going so far as to tie the feather duster to the end of the broom handle so as to get at the dusty pleats visible along the topmost edges of the curtains – Joyce turned her attention to the more taxing business of the floors. Hoovering was bad for her back, always had been – something to do with the angle, the slight bend involved in order to get the necessary push behind the machine – so she took it very steadily, pausing for a little sit-down or a strong cup of tea when the pain became too intense. She saved the floors for the next day; the last job of all and by far the worst: using a wadge of old newspapers to protect her knees, she scrubbed the tiled floors of the bathroom, kitchen and utility room by hand, as she remembered her mother doing, in the days when a bucket of soapy water and a tough bristled brush had been the only things for mud and grease. She used matchsticks to gouge out the grime between the tiles themselves, before running along their edges with her thumbnail to get into the smallest cracks, and finally rubbing them down with a jay cloth in order to work up a bit of a shine. The worst, most clogged-up area was by the back door that led into the garden and behind the downstairs loo, where scummy dirt had been joined by patches of black mildew and where each floor tile was badly cracked, cobbled together like a lumpy mosaic.

While acknowledging that Kate was busy – far too busy in her humble opinion – Joyce could not prevent the judgement forming, very early on into her stay, that her daughter-in-law spent far too little time doing anything in the home but cooking. Though she knew well enough that it was all the rage these days for women to be tearing round the country with careers and such things, she could not bring herself to believe that it was the way God had meant things to be. The result was neglect, she thought, pausing from her assault on the mildew to wipe her handkerchief over the moisture that had collected in the clusters of vertical lines along her upper lip. She dabbed her nose and prinked her hair with the tips of her fingers, hating the floppy shapeless feel of it, the way the perm was losing hold. Without mothers to hand children went wild, husbands turned sulky and houses grew dirty, she thought with a sigh, carefully refolding her small handkerchief so that the embroidered monogram, *JL*, was restored neatly to the top left hand corner of the last square.

On returning to her labours, her back protested harder than ever at the discomfort, so much so that she found herself resorting to conversations inside her head to keep her going. I know I'm doing the right thing, Dick, she said to him, I know you're proud. And after a while, when the pain was gripping her entire waist like a girdle of knives, she heard a voice which she recognised not as Dick's but as her father's. 'Cleanliness is indeed next to godliness,' he boomed, scrutinising her hard, towering over her as he always had, when scrubbed pink palms were held up for preprandial inspection, as the clock in the hall chimed twelve.

Accepting the invitation to come and stay with Nicholas and Kate had all been part of the terrible blur that followed losing Dick. After so many years of living with a man who thought with enough conviction for the two of them, a man whose routines and demeanour she had allowed to become the very backbone of her life, it had been hard to think quite how she should carry on alone – indeed it had been hard to think at all. Feeling so desperately adrift, especially after Alison had gone, Joyce had sunk into a self-defensive habit of acting without the consciousness of being in the act, of only being aware of doing things as she did them. It was a way of not thinking, a highly precarious, shocked state of mind which had ensured that she was quite powerless before Nicholas' cajoling. He had sounded so like his father, commanding in that gently gruff way, that at the time it had been an unqualified relief to submit to his invitation, to relinquish the daily burden of having to decide how to live each second on her own. To be absorbed into another family, to be caught up in the bustle of other people's lives had seemed irresistibly attractive, holding out alluring possibilities of losing oneself even more deeply – of burying sadness – along the way.

But in the end nothing had worked out as she had hoped. If anything, being surrounded by the unfathomable mystery of her son's marriage (though Joyce had long since acquired the wisdom to accept that most people's relationships were incomprehensible to everyone but themselves) with all its charging about and door-slamming and general chaos, had only served to exacerbate her own sense of unenviable inactivity. It was not comforting to be a bystander to busyness that was not her own, busyness to do with teenagers and twenty-year-old marriages – an era which Joyce herself had long since left behind and to which she had no desire to return.

And she missed Worthing terribly, the familiar walks along the front, the coach loads of tourists and chattering exchange students, the afternoon bridge at the old people's home on the corner, Mrs Bunting and Julie at the hairdresser's. Being away from all that, without the familiar bus routes or Joe from the minicab company, without any of the structure or scenery which had formed the backdrop to the last quarter of her life, had left

Joyce feeling marooned. Loneliness, as she quickly discovered, was far worse amongst crowds, its echoes far harder to bear when they reverberated along the hectic corridors of other people's lives.

Though it had taken a while for the picture to clear, Joyce had bravely come to accept that it had all been a dreadful mistake. In addition to her own troubles, she sensed dimly, somewhere between all the family commitments, the rushed meals and brief exchanges, that there was some kind of deeper crisis going on in the household, a crisis to which she feared – in her worst moments – that her presence might be contributing.

So when Betsie Hall's letter had arrived, a pearly white surprise amongst the meagre offerings of forwarded brown-enveloped bills and fat circulars about investments for pensioners, it had felt like a gift from heaven. The Halls lived at the other end of Worthing, nearer the rural side of things, in a street which had its own post office and a small pond beside which you could sit on a bench dedicated to someone called Emilia Esterhaze and watch the ducks. Dick and Betsie's husband Stan had been good friends for years, and in happier years gone by, before Stan's illness had confined him to bed, the four of them used to meet up quite regularly at the bowling club or for occasional pub lunches on a Sunday. Betsie was a good sort, a little livelier than Joyce – much readier with her tongue – but nonetheless kind and well-meaning. The letter explained that Stan had passed away and invited Joyce to come and stay. After the loneliness of her summer months, the idea of spending time with someone like Betsie – someone at least in a similar predicament to herself – shimmered before Joyce as one of the most glorious opportunities of her life.

The only remaining problem was how to tell Nicholas and Kate without hurting their feelings. If they realised how unhappy she had been they would only feel guilty. And since, Joyce suspected, it was probably some kind of guilt that had prompted them to invite her to stay in the first place, that was the very last thing she wanted. With schoolgirl excitement and sneakiness, she had rung Betsie to arrange things while Kate was in London seeing her brother, during the afternoon when Nicholas disappeared on a mysteriously long shopping trip, returning – much to her unexpressed wonder – without any parcels at all. The excursion to Devon had fallen into her lap like the final piece of the puzzle: it gave her ample time to pack up and clean, time to make her departure without interruption or confrontation of any kind – a perfect conclusion for Joyce, who was of a class and generation brought up to believe that storage rather than the expression of vehement feeling was the hallmark of good behaviour. Over the years she and Dick had perfected the art of bottling up their disagreements, riding them out in silence, so that barely a cross word had to be said out loud. Though she did not imagine Nicholas or Kate would be exactly cross with her, she nonetheless feared what they might say, just as she feared all that persuading and questioning and explaining that would necessarily follow.

Instead, she wrote them a letter, the very last chore before pulling the door behind her and posting her key through the letter box. The taxi driver held the car door open for her while she levered herself onto the back seat; though her fingers throbbed and her lower back was now stiff as well as sore, Joyce felt a great calm inside. Time, in her experience, was the most powerful of instruments. After a couple of weeks with Betsie, she was sure that Nicholas and Kate would see that the moment had passed for trying to persuade her to come back. She might even decide to go home, she thought with a thump of her heart, the idea of it filling her with sudden longing: the joy of her own small kitchen, the cosy warmth of the electric fire positioned exactly right, beside the footstool where she liked to rest her feet while she knitted or dozed in front of the telly.

Joyce closed her eyes, letting her body roll with the swaying of the taxi as it cruised, several miles too fast, round the narrow country roads. She thought of her bed – the familiar grooves of it – twenty inches from Dick's, the shared bedside table slotted in between, their glasses cases either side of the tissue box, their tin of cod liver oil capsules in the middle of the drawer underneath. She closed her eyes, living the scene. The taxi driver, assuming his elderly charge had fallen asleep, lit a cigarette and pressed his foot harder on the accelerator. If he had glanced a little more carefully in his rearview mirror he might have observed that his passenger was not asleep after all, that, as her head lolled to one side it was not rheumy old eyes, but tears, that wetted his upholstery.

31

'This might have been quite nice on our own,' whispered Kate, nestling against Nicholas on the second night, slippingy icy hands under his back.

'You could be right there,' he conceded with a half smile, flinching at the cold of her but letting the hands remain where they were.

A totally unforeseen sense of unity had been engendered by the increasingly undisguised discord raging between their hosts. Like survivors of a flood washed up on higher ground, the Latimers had spent a good proportion of their day watching Victoria and Frank flounder in far deeper and more embarrassingly visible waters than they had ever known, waters in which even the most basic strokes of politeness or fellow-feeling had been sacrificed to the uniquely intense brand of vitriol reserved for the intimate.

The show had begun at breakfast when, as Kate had so accurately predicted, the four of them spooned cereal into their mouths with sheepish expressions on their faces and pulsating heads. Nicholas, who had fallen asleep in the small hours only to be woken up somewhere around six by an unlatched window banging open and shut in the intermittent blasts of cold, salty air, had gingerly emerged from his bedroom imagining that no one could be suffering more acutely than he. Four mugs of black coffee later, with his body still shaky but out of pain, he was beginning to change his mind.

By far the most obvious victim of the previous night's revelry was Victoria, who arrived at the breakfast table last of all, clad in nothing but a short, peach-coloured robe and dark glasses, looking like some fading film star protecting evidence of her latest facelift, or wary of having bloodshot eyes captured on celluloid.

'Christ,' muttered Frank, whose own face looked very lined, as if it had been pressed unnaturally hard into the creases of his pillow for the entire night, but who had, until the appearance of his wife, been putting on a brave show of holiday heartiness, 'you could have got dressed.'

'I am dressed, darling.' Victoria tugged ineffectually at one side of her flimsy attire, succeeding only in revealing a stark glimpse of untanned flesh on the mound of one breast. 'When you gave this to me, was it your intention that I should never wear it?'

Nicholas and Kate exchanged glances, before burying their faces more deeply into their bowls and making an unnecessary to-do about passing milk and sugar.

From this disheartening start matters proceeded to get steadily worse. The rain, meanwhile, continued to pour with equal steadiness outside, leaving the four of them to thrash around for survival, like beached fish.

Kate, remembering the way in which Victoria had once been able to confide in her, made several bids throughout the morning to get her on her own, throwing out breezy comments about feeling rotten and having bad patches in marriages. But Victoria, sealed tight behind the inscrutable lenses of her sunglasses, resolutely refused to pick up any lines of assistance slung her way, preferring instead to focus her energies on baiting Frank, going about her task with all the shamelessness of an angry child. A hasty walk to the clifftop, snatched between downpours, followed by a game of Scrabble did nothing to lighten the atmosphere. Kate and Nicholas, having each tried in their various ways to be sociable, gradually withdrew to the sanctity of the sofa, where they sat like banned players, spectators to an ugly game, with nothing but the flopping covers of the day's newspapers as protection from the cruelties of the sport going on around them.

'If Frank wasn't quite such a skinflint, we could have been sitting in the Italian sunshine somewhere instead of cowering inside from English summer gales.'

'What dear Victoria has omitted to mention is the state

of our bank acount, which thanks to the haphazard spend-spend-spend approach of the one member of the team who contributes nothing to the family income, is badly in need of reinforcements.'

'I'd have thought, being a bank manager, of all things, you might have worked out our family budget slightly more efficiently. And what, might I add, am I expected to work at? Since I was forced to give up my career in order to bear your children.'

'Our children. It takes two, in case you've forgotten.'

'Do you know, I almost have.'

Silence, while Nicholas scribbles in several quick crossword clues and nudges Kate for some help.

'I hardly call being a hotel receptionist a career.'

'I was doing hotel management. It was part of the course. I only had eighteen months to go.'

'You hated it.'

'I loved it. It was what I'd always wanted.'

'Yes, after hairdressing, aromatherapy and . . . what was it? . . . psycho . . . physio . . . one of those.'

'Physiotherapy. At least I've tried a few things in my time. At least I haven't settled for the first bloody thing I started aged sixteen as if that was the only thing life could ever possibly have to offer.'

They were in a world of their own, a world in which all concessions to social decorum had been abandoned, and in which any timid interjection from either of their guests was barely heard, let alone responded to. There were no martini cocktails that night, no chewy bolognaise and tangy wine with a dash of footsie-footsie between chair-legs. Instead Kate, on seeing that neither of their hosts had any intention of removing themselves from in front of a badly zig-zagging television screen, slipped quietly off to the kitchen to see what she could do. After a brief survey of empty cupboards, she managed to cobble together a salad, using a variety of leftovers from the fridge and some drenched herbs from an overgrown patch just to the left of the back door, sticking the whole lot together with generous dollops of mayonnaise. To complete the feast she put a batch of stale rolls in the oven and then smothered them in crushed garlic and butter. The four of them ate in the sitting room with plates on their laps and glasses of water at their sides, watching a film about a man who had been kidnapped by aliens and apparently returned to earth disguised as a gorilla.

'I still don't understand why the gorilla didn't die,' said Kate sleepily, enjoying the way her hands were warming under Nicholas' back.

'The gorilla was part of the experiment.'

'What experiment?' She yawned, her head filling with images of hairy-faced men in white coats.

'They were trying to see if a gorilla could exist on Mars, weren't they?'

'Were they?'

They looked at each other and laughed out loud, before clapping their hands to their mouths and glancing guiltily at the door, as if humour had been banned that day for all residents of the house.

'By the way, I told Frank we'd have to be away first thing tomorrow,' said Nicholas, when the light was out and they were both lying in the darkness, the rain still beating hard overhead.

'Oh, well done.' Kate squeezed his hand before turning away from him, tucking herself up into a cosy ball, her hands pulled into her chest.

'I said we were worried about Mum.'

She giggled sleepily, murmuring 'You're marvellous,' before letting herself fall headlong into the most heavenly deep, dark, cushioned ravine of a sleep.

Nicholas, smiling too at the simple accomplishment of his white lie, followed not far behind; the noises outside which had seemed so disruptive the night before now beat a lullaby in his head, drumming out worry like a drug.

The next morning brought sunshine in several rather curious forms: while the real stuff poured in through every seaward facing window in the house, showing off a sweep of glistening green hilltops and the glimmering innocence of the tranquil sea, brightness of a more dubious variety was being displayed at the breakfast table. Victoria, this time sporting an unquestionably respectable pair of khaki shorts and matching brown T-shirt, made real coffee for them all, humming merrily between concerned queries about whether everyone had slept well and chirruping about the shame of Nicholas and Kate having to leave, just when the weather had improved so dramatically.

In mutual, silent support, Nicholas and Kate stuck to their guns, even elaborating their concern about Joyce with little stories of her frailty and forgetfulness. Phoning was no good, they protested, when Victoria suggested it as an alternative to leaving a day early, since she always said everything was fine. They really shouldn't have come at all, put in Kate, though it had been marvellous to get away.

Kate was packing up the last of their things, checking under the bed and rinsing blobs of shaving foam and toothpaste from the sides of the basin, when Victoria appeared in the doorway behind.

'Are you sure we can't persuade you to stay?'

Kate shook her head, smiling her gratitude at the offer, having long since run out of original ways of expressing their need to leave.

With a theatrical sigh of resignation Victoria followed her downstairs.

'Shame we were all a bit cranky yesterday,' she said lightly, just as they reached the landing, before the final four steps down into the hall. 'Hangovers all round, I guess,' she added with a rueful grin and a sidelong look which felt like a plea for concurrence.

'Absolutely,' agreed Kate hastily, feeling like someone who has witnessed something vile and been sworn to keep it a secret.

It turned out that Frank had said something along similar lines to Nicholas, while they were standing in the garden admiring the revelation of the sea. 'Can't take her booze, Victoria, I'm afraid – puts her in a mood for days sometimes . . . but still, we all have our little weaknesses, I dare say . . .'

'Oh indeed we do,' said Nicholas, staring hard at the view, 'indeed we do.'

32

They didn't see the note at first, since it had fallen from where Joyce had propped it by the teapot and was lying face down beside the jar of tea-bags. Nor, in their eagerness to get inside the front door, each of them laden with bags, damp raincoats and Wellingtons, had Kate or Nicholas noticed the key lying on the doormat, an omission made forgivable by the fact that it had bounced awkwardly upon landing and was actually lodged in a gap between the mat and surrounding carpet.

The teapot had seemed to Joyce to be the most obvious place to leave an item of such importance, since for her tea was one of the linchpins of life, cups of it through the day acting like fence-posts along a narrow road, comforting indicators of passing time. Nicholas and Kate, however, not having reached a comparable stage in their own lives where hot drinks were concerned, and feeling thirsty from their long drive on such a warm day, went not to the teapot but to the fridge to seek refreshment. It wasn't until Kate had pulled out a bottle of beer for Nicholas and a can of something sweet and fizzy for herself, that she first noticed that the kitchen looked different. It sparkled. There was no other word for it. And upon registering this fact, Kate's mind lumbered on towards consideration of the only person who could possibly have been responsible for such sparkle.

'I say, Nicholas, look at this place. Your poor mother must have spent the whole time cleaning.'

'Where is she anyway?' he asked, looking up from a letter he was reading, peering over the tops of his spectacles at her. 'Hmm, looks lovely,' he said, returning to the letter, which was from the managing director of Freeman Lyle, informing him and all other employees that times were hard, that belts had to be tightened and that there would be no company summer party that year. Impressed by the unmistakable thread of desperation behind such a cut-back, Nicholas found himself in the unusual position of wondering if – and hoping that – he still had a job.

'Well I assumed she was upstairs having her afternoon nap.' Kate eyed the ceiling, as if seeking confirmation of the idea. She felt a twinge of guilt at not being able to muster any enthusiasm at the thought of greeting Joyce. It was a comfort that Nicholas too seemed unmoved by the idea of seeing his mother again. 'I'll give her a knock in a minute – take her up a cup of tea.' As she spoke, Kate put down her can and wandered in a rather dazed fashion round the kitchen, staring in wonderment at the glistening surfaces, feeling that it would be wrong to touch or use any of them ever again. Putting off the chore of unpacking, she went out into the garden, her heart warming, as always, at the sight of the busy patterns of flowers and their backdrop of soft grey stone, the perfect foil for such an array of colour. Walking slowly across to the nearest of the beds, she began idly plucking at dead heads and bending down to pull out any particularly loose looking weeds. The soil was so wet that most of them came out easily, right down to the finest tip of their spindly-fingered roots. Squatting down, Kate began to apply herself more earnestly to her task, until there was such a pile of weeds beside her that it seemed only sensible to fetch the wheelbarrow. How neglectful she had been this year, she scolded herself, as she strode across the lawn to the shed where they kept garden tools and the children's old bikes. This time last year the garden had been a real picture, she recalled, indulgently letting images of the past rise up before her like snapshots of some halcyon era, an unappreciated, irretrievable time when troubles had been mild and manageable.

Stepping carefully between the lavender bushes, she began to tend to the roses which had been in full bloom when they left for Devon but which now looked uncomfortably laden with the moisture of so much rain, their stems bent right over, their delicate heads flopping down as if offering themselves up for execution. Taking pity, Kate pulled off the heaviest looking ones, tossing their pretty velvet petals into the barrow with a shiver of sadness that they should have been cheated out of their prime.

By the time she had completed her circuit of the garden the barrow was quite full; behind her lay deep wheel tracks from where she had steered it through the long lush hair of uncut grass – it apparently having celebrated the rainy weather by growing two feet in as many days. Though the air was warm, there was a refreshing breeze that whisked up the corners of her skirt and fanned her hair back from her face. She took deep breaths as she walked, drinking in the sweet smells roused by the rain, loving being back in her own home, relishing the curious sensation of having been away for weeks and weeks.

A tune began to play inside her head, a snatch of something classical and Mozarty which she couldn't place but which she knew came from distant days of hard benches and school choirs. She started to hum it quietly at first, but increased the volume as her confidence grew. By the time she reached the safe distance of the compost heap in the furthest corner of the garden, she was performing with all the panache of an international opera star, serenading her barrow like a lover, flinging out her arms as if to embrace the sky.

She did not see Nicholas leaning out of a sitting-room window watching her, a man in a trance. Though the sound of Kate's voice was what had drawn him, it was not her wavering treble that held him spellbound, but rather the entire scene: the sun-drenched garden, the woman in a skirt and wellingtons at the far end of it, mud on her bare arms, her head tossed back, singing for all she was worth at the sky. It was like staring into a painting that had come alive, though the picture before him was one of such pure elation, such private joy that he shrank like an intruder from its edges.

With a final flourish of her barrow, and a note that felt – though it almost certainly wasn't – as high as a top G, Kate pitched the last of its contents onto the heap and then, panting slightly, brought the note to an abrupt end. Behind her, Nicholas withdrew, his heart brimming with emotion – with envy for such a capacity for abandonment, and with love too, such a fierce love that he had to stop to catch his breath, as if winded by the force of it.

To get through the moment, he busied himself with taking their bags upstairs, whereupon he noticed that the door to his mother's bedroom was wide open and that the bed had been stripped down to nothing but its shamefully grubby mattress. A pile of freshly laundered sheets had been placed on one end, beside the pillow and a folded pink blanket. Nicholas' first reaction was to search the tiny room harder, as if he fully expected to find his mother crouching in one corner of the wardrobe or coiled up in the bottom of the chest of drawers. Next he checked the bathroom. Then he ran back into the bedroom and pushed open the window.

'She's gone, Kate, she's bloody well gone,' he shouted.

'Who's gone?' she called up stupidly, one hand to her forehead to shield her eyes from the sun.

'Mum – she's bloody well gone, I tell you. There's nothing here – no clothes – nothing. She's disappeared.'

While they searched the house, Nicholas wondered, rather hysterically, whether it was a crime to lose a mother. Kate followed him round in a daze, wanting to be supportive but not as yet able to think of anything helpful to say. Seeing that not only the kitchen, but the entire house had been tidied and scrubbed clean, she sensed a finality behind Joyce's absence which filled her with both worry and relief.

'She must have gone home, I suppose.'

Nicholas ran to the phone and dialled Barnet Street, letting it ring scores of times before silently shaking his head and putting the receiver down.

'I could drive over there and check if you like.' Kate, pleased to have thought of something positive and helpful to do at last, held her hand out for the keys. 'I'm sure there's some simple explanation for all this. She's almost certainly gone back to Worthing, but is out shopping or something and is planning to ring us tomorrow, which is, after all, the day we were expected back.'

Nicholas regarded her hopefully. 'Do you think so?'

'Absolutely. If you give me the spare key I'll drive over right now and check. Don't look so worried.' She went over to where he was sitting and fondly stroked the stiff brush of his hair with her fingers before squatting down in front of him and guiding his face to meet hers. 'She's fine, I know she is. Nothing can have happened – she clearly intended to leave – I mean look how beautifully she tidied up for us. Obviously she's just had enough of family life for a while – wanted to be alone – that kind of thing.'

'But why didn't she say?' Nicholas stared glumly at the carpet.

Kate took his hands and pressed them against her cheeks. 'Dearest Nicholas, your mother doesn't exactly have an impressive track record for saying very much, does she? Wanders round in a world of her own most of the time. Who knows what she's really thinking or planning? I am sure everything will become clear very soon.' She kissed each of his palms in turn and stood up. 'Now then, would you like to go to Worthing or would you prefer to be on standby here for phone calls and so on?'

'I don't mind . . . I'll stay here, I think. It's very good of you to go, Kate, thanks.' After rooting around in his pockets he held out the keys for her. As she took them he grasped her fingers. 'I love you, Kate,' he said, his voice croaky.

'I know,' she murmured before he kissed her, 'I know. You'll see, it will be all right.' Though she only meant it would be all right about his mother, her words resounded in Nicholas' ears with reassurance for far more than that.

After Kate had gone Nicholas trailed aimlessly round the house picking things up and putting them down, before finding himself near the kettle. More for something to do than anything else, he filled it with water and looked round for a mug and a tea-bag. At which point he noticed his mother's letter, which had by now fallen victim to several general splashes of tap water from the sink, leaving the ink so badly smeared that only the capital letters of their names were clearly distinguishable. Nicholas tore it open with fear in his heart, letters and disappearing acts being intertwined in his mind with scenarios of the most gruesome kind.

My Dears,

I am sorry to leave you without warning, but I thought it might make it all easier. It has been so very kind of you to have me all these weeks, but I really feel the time has come for me to leave you in peace. I won't tell you quite where I am for the minute, as I don't want you to fuss about having me back. Don't worry about me, whatever you do.

I hope you had a lovely time in Devon.

Love Mum

PS I'll post my key back through the letterbox.

Nicholas' first reaction was to screw this enigmatic communication into a tight ball and hurl it at the side of the fridge, where it hit a magnet of a ladybird that Millie had made and ricocheted neatly into the fruit bowl, lodging between a black banana and a tired looking lemon. How astonishingly childish, he thought, stirring his tea viciously, noting surfacing blobs of cream with distaste, how ridiculously naive to imagine that she could slip off like that without it mattering. It was like having another child to worry about. Three was bad enough; his mind paused for a fond flicker of longing for the children before being distracted by the more immediate problem of his tea. It looked oily and unappealing, the cream blobs having dispersed into dancing circles of buttery globules. After an apprehensive sniff Nicholas took a sip, made a face and tipped it down the sink. He was on the point of pouring away the soured contents of the offending milk bottle when the phone rang. He picked it up at once, expecting it to be Kate calling to say that the house in Barnet Street was empty.

'I've found a letter from her,' he blurted, 'half-soaked. It was by the tea-bags.'

'What letter?'

On recognising Joanna's voice Nicholas experienced a dismaying, gravitational wrench in the pit of his stomach. 'My mother has disappeared – we're rather worried – though she says in a letter that she's fine.'

'Well I expect she is then.' The sentence was laced with controlled impatience. Joanna had not called her new lover to discuss the whereabouts of a truant mother. 'Have you missed me?'

'Missed you?' Nicholas ran his fingers through his hair and turned nervously to face the door. 'Well I . . . the thing is you're not supposed to call me at home . . . I mean, it's sheer luck that I'm here on my own. Kate's trying to find Joyce.'

'Who's Joyce?'

'My mother.'

'I see.' There was a silence. 'Clearly I am being the most horrible nuisance . . .' she began in more quavering tones.

'No, no . . . I mean, it's just that this really is not a good time, Joanna. We've got this sort of family crisis on—'

'When can I see you then?' she cut in; 'the sooner we straighten that out the sooner you can go back to your crisis.'

Realising with another plummeting feeling that it would cause him no lack of sleep – that it might in fact improve his sleep considerably – if he were never to see Joanna Wyrral again, Nicholas at first took refuge in silence. This wasn't something that could be said over the phone. Neutral ground, he thought frantically, somewhere safe and impersonal, somewhere that would ease the trial of having to extract himself from this unfortunate situation.

'I presume your mother's place is out of bounds?' Joanna volunteered slyly, wanting to remind him of the time they had spent there, sensing that his appetite for her was somewhat in need of sharpening. 'Henry's around, but . . .'

'I might be able to get away tomorrow,' Nicholas interjected, his mind grinding along rather less erotic tracks. 'I should think I'll be able to slip away, but after that it gets more complicated because the children will be back and then my holiday ends and . . .'

'You're not making excuses, are you, Nick? The thing is,' there was a pause, 'I'll go mad if I don't see you.'

'Oh no,' he almost shouted in panic. 'No excuses – far from it – not at all. Let's say tomorrow afternoon then. In the pub car park. We'll . . . er . . . take it from there, as they say.'

'Sounds good to me.' Her voice was breathy with relief. 'Shall we say two o clock? Would that fit in with . . . ?'

'Yes, yes – absolutely fine,' Nicholas cut in impatiently, wanting only to end the conversation, wanting only to end the whole confused business, but still clinging to some unwritten code of honour which forbade the undertaking of such things over the telephone.

Kate rang a few minutes later to say that the house in Barnet Street looked quite uninhabited. When he read Joyce's note out to her she reacted with comforting expletives of frustration and outrage, before going on to say soothingly that there was clearly nothing more they could do for the time being and would he like her beef in cream sauce for dinner that night. It was a dish which, along with several others that involved more than a smattering of onions, peppers and cream, had been jettisoned from the family menu in recent months on account of Joyce's often embarrassingly audible war against the ravages of indigestion. Nicholas, while sympathising with his mother's clearly very painful eructions, had, as he now realised with a gastric pang of his own, missed these ingredients terribly. The prospect of reacquainting himself with them, over a glass of red wine or two, with a wife who suddenly seemed genuinely concerned about his happiness, warmed his heart beautifully. So beautifully in fact, that he not only unpacked all Kate's clothes as well as his own, but he even put the dirty ones in the washing machine, and laid out a fresh piece of newspaper by the back door to serve as a mat for their muddy boots. With such monumental domestic achievements under his belt, Nicholas then felt inspired enough to sidle past the exercise bike, giving the seat of it a hearty pat on the way – like salutations for a much missed friend – before settling himself in front of the screen of his computer.

As Nicholas slid the disc into the narrow post-box of a slit and listened to the mechanical whirring that preceded the appearance of any readable image on the screen, a small flutter of eagerness beat inside his stomach. The shadow of an inspiration began to form: the troublesome old mother walking out on her son was a twist he hadn't thought of before, and rather a good one too. Then there could be an accident, he mused, his fingers tapping the keys, something not fatal but bad enough to make everyone feel terribly guilty and then terribly close. Nothing quite so unifying as a family crisis, he thought with a smile, while the words spilled onto the screen.

33

'Perhaps we should tell the police,' Kate suggested after a couple of mouthfuls. Having eyed the price of some rather fatty rump steak for a few minutes, she had, in a rush of impetuosity, seized a bulging pack of fillet pieces instead. After browning these extravagances for just a few seconds in sizzling butter and oil, together with a selection of vegetables and spices that would have made her mother-in-law's guts burst at the seams, Kate had stirred them into the most alluringly velvet of her cream sauces. Nicholas found it hard not to groan as he ate, tasting as if for the very first time the sheer pleasure of the texture and flavour of such food; each mouthful seemed to dissolve on contact with his teeth, requiring only the most lazy, languid chewing before slipping effortlessly down his throat.

'Do you think so?' He wiped a dribble of sauce from his chin with the tip of his little finger and took a generous sip of wine. He had found a dusty bottle of claret in the cellar, the last of a very fine case which Harry had given them the Christmas before, together with a book they never used, called *Knowing Your Grapes*. 'But what exactly could we say? Missing persons – that sort of thing?' His wide mouth began to form into an unmistakably devious smile. 'Mother walks out on forty-six-year-old son, eh? Home alone Dad in despair.' Once Nicholas started to laugh he found it rather hard to stop.

'Mother Missing in Rural Riddle,' volunteered Kate, between her own fits of laughter.

'Gregarious Granny Rides Again!' he shouted, banging the flat of his hand down hard on the table and then, sensing that complete hysteria was about to take hold, that, though he was still laughing, the water in his eyes might, in an instant, be transformed into tears, the laughs to sobs he staggered across the kitchen in search of something appropriate on which to wipe his face. Tearing off two squares of kitchen paper from the roll beside the sink, he buried his face in it and breathed deeply. 'Oh dear.' He looked up, shaking his head. 'Poor Mum – oh dear, poor Mum.'

Kate, beaming, motioned at him with her glass. 'Come back here and eat before your steak goes clammy. It's a fiver a mouthful this stuff, you know.'

Nicholas, more or less composed, returned to his seat. 'Do you know,' he ventured after a few moments, 'my first thought was that she might have killed herself?'

'Perhaps she has.'

'Kate – don't.'

'Well that silly letter is so ambiguous.' Spearing a small piece of fillet with her fork, Kate ploughed a slow furrow through her pool of sauce. 'Perhaps the reason she says we're not supposed to worry about her is because she's in heaven.'

Nicholas felt the pulse of a giggle returning, as irrepressible as a bad cough. 'God, I feel so wicked,' he choked, wiping under his eyes with his fingers, 'I don't know what's got into me. I should be worried sick.' He straightened his back and assumed an expression of utmost gravity. 'I am worried sick,' he announced, before his mouth quavered at the sides and the urge to smile defeated him again. He shook his head. 'Anyone but you . . .'

'Anyone but me what?'

'Anyone but you would think I was mad or evil.'

'Oh I think you're both those things,' she replied wickedly, getting up to clear their plates and fetch the cut-up strawberries and peaches which she had tossed in a tablespoonful of sweet liqueur. 'It's just that I'm the same, so it would be a bit hypocritical to mind, wouldn't it?' She handed him a carton of double cream to open and sat back down. 'Besides which I think Joyce is perfectly all right. And – I'm sorry but I have to say it – I think it's marvellous to have you to myself for once.' On the point of serving out the dessert, Kate suddenly pushed back her chair and ran to fetch her handbag from the hall.

'What do you make of these,' she asked, smiling, holding up a pair of large, gold-hooped earrings which Nicholas immediately – with a heart-thump that was certainly audible to himself – recognised as Joanna's. One had caught in her hair, he remembered, prompting her to insist on interrupting proceedings in order to take them off.

The inside of Nicholas' mouth, which had so relished the mingling of sauce and wine, dried in one instant to the texture of used sandpaper. Unable to speak, he raised one arm and swung his head in a show of mute wonderment.

'I found them at your mother's place – on the floor beside the spare bed. Odd, isn't it? I mean,' Kate swung the loops round her index finger, 'they don't exactly look like Joyce's cup of tea.'

For one awful moment Nicholas thought she was playing with him, like a lazy, grinning cat with a bouncy fool of a mouse pinned under one claw by the tip of its sinewy tail. He watched her face closely: maybe that lovely smile, which he was so very tempted to start to trust again, was false after all, a trick to lure him into some macabre game of treachery and confrontation.

'Not Mother's style at all,' he agreed meekly, waiting for the axe to fall, his fingers fumbling so badly on the lid of the cream that Kate tut-tutted and took it from him, applying her more expert feline nails to the task.

'I suppose they must be Alison's from when she stayed,' she continued, not looking up from the carton, so that the flush of relief that gushed and ebbed from Nicholas' face passed without observation.

He wagged his head like an eager dog. 'Alison's exactly – that has to be it.'

'Except,' said Kate, thoughtfully raising a heaped spoon of fruit and cream to her mouth and focusing her shining brown eyes directly upon his, 'I didn't think she had pierced ears.'

'I thought all women had pierced ears,' he remarked, daring for the first time in this unsettling exchange to lift his eyes from his food.

'Oh no, not at all. I only had it done because of a pact in the fifth form – though several cowards dropped out when they saw the horrible gun thing that they use. One girl – Jemima something – actually fainted on the spot. The holes they make are gooey for a long time afterwards – you have to wear special little earrings daubed in antiseptic, so you go round smelling like a bottle of TCP and can only sleep lying on your back because it hurts too much to be on your side.'

'My goodness, I had no idea it was so gruesome. My poor Kate, what a brave little fifth-former you must have been,' he teased, gently nudging the subject away from the quicksand, at the same time rather relishing the thought of Kate in school uniform.

Kate made a face. 'Coffee, darling? Or some of your mother's evening herbal tea? She has left us a whole boxful of the raspberry flavour you love best.'

Nicholas, who as she well knew, could not abide even the faintest whiff of any of Joyce's aromatic late-night drinks, grinned, pretending to give the matter weighty consideration. 'Strong black coffee for me tonight, please. There's a late film about aliens and spaceships starting in five minutes – and I don't want to miss a second.'

'Goody, more gorillas,' said Kate, happily abandoning the kitchen to its mess and following him through to the sitting room. She carried two mugs of coffee while Nicholas brought what remained of the wine and a large bag of lemon bonbons which he had discovered during the course of an unsuccessful cupboard-rummage for chocolate.

'Those are Millie's sweets,' scolded Kate, kicking off her shoes and nestling against him on the sofa. 'A boy called Henry gave them to her on the last day of term and she has been saving them ever since.'

Nicholas flinched imperceptibly at the name Henry, an unwelcome flash of the task that awaited him the next day beaming across his mind. 'Is Henry a boyfriend?' He put a bonbon in his mouth, noisily licking the sweet yellow dust from his finger-tips. Kate took one too.

'Henry is apparently in love with Millie, but Millie isn't sure,' she said, her voice full of sweet. 'She says she's not ready for a serious relationship.'

'She didn't.'

'She did,' Kate insisted, laughing.

They both watched the television in silence for a few minutes, where several characters in silver suits were punching panels of coloured buttons and talking in clipped monotones about incomprehensible technical problems and unlikely intergalactic threats.

'Where are the gorillas?' asked Kate, hugging her mug to her chest and breathing a sigh of drowsy happiness.

Nicholas turned and smiled at her. 'I had convinced myself you had a lover, you know.'

'A lover?' Her brown eyes opened wide. 'Really, Nicholas . . . how absurd.' She shot him a brilliant and disarming smile. 'I don't have the time for such things.' An image of Max Urquart sprang into her head, sitting up for attention like a cardboard figure in a children's pop-up book. She forced her mind to turn the page, to move on from the memory. 'You don't still think it, do you?'

A longish pause. 'No,' he said slowly, 'I don't think I do.'

'Well, thank goodness for that. It's been a lousy summer, hasn't it, my love, what with your father dying and . . . everything else? I sometimes feel . . . I wonder . . . have I been neglecting you dreadfully?'

'Dreadfully.'

They smiled at one another. 'Oh Nicholas . . .' she sighed, wanting to say so much, but wary of destroying the tentative peace that had so magically returned by daring to refer to it. 'I don't know what's been going on exactly, but today I really feel as if—' He put his hand across her mouth and shook his head at her.

'Let's leave it there . . . please? I'm an old fool, who loves you terribly.' He nuzzled her jumble of hair with his mouth, pulling her close. 'Keep an eye open for large hairy primates, my love,' he murmured, 'or you might lose the thread. I think the tall one on the left is going to be trouble – there's a distinctly malevolent gleam in that reflector mask of his. The others don't know it yet, of course, but he'll be the traitor, you mark my words.'

Kate, who hated science fiction in any shape or form, but who loved this long-neglected pastime of snuggling on the sofa with her husband, let her head fall onto his shoulder and closed her eyes.

Harry took a desultory sip of his champagne and scowled at his race-card. Thanks to his habitual – and quite absurd – sense of social obligation he had bet on each of Rupert's horses that day and lost every time. Alicia, on the other hand, who had followed up on a splendidly feisty approach to Rupert by backing all the names he scorned most, had so far won money in every race. Having originally been both thrilled and relieved to see the teasing banter with which Alicia adroitly handled his friend, Harry was now beginning to feel the stirrings of discontent. Pregnant women were supposed to wilt and moan, he thought huffily, folding his arms and watching while Alicia chinked glasses with Rupert and told him that if he was very lucky she might be able to think of someone who could recommend him a new trainer.

'How are you feeling – not too hot or tired or anything?' interrupted Harry, leaning forward to get her attention, touching her bare skin lightly with his fingers, two gentle strokes near the small mole in the crook of her arm.

When she turned to him her face was infused with eager contentment. 'Oh no. I'm having the most wonderful time, Harry – this is such a treat. It's years since I've been to the races. Not since – well, never mind – not for a very long time anyway. And I can't think how you've kept lovely Rupert under wraps all these months – he's quite a treasure.'

Rupert Kershaw, who had imbibed ten glasses of champagne to Alicia's one and who had been mulling over the confusing experience of finding someone whom he fully expected to loathe so contrarily engaging, shrugged his shoulders at Harry's frown.

'She's got the golden touch, your lady, Harold, the golden touch.'

'Not since when?' persisted Harry, ignoring Rupert, whom he thought had been unforgivably boring, and increasing the pressure of his grip on Alicia's arm.

'What, darling?' Alicia put her face close to his and pressed the tip of his nose with one finger. Her cheeks were ripe with colour, but smooth and dry. Her lips were faintly pink, like her dress, which hung in large, loose folds, cleverly disguising the eight-month bulk underneath. 'You haven't been to the races since when?' repeated Harry, blinking at her.

'Since the days when I went around with the kind of people who did that kind of thing all the time.' She stroked his cheek with the back of her fingers. 'They were very boring, Harry, not like you at all.'

'Nor me,' put in Rupert, who was beginning to feel left out.

Alicia flopped back in her chair, resting her arms across the mound of her stomach and feeling – for the first time that afternoon – a trifle tired. An insecure Harry was so much more demanding, she had found, though the discovery did not dishearten her in the least. As a result of Kate's timely piece of advice, Harry now persevered in the apprehension that Alicia might one ·day abandon him for good, a small Damoclean thread of a belief which had produced the most astonishing and fruitful results, a virulent capacity for jealousy being among the more prominent and least attractive. Not only was Harry showing niggling signs of envy over meaningless prattle with acquaintances like Rupert, but he had also taken to interrogating her about relationships begun and ended so long ago that Alicia herself had genuine difficulty remembering the true sequence of events. After a few turbulent grillings about such things, during which she perceived that this new, curiously retrospective envy of Harry's needed only the merest morsel of information to flicker into life, she had abandoned honesty altogether and opted for outright denial or dismissal instead. More recently she had even dared to deliver a tender but strict little speech about soon having to share her with Baby and the two of them not having time for such silliness. Harry, who had a secret and terrible dread of how he might react if he saw another creature sucking the berry-red topping of one of Alicia's creamy domed breasts, even if that creature were their own child, had nodded with uncharacteristic meekness, unreassured, but so totally ill-equipped to deal with this recent onslaught of unfamiliar and exacting emotions that acquiescence had seemed the only response possible.

Weary of flattering Rupert, whom she secretly thought pompous and dull, Alicia reached under the table and took hold of Harry's hand, taking two of his fingers in her fist and squeezing hard. Harry moved the fingers appreciatively in response, enjoying the familiar pulse of arousal that the touch of her evoked, feeling all the better for it.

They were sitting on a green and white striped canopied terrace reserved for owners and trainers, overlooking the final furlong of the racecourse. Immediately below them a colourful cross-section of racing devotees swarmed between gesticulating bookies, queues for the Tote windows and the yawning entrance to the grandstand. To their left, covering the bottom half of a small hill, were gathered those punters with picnics as opposed to fat wallets or invitations to hospitality tents to see them through the day. Over to the right lay the paddock, filled with prancing contenders for the next race, its ring of white fencing looking impressively polished beside the lush oval of well-tended grass within.

For a while the three of them sat in silence. While Rupert fought the urge to fall asleep, his head jerking comically between snoozes, Harry stared unseeing at the rippling movements and colours of the crowds below, his mind lazily anticipating how he would make love to Alicia later on that day, how he would cup the beautiful swells of her in his arms, how slow and tender he would be. Though they had dutifully watched the parade of horses and exchanged chit-chat about form and odds before the start of the previous races, Harry, disgruntled at having lost three sizeable sums of money in such quick succession, had declared his intention to abstain from the next two. Rupert, who had no more runners that day anyway, had made no protest, while Alicia had been secretly grateful for the opportunity to sit down.

She would have liked to have put her feet up, to get her ankles above the level of her hips and put a stop to the increasingly uncomfortable sensation that all the excess liquid in her body was steadily draining down towards her toes. Pushing her chair back a few inches, she cast a surreptitious glance at her feet, needing to see that the slim legs of which she was justifiably proud, were still there, that the neat nodules of her ankle-bones had not after all drowned in a sea of inflated flesh.

I'm sorry but I'm not sure I'm going to last the day, Harry darling,' she whispered, her warm breath close to his cheek. 'You stay on for some fun with Rupert, if you like – I can get a taxi or something.'

'Not on your life,' he whispered back. The two of them looked across at their host, whose head had finally tipped into a position which, while clearly not ideal for sleep, was finely poised so as not to overbalance and awaken its owner. 'We'd better give him a few moments,' muttered Harry impatiently, suddenly wondering why he had used this precious day off to do anything other than lounge around the flat. Alicia had been staying there quite a lot recently, sometimes two nights on the trot. A couple of her dresses now hung in the wardrobe; a robe shared the peg on the bedroom door with his dressing gown, just as a toothbrush shared the tooth mug and a pot or two of her creams flanked the shelf where his electric razor and comb were housed. Nothing had been said about these items or their presence in his flat. It was as if they had grown there themselves, taken root without any organisation or prompting at all. Instead of minding, Harry found that when Alicia stayed away he rather liked to see the dresses there, hanging loose and free beside his array of dark suits, their colours so bright, their folds looking silky and mysterious.

On occasions, Harry even caught himself thinking about all the things she had bought for the baby – the pram with blue elephants on the hood and what looked like a large cat basket draped in flowered cotton. Harry could remember these things from what felt like ages back, during the time when he hadn't wanted to know. Now he caught himself wanting to know rather more: Did the basket-bed have wheels, for instance, or just those floppy handles at the side? Exactly how transportable was it?

And if the basket-bed found its way to Fulham on a social call, where could it lodge? The large tea chest at the foot of his bed leapt helpfully to mind. It was solid and rarely opened. Perhaps the basket and its unimaginable contents could perch there, while its mother lay in his arms, while everything else carried on as before. A basket wasn't much to have to take on board after all, he reasoned, given that its bearer was still so irrefutably desirable.

'I need to powder my nose – again – sorry,' said Alicia, using both hands to lever herself from her chair. 'Won't be a tick.' She got up and walked stiffly towards the back of their canopied haven, resisting the downpull of her belly by keeping her head high and placing one foot firmly in front of the other. Behind her, as she guessed correctly, her lover watched, marvelling at her poise, at the grace that could accompany such extreme distortion of a body.

Bored and in danger of feeling sleepy himself, Harry picked out a large ice-cube from the champagne bucket and popped it in his mouth before returning his attention to the milling crowds below. Almost immediately, his eye was caught by a familiar figure, bobbing in the densest part of the spectators round the paddock. It occurred to Harry, while his eye remained tightly trained on this unexpected find, that it was somewhat bizarre – something between luck, coincidence and fate – to have spotted such a small blob within so large a mass of humanity, and that, had he been instructed to scour the landscape for his brother-in-law he would almost certainly have failed. His other train of thought upon recognising Nicholas related to the woman whose hand he was holding; for the woman was certainly not his sister, nor did she strike him – given an outfit that appeared to comprise nothing more than white jeans and a pink T-shirt – as a plausible member of the marketing fraternity of Freeman Lyle or any other institution that could have been ascribed to his brother-in-law's business practices.

'Oh fuck,' said Harry under his breath, crunching on his melted pebble of ice and squinting to try and sharpen up the image. Just a couple of feet behind him, slung round Rupert's neck, were some high-calibre binoculars; but Harry was reluctant to turn round even for a second, for fear that he would lose Nicholas to the crowd. Instead, he leant his arms along the railings beside his chair, resting his chin on his hands and staring so hard his eyes began to ache from the strain. The woman now had her arm round Nicholas' waist; her head rested on his shoulder. Then they began working their way back through the crowd, heading away from the paddock towards the wide entrance to the grandstand directly beneath where Harry was sitting. As they drew closer Harry found himself pulling back slightly, so that only the top half of his face was visible over the tops of his hands. It was ridiculous of course; he was still much too far away and high up to be noticed; but he took the precaution nonetheless, out of some protective instinct – though quite whom he was protecting and from what he was by no means sure. Just before they disappeared from view, the woman, who had wide hips and long wheat-coloured hair, released her grip on Nicholas' midriff and set off walking a few steps ahead of him, as if leading the way. Nicholas, apart from looking up sharply once, almost as if he was suspicious of an observer, continued to walk with far less flounce than his companion, almost doggedly, Harry thought, like a man grimly determined upon a fixed course.

It wasn't until they were out of sight that the first rush of filial outrage set in. Kate, he recalled, had recently implied that there were a few problems in her marriage, but nothing so monumental as this. Though Harry had conducted several liaisons with married women in his time, and though he still distrusted the disciplinary aspects of marriage with every hormone in his body, he felt not the slightest compunction about judging Nicholas in the most scalding terms. It was the notion of Kate – good, strong, reliable, capable Kate – as a victim that somehow appalled him the most; the thought that someone as absurd and awkward and shambolic as Nicholas should have the capacity to belittle his big sister in such an uncompromising way filled him with a panicky horror, a horror whose roots were tunnelled deep into the past, wound round years of sibling solidarity and disputes in which blood ran thicker than reason.

She deserves better, he thought bitterly, taking a last deep inhalation of his cigarette and dropping the glowing stub into the empty bottle, where it sizzled briefly in the shallow puddle of warm champagne before being extinguished altogether. 'She's always deserved better,' he muttered, looking round for Alicia.

'I'm taking you to the races,' had been Joanna's initial, discouraging response to Nicholas' confused and lengthy speech on the subject of untying extra-marital knots. In spite of rehearsing with stunning lucidity into his rearview mirror while coasting along the smooth, freshly tarmacked section of the A24, his final performance succeeded in articulating only the most garbled version of the arguments. While part of this incoherence stemmed from an honourable fear of hurting Joanna's feelings, Nicholas was also struggling under the weight of a genuine confusion as to what exactly had been happening to him that year and why. A crisis had come and gone; he had been whirled along in the eye of a storm and deposited dazed, but happy to be alive, in a territory in which he was still trying to get his bearings. Relating these sensations to particulars was hard. To have said, for instance, that getting drunk and giggly about losing his mother was not something he could have done with anyone in the world but Kate, that the thought of seeing the children again – the thought of getting the family back in one piece under one roof after such an abominable summer – thrilled him beyond expression, would not, Nicholas felt, have advanced his cause with much understanding where his lover was concerned. So instead he took refuge in euphemisms like 'seeing things through' and 'making a go of it' – blunt instruments which did little justice either to the complexity or intensity of his emotions and which bounced off Joanna's broad back like rubber arrows.

'You're in a mood,' she said, accompanying this deflating observation with a lavish squeeze of his upper thigh, 'I can tell. Punting will knock it out of you – never fails. My treat, of course. Henry gets season tickets every year. He loves the horseflesh. I love it too, but more than anything I like winning money.' She slapped her own thigh hard and laughed, rather manically, so that Nicholas began to wonder whether she'd poured vodka instead of milk on her cornflakes.

'Joanna, going to the races is not going to solve anything.' He stared helplessly out of the window at the countryside whizzing by, eyeing livestock and trees with envy, despising himself for managing the situation so ineptly. 'I've got to get back . . .'

Though they had passed a large black and white arrowed warning sign, beyond which the road disappeared in a sudden swoop to the right, Joanna chose that particular moment to pull out and overtake the caravan which had been lumbering along in front of them for several miles.

While Nicholas sucked in his cheeks, quite losing the thread of his sentence through this impetuous and unnecessary endangerment to life, Joanna pressed her foot hard down on the accelerator and swung her body as they turned, like a cooperative pillion rider on a motorbike.

'God, I love this tank,' she cried, as they emerged safely onto an open stretch of road beyond the bend, the caravan already no more than a receding white speck behind them. 'Nearly there now. What were you saying?'

'I was saying,' replied Nicholas, with some venom, 'that it's all over. You and me. Finished. Big mistake, the whole thing.'

It was some moments before he realised she was crying, an observation which caused him more alarm for their safety than on any other account, since Joanna, in the heat of her emotion, now seemed to have abandoned any conventional left-handed approach to motoring and was instead steering a wavering course down the middle of the road, two fat wheels either side of the central white lines.

'Look – I'm sorry you're upset – I say, shall we stop and talk this over for a moment?'

She shook her head and sniffed hard, at the same time jerking the car over to the left so as to allow a crawling Morris Minor to pass on the other side.

After several very tense minutes she at last seemed to calm down, easing her foot off the accelerator and allowing her vehicle to proceed with more comforting proximity to the grass verge on their own side of the road. Nicholas unclenched his hands and tried to think of a new, more easily digestible way of saying what he had said already.

'I'm not going to be like that woman in the film,' she blurted, clearly embroiled in a complex train of thought of her own. 'I'm not going to go round killing your daughter's rabbits or assaulting you with kitchen knives, but I would just like to make the point that I know how Glenn Close felt. You can't just pick people up and drop them again, Nicholas, like damaged goods or toys or something. I mean,' she sniffed again, more volubly, and wiped her nose on her sleeve, 'I was developing a real . . . need of you . . . you know?'

Nicholas, on the basis of his own reactions to their infrequent and hurried coupling, with its almost total lack of emotional input, found this rather hard to believe, but guessed he might be ill-advised to say so. He studied her for a moment out of the corner of his eye, looking for signs that she was acting up, laying it on thick, just to make him feel bad. But the tear-stained cheeks looked real enough. And the sniffs certainly were unpleasantly authentic.

'All I'm saying is,' she went on, 'let's have this one afternoon together – like some kind of goodbye present or something. It would mean a lot to me, Nick.' The hand returned to his thigh, its greedy squeezing reminding him of the faintly distasteful appetite with which she had approached love-making, the neediness of her, the way she'd run her hands over him even after they'd finished, showing him she wouldn't say no to more. Some of her embraces had felt like being eaten alive.

He lifted her hand off his leg and returned it firmly to her own lap. 'Joanna, I just can't see that it would do any good—'

'No, perhaps not,' she cut in, her voice now very sharp, 'but it might mean the difference between, say, telling your wife, and not.'

Nicholas caught his breath determined, through an animal instinct for survival, not to show fear. It was absurd of him, he supposed, not to have anticipated such an obvious, cheap ploy. Though the easiest retaliatory response would have been to threaten to tell Henry, Nicholas somehow suspected that such an attempt to turn the tables would not have the equivalent effect and might only serve to sharpen her appetite for revenge. 'I'd rather you didn't,' he said casually, as they bumped across a field towards dense rows of parked cars. In the distance he could see the square concrete top of a grandstand, the rest of it obscured by a plump hill, crawling with people, like busy termites on an ant-hill.

'Well let's enjoy our afternoon then, shall we?' Joanna yanked up the handbrake and turned to look at him. Though her streaky fair hair was fluffy and clean, her face now looked oily and blotched. All her customary blue make-up had been largely washed away by tears, leaving her eyes looking quite faded, like washed-out denim. Opening her handbag, she pulled out two triangular cardboard badges, dangling from safety-pins on silky red strings. 'Members Only,' she said, shaking them at him and looking smug.

'Super,' he said flatly.

As if genuinely oblivious to his state of mind, Joanna then made a great show of pinning his badge to the breast pocket of his shirt, undoing an extra button and putting her hand right inside in order to make an unnecessary detour through the hairs on his chest. 'I say, you've got a grey one here,' she remarked, as she was doing the button back up again. 'Shall I pull it out?'

He pushed her hands away. 'No, thank you. I am a forty-six-year-old father of three. I'm supposed to have grey hairs.'

'Touchy, aren't we?' She pinned her own badge on herself. 'Let's not ruin the day with bad tempers, okay?'

This was such a monumental understatement of the situation that Nicholas was tempted for a moment to let out a crazed laugh.

'I think this is a very grown-up way to end things, personally, very . . . civilised,' she added, as they made their way across the field to the entrance to the racecourse.

Nicholas, who felt there was in fact something deeply uncivilised – something almost sinister – about the whole business, trudged after her, his member's badge flapping against his shirt.

'I can stay till four o' clock,' he panted, 'and that's it.' He thought with a mixture of panic and yearning about Kate, to whom he had lied so easily, so glibly that morning. He had research to do at Chichester library, he had said, knowing that where his writing was concerned she would never dare to show anything but the utmost support, even if, deep down, she had come to believe that he was wasting his time. It was his last lie, he reassured himself, his last strike against the way she herself had been behaving. Though he no longer believed that she had actually had an affair, there was no doubt in Nicholas' mind that

Kate had taken some kind of time-out that year, unjustified, threatening time-out which had greatly contributed to his own unhappiness and all its awful consequences. Just a couple of hours, he told himself now, falling into step beside Joanna, just a couple of hours, then life could go back to normal.

Between placing bets and leading Nicholas from one area to the next, Joanna consumed a choc 'n nut ice-cream, two smoked salmon sandwiches and a Mars bar, offering each item of food up to his mouth many times, as if they were playful lovers still at the stage of chewing different ends of the same piece of spaghetti. Unable to enter into the charade with the somewhat chilling élan being displayed by his companion, Nicholas divided his time and energies between eyeing the crawling minute hand of the clock tower on the grandstand and defending his body, tactical assaults of affection being a key element of Joanna's game.

Aside from not feeling remotely inclined to continue with the physical side of the relationship, Nicholas entertained considerable fears about being seen. Though he knew no one who liked racing, it was the kind of venue, he felt, where one ran into old friends. To have explained a forty-year-old blonde in clinging white trousers would have been hard enough, let alone one who patted his bottom and kept slipping her hand up under his elbow with all the insistence of a disobedient nymphet. His instinct in consequence was to burrow into the thickest parts of the crowd and to scan the faces of everyone they passed. Every so often his heart would lurch and settle again, as a figure whom he had imagined to be familiar turned out to be unknown after all.

Joanna, on the other hand, though far more likely to bump into someone she knew, appeared to share no such qualms. 'You're having fun, aren't you? – go on admit it,' she urged, sliding her arm round his waist when they had returned for the third time to jostle round the white perimeter of the viewing paddock. 'Have a bet on this one – please, Nicholas, darling – a last kindness for Jo-Jo. It's no fun doing it on my own.' She pinched a handful of waistline flesh between her fingers, causing him to flinch in a spasm of ticklish pain.

'No,' he gasped, trying to unfurl her fingers from his shirt, irritation now seething so close to the surface that he felt seriously tempted to hit her hard across her face. 'For Christ's sake, Joanna, stop it, can't you?' As he tussled with her, he accidentally elbowed a tweed-capped gentleman to his left, who turned and scowled, annoyance flaring in his yellowy eyes.

Joanna, meanwhile, continued trying to seize sections of Nicholas' midriff with her hands, giggling as if they were indulging in some kind of erotic foreplay.

'Right, that's it,' hissed Nicholas loudly through clenched teeth, causing the elderly man to cast him another withering glance from under the peaked brim of his hat. 'I've had all I can take. I am going. Now.' He turned, but Joanna, keeping her arm about his, turned with him, still smiling at the game. 'And how are you going to get away without me? I've got the car remember.'

'I'll walk if I have to.' It was hard work, pushing their way back through the crowd towards the grandstand. Joanna's arm remained, leech-like, across his back, though her fingers clung now to the material of his shirt instead of his body itself. 'This is not some kind of joke, you know.'

'I know.' Her bottom lip trembled. 'I just don't want to lose you, I—'

'Oh don't start on that, please don't start on that.' He had long since lost any sense of the character of this woman, of how her mind worked, of what flicker of a mannerism or attitude had prompted him to allow her to be anything more than the owner of a large dog whom he had once passed on a walk and then nearly run over on a zebra crossing. She was totally unknown to him, frighteningly so, since the sea-changes in her behaviour evinced undertows of hysteria against which he knew himself to be powerless. For a moment he caught himself wondering about the horse-loving Henry, experiencing a stab of pity for any man misguided enough to set up permanent home with such a confused and tumultuous package of emotions.

'Oh fuck off then,' she said suddenly, letting go of him and striding out in front. Unaware that his actions were being scrutinised by his brother-in-law, Nicholas, surprised but relieved, followed the cast of her shadow until it was swallowed up by the cool dark tunnel of the entrance to the grandstand.

Joanna said no more. When they got back into the car, she

switched the air-conditioning onto full, its icy swish conveniently drowning out any vestigial sense of the need to talk. Nicholas, chilled but grateful, sat rigid beside her, barely moving, barely breathing, throughout the laborious process of queueing behind other early leavers and joining the main road back to Worthing. Though possible sentences began to form in his mind, especially when they hit the ring road and he knew the sanctity of his own car was just a few minutes away, he resisted the urge to speak, fearful of triggering another mood-swing and making an appalling afternoon even worse. It was hard though, particularly during the very last moments, when he was climbing down from her car and she sat motionless, staring ahead through the windscreen at the sea.

He was unlocking his car door, his fingers trembling with after-shock, when Joanna wound down her window and shouted at him.

'Just don't put me in one of your fucking stories,' she yelled, all teeth and hair, 'or I'll sue you for every fucking penny!'

The tyres screeched on the hot tarmac as she drove away. Nicholas got into his own car, which smelt unpleasantly of over-heated plastic, and sat for a few moments with the door open and one leg still on the ground outside. The idea of using Joanna Wyrral as fodder for his stumbling literary attempts had never occurred to him. He tried for a few moments, while the stale, belting heat around him merged with the fresher warmth outside, to imagine what he might say about her. But nothing came to mind, beyond hazy pictures of an imagined Henry and more vivid, less sympathetic snapshots of dribbling dogs and horses. He shook his head, pulled his leg inside the car and gingerly placed his hands on the hot steering wheel. Its temperature was such that he had to drive for the first few minutes with the edges of his palms. By the time he had rejoined the ring road, he was able to grip the wheel more firmly. Leaning over, he wound down the window on the passenger side as well, creating a swirling channel of air through the front section of the car. A few miles later he picked a tape at random from the glove compartment of the car and slotted it into the radio cassette player. Strains of Nessun Dorma were caught and carried on the summer breeze as Nicholas sped homewards, his heart full of an inexpressible sense of there being a way forward, a fresh and mysterious desire to get on with life, in spite of it being quite riddled with imperfections.

35

Nicholas Latimer's operatic surge of post-traumatic relief was brought to an abrupt halt by a juddering at the rear of the car, followed by the unmistakable lop-sided wobble of a blow-out. Cursing loudly, he pulled over to the edge of the road and got out to inspect the damage. The lower half of the back left-hand tyre had subsided onto the ground, its shapeless mass looking as hopeless as a melted black sack. That he was just a couple of miles from Elhurst only sharpened Nicholas' sense of ill-fortune. Overhead, as if to accentuate his plight further, grey clouds as big as ships were tacking across the sky, blocking the sun with their sails and casting long shadows on the earth below. Nicholas shivered. Although only five o'clock it felt much later. He would have to hurry.

Nicholas had never liked changing tyres. Each time the necessity arose, he approached the task with all the clumsy caution of a first-timer, forgetting the simplest things, like which way up the jack went and whether the nuts undid in a clockwise or anticlockwise direction. Reassuring himself that what had been done before could be achieved again, that all it took was a bit of common sense and brute force, Nicholas resignedly opened the boot and set about ejecting family debris – polythene bags, hairless tennis balls, bits of cardboard box and old rope – under which lay the release clip for the spare tyre compartment. The last time he had done this, he reminded himself, there had been suitcases, fishing rods and swimming things to contend with as well, since the puncture had struck during their drive back from the Loire to Calais – a nightmare of a journey which he now deliberately recalled in some detail, in the hope of diminishing his current predicament by comparison. They had set off so late that Millie's vomiting had to be accommodated with the meagre aid of a sandcastle bucket and three used tissues; Nicholas had driven like the maniacs he usually spent half the holiday cursing, only to find on arriving at Calais, that they had got the clocks wrong and had a whole hour to kill before the sailing of their ferry.

A cold wind started whipping through the trees of the wood to his left; bending over the back of the car Nicholas could feel his trousers blown flat against the calves of his legs, while his shirt billowed like a straining windsock. The sun had shrunk to a small torchlight of yellow, barely visible behind its screen of grey.

He extracted the spare tyre from its deep niche with difficulty, the weight of it surprising him; as he felt his knees click and his lower back wrench stubbornly at the unfamiliar exertion, Nicholas was reduced to some imaginative swearing at designers of motor vehicles in order to jolly himself along. Having at last got the tyre balanced on the edge of the open boot, he let it bounce heavily onto the ground, almost crushing his toes as it landed.

The jack, a curious piece of metal, with pieces flapping uselessly either side of it, took its usual time to sort out. Some ten minutes later, after several sessions of trial and error, Nicholas successfully began to lever up the car, feeling as he did so a few preliminary spits of rain on the back of his neck. 'Thank you, God,' he grunted through clenched teeth, cranking the jack with a fresh burst of energy.

It was only after the car had reached an extremely satisfying height from the ground that it dawned on Nicholas that he had yet to unearth the tool that undid the nuts on the wheel. Returning to the open boot, he spent several minutes rummaging around. It was not there. Nor was it in the heap of family mementoes sitting on the gravelled edge of the road. Searching under the seats, in the glove compartment and in the door pockets proved equally fruitless. In a last flurry of desperation he even resorted to scanning the baffling grey intestines of the main engine; but the wheel-spanner was not to be found nestling there either.

As the spitting grew more persistent, so did the wind, beating viciously through the trees, as if eager to steal a march on autumn and bring down as many leaves as it could. A few of the weaker ones were already fluttering hopelessly to the ground.

Quickly locking up the car, hurling everything back onto the back seat, but leaving the jack as it was, Nicholas set off at a trot in the direction of Elhurst. There was a public telephone outside the post office; he would call Kate from there and get rescued. After an initial light-footed sprint he began to feel puffed and panicky. It was much further than he had thought. Kate would be seriously worried. Though he tried to keep up a slow jog, a seering stitch in his left side eventually forced him to slow his pace to a fast walk; he took big, unsatisfactory gulps of wet air as he strode along, occasionally looking over his shoulder in the hope of thumbing a lift. Given his bedraggled appearance, not to mention the general tenor of his day, it came as no surprise that none of the handful of cars that drove by on his side – their wheels spurting puddles at his legs – elected to stop.

It was only as he passed the entrance to their impressive driveway that Nicholas remembered the Sullivans; their house was only yards away compared to the good mile or two still lying between him and Elhurst post office. Without hesitating he turned off left and – his pulmonary batteries recharged by this unexpected change in fortune – jogged all the way up to their front door.

Mary was praying when the door bell rang, a relaxing occupation to which she had resorted with increasing frequency in recent weeks, slipping in and out of it when she was on her own, taking up the threads of silent conversation and supplication with an ease that bore testimony to her solitude.

When she answered the door, Nicholas noticed her gold cross at once, dangling over the top of a high ruff of a shirt collar that made him think of choirboys. She looked terribly old, he thought with a start, as if she had nose-dived into a sector of middle-age for which he was not even yet preparing. Her ashen hair seemed to cling to her head, falling in unnaturally tidy flat strands that suggested no spontaneous or unscheduled movement of any kind. The ends of it fluttered pitifully in the flurry of wind that whirled in through the open door. Though she smiled on seeing him, her face looked pasty and lined, as if all the moisture had been drained away for good, leaving a cracked white delta of a ruin behind. Nicholas, until that moment brimming with a sense of his own personal misfortune, was taken aback. Though he had never liked Mary Sullivan particularly, the way she fawned on Kate, the way she was too painfully timid to hold or at least voice an opinion of her own, seeing her now, as no more than a husk of the young woman she must once have been, prompted a swell of pity. She must be sick, he thought at once, smiling back, beginning to apologise and explain.

Mary was very kind. She fetched a towel and made him tea, all the while murmuring sympathetically at his repetitive accounts of what had happened.

'Angus bought me one of those portable telephones for the car, in case such a thing should ever happen to me . . .' she said, while Nicholas dialled home and then raised his cup in grateful salute to her while holding the receiver to his ear. She spoke in a distant, dreamy way, as if remembering someone from the past, . . . 'though I've never used it once.'

'That was thoughtful of him,' said Nicholas absently, his mind now focused on the phone call, on how he would reassure Kate. He held his breath while he waited to hear her voice, infused with a sudden need to hear it, like a longing for a sweet, familiar refrain.

Mary began rearranging the long stems of some pink and purple flowers in a vase in the middle of her kitchen table. The lady on the course had said never to fill a vase too full and to vary the lengths of the stems, so as to give shape as well as colour to a design. In spite of Mary's efforts to follow such advice, all her flowers still insisted on flopping outwards in an uninspired circle round the perimeter of the cut glass, as if yearning to be released from it altogether. While in the middle of the circle sat a big empty hole, begging to be filled.

Angus had been gone for four weeks, three days and – she checked her watch – eleven hours. He had telephoned twice in all that time, the most recent occasion being the night before, just as she was on the point of raising the first forkful of an omelette to her lips, eggs being her staple diet when she was on her own. She missed the company of her husband too much – was too grateful for the call – to say that he was interrupting her meal. Instead she sat and watched her plate while Angus talked, noting the way the lovely soft yellow of the egg seemed to shrink and congeal as it chilled, while the patches of butter, so enticing when melted, hardened round its edges like yellow mould. She supposed it was odd of her not to complain. Even for Angus four weeks away was a long time. During the phone call he had said that business in Spain was exceptionally good, that he was thinking of investing in property over there, that it would be nice to have a staging post in Europe other than a hotel.

'You mean we should live in Spain for some of the year?' she had asked, not sure whether such a notion filled her with hope or fear.

Not at all, Angus had retorted, actually living in Spain was not what he meant at all; leaving Mary to feel that another invisible seam of their marriage was coming apart, that one day she would wake up and find him gone altogether. Her instinct in the face of this was to cling more grimly to what she had. She told him she missed him. Angus said he missed her too, that he would be home soon – the following week perhaps – that he would call again, that she should look after herself.

After the call Mary stared hard at her lifeless slab of cooked egg. She had been looking forward to eating it, to tasting the moist salty warmth of it on her tongue and throat. After a few moments she pushed the plate to one side, realising with a little start that it was better when Angus didn't call at all: silence as well as absence at least allowed her to dig down into a high-walled groove of her own – a safe, deep trench that blocked out all those debilitating preoccupations with the desirable things that were absent from her life, the things that other married women seemed to take for granted.

Filtering out thoughts of Max Urquart was a harder task, often only manageable with the help of the Almighty. For the dark, glinting looks of the Elhurst bookshop keeper had, amidst the other fervent goings-on in Mary's head, assumed a somewhat devilish tinge. The significance of his visit to her house had swelled in consequence, introducing a fresh pulse of failure to her life, coupled with a new, rawer sense of shame and sin. Max Urquart – she could see now – had been sent as her temptor and tormentor, as rightful castigation for a woman with all the wherewithal, but none of the tenacity, to be happy.

Nicholas scowled accusingly at the phone. 'Kate doesn't seem to be there – most odd – I really can't think where she can be.' He tweaked an earlobe and shook his head.

Mary hesitated. She should offer to drive him home, she knew, but the thought of it filled her with dread. In recent days she had barely gone out at all. The prospect of having to make further conversation with Nicholas, of maybe even meeting Kate, made her tremble. She twiddled her thin necklace round and round her fingers until the small crucifix was pressed tightly against her throat, its edges leaving faint imprints on her papery skin.

'I could always give you a lift . . .' she faltered.

Nicholas leapt off the stool. 'Mary, you brick, could you really? Are you sure it wouldn't be too much trouble? Won't Angus get back and wonder—?'

'Angus is away. I'll get my coat.' She returned after a minute or two wearing a long grey mackintosh and what looked like a square of cellophane across her head; it flattened her hair in an unnatural way that reminded Nicholas of a face pressed up against a window. She held out a brown umbrella with a handle carved in the shape of a duck's head. 'Take this. It's pouring outside. You'll get soaked just walking to the car.'

Nicholas shook his head and turned up the collar of his shirt. Something about the see-thru plastic stretched across Mary's head made him want to get wet. 'A few drops won't harm.' He rubbed his hands briskly together as he followed her out of the house and round the side to where a smart red Subaru was parked neatly by a high latticed fence.

Mary's worries proved groundless. Nicholas barely said a word and when they arrived at his house it was immediately clear that no one was home. He thanked her quickly and slithered out into the rain. At the last moment, as he was on the point of slamming the door shut, he pushed his head back inside the car.

'Do come and see us, Mary – I mean you and Angus – I'll get Kate onto it. She's the big chief when it comes to our social life. I'm just one of the Indians.' He offered her a parting grin, wondering to himself if it was cancer that could make a woman look so drained.

Mary twitched her head in response, certain that such a thing would never happen, certain that she had already floated too far away from other people ever to be retrieved or noticed again.

When Nicholas saw a large folded piece of white paper pinioned under a mug in the middle of the kitchen table, artfully positioned (unlike his mother's farewell notelet), so as to be unmissable, he stopped in his tracks, putting one hand on the wall and the other round his stomach as if to steady himself after a physical blow. Of course, of course, he thought, his mind racing. This is it. Joanna phoned while I was on the way home. Of course she did. She told Kate. And so Kate has left me. This is my punishment. What I deserve.

Though only a few seconds passed before he actually reached the note, the pulse of time had slowed to an intolerable crawl, as if it too felt that Nicholas' come-uppance should be savoured to the full. Nicholas studied the paper for a moment before unfolding it, partly to delay confirmation of his fate and partly because he was struck by the obvious haste with which she had written his name. Kate had beautiful handwriting, all legible, neat curls and italicised capitals, yet the word *Nicholas* had obviously been dashed off at great speed, without any care at all. It was an unnecessary insult, he felt, after twenty years of marriage, to be rejected with such haste. The rest of the writing looked equally rushed. With a heavy heart, he began to read.

Dear Nicholas,

I am so sorry to rush off, but wait until you hear why. Alicia – Harry's girlfriend – has gone into premature labour. They are trying to let it all happen naturally but apparently there might be complications. Harry rang in a flat spin and I felt I just had to go up and hold hands and so on. He says there's no question of Alicia's mother or anyone coming down from Scotland. Please don't be cross at me for over-reacting, Harry did sound in such a panic.

If things get late I'll stay at Harry's and come back tomorrow morning.

Please could you pull a few things out of the deep freeze in preparation for the marauding hordes – Millie is due to be dropped off quite early and both James and Grace are supposed to be home

*by lunchtime. They've all got lifts so you shouldn't have to meet
any trains.*

*Darling, I am sorry to disappear like this, especially when we were
having such a lovely time together. I know you didn't want me to
say anything outright about it, but I have this wonderful feeling that
we've come through a sort of dreadful crisis and I'm so thankful. I
love you very very much.*

Hope the research went well.

All my love Kate.

PS. I'll phone with any news

*PPS, I nearly forgot – Joyce rang. She's fine and staying with
someone called Betsie (y?). I told you it would all be all right. Love
you lots. K.*

Nicholas put down the letter and sat very still.

So it was going to be all right after all. He had a wife who
loved him, a mother who was not dead, children who were
coming home.

In something of a daze he walked over to the fridge-freezer and
pulled out two plastic cartons. Although Kate was an avid devo-
tee of labelling frozen family meals it was some eight months
since the freezer had been defrosted, a domestic oversight which
meant that each box was too caked in immovable layers of icy
crystals for Nicholas to be able to decipher any writing on the
lids. Stacking the cartons beside the sink, Nicholas reached for a
glass and poured himself a generous whisky. He was just trying
to dislodge the tray of ice-cubes from its igloo-quarters when
there was a knock at the front door, followed by the voice of
his son calling through the letter flap.

'Hey, anyone home?'

Nicholas opened the door. A car in the drive hooted twice
and drove away. James, a heavy rucksack on his back, his nose
pink and peeling, though the rest of his face was a nutty brown,
grinned at his father. 'Surprise,' he said matter-of-factly, tapping
Nicholas' stomach with the tip of his cricket bat. 'I thought no
one was here for a minute. Where's your car?'

'It's a long story,' replied his father, relieving him of the rucksack and patting him affectionately on the shoulder. He would have liked a hug, but these days took the cue for such things from James himself. The two men went into the kitchen. 'Your mother is, by all accounts, helping your uncle and his girlfriend give birth in a hospital in London. Your grandmother has gone to live with someone called Betsie. Your sisters are coming back tomorrow.' He took a swig of his whisky. 'And my car is punctured and abandoned on the other side of Elhurst. How was the tour?'

'Brilliant.' James stretched up his arms and grinned expansively. He had the same grin as his father, the same elasticated lower face that could sometimes give the impression of being amused even when he wasn't. 'It was bloody marvellous. Apart from the last bit – so much rain – that's why we're back a day early. It seemed pointless hanging round when everything was just about wrapped up anyway.'

'Like a drink?'

'I'll have what you're having,' he said, meeting Nicholas' gaze with a flash of challenging insolence.

'Oh, you will, will you?' replied his father, but tenderly. He got out a fresh glass and poured out an inch of whisky.

'Don't know how you can bear to drink it without ice.' James marched over to the freezer, only to encounter the arctic conditions which had defeated Nicholas a few minutes before.

'I'd love a lump of ice, but as you can see, there's a problem. You'll need a chisel to unstick that lot.'

Without a word, James pulled a large pen knife from his jeans pocket and began attacking the ice with a long blade with mean jagged edges. After only a couple of minutes he folded the knife away and eased out the tray of ice-cubes. 'Voilà,' he said, looking smug.

They took their whiskies into the sitting room. When their glasses were empty Nicholas returned to the kitchen to fetch the bottle.

'Mind if I smoke?' asked James casually, pulling out a squashed packet of cigarettes from the back pocket of his trousers.

Nicholas shook his head and watched, faintly intrigued, while his son produced a large silver lighter which, judging by the ferocity and smell of its flame, was powered by diesel. James tilted his head back against the sofa and inhaled deeply, looking for an instant so like his uncle Harry that Nicholas recoiled. He didn't want James to turn out like Harry. Or did he? Harry's life certainly had all the trappings of success: lots of girlfriends, money, a handsome flat. Why the hell shouldn't he want James to have the same? Why, for instance, should he want James to turn out like him, full of uncertainty, insecurity and half-success? Because, he answered himself dreamily, I am not entirely selfish and I have known spells of great contentment. Nicholas closed his eyes and smiled, enjoying the seeping feeling of the alcohol in his limbs, the way its warmth edged out the tension, the way now, even watching James blow perfect smoke-rings at the lampshade beside him filled him with nothing but joy.

'I notched up a century last Thursday.'

'I say – well done – that's tremendous.' Nicholas reached across the sofa and squeezed his shoulder.

'The bowling was lousy . . .'

'I bet it wasn't. Congratulations. I hope you celebrated afterwards.'

'Oh yes,' said James quietly, trying to stop a smile from turning into a complacent grin. 'We celebrated all right. Had quite a party in fact.' He tapped the ash into the lid of his cigarette packet and took another deep drag. 'There were rather a lot of what you might call camp-followers – girls and so on – so we had an instant party whenever we wanted. The masters were so lax, I couldn't believe it – I guess they wanted to have a good time as much as the rest of us.'

Girls and so on, thought Nicholas, nodding his head and eyeing his son with fresh admiration. So that was it. No wonder the boy looked pleased with himself. He was debating how to pursue this subject further, whether showing a flicker of parental interest would be appropriate, when James made a good job of changing the subject anyway.

'Have you heard from Grace at all while she's been away?'

'No – I mean, I think she spoke to Mum once or twice – why?'

James shifted his position, looking uncomfortable. 'It's probably nothing.'

'What's probably nothing?'

'It's just that I phoned her from a call-box one night – for a laugh, you know, – and she sounded really upset. Wouldn't tell me why, but I got the impression something had happened. Then I ran out of coins.'

'What sort of something?' Nicholas was on the edge of the sofa now, rolling his empty glass between his hands and staring hard at James.

'Dad, I really don't know.' He squeezed the smouldering end of his cigarette butt between his finger-tips and then balanced the cork tip carefully on the table, dirty end up, before wiping his hand absently on his jeans. 'They're a funny lot after all, aren't they?'

'Who?'

'Girls – women and so on.'

Nicholas, in spite of the new beat of worry drumming inside his head about Grace, could not help smiling. 'Oh, women and so on, I see. Yes, they certainly are a funny lot. And they get a lot funnier with age, I can tell you,' he added, thinking with tipsy fondness of his marriage.

James glanced up sharply, as if he had just been presented with a great truth. 'Do they?' He looked alarmed. 'I don't think I could cope with much more. I mean – there's one girl – I sort of met her on tour – and she's great and everything, but so . . . so dramatic. Like everything is this one big emotional crisis.'

Nicholas, aware that they had embarked upon the sort of father-son conversation for which he had sometimes longed, hesitated before responding, terrified that anything he said might only sound middle-aged or patronising. 'Women are big on emotions,' he said at last, 'they never seem to think we men have enough of them.'

James flexed his face into a thoughtful frown, absently chewing one half of his bottom lip. 'Grace certainly did sound . . . well . . . charged up about something. But then I guess she must be about the same age as my . . . as this girl I know, so what I'm trying to say is that she's probably getting emotional about something that doesn't really matter at all.' He stared, clearly perplexed, into what remained of his whisky. 'Probably best to leave women alone when they get like that, I suppose, let them come to their senses. Do you think?'

Nicholas, who had completely lost track of whose emotional crisis was under discussion, whether James's concern was for the mental enigma presented by his sister or his girlfriend, nodded keenly. Anxious, above everything else, to keep this unexpectedly frank – if somewhat fuzzy – line of communication between generations open, he ventured to agree that leaving women alone in such circumstances was indeed the best – the only – thing to do.

While James sat contemplating this jewel of parental wisdom Nicholas' mind skipped back to the question of Grace and whether there was anything to worry about. I need Kate, he thought, the force of all the whisky suddenly overcoming him with a sense of not being able to cope alone, I need Kate to sort this one out tomorrow.

'Mum will be back tomorrow,' he said aloud. 'She'll see to Grace. She'll put everything right.' He turned to James in search of an echo of agreement, only to find that his son had fallen fast asleep, his chin on his chest, his glass in one hand and his cigarettes in the other. The sun had prompted a smattering of freckles to spring up across the bridge of his nose, faint ginger smudges beneath the raw pink skin, reminding Nicholas with an ache of nostalgia of the little-boy version of this child. Part of his brown bush of hair, which showed all the signs of developing into the obstinate spikes with which Nicholas had to contend, had flopped forward over his forehead in a perfect kiss-curl which – had he seen it – would have shamed him beyond words. Nicholas touched the hair tenderly, fearful of waking its owner. Then he gently eased out the glass and the cigarette packet from the loose grip of James's fingers and placed a large cushion up beside his head. James groaned and nestled down into the sofa, pulling his legs up and hugging the old velvet cushion to him like a lover.

36

'Your breath smells funny,' remarked Millie, screwing her nose up in disgust and wriggling further under the duvet.

'Hello, Millie,' croaked Nicholas, rubbing enough sleep from his eyes so as to be able to focus on his watch. 'Where did you spring from? Have you had a lovely time?'

'Lovely, lovely, lovely,' she sang, tugging at the bed covers until her father's bare chest and crumpled pyjama bottoms were totally exposed to the chill of the morning. 'Clare's Mum brought me. They've gone to visit her Aunty Pat now. She lives in Woking with one cat and two dogs.'

'Lucky old Aunty Pat.' Nicholas kissed her head before rolling out of bed and drawing back the curtains.

'James let me in. He said he slept last night on the sofa. Did he really? Can I do it tonight? Where's Mum?' Millie was now curled up like a cat amongst the bedclothes, with pillows propped behind her head and under her elbows.

'Mum's in London – back this morning.' Nicholas yawned and stretched. 'Looks like you might have a little baby cousin – that's why she's up there.'

'A baby,' Millie squealed, 'a real live baby cousin – I can't believe it.' She clapped her hands, her heart thrilling with a surge of maternal feelings. 'So Uncle Harry's a daddy now.' She frowned. 'Should we still call him uncle?'

'I should think so.' Nicholas tweaked the point of her chin and pulled on his dressing gown. 'Breakfast time.'

'But I had breakfast ages ago. I want lunch.'

'Come and have lunch then, I don't care.'

Millie clambered onto his back, demanding a piggy-back ride

down the stairs. 'We're both getting too old for this,' he groaned, gasping at the vice-like clench of her bony knees round his waist and the surprising weight of her. 'You'll have to start giving your Dad piggy-back rides soon, young lady – that's the way it works, you know.' He successfully negotiated the corners on the landing and started down the main stairs. 'From here on in the whole family system goes into reverse – the children have to start looking after the parents, bringing them the papers in bed, ferrying them about the place and all that sort of thing.'

'Like you looked after Granny?'

Nicholas who had only been idly teasing, felt caught out, both because of the familiar tickle of guilt about the barely disguised ill-humour with which he had played host to his mother and because it seemed unimaginable that he should ever find himself in a comparable position. Seeing one's parents grown rickety and dependent was one thing; accepting it as a likely future for oneself was quite another.

'Sort of like Granny, yes,' he said thoughtfully, depositing Millie onto a kitchen chair and rubbing the base of his spine where a dull ache was nagging, no doubt from tugging at tyres in the rain the day before.

'But James said Granny has gone to live with a friend called Annie.' Millie helped herself to a handful of cereal from an open packet on the table as she spoke, and then began picking each frosted flake from the palm of her hand individually, like a bird with a spread of crumbs.

'Betsie. Granny's gone to live with someone called Betsie.'

'I suppose she'll have more fun with a friend her own age,' put in Millie with her mouth full, delivering the comment like an adult remarking upon the playing habits of a small child.

Nicholas grinned, loving this nine-year-old capacity for seeing to the heart of things, the enviable simplicity of one not yet old enough to be burdened by the middle-aged baggage of paranoia or guilt. 'Yes, I expect she will.'

Nicholas was seated at the kitchen table, still in his dressing gown, when Grace walked in some forty-five minutes later. Compared to the healthy glow of James and Millie their elder sister struck him as painfully pale, with a new and ugly puffiness to her cheeks and eyes. Her jeans, Nicholas noticed, looked very tight, especially round the thighs, where white stitching was visible along the seams.

'Grace, love, hello,' he said, getting up and kissing her at once. To his surprise she put her arms round his neck and held on tightly for several seconds.

'Hello, Dad. God, it's good to be home.' She swung a green suede tasselled bag from off her shoulder and dumped it on the table, knocking over two cereal packets in the process. 'Christ, I'm starving.' She went to the fridge and began rooting around for food.

'How was France then?' Nicholas folded away the paper and crossed his arms, wanting to hear what she had been up to, wanting above all to be reassured that James's comments the night before had been groundless.

'Okay, I guess.' She peeled a lid off a pot of yoghurt and licked the lid. 'Where's Mum?'

'London. Uncle Harry's girlfriend went into labour last night. There were complications and Mum went up to help. She'll be back any minute, I expect.'

'Any minute?' Grace, a spoonful of pink yoghurt at her lips, eyed the door with uncertainty, as if the idea of her mother walking in did not fill her with entirely positive emotions.

'So are you fluent then?' he teased, prompting only a scowl and a vigorous shaking of the head. 'Say something, go on, let's hear you.'

'No way.'

'Come on,' he cajoled, 'I want to hear that we got our money's worth. It was a considerable investment posting you over there, you know; don't think I'm going to let you get away without proving that at least some of those wads of money were well spent.' Since Nicholas was brimming with good humour, it came as something of a shock to see Grace put down her half-eaten yoghurt and bury her face in her hands. Her finger-nails were coated with chipped red nail varnish, he noticed, and her hair, the lower half of it still streaky white, looked lank and greasy.

'Grace, darling, I didn't mean . . .'

When Millie appeared in the doorway Nicholas shooed her away, before cautiously approaching Grace's heaving shoulders, not at all sure he was up to the task of calming them. It was a long time since his eldest daughter had shown him anything but disdain, a long time since she had wriggled on his lap, like Millie still sometimes did, spilling out her thoughts in an easy stream of confidences and giggles. But then Millie was different, easier somehow, always had been. He bent down beside her chair and put a tentative arm round Grace's shoulders.

'Hey, what is all this?' he enquired softly, pulling her more into the curve of his arm so that most of her tears were soaked up by the towelling sleeve of his dressing gown. 'Come on now, it can't be that bad. Mum'll be home soon, she'll sort it all out,' he added, looking longingly at the door. It was odd that Kate hadn't phoned.

At the mention of her mother, Grace raised her head, her whole body hiccoughing with sobs. 'Oh no, please – I don't want to tell Mum about this.'

Nicholas, who had never once entertained the revolutionary idea that a fifteen-year-old daughter would wish to confide the woes of female adolescence to anyone but a mother was amazed.

'Well of course, if you don't want to . . . but I still don't understand what this is all about.'

Without uttering a word, Grace, still weeping, but less intensely now, pulled her bag towards her by its tassels and began pulling things out of it. A camera, a pink comb, a powder compact and a large pad of paper were extracted before she found what she was looking for: a long white envelope, with the words *Mme Latimer* written in ornate, loopy letters across the front of it. Nicholas, aware that receiving letters of importance had been something of a theme in recent days, took it from Grace's hands with some trepidation.

'What's this then?'

'Read it and see,' said Grace, gloomily. 'No, hang on,' She grabbed his arm. 'Before you read it, let me just tell you something.' She swallowed hard and looked down into her clasped hands. 'I hated France. I have never hated anything so much in all my life. Mathilde was a stuck-up prat, her father a slimy bully and her mother a nagging, neurotic bitch.'

Nicholas opened his mouth to speak, but felt bound to close it again when it became apparent that Grace had not finished.

'I don't think I learnt a word of sodding French. All I did was eat. Look at me,' she smacked the bulge of her stomach hard, 'it's disgusting. But they all ate like pigs and there was nothing else to do,' she went on miserably. 'And now I'm fat. God knows what Megan will say when she sees me.'

Nicholas, anxious not to add eating disorders to the list of concerns already cramming his head, put the letter to one side and knelt down beside her, only part of him registering the shock of the cold tiles on his bare knees.

'Grace, you are not fat. And if Megan or anyone else dares to suggest anything of the sort then I shall personally clobber her. The teens are a classic time for weight gain, especially in girls,' he went on breathlessly, not unimpressed by how knowledgeable he sounded; 'your mother always says that it wasn't until at least eighteen or nineteen that the puppy fat really started to fall away. And look at her – she's done jolly well considering she's had you lot and since made something of a living out of preparing food.'

A small smile quivered at the edges of Grace's mouth. 'Did she really say that – about being fattest in her teens?' She peered at him from under wet lashes, her brown eyes, so uncannily like Kate's, now full of hope.

'Absolutely.' Nicholas slapped his thigh to emphasise the point. He was sure Kate had once said something like that, or something very much along those lines anyway.

Grace took a long, deep, shaky breath. 'And now you'd better read that letter. I warn you, it's not good, Daddy, not good at all.' She pushed her unfinished yoghurt away and sat with her face hidden by her hands while he read it. Though Nicholas struggled with the erratic grammar and misspellings, there was no getting away from the dismaying gist of its contents.

Dear Madame Latimer,

I was not wishing to worry you while we have Grace in our hous, but I think I must tell you something of which she has done. We have Grace like our own dauter, but it was a bad thing and quite serious I think. My husband also. Your dauter has been taking some things from the shops. It was by an accident that I found this after we are going to Montpellier for one day. She take a shirt and cosmetical things also and pade no monay for these things. I talk to Grace alone. I do not want Mathilde to learn these sins. My husband also talk to Grace and she say sorry, so we think eh bien we will not do more about it. But I feel as a mother I must tell you these things about your dauter Grace. We look after her well, do not worry. I am sorry to write you this sad things.

'Shoplifting?'

Grace nodded, not looking at him, but picking at the ragged shorelines of her nail varnish with her thumb-nail.

'Have you done it before?'

She nodded again. 'Once.'

If his daughter had not already shown such vehement signs of regret and unhappiness, Nicholas would almost certainly have shouted these words, instead of delivering them as he did with icy reserve. He wished he had some way of grasping – other than by guesswork and a shiver of intuition – quite how serious the problem really was. Kleptomania could be a disease, he knew, he had read of people who needed to trawl superstores regularly, regardless of wealth, like addicts needing the pump of a needle.

'Will you do it again?'

Grace looked at him for the first time; her eyes were badly bloodshot and red-rimmed; underneath them hung dark, puffy semi-circles of fatigue, circles that had no business being on a fifteen-year-old face, Nicholas thought, his heart lurching. 'I will never do it again, Dad,' she said in a small voice. 'I promise. Never. It started as a dare with Megan – I didn't even like it,' she was talking in a rush now, her eyes on the twisting fingers in her lap. 'I mean it was just too scary for words. But then in France – I don't know – everything somehow got on top of me and I just caught myself deciding to give it a go, just to see if I could get away with it. When Madame Labrousse asked to look in my bag when we got home it was so awful,' she whispered, 'I felt terrible, worse than I ever have in my life before.'

Nicholas, whose knees were aching, stood up and went to sit opposite her. 'I ought to tell your mother . . .'

'No, please, please no.' She grabbed his hands. 'It would somehow make things even worse if she knew too. With you it's a bit different – I don't know – I just felt deep down that you wouldn't be quite so shocked as Mum, that you would handle it better, not go over the top – give me another chance sort of thing.'

Nicholas, in spite of the dire circumstances in which this compliment was being delivered could not suppress a twinge of pleasure. 'Really?' He raised his eyebrows and then brought them together in an attempt at a severe frown. 'Or do you just mean Dad's a soft touch?'

Grace had kept hold of his hands and was looking so serious that he began to wish she would smile. 'No, Dad, that's not it at all. I just know you won't make any more of a big deal of it, now that it's over.'

'Is it over?'

'I promise.' She hung her head.

'Because if anything like this ever happens again, not only your mother will hear of it, but the local constabulary too. Is that understood?' He raised his voice to underline how fierce he meant to be, though inside he trembled at the sight of her, at the shame etched on the sad, blotchy face, at all the awful vulnerability of being adrift between generations.

'Understood,' she echoed. 'Thanks, Dad, you're the best.'

Nicholas, who could not at that moment speak thanks to a lump the size of a golf ball jamming his throat, got up and put his arms round her.

'Now you go and get straightened out upstairs, my girl,' he growled at length, 'so you're all bright-eyed for your mother. We'll tell her you were reading Proust by the end, eh?'

Grace nodded almost eagerly, before trailing out of the room, dragging her large green shoulder-bag behind her like a reluctant dog.

37

The hospital canteen had run out of everything but pork pies and leathery white sandwiches with slabs of shiny orange cheese hanging out of their sides, lolling on the plates like hot tongues. Harry, after scouring the shelves and glass cabinets for something resembling alcohol, banged his hand down on the counter with impatience, catching the edge of their tray as he did so and knocking over one of the two green bottles of fizzy water which they had selected in preference to stewed tea; it rolled along the counter towards the lady with a blonde bee-hive hairstyle who was manning the till.

'No smokin' over here, sir,' was all the woman said, as she righted the bottle and began lazily totting up their purchases. She pointed with her chin towards the far corner of the room, where three despondent nurses were seated down one end of a long table under an umbrella of blue smoke.

'That is where I am heading, my good woman,' replied Harry testily, his freshly lit cigarette waggling unattended in one corner of his mouth while he fished inside both trouser pockets for the considerable quantity of change required to meet the cost of water, two plastic beakers and one packet of four miniature digestive biscuits, the latter having been extracted, with some triumph, by Kate from a basket of sugar sachets.

'I hardly think I can be disturbing other patrons,' argued Harry, by way of an indirect reference to the fact that the canteen was almost deserted. The jigging of his cigarette, now affixed, in Andy Capp fashion, to his lower lip underscored the unnecessary insolence of this remark. Kate, fearing that her brother was on the verge of being very rude, chipped in.

'Go on, Harry, go and sit down, I'll settle up here.' She pushed him towards the tables and handed the woman at the till a crisp five-pound note. 'He's expecting his first child,' she confided, lowering her voice, having judged – correctly, as it turned out – that such information would redress the situation considerably.

'Oh, I see.' The woman, who had a heart-shaped face with sad grey eyes, nodded knowingly and patted the airy wings of her hair. 'First time nerves, eh? Good luck to you and your wife, mister,' she called after Harry. 'Children don't change a thing, you'll see,' she added with a cackle.

Harry, taking a seat at the opposite end of the table from the nurses, scowled as his sister approached. 'I just don't understand how they can let it all stop – just like that – after so much time and all those hateful contractions and so on.' He stubbed out his cigarette in a flimsy tinfoil container and began running his fingers through his hair, covering all areas of his head, as if coiffuring himself after a swim. 'Christ it's a grim business.'

Alicia, who had endured several hours of racking contractions at very irregular intervals was at that moment asleep, all pain and movement in her abdomen having suddenly and mysteriously ceased. While the doctors claimed to be unperturbed by this turn of events, Harry, who had imagined them all to be galloping down the final furlong of childbirth, was left in a frenzy of anxious frustration, incredulous that after such a fast and furious start – the marks of Alicia's long nails were still deep and pink in the palms of his hands – they could simply allow the process to stop. There fluttered too, on the fringes of his consciousness, an unsettling vision of his half-born child, stuck kicking for life in some dark intestinal tube, with no air to breathe, no prospect of release. Though Alicia herself was too grateful and exhausted to do anything but fall asleep, Harry strutted and ranted for a time, doing his best to be demanding and assertive, but receiving only back-pats and bland explanations for his pains. After a while the doctor in charge raced off to answer a call on his bleep, leaving only a baby-faced midwife with buck teeth to continue the business of soothing the harassed father. The nurse, whose sing-song voice and bouncy pony-tail did nothing to eradicate Harry's impression that the person now in charge of the situation was no older than his teenage niece, reiterated the official view that, since the pregnancy was still three weeks short of term, it would be better to let the contractions restart of their own accord. It meant Mum could have a rest, she concluded, and Dad could have a cup of tea.

Harry, who was in serious need of something far more anaesthetising than tea, and who shuddered at hearing Alicia and himself referred to in such domesticated and frumpy terms as 'Mum and Dad', accepted this dismissal reluctantly, only managing not to protest again because of a firm sisterly hand on his elbow steering him towards the lifts.

Though not regretting for a moment that she had come, Kate was finding it a lot harder to be attendant at the birth of someone else's child than it had been to deliver her own. This was not simply because, like Harry, she felt helpless and out of control, but also because of the realisation that she had to walk a tightrope between interference and help. Even Harry's angry reactions struck her as part of a process over which she had little right to intervene, cigar-twiddling, corridor-pacing fathers, being all part of the traditional natal scene. In addition to which, she was considerably better educated than her brother as to the hazards of unpunctual babies and could therefore sense the possibilities of danger hovering behind the battened down smiles of the medical staff. While keeping such thoughts firmly to herself, Kate felt justified in prolonging her presence in the hospital a little longer and in dragging Harry away from Alicia's bedside – if only to charge him up with gaseous water – before the inevitably tense elements of the final haul, whatever that haul might be.

Harry swigged straight from the bottle and stifled a burp. Bored with his latest cigarette, but unwilling to stub out one so far from the cork, he began pressing the burning tip against his plastic glass, creating pock-marks of congealed plastic, like acne scars on a shiny face. One of the nurses sitting nearby, a girl with eastern features and a high bun of glossy black hair, watched him for a while, trying to catch his eye. Kate, noticing this, was relieved – and quite impressed – that her brother failed to observe, or perhaps chose to ignore, the attentions of such a striking female. There was a time when Harry, on spotting three women under the age of thirty-five sitting together without attendant males, would have felt almost duty bound to ply them with his charms, driven if not by attraction, then by an antediluvian mind-set, to do with the testosterone-charged impulses that reigned supreme in less civilised areas of the world.

Even though it was nearly two o'clock in the morning, Kate felt beady-eyed and alert. She watched Harry in silence for a while, smiling to herself at his obvious distraction, at the concentration which he applied to the systematic torturing of his beaker. It was looking like the surface of a planet now, heaving lumps and holes of alien matter, ringed with brown and yellow.

'Cheer up, Harry,' she said at length, 'they said they'd come and get us if anything happened. If nothing has started by morning they might even let you go home.'

Harry groaned. 'That would be the worst thing – to have to go through all this again on another day.' He tossed his cigarette, its end now gooey with melted plastic, into the corrugated insult of an ashtray and leant backwards, struggling to fit his long body comfortably into the chrome S-bend of his seat and stretching his long legs so far under the table that they got tangled up in Kate's own legs, tucked back neatly under her chair.

'Do I take it from this that you are almost thrilled at the prospect of becoming a father?' The question slipped out almost by mistake, borne along by the new dimension of intimacy that their situation allowed.

'Thrilled?' Harry shook his head and frowned. 'Not at all. Appalled, more like – or terrified, I suppose.' He turned his empty water bottle on its side and began rolling it back and forth under the palm of his hand, as if flattening some invisible piece of pastry. 'And curious.' His smile came without warning, infusing his handsome face with life and light and making Kate grin back in happiness for him. 'Horribly curious. Poor little mite. What an ordeal. And for Alicia too,' he added hastily, his face collapsing into a frown. 'You know, that girl really has . . . I'm not saying . . . I mean marriage is definitely not on the cards, but I have to say that I've come to . . . appreciate Alicia in a way that I never imagined possible.'

'But no marriage?' Kate's eyes twinkled in sceptical disbelief as she welcomed a recollection of the vastly improved state of things at home: how good it was to feel so absolutely back on track again, after so long. And it struck her then with fresh force quite what a dark tunnel the last few months had been, what a marvellous relief it was that they seemed – somehow or other – to have pushed on through to the other side. Letting her eyes glaze over, she drifted off on dreamy thoughts about home, floating away from the seedy green and beige surroundings of the hospital canteen, with its faint smell of chip fat mingling with Harry's interminable smoke. Her eyes closed for an instant. It would be good to see the children again, and Nicholas . . .

'I don't know if now's the time,' Harry was saying, pulling the last but one cigarette from his packet and lighting it with a deft flick of a small gold lighter which he dropped back into the breast pocket of his shirt, 'I mean it's never going to be the right time to tell you something like this, something so . . .'

'So what?' asked Kate, blinking, forcing her brain back into focus, fighting a sudden sledgehammer of a desire to sleep. It dawned on her that Harry was trying to say something important. Suspecting that it was to do with the daunting business of confessing to feelings for the woman who was about to bear his child, she sat up straighter in her chair, aiming for an expression that looked sympathetic, but at the same time not too unattractively eager. There would be no point in gloating; it was truly wonderful that Harry, of all people, had at last discovered something like love.

'I mean, you did say that there were problems, after all . . .'

'Problems? With what?' Kate took a sip of water from her own unmutilated beaker and folded her hands together. She was going to have to concentrate harder, she told herself, wondering at the same time whether it was her sleepiness or Harry's uncharacteristic state of high emotion that was causing the direction of their conversation to grow suddenly so opaque.

'Marriage.' Harry swallowed the smoke rather than inhaled it, before letting it drift out of his nostrils in delicate squirls. There was still time to pull back, he told himself, still time not to say anything. He looked across at his sister. Her wide brown eyes, though framed with lines of tiredness, shone with trust and warmth. Her hair, which had been tied back with a black velvet ribbon when she arrived, had long since broken free and was hanging in a not altogether unattractive mess around her face, though the glimmers of grey were clearer than he remembered them being before. Touched by the vulnerability of her, he looked quickly away. Honesty did not – in Harry's experience anyway – always lead to the best results. If he made no mention of Nicholas' girlfriend then Kate could continue in whatever haze she currently lived her life, fussing round with children and shopping and cooking, happily oblivious to a deception which might in the end prove meaningless.

'I'm rather keen on marriage at the moment, actually,' said Kate with a secretive smile. 'Nicholas and I . . .' she sighed happily, not daring to embark on the challenge of affirming middle-age love without sounding corny or insincere.

Something about the trust she was showing pushed Harry back towards his original resolve. He simply could not bear to see his sister duped – into happiness or anything else. 'About Nicholas,' he began, before clearing his throat to play for one last second of time, aware of Kate's eyes upon him, 'it's just that – Christ, there's no easy way to say this, Katie – but – the fact is I saw Nicholas with someone else – a woman – at the races.'

'The races?' Kate, secure in her knowledge that Nicholas had been nowhere near a racecourse in the last ten years at least, let out a laugh of genuine incredulity.

Harry was torn between wanting to protect her from pain and a by now overpowering need to tell her the truth. 'Katie, try not to mind too much – you know men and all that – not that I'm saying it's okay – far from it – I'd like to thrash Nicholas within an inch of his life—'

'But Nicholas never goes to the races,' she laughed, patting his hand, 'he's petrified of horses – he fell off once when he was ten years old – broke three ribs and got a rusty metal nail in his arm. He must have told you the story – he nearly died of blood-poisoning. He's still terribly proud of the scar – you know Nicholas . . .'

Harry, forced by her obtuseness to be cruel, lowered his voice to a grey monotone to deliver the information again, this time leaving no room for disbelief. 'I saw Nicholas at Ferndown Racecourse this afternoon. He was with a woman with long blonde hair. They were holding hands. They looked very . . . close.' He sat back and folded his arms. 'I'm sorry, Kate, but there it is.'

Kate stared at a brown circular stain on the table and said nothing.

'Look,' went on Harry more urgently, 'if it was me I would like to know. To have someone cheating on you is frankly unacceptable – in my book anyway – especially . . . I mean, especially as . . . as it's you, Katie; he faltered, struggling, now the moment had come, to justify exactly why he had felt so compelled to tell her of Nicholas' indiscretion. At the back of his mind there skulked a dislike of his brother-in-law which – at this moment as at all other moments – he did his best to quell. Even Harry stopped short of nurturing unseemly shivers of anticipation at the novel prospect of turning his sister against a man whom she clearly loved, even though that man was a creature whom he himself had never admired and whom, deep down, he had always deemed too unglamorous, too average to be worthy of her.

'You must be raging,' he began, but stopped again, since Kate appeared to be nothing of the sort. Her face, usually such a picture of the thoughts inside, stared back blankly into his, registering no emotion that he could recognise.

'Oh there you are,' came a soft voice behind them. 'I thought I'd find you down here. The tea's always warm anyway,' she added, clearly disregarding their bottles and beakers. The little nurse followed this by offering them a rabbit-smile and mouthing salutations at her colleagues down the other end of the table. She hovered by their chairs for an instant, before inclining her head towards them and speaking in a faintly bored, lilting voice, as if she were a waitress listing specials on the day's menu. 'Mum's in labour again, but there are indications of foetal *distress* so Mr Grant is going to do a caesarean section. They're getting her ready now. You can get scrubbed up too, Mr Melford; if you would like to, that is. Shall we go?'

Harry, visibly overcome by the thought of being invited to watch somebody apply a scalpel to the honeyed flesh of Alicia's belly, managed something between a shake and a nod, while the blood drained from his face and his lips shrank to a colourless line of grey. He swallowed and looked at Kate, as if only she could confirm the appropriate role expected of a man in such circumstances. Kate, pulling her eyes away from the brown stain, said nothing to Harry, but got up obediently to follow the nurse from the canteen. She trod very carefully across the thin carpet tiles of the floor, stepping between lines and holes and marks as if her life depended on it. 'Tread on a line, marry a swine, tread in a square, marry a bear,' chanted a voice inside her head. Kate found herself wondering why she had always preferred the thought of bears.

'What sort of foetal distress?' she asked, while the three of them stood watching the red light of the lift button, which Harry had pressed at least ten times in a futile effort to hasten its arrival on the fourth floor.

'The heartbeat was a little slow, that's all.' The moment the furthest set of doors slid open the little nurse hopped inside and pressed a button to keep them that way. Harry and Kate hurried inside behind an orderly pushing an empty wheelchair. After a cumbersome start, the lift suddenly picked up speed, making their tummies turn in unison and causing Kate to feel so giddy that she had to put out one hand to steady herself until a few moments after they had stopped.

'But the heartbeat,' Harry was muttering, 'that's terribly important, I mean . . .'

'Its rate has slowed down slightly, that's all.' The nurse led the way out of the lift, her flat white shoes squeaking on the brown linoleum floor. 'The operation is very quick – baby will be out in fifteen minutes flat – it's the sewing up that takes the time.'

Harry, casting a sidelong look at Kate, pushed uselessly at the long floppy sides of his hair. But his sister's eyes were pinned to the crisp white back of their guide, like a face transfixed by a blank screen.

Things happened very quickly after that. Alicia, who had been calm in the storm of pain, was panic-stricken at the thought of an operation. While they waited for the epidural to numb the lower half of her body she clung to Harry's hand as a drowning person might cling to a log, her face fixed in an expression of unremitting terror. Harry, equally terrified, clung back, licking his lips and trying to smile.

Kate, functioning as if from within a deep dream, forced herself to approach them and go through the motions of reassurance. Though she could not bring herself to look at Harry, she was able to take hold of Alicia's free hand and speak with soothing, artificial confidence about the breeze of having babies on operating tables, the scores of women who had caesareans every minute of every day, the added safety for the child, the speed of delivery. Kate was still listing positive things when she was politely ushered from the room by a nurse carrying a white metal bowl containing some water and a razor.

'I've got to shave Mum now – won't be a tick.'

Kate slipped away, leaving Harry to gasp in silent horror while one of the most prized, secret parts of his lover was, with a few deft strokes, laid bare to the world.

'It'll itch a bit when it grows back, I'm afraid,' commented the nurse matter-of-factly, as she dabbed Alicia dry and pulled the theatre gown back over her legs. 'And of course it will help hide the scar.'

'You cut that low?' asked Harry in a strangled voice.

A look of real concern flashed across the midwife's face. 'Are you sure you're up to this, sir? We can't have fainting Dads in theatre – not that it hasn't happened in the past – but if you feel that you can't Mr Grant would much prefer it if—'

'Oh Harry, please be there, please.' Alicia sounded as though she was praying.

'You don't have to peak over the screen,' put in the nurse helpfully, 'just stand by Mum and hold her hand. You won't see a thing – until baby comes out.'

Harry gulped. 'I expect I can manage that.'

'Come and get scrubbed up then. The doctor's on his way.'

38

After welcoming the safe arrival of Lilly Anastasia Melford Browning, some time around four o'clock that morning, Kate took a taxi back to Harry's flat, leaving her brother to stare in open-mouthed wonder at the small pink package of a daughter sleeping in a plastic bubble-cot beside her mother. Lilly was so perfectly formed and of such a respectable weight that it was generally agreed that Alicia had got her dates muddled. Apart from a faint glow of jaundice the doctors could find nothing to worry about at all. Harry had been rendered gratifyingly speechless by the whole thing, while Alicia, after some emotional murmurings about how he now had two girls to look after instead of one, had drifted off into an exhausted sleep.

Kate had accepted Harry's offer of spare keys and slipped away. To see her philandering brother filled with the incommunicable joy of parental wonderment, to see him – possibly – on the threshold of a glorious phase of life through which she herself had long since passed only served to heighten her sense of desolation. Nicholas had looked like that too, at Grace, at James and at Millie. Now he was screwing a woman with blonde hair.

Once the initial numbness of shock had worn off, Kate found herself whirling through the gamut of possible reactions to such a thing, without being sure that she truly felt any of them. It was almost as if muddled preconceptions about how wives were supposed to react in such circumstances prevented her from settling upon a genuine response of her own. That it had happened to so many others, that in time-honoured tradition, she, the wife, had suspected nothing, almost bothered Kate more than the disloyalty itself. To realise that her life, which secretly, deep down, she had always believed to be special and different and hallowed, was in fact as flawed as everybody else's, to accept that she and Nicholas were, like most of the world, incapable of hobbling along faithfully towards their graves without falling into deceit and dishonour, was depressing beyond words.

As she leant back against the hard leather seat of her taxi Kate was assailed by memories of the Armstrongs, how she had counselled Victoria all those years ago, secretly, complacently sure that such a pain would never be hers, quietly pitying the compromise of having to forgive such a thing, safe in the conviction that she would be incapable of accepting such imperfection for herself.

And then there was the shame, something that Victoria had not mentioned, the shudder of social embarrassment at having failed to earn the life-long fidelity of her man.

Once in bed, Kate slithered easily into a coloured tangle of a dream full of nameless faces and the cries of newborn children. When she awoke, she felt unrefreshed, as if only moments had passed since placing her head on the pillow. In fact some eight hours had elapsed, during which Harry had been back to the flat and returned to the hospital. There was a note from him on the back of a brown envelope beside her pillow, explaining his whereabouts and thanking her for her support. No mention of Nicholas though. Typical, she thought, tearing the envelope into pieces and dropping them one by one into the waste-paper bin. He couldn't think what to say, so he didn't say anything at all. Though he had taken upon himself the responsibility of delivering the axe-blow of information, he felt no compunction about escaping involvement in its consequences. It showed a certain neglect which, even given the other momentous event of that night, Kate found hard to forgive. Wearily, she pulled on her clothes, not bothering to check her appearance in the mirror before leaving the flat. Just as it had felt wrong to sleep so soundly, she felt a stab of impatience at the realisation she was hungry, as if cheated wives had no right to appetites; as if they should be too haunted and overcome by emotion to need food.

Ignoring the rumbling of her stomach, Kate walked fast, driven by an instinctive anxiety to put as much distance between herself and Harry's flat as possible. Having thought she was going to get a tube, she found herself passing first one, then another sign for the Underground without paying any heed to them. Taxis with yellow lights cruised by, their drivers craning their necks for any sign of a customer. Kate walked on, staring only at the ground, aware of no physical sensation except the start of a blister under the heel strap of her left sandal.

She stopped walking only when an image of Max Urquart flashed across her mind. If she had managed to say no, why the fuck hadn't Nicholas?

Looking up, Kate saw that she had stopped outside the wrought-iron gates of what was clearly a small museum or art gallery. At the top of a flight of broad stone steps a man in a dark blue uniform with a red pin-stripe down the sides of his trousers was propping open the front door with a large rusty bell.

'Five minutes,' he called down to Kate, holding up all five fingers of one hand, to emphasise the point and twitching his head in a way that could have been a wink, but which was suggestive of something less controlled. Kate, whose hovering at the gates bore no relation to anything so logical as the desire to go in, started to walk on, before stopping and turning to lean her back against the wall. A sign across the road told her she was in Gilbert Street, wherever that was. It didn't matter. She had no desire to go home, no sense of what to do at all.

I was attracted to Max for emotional reasons, she thought bitterly, because I was lonely and worried, and not out of any celebratedly male predilection for mindless lust. But the neat equation failed to convince and she set it to one side. It simply wouldn't do. She was as lustful as the next woman. And Nicholas could be beautifully emotional about sex, she thought sadly, remembering them suddenly as they were, as they could be, when things were good. While recognising such sentiments to be indulgent and unhelpful, it was an image that held, an image which she felt deeply reluctant to surrender, in spite of everything.

'Nice day for it,' commented the man when Kate walked up the steps, half of his face seizing up again, though he covered it up with a quick smile and a twiddle of his moustache.

It was a small art gallery, containing paintings which, while not recognisably famous, looked as though they easily could have been. Even though Kate had heard of none of the artists, there was some relief in the sensation of being taken out of herself as the pictures caught her eye, forcing her to imagine the stories of lives and times other than her own. After walking down a narrow hallway lined with country scenes and seascapes, she entered a large room whose furthest wall was dominated by a ceiling-high portrait of a grand lord and lady, as puffed and pompous as peacocks; their disciplinarian expressions fixed so sternly upon Kate as she approached that she felt compelled to sit down on the leather viewing bench and stare them out. In the background, tiny dancing figures of children could be seen, holding hands and laughing, while a liver-spotted spaniel dog pranced at their feet. Kate, thinking of her own children, bit her lip and swallowed hard. Someone else had entered the room behind her. It wouldn't do to cry here, she thought, clenching her jaws and blinking hard, not in public. The person sat down on the other end of the bench, facing the opposite way. If this was a film, Kate told herself, this stranger would be dark and handsome and know instinctively that I was sad. He would lean across and say something soft in my ear, he would take me away for coffee and compassion, he would mend my life forever. But as she rose from the bench and stole a look sideways she saw that the stranger was an old woman in a squashed mauve felt hat, with a sagging, toothless jaw and a twitching pink scratch of a smile. The woman nodded in response, raising her walking stick an inch or two off the ground. So much for real life, thought Kate grimly, moving away.

It was time to go home. There was nothing else to do, after all. While she dreaded the thought of seeing Nicholas, the sickening idea of having it all out, of going through the motions of an experience she had never imagined for herself, she did long to see the children. The two weeks since they had all gone their separate ways suddenly felt intolerably endless.

On the train some of the shame began to ebb away, only to be replaced by a horrible tide of curiosity. A woman with long blonde hair. What aged woman? What sort of hair? Permed, curly or straight? Was she thin or fat? Were her eyes brown or blue? Was she married? Did she groan in the throes of passion or suffer her pleasure in silence? Did she do things with Nicholas that Kate had never thought of? Even while a hard, critical core of her acknowledged such questions to be painful and futile, merely the furious musings expected of betrayed spouses, Kate found it impossible to stem their flow. The curiosity had to be suffered, to be endured like everything else.

She remembered reading about a jilted middle-aged wife who cut all the arms off her husband's Savile Row suits and left his vintage wines beside the milk-bottles of their neighbours. Kate allowed her mind to dawdle along similar lines for a time, but without mustering any enthusiasm for embarking on a similar course of revenge. Nicholas' suits were bought in sales and had patched-up pocket-linings; what meagre wine stocks they had came from the supermarket and if she rammed his company car at their front door his employers would almost certainly provide him with another one. And then the front door would need fixing. The realisation that she was not even up to the drama of a hysterical response seemed to break the barrier inside, allowing Kate's thoughts to sink at last down to the level towards which they had been driving all day, a level that brought the first tears, the first sense of genuine loss. It didn't matter if he explained, if he said he was sorry and wanted to try again. It didn't matter if it turned out to be only lust and not love. A light had been lost. A door to a dark room had been opened, a door which could never be shut. Even with forgiveness, knowledge of the deed could not be undone. And as the countryside blurred before her streaming eyes, Kate wondered how she could ever learn to live with such a knowledge, what possible aspect of the situation could give her the strength to return and carry on.

Nicholas, meanwhile, was busy making preparations for his wife's homecoming. The third load of holiday washing was already in hand, thanks to some help from Grace, who knew which buttons to press, and to James who, clad only in shorts, sunglasses and his Walkman, had spent considerable time hanging curious items from his sisters' wardrobes on the umbrella clothes-line planted in the least conspicuous corner of the garden. His cricket things, too stained to qualify even for the washing machine – as his elder sister gleefully informed him – had been crammed into a bucket of cold water and bleach which Millie kept stirring with a wooden spoon, two fingers ostentatiously sealing her nostrils, as if she were minding a cauldron of some unspeakable brew.

The cartons which Nicholas had dutifully extricated from the frozen claws of the deep freeze turned out to contain nothing but sludge of the most unpromising kind. He stood pondering the smeared, illegible labels for some time, until he was joined by a daughter at each elbow, all the children by now having warmed to the morning's theme of getting everything in the house straight for their mother. While Millie contented herself with clutching at her throat and producing a series of melodramatic gagging noises at the sight of so liquid a meal, Grace and her father attempted a rather more intelligent debate as to the possible nature of the ingredients confronting them and how they might be transformed into food. After a sniff or two, it was generally agreed that the pinky grey one comprised puréed fruit of some kind, though opinions remained severely divided over its greeny brown companion; Grace swore it was an inedible chicken giblet concoction fit only for animals or the bin.

In spite of such discouraging cynicism on the part of his daughters, Nicholas, driven by the strong and steady pulse of inner guilt, clung to his resolve to have a meal – quite which one he neither knew nor cared – on the table for when Kate returned. Like a recently confessed sinner he had entered a period of atonement and was following his best instincts for setting things right. The preparation of food, filling the washing machine and unpacking their clothes, were the most obvious gifts of repentance he could deliver to a woman as domestically inclined as his wife, especially given the awkward fact of trying to make up for something about which she knew nothing at all. The idea of telling her about Joanna was as appealing to Nicholas as it was abhorrent. Though he would have loved to get it off his chest, to absolve himself completely, he knew that in the end fear would prevent him – fear of losing her in the process. There thrived too, in the midst of these selfish anxieties, a more noble reluctance to hurt Kate: it would, he felt, be not unlike firing a potentially fatal shot after a war had been fought and won – an image which encouraged his resolve to seek refuge in silence.

How close he had come, he realised, pressing the lids of the cartons back into place, to losing everything. From the safe-haven of hindsight, his liaison with Joanna Wyrall seemed the tail end of a long chain of disasters, a chain whose beginnings were linked to a crisis of confidence, a debilitating affliction to do with loving a wife too hard, followed by the unforeseeably shocking experience of losing his father. Blowing on his cold hands – the tips of his fingers had turned yellowy-white from handling the frozen boxes – Nicholas tried for an instant to recall the miserable envy that had so smothered him earlier in the year, the strangling self-hatred that had accompanied the belief that his beloved wife was beginning to take off from him, beginning to find her feet in an alien zone far beyond the safe apron-anchored environment of their home. Why didn't it seem so bad any more, he wondered, as the old panic refused to surface, stirring only as a dim memory of a threat gone by? 'Because I trust her,' he murmured to himself, wiping his hands on a towel, at the same time marvelling at the mercurial qualities of such an emotion, how it could reappear just as mysteriously as it had once slipped through his fingers. He hung the tea-towel carefully back on its hook beside the fridge and took a deep, contented breath, relishing his new peace of mind, acknowledging that it tasted sweeter for having been absent for so long.

Despairing at the frozen sludge – though he made a show of welcoming Millie's plan of stirring cream and sugar into the pink one – Nicholas next resolved to make an excursion into Elhurst for some of Mrs Edwards' home-made pâté and a couple of sticks of French bread. The cartons, left to their own devices, now began to defrost in earnest; their dense coats of ice-fibres sliding like mini-glaciers down their sides, forming a large pool of surrounding water which soon reached the pages of Kate's kitchen pad, ill-advisedly parked nearby; its clean white pages bulged and bulked as the water worked its way through, crawling towards its white middle like a slow tide on an empty beach.

Once he had got dressed Nicholas, driven by a rather pleasing curiosity as to the progress of various projects and the state of his in-tray, decided to ring the office. As he dialled the numbers, feet up on the kitchen table and a fresh mug of coffee in hand, he marvelled at the unfathomable way in which all the routines of his existence were suddenly springing to life again, as if injected with new zest, taking shape in a way that made him want to embrace rather than despise them. He sipped his coffee and smiled. After the misery and madness of the summer it was such a relief to rediscover the shape of his old life, waiting for him like a patient shadow, ready to be stepped into and swept along as before.

Janice, after answering the phone in her usual clipped, efficient tones, promptly burst into tears. Amazed at such an emotional display from one whose office chit-chat did not usually extend beyond the frustrating vagaries of the photo-copier, Nicholas, suspecting rebellious hormones of some kind, at first suggested that he call back at a more appropriate time. But Janice insisted that she was fine, managing then to contain her sobs sufficiently to explain that she, along with twenty other members of staff from all levels of the company, had just been made redundant and would be leaving Freeman Lyle at the end of September. While he was on holiday there had been big cuts across the board, she wailed, heads had rolled on all sides and everybody was in shock.

Nicholas replaced the receiver with a trembling hand, breath-less at the sense of his own good fortune. It seemed incredible that not so very long ago the idea of his job had filled him with nothing but gloom. According to Janice, several of his colleagues were on the hit-list, a fact which only heightened Nicholas' appreciation of his luck, at the same time encouraging the revolutionary notion that he might, after all, be valued quite highly, that somewhere along the line his contributions to the research and development of domestic products were having an effect that mattered.

This news from work fuelled Nicholas' domestic good inten-tions still further. Armed with Kate's secateurs, he marched out into the garden and cut a whole bucketful of flowers, careful to spread his collection so as not to denude any single plant entirely. With the girls' help he then arranged these in several vases which they distributed around the ground floor of the house.

'Anyone would think Mum was having the baby,' remarked James, eyeing a heap of lupins and roses in the middle of the kitchen table. 'It'll be boxes of chocolates next.'

'Chocolates. Good idea, James. We'll get them in Elhurst at the same time as the bread and cream and so on. You can be our chauffeur.'

James, whose bird-hopping efforts behind the wheel of a car had so far been reserved for his mother alone, couldn't believe his luck.

'Wow – your car – thanks, Dad.'

Leaving Grace jigging cheerfully to a metallic humming emanating from her brother's earphones while hanging yet another basketful of washing out in the sunshine, they set off for Elhurst. By squeezing his knee-caps hard, Nicholas managed not to scream once, not even when James stalled halfway over the crossroads by the pub, and then, panicking at the fast approach of a green bus, tried to start up in second gear. Millie, who had invited herself along for the ride, sat quietly in the back throughout these adventures, chewing gum and reading a comic, as if it were a drive like any other, with nothing beyond the tedium of red traffic lights and crawling tractors to contend with.

After shopping and laying the table there was nothing more to do. Nicholas put a bottle of wine in the fridge and took a mug of tea to his desk. The children, still charged with the novelty of being back home, went about their own lives without disturbing him or each other. After a two-hour stint of startling creativity – his short story was all but finished – Nicholas felt wholly justified in treating himself to some cricket. He found James already there, lying on his stomach on the floor in front of the television with a cushion under his elbows and a can of beer by his chin.

'I don't suppose I can light up, can I?' he mumbled, as his father sat down behind him.

Nicholas sighed, torn between wanting to develop the thread of a bond strung between them the night before and parental feelings of an infinitely less tolerant kind. 'Outside only, okay?' He threw a cushion at James's back. 'If Mum agrees.'

James threw the cushion back, turning his head enough for Nicholas to see the grin.

'And never at school.'

'Oh no, Dad, never at school,' he echoed in a mischievous tone. Nicholas was just pondering whether he had been taken sufficiently seriously on the matter when Grace put her head round the door to ask if she could use the phone. Nodding his head in wonderment – Grace *never* asked if she could use the phone – Nicholas' attention was then distracted by an astonishing catch from a towering black fielder on the boundary line. He sat forward eagerly to watch the replays.

'Bravo', shouted James, rolling on his back and sticking his legs in the air. 'I think that calls for a celebration.' He patted the pocket where his cigarettes lived and got up to go outside.

By the time Kate got to Westbury station, some ten miles from Elhurst, she had thought through so many possible explanations and consequences that her head hurt. She had even, driven by a desperation that she despised more than anything, begun to fantasise that Harry might after all have been mistaken, that Nicholas was simply not the kind to go in for sexual infidelity, he was too disorganised for one thing – and too honest. Though such thoughts buoyed her for a time, they were soon drowned by keener recollections of their torturous summer: Nicholas' impenetrable gloom, the wedge of separation so badly reinforced by the presence of his mother. She wondered now if Joyce's arrival had coincided with the start of Nicholas' affair, or whether it had been going on long before.

But as she turned onto the main Elhurst Road, something in Kate, unaccustomed to or unimpressed by the role of victim, started to rally, a dubious emotion which felt like vengeful bravery surging inside. It surged all the harder when she recognised the start of the roadside fencing that led along to the entrance to Mill House. With a vague sense of an appealing circumstantial symmetry of which only she could be the architect, Kate turned off the road, her head reeling with jumbled recollections of Max Urquart, how impressively direct and intuitive he had seemed, how desirable he had made her feel, how he had once promised to be her friend. She pulled up several yards from the house, half in the shade offered by a fine yew hedge which curled round the edge of the drive and for several hundred yards along the road.

Here is an answer, she told herself, here at least is a way

through. She quietly closed the car door and started towards the house. Though she had never felt less desirable in her life, though her heart fluttered with longing for the old equilibrium of her marriage rather than for the harrowing prospect of throwing herself at the feet of a man she barely knew, Kate walked steadily towards the lion mouth knocker on the door.

Something about the stillness that crouched around the house made her turn away at the last minute and follow the path round the side instead. She ran her hand along the warm stone of the wall as she walked, rubbing it with her fingers, as if the sun-soaked brick had the power to energise and inspire. In the garden at the back the sun, already sinking fast, fired its beams across the river at blinding angles, striking Kate's eyes and bouncing off the line of sitting-room windows behind her. She put her hand to her brow, squinting into the glare, expecting to see Max Urquart any minute; but as her heart quickened so did her courage begin to fail, rational voices breaking through her resolve to question the confusing nature of the consequences that would follow on from this show of daring. Green spots danced before her eyes as she turned back to face the shadows along the wall.

She had just stepped past the smallest of the sitting-room windows when a movement inside caught her eye. An instinct from nowhere made her jump to one side and press her back hard up against the wall. She could feel the gritty stone pressing against her skin through the thin cotton of her dress. Her breath was coming hot and fast, in strange spurts of its own. Edging forward carefully, she peered round the side of the window. It was clear at once that Max had no idea she was there. He was standing near the sofa, holding a cardboard box under one arm, using the nail on his little finger to scratch the inside of one nostril with the unmistakable relish of one who imagines himself to be alone.

Kate snatched in her head like a snail. A man like Max Urquart wasn't designed to be seen picking his nose.

Her mind slowly registered the fact that his sitting room was in complete disarray: books, papers, ornaments, boxes and pictures were piled up on every side, though whether these items were in the process of being packed or rearranged was – from her limited vantage point – unclear. Max was now making a tour of the furniture, picking things up and putting them down again without any apparent sense of purpose, looking pensive, and not particularly happy. He was wearing a rust-coloured, round-necked canvas top of the kind that Kate associated with male models lounging on sailing boats, together with elegantly crumpled knee-length white shorts and a pair of faded brown espadrilles which flopped soundlessly as he walked. The rounds of his heels looked very white against his tanned ankles. As she watched, Max knelt down in front of an impressively small black box of a music system and began fiddling with knobs and an assortment of silver discs. After a minute or two a blast of tinny music rocketed into the hot silence of the late afternoon, making Kate jump like a startled cat, gripping the wall behind her with her nails.

I may be mad, she told herself, but I have to do this. I have to do this or leave at once.

Boldly, she stepped into the frame of the window and raised one hand to tap on the glass.

As she did so a woman entered the far side of the room, an exceedingly tall woman in high heels and a silky green nightgown of a dress that rippled down to a point just above her knees. Kate, catching her breath, immediately shrank back out of sight. The woman looked expensive: the gold straps of her shoes, the heavy baubles dangling from her ears, the silver clasp pinning her mane of fair hair into a tumbledown bun shimmered with the unmistakable aura of serious money. She said something, and Max bent down to the music machine again, taking out the CD and replacing it with another. A slow jazz-like tune began to pulse from the miniature speakers, a snaking trumpet of sound that wound its way round the room and out through the windows to where Kate still remained, one cheek pressed hard against the wall, her eyes closed, now praying she could wish herself away.

When she opened them again, the window was still there, its glossy white frame just inches from the tip of her nose; there were tiny specks of paint on the surrounding stone, she noticed, nestling amongst buttons of green moss; the glassy view of the interior beyond was like a picture on a wall, a portrait of two strangers whose lives could only be imagined. Adjusting the focus of her eyes with some difficulty, she saw that Max was now on all fours beside the stereo system, apparently pinioned there by the woman's foot, one beautifully arched, gold latticed shoe having been placed on top of his back, its sharp heel pressing between his shoulder blades like a poised knife. Max's head was turned back and up towards the owner of the shoe, smiling like an obedient dog. When the woman at last removed her foot he stood up at once and circled her in his arms, pressing his hips into hers as they both began to sway to the music, moving only slightly, as if the rhythms they followed pulsed from deep inside.

Suddenly, Max pulled away from his partner and strode over towards the window. Kate stepped back at once and began sidling towards the corner of the house, clumsily groping her way, crushing clusters of flowers underfoot in her desperation to get away. Max stood at the window for a few seconds, squinting at the slanting rays of the sun, his face otherwise impassive, before roughly pulling the curtains across the glass. From there he proceeded round all the other windows, tugging at each set of curtains in turn, until Kate was shut out completely with only the sunshine and the faint drone of insects for company.

She walked doggedly back to her car, weighed down by the deflation of disillusionment and defeat, half expecting Max or his baubled lady-friend to come charging out of the house after her. In spite of her quick reactions she was convinced she had been seen – something in Max's face, a tic of irritation as he spun round, before striding over towards her window. Misery overcame any remaining energy she had to care; though even in the blur of hopelessness she recognised that luck of a kind had been her guide. What a fool she might have made of herself if the woman had not appeared when she did. And how pathetically absurd to have imagined that a liaison of any sort with a man like Max Urquart, an unknowable, weird man, clearly with a dangerously selfish agenda of his own, could have offered her any solutions. Such people came from another world, a world which – in spite of any surface allure – she had no wish or hope of penetrating, a world in which creatures like her and

Nicholas would always have bobbed about like bright corks on a dark sea.

After nosing back up the drive towards the main road, Kate paused at the top, letting the engine idle for a few moments while she pretended to herself that she had a choice, that she had the freedom to turn left or right.

At length she rammed her foot down on the accelerator and skidded off in the direction of Elhurst. Of course she had to go home, of course she had to. She wanted to see her children. And, strangely enough, she wanted to see Nicholas too, to get on with the business of confrontation and settlement – to play the part of the wronged wife and see where it led.

It was only much later that it occurred to Kate quite what an influence Mary Sullivan had on the way things turned out. For without Mary, there wouldn't have been Mary's Subaru, emerging at full pelt round the corner, its crimson metallic body well over the white line that divided the two halves of the road. There was just time – a long, languid second or two – for Kate to register the identity of the owner of the oncoming car and for her to think, with the cool precision sometimes induced by a split second of monumental danger, that she probably would not die, before their vehicles collided, diving off opposite sides of the road with all the well-rehearsed symmetry of formation flying.

As it happened, Mary was as distraught as her erstwhile friend that afternoon, though for very different and rather more convoluted reasons. After spending an entire day roaming through the rooms of her large house like a lost spirit, tweaking at chair covers, polishing away imagined fingerprints on window-panes, flicking through magazines, racking her brain for someone to call or write to, Mary had arrived at a new pinpoint of desperation, even for herself, something beyond the limits of what she could normally endure. The breaking point had been reached when she fell to her knees in the kitchen, needing the comfort of prayer, seeking the meditative, floating state of mind in which the voices inside her head at least felt directed towards something more receptive than silence. But the sedative did not work that day. All her silent expressions of unhappiness met with nothing more encouraging than echoes of themselves, reverberating mockingly round her head, like the mimicry of malignant beings.

Mary's instinct in the face of this was not simply to run away, but to seek sanctuary. A vision of Chichester Cathedral had risen up through the grey mire of her desperation like a beacon of hope – the closest thing to divine inspiration she had felt for days – an invitation to peace. Almost smiling with relief, she had at first been happy to let the image shimmer inside her head: the solid stone tower pushing so effortlessly towards the heavens; the cool, elegantly arched interior ringing with the whispers of generations of souls who had been lost and found. Was it wrong to feel closer to God in such surroundings, she wondered, in a place where even the echoing tip-taps of tourists' feet sounded hallowed, a place where the swelling notes of the organ reached outwards and upwards towards heights of religious emotion that squeezed her heart into pulses of unutterable conviction? Groping in her handbag for her car keys, emptiness storming inside, Mary had felt a need for such draughts of conviction with all the thirst of true despair.

So it was that two women, normally given to abiding by both speed limits and the dictates of painted white lines, found themselves careering towards each other with a potentially fatal lack of control.

Mary, whose car – like most cars – had not been designed for the purpose of plummeting head first into deep ditches, came off worst, suffering a fractured pelvis and a broken ankle. Kate, whose stopping point was the rather more welcoming embrace of the yew hedge, followed by a field, emerged much more obviously intact, with only mild concussion and whiplash to show for the adventure. Three cows eyed her lazily as she eased herself from the front seat, their jaws grinding steadily, a look of disdainful enquiry on their wide brown faces. On the way to the hospital and for days afterwards, Kate remembered that look, how reassuring it had been and yet how belittling. It put things in their place rather, to be frowned upon by a cow.

The immediate result of this wholly unforeseen circumstance was to deflect everybody's attention from the preoccupations which had been so intensely attendant upon them before the accident happened. Sitting in the back of the ambulance with Mary laid out like a corpse beside them and Nicholas holding her hand, his face knitted with concern, made questions of marital fidelity seem remote and impossible. And in the hospital too, drowsy with shock and pain, there was nothing Kate wanted to do except close her eyes and sleep.

The next morning the children, sporting funereal faces and bunches of flowers snatched from the vases that Nicholas and Grace had so thoughtfully arranged around the house the day before, trooped in to the ward, each one clearly jolted by the hitherto unabsorbable fact that not even their own mother was immortal. Kate, moved very deeply at the sight of the grim-faced trio, did her best to jolly them along. Nicholas helped her out, managing marvellously to be funny about serious things, striking just the right balance between merriness and reassurance, lifting the spirits of them all. Kate, who could not suppress a pang or two of misplaced pleasure at finding herself so much the centre of attention, especially where her husband was concerned, watched him with curiosity, thinking that if he was merely playing the role of the concerned spouse and supportive parent then he was really doing it extremely well.

In a ward reserved for more serious injuries, Mary too, albeit through a haze of sedated pain, sensed that the crash had somehow jettisoned her back into an existence with which she had been in danger of losing touch. Not only did Angus fly home at once, appearing at her bedside with a bag of quite inappropriate things from the bedroom and bathroom cupboards, but she also found herself tied up in the lives of the Latimers once again. Kate's children came by with their father a couple of times, shyly asking about her plaster cast and depositing bags of green bananas and purple grapes beside her water jug. Then, on the second day Kate herself came, shuffling along in her dressing gown and slippers, her face looking grey and creased, but her smile as warm as ever.

What a way to bump into each other after so much time, she said, laughing easily, making Mary want to laugh too, though she couldn't because any movement below her rib-cage caused a girdle of pain to lock round her hip joints. Though they talked in some detail of the accident, how each had tried to swerve, of the shocking clash of metal, the impact and the noise, enjoying the relief of a post-mortem on a shared horror, the events and emotions of the recent past were – as if by some tacit mutual agreement – never once referred to by either of them.

Even after Kate was discharged, she returned to visit Mary every other day at least, bringing books and needlework – all the things which Angus couldn't find or forgot and which Mary was too fearful to bully him about. Angus did not like seeing her ill, she could tell. Though he went through the motions of support, she sensed his repulsion, his impatience with her condition – so much so that she spent half of her husband's visits apologising for being there.

It was over two weeks before Mary was allowed home, swinging stiffly and painfully through a pair of elbow-crutches that left the palms of her hands aching and raw and her arms shaking from the strain. Thanks to a hormone imbalance related to ovarian cysts from which she had suffered since her twenties, Mary's bones proved uncooperatively brittle about healing – a fact which had Angus raging ineffectually about the incompetence of modern medicine and which left Kate marvelling at how frighteningly little she knew of someone with whom she had supposedly been conducting two-way conversations for years.

The subject of Max Urquart came up at last, with merciful ease, thanks to the appearance of For Sale signs outside both his properties.

'We were quite good friends for a time,' confessed Kate, after she had casually mentioned the signs, dropping them into the conversation like pebbles in a still pond, watching for the ripples of disturbance they might cause. She had brought Mary some homemade raspberry flapjacks and was busy making a Thermos of tea to see her through until Angus returned from golf. 'He offered to teach me how to use a computer – to help me straighten out the manuscript for my book – get it looking more professional – you know the kind of thing.'

Mary nodded, not looking at Kate but fiddling with a loose thread in the padded section of one of her crutches. 'Oh I know. He made friends with quite a lot of people, I think. Had a sort of . . . of charm about him. Put me onto a couple of lovely books . . .' Her voice tailed off at the recollection of the humiliation of his visit to her house. 'Though I'm not sure I really liked him in the end,' she added quietly. 'I got the feeling he was one of those who secretly mocks other people – who deep down despises everyone but himself.'

Kate, surprised by such a penetrating expression of criticism from Mary – Mary, who was usually maddeningly incapable of seeing the bad side to anything – silently wondered what could have happened for her to form such an opinion.

Their eyes met for a second but Mary looked quickly away, before beginning to haul herself upright, her lips tightening at the re-ignition of pain caused by so laborious a movement.

'He's gone back to Suffolk by all accounts. Grand reunion with his old flame,' said Kate dryly.

'That's nice for him. Nice that he should have someone after all.'

Again Kate tried to catch Mary's eye to see if there were any hidden layers of meaning to be extracted from the remark. But Mary was now busy fiddling with the strings of her apron, whose wide pockets were an invaluable form of transportation for anything she needed to carry with her round the house – usually spray cleaners and dusters, though on this occasion Kate had taken out all cleaning aids and replaced them with a novel, a historical romance which had recently been serialised on the television and which she knew Mary had enjoyed enormously.

'You must learn how to spoil yourself, Mary,' she scolded fondly, following her out into the garden with the Thermos of tea and a Tupperware box full of biscuits. 'You're to stay in the garden for the next two hours at least. That's an order.'

As she watched Mary gingerly lower herself into a garden chair Kate found herself questioning whether the emotional stoicism of such a woman was something to be pitied or admired. The thought led her round to the raw, unresolvable question of marital fidelity. She wondered if Angus was unfaithful as well as unkind. Some of the pity must have seeped into her expression. For Mary then said, very quietly, 'You must understand, Kate dear, I'd be nothing without Angus. I'm one of those women who is defined by her men. Not like you. You're not like that at all. You have the freedom to make choices about such things.'

After opening her mouth to make a hurried, automatic denial of such a claim, Kate meekly closed it again. Mary was right. Life without Nicholas would be hard and sometimes empty; but it would be possible. She could envisage it with almost frightening clarity. She could cope alone. Something about her, some inner strength arising from her upbringing, or perhaps simply from the lottery of genetic make-up, ensured that she was and always would be a survivor of the most fundamental kind. Like Harry, she thought grimly, though the comparison was not one that she relished.

This liberating realisation brought with it a real sense of power. Not a vicious, vindictive power, but an unshiftable, deeply rooted sensation of absolute confidence in herself. Recognising that she was not trapped after all, that she had the inner resources to choose a response to the way Nicholas had behaved, made Kate feel quite giddy with a fresh awareness of the strength of her position.

She tilted her face up to the sun and closed her eyes, smiling. 'Enjoy this while it lasts, Mary,' she instructed with teasing severity. 'Siberian winds are on their way apparently. I heard it on the news this morning.'

'Then we'll be longing for all that sticky heat again, I suppose,' sighed Mary, laying down her crutches carefully in the grass beside her chair.

'Not me.' Kate shook her head firmly, ugly snapshots of the summer flicking inside her head. 'I'm ready for the winter.'

When Kate came home from hospital Nicholas, happily oblivious to the degree with which his actions were being scrutinised, felt nothing but the sweetest relief. Watching her joke bravely about the constrictions of a neck-brace, seeing the way she walked – with a stiffness that she tried to disguise – he was gripped with a tenderness that felt keener than love, a tenderness quite beyond expression. Since flowers, laundered clothes and hoovered carpets seemed only the most pitiful manifestation of such a feeling, he added to these attentions by treating Kate like a fragile ornament, showing a gentle attentiveness which aroused her suspicions but which touched her too in the irritatingly vulnerable spot that yearned for such things.

Though she scoured each day for the right moment to confront her husband about his indiscretion, it was something against which every other incident in their lives continued to conspire with an efficiency that was almost sinister. September had brought not only the frenzy of getting the children back to school with the right number of pencils and shoes, but also the final throes of the laborious production of her book, visits to Mary with sympathy and freezable meals and trips up to London to visit Lilly and Alicia. Though Kate rarely saw Harry himself, it was clear from the way Alicia spoke that the two of them had entered the early stages of parenthood with all the gooey wonderment of first-timers in the grip of a genuine belief that such a joy is a gift reserved for them alone. While pleased for them, Kate quickly began to find such parental euphoria faintly irritating, a reaction which she secretly interpreted as a happy sign that she herself was more than ready to move on from such things, that those soon-to-be-redundant hormones of hers were not something she would miss very greatly.

By far the greatest hurdles to Kate's desire for a confrontation with her husband were subtly and unwittingly erected by Nicholas himself. While having the sense to be suspicious of her own powers of judgement, Kate could see that something in him had changed – his smile, his whole bearing, shone now with a fresh sense of purpose. Wary that it might be the presence of another woman that had wrought so pleasing a transformation, Kate raised every intuitive antenna she possessed in order to try and understand its origins. But the more she watched, the more she became convinced that the blonde, if she had ever existed, certainly no longer did so. There simply wasn't time for it. No matter what time of day she called, Nicholas was always in the office – a new, much keener appreciation of his pay-packet having arrived now that the realities of the recession had knocked some of the stuffing out of his own company. And he was always available to talk to her, just like in the very old days, when they had phoned each other at work every two hours at least, needing, in those early frenzied times, to feed off each other's voices like bees at a flower. As if this wasn't enough, Nicholas had also taken to arriving home a good hour earlier than he ever used to, presenting his family not with sullen humphs, but with the eager smiling face of a man at ease with his life, with no dread of the future. Though the children seemed oblivious to these transformations, Kate found it impossible not to be astonished by the unlikelihood and cheek of them. But she also found it impossible not to love them too, since they heralded the re-emergence of a man whom she had come to believe had been lost for good and whom she had always loved very dearly.

As time bubbled away, her sense of urgency about the matter began to recede, so much so that she sometimes forgot to think about it at all. And when she did think about it, Kate found any remaining anger that she had, forming not in arrows at her husband, but at her brother. What right had Harry to stick his finger in her marriage like that? Harry of all people. A man so far incapable of sustaining a relationship of his own for more than a few months. A man so scared of commitment that he had virtually forbidden Alicia to rent out her own flat, just so there was still a permanent bolt-hole, should the need arise.

The more Kate thought along these lines, the more bitterly convinced she became that during their faintly surreal pit-stop in the hospital canteen on the night of Lilly's birth, Harry had committed a crime far more heinous than anything her husband might or might not have done himself. How selfishly wrong of a brother, how treacherous, to chuck a spanner into the machinery of something as delicate and finely poised as a marriage, to jeopardise the stability of a construction based on a set of principles which Harry himself had not the slightest intention of understanding or emulating, and to which he clearly attributed little value or respect.

It wasn't Elizabeth Hale's custom to give parties for minor authors of cookbooks, but since it was Kate and since she felt guilty about the innumerable cock-ups that had plagued the production of the book, she felt bound to make some gesture of amicable compensation. Though she by no means regretted bumping into her old schoolfriend and sparking her into action with suggestions about gathering recipes, dealing with her on a business footing over the months had made her realise that no great sisterly intimacy was about to be reborn. Kate had never been sufficiently involved in the working world to empathise with all the strains and complications that confronted Elizabeth daily. Kate didn't know about juggling careers with families, philandering nannies, impossible deadlines, compromising with art directors and prioritising phone-calls. Kate had apparently expected the finsihed book to slip out with the ease and control with which she produced one of her delightful meals.

Elizabeth gave Kate five weeks' notice, boldly instructing her to invite everyone she could think of – including aged aunts and ex-lovers – confident that her spacious Camden house could accommodate whatever resulted. Thanks to the uninterrupted flow of two substantial salaries, the Hales afforded a hefty mortgage on a property which not only boasted six bedrooms, but two double reception rooms as well, not to mention a glass-roofed conservatory that led onto a 100-foot garden at the rear. Early November was a dodgy time for gardens, Elizabeth knew, though she did have fond memories of an outrageously warm Guy Fawkes night several years back, when scores of friends had continued partying outside long after the fizzle of the last firework.

It came as something of a shock when Kate Latimer presented her with a list of only fifteen names – and that included her children. After a couple of days pondering the rather sticky issue of whose party it was anyway, Elizabeth flung invitations at work colleagues like confetti. It wouldn't do to have too small a party, she felt, not for an editor of her stature, with her aspirations.

With the date fixed and the task of acquiring drink delegated to her husband Charlie, there only remained the challenge of negotiating with the delicatessen round the corner, where air-conditioned glass cabinets boasted an array of bite-sized puff-pastry savouries and fragile towering desserts which Elizabeth hoped even Kate Latimer would find impressive.

It wasn't until Kate asked him to do battle with the zip on the timeless black velvet creation which she had wheeled out to dazzling effect for every function of any importance to which they had ever been invited, that Nicholas noticed Joanna's earrings. They hung with chilling impudence from his wife's dainty earlobes, winking at him as their gold hoops twirled in the bright light of the bathroom mirror. His first instinct was to remain silent, banking on a well-established male tradition of failing to notice such things. Kate, holding his gaze in the glass in front of them, caught hold of one of his hands as it reached the top of her neck.

'So, what's the verdict?' she asked, her face shining with bold pleasure at her reflection.

Nicholas coughed and gently tried to withdraw his hand, taking care to caress her back as he did so, partly so that no inference of rejection could be drawn by the gesture and partly because the plunging V-line of exposed flesh was so tempting. He could feel her shiver as his lips touched the downy hairs on the nape of her bare neck. Her skin smelt faintly of lemons.

'You look stunning,' he murmured.

'And you don't mind?'

'Mind? How could I mind?' His lips were making their way across the top of her back towards one of the slim shoulder-straps that held everything in place. 'You look good enough to unwrap,' he whispered, taking an edge of the strap between his teeth and starting to draw it down over her shoulder.

Kate, faintly guilty about the earrings which she had been meaning to post to Alison for weeks, was momentarily distracted by the recollection of an occasion, not so very long ago, when the sight of her dressed up for a trip to lunch in London had prompted rather less positive reactions from her spouse. She opened her mouth to make the comparison, but then closed it again. The moment was too good, the evening too special, to sabotage it with such a provocative reference to the past. 'Not now, Nicholas,' she whispered instead, closing her eyes and offering not a twitch of physical resistance to the downward journey of her dress strap.

'Are we going or what?' announced Grace from the doorway behind them. Both parents straightened and turned at once, drawing in their breath at the sight of their daughter's tight leather mini-skirt, buttoned at the side like a bulging purse and accompanied by a low-necked top which parcelled her small breasts and rib-cage with an effect reminiscent of taut cellophane. Though the weight gained in France had by no means been entirely lost and though the skirt clearly left little room for sideways manoeuvre of any kind, Grace wore the outfit with considerable aplomb, assisted by the stately effect of extremely high heels. She'd had her hair cut brutally short just before the start of term, so that only the tips of it bore evidence of the bleach, the overall effect being a dramatic and not unattractive hedgehog style which she had accentuated with the skilful application of some gel.

'Well, you're clearly ready for a party,' remarked Kate with a smile which she hoped reflected none of her alarm.

'Gorgeous lady,' added Nicholas, nodding his head appreciatively and earning a smile of gratitude which he knew linked directly to their private discussion on her return from France. The trust which had fluttered into life on that day was something that he had since nurtured like a rare species of flower. 'Gorgeous,' he said again, kissing her on the forehead, mindful both of overdoing his affection and of disrupting any of the rather too generously applied layers of make-up below.

The first thing that greeted them was a display of Kate's book on an oval-shaped hall table positioned before a stately Victorian mirror framed with wreaths of twisted gold. The books had been placed in a variety of positions, so as to show off as many different highlights as possible, including the back cover photograph of Kate in a green apron holding out a magnificent vegetable quiche, an oil palette of colours and shapes that looked far too perfect to eat. Though a modest display, the overall effect was cleverly magnified by the mirror behind; Kate with a squeal of self-conscious embarrassment turned away and burrowed her face into Nicholas' shoulder.

'The price of fame, darling,' he said with a happy laugh and a nod of approval over her head at Elizabeth who stood behind with arms stretched out for coats and scarves.

'You look lovely, Kate,' she murmured, helping to ease off the rather tatty navy overcoat and cooing at the revelation underneath. 'I'm just so glad you're completely over that horrible accident. How's the other woman?'

'Home – at last – but not up to coming tonight, I'm afraid. She's something of a prisoner in her own home,' Kate murmured, thinking as she spoke that as much could have been said of Mary before the accident as after; 'so I'm helping out as much as I can – though the husband clearly thinks I'm a pest.'

'Bugger husbands,' said Elizabeth cheerfully, steering them all towards the main sitting room, where a clutch of guests, none of whom Kate knew, were already standing in a self-conscious circle by the mantelpiece, sipping drinks and making dainty inroads into the trays of inviting tidbits that surrounded them.

'We bought one crate only of the decent stuff – so enjoy it while it lasts – which won't be long with this pack of jackals,' boomed Charlie Hale, crossing towards the Latimers with a full tray of champagne flutes and beaming through the bushels of his beard. 'After that it's fizzy wine, I'm afraid.' He winked at Millie, who, having seized the chance to wear her new purple leggings and a lovely mauve stretch-top of Grace's which she had coveted for years, was now having second thoughts and wishing she had stuck to jeans. Sensing that her mother might be in demand, she was skulking at her father's heels, shifting awkwardly from one foot to the other, trying not to catch anybody's eye. While Grace concentrated on looking bored instead of petrified, keeping her nose in the air and twiddling her champagne glass as if she endured cocktail parties every night of the week, James, equally anxious to avoid giving any impression of social unease, sought refuge in the lighting of a cigarette. Blinking the smoke from his eyes, he then deftly scanned the room for any signs of a female under the age of forty – apart from his sisters – his confidence in such investigative procedures having advanced considerably since the off-pitch successes of the cricket tour. Only a few moments' scrutiny was rewarded by the sight of Charlie and Elizabeth's eldest daughter down the far end of the room, leaning with studied fifteen-year-old nonchalance against the closed lid of a shabby upright piano. Gripping his glass tightly, James set off on the long walk across the room, looking firmly at the deep blue of the carpet, so as not to lose courage.

Just as Nicholas and Kate were running out of things to say to a young bespectacled editor with protuberant, faintly transparent ears and a somewhat disconcerting passion for the subject of boxing, a whole new wave of guests arrived, bearing upon it a decidedly harassed looking Beth and George. Though Kate had spoken to them many times on the phone since the accident, mainly persuading them not to feel the need to assist directly in her convalescence, she hadn't actually seen them since their cruise.

'Nowhere to park the bloody car,' bellowed her father, seizing a glass from a passing tray with unseemly enthusiasm and swigging greedily. He looks very tired, thought Kate, unable to suppress the unwelcome thought that her own father might be the next one to go, if her waif of a mother-in-law didn't beat him to it. In view of such macabre reflections she found herself more than usually thankful for her stepmother's at times irritating, boundless – and peculiarly American – energy.

'I keep telling him, you have to live here to earn a parking space,' gurgled Beth, nudging George with her elbow and raising one very heavily-pencilled eyebrow at Kate. 'Congratulations, by the way, you wonder-woman you. I hate women like you – they make the rest of us look so dumb.' She smiled broadly as evidence that the criticism was kindly meant. 'When's the sequel due?'

'Sequel? Oh heavens – there's not going to be another one.'

'But it might be a best-seller – top rooky chef of the year – what do you say, George?'

'Absolutely,' agreed George, though in truth he was struggling over the swell of noise to catch anything that anybody was saying.

'Well, I'm a one-book woman,' declared Kate, sticking her chin out, memories of marshalling her culinary ideas still hopelessly linked to the tensions of the summer. 'I really can't imagine how I'd ever want to do another.'

'But here's to Kate, I say,' bellowed George, raising his glass and winking at his daughter. 'Tremendous stuff.' Everyone chinked glasses and made agreeing noises. Kate touched glasses with her husband last of all.

'You think up as many or as few bloody recipes as you want to, my love,' he whispered, 'don't let any of these bullies get to you.'

'I'm not sure we'll manage carriages at midnight, Katie,' put in George, fiddling with his hearing aid, 'bit of a drive back and I've got this infernal cold – can't take the pace these days. And I'm under strict instructions from my little Hitler of a nurse here to be a good boy and get lots of early nights.'

'Oh George, you silly.' Beth eyed him tenderly and then linked her arm through his. 'Now, who shall we bother next, honey? – it's not often we get to party – we've just got to make the most of it.' And the two of them sailed bravely off into the throng, leaving Kate and Nicholas time to exchange brief looks of mutual concern before they were assailed by someone else.

The room had suddenly filled up. Even with the double doors open, the guests were now packaged so tightly together that any circulation was impossible without considerable elbow-tunnelling and apologies for squashed toes.

Elizabeth, worried for her ornaments and carpets, chimed a fork against a glass and announced that there were two empty rooms on the opposite side of the hall and would people please use those as well. After a fractional pause, the buzz of conversation resumed and everyone stayed where they were.

It was the food photographer who tapped Kate on the shoulder next. Nicholas' stomach gave a little twist at the sight of him, registering with distaste the streaked blonde helmet of hair, the satiny black shirt, open to the navel and beneath that some ballooning Aladdin-style trousers tucked into what looked like a pair of riding boots.

'Jake, isn't it? Good to see you.' Nicholas wrenched his mouth into an expression which he hoped looked polite, if not exactly friendly, and gave Jake's heavily ringed right hand a hearty shake, holding on longer than he would normally have done, out of some perverse sense that Jake himself was not a hand-shaking sort. Kate received a kiss, an affectedly languorous one, Nicholas observed, just millimetres from her lips, when there were vast expanses of infinitely less provocative face-zones from which to choose. He was on the verge of allowing himself to be annoyed by such an unwarranted flourish of familiarity when he became aware that Jake's attention had shifted entirely away from Kate and was being directed instead, with almost visible steam, towards Grace, who, until this moment, had hovered at her mother's elbow saying nothing at all.

'Wow,' breathed Jake, 'that's some outfit.'

Grace, squirming with evident pleasure, said thank you and where had he got his trousers. Jake, suddenly looking and sounding a decade less than his twenty-seven years, said he had picked them up in the King's Road years ago but they still kept falling out of his wardrobe begging to be worn. Grace said she was really interested in clothes and was thinking of studying fashion after she left school. Jake said this sounded like the coolest idea he had ever heard and some of his closest friends were in the fashion industry and if she ever needed introductions of any kind he would be only too glad to help. Grace said that sounded fantastic and what did he do. Jake, with Spielbergian modesty, said he was in films, but sometimes resorted to paying bills with still-life photography. Grace's eyes, two pools of admiring awe, opened wider still. Her parents quietly side-stepped away.

Once they were out of ear-shot Kate groaned. 'I suppose it will be unwanted pregnancies and acid-house parties next, whatever they are. I'm not going to be any good at this bit, I can tell.'

'What bit?' Nicholas plucked a cocktail sausage from a nearby plate and popped it in his mouth.

'The teenager-to-adult bit. Babies and youngish children are my forte – but not this stuff.' She gestured with her glass at the room in general. 'Grace looks like a tart on the make, for God's sake.'

'Oh I don't know,' – Nicholas cast a critical look in the direction of his daughter, whose face was now only six inches or so from the carefully nurtured chin-stubble of the would-be movie mogul – 'I think she looks all right. Striking, mind you, but all right.' He chewed his sausage thoughtfully. 'Funny you should say that, you know, because I think I might be finding precisely the opposite to be true. Squawking toddlers were the hard part. But now' – he hesitated, momentarily tempted to confide Grace's secret to Kate, not because he felt she needed to know, but simply to demonstrate the point he was trying to make – 'I'm just beginning to think that I understand the children rather better than I used to. I like all this grown-up stuff – I feel I know more where I stand.'

'That's just as well,' replied Kate, cheerfully, 'then at least one of us is on top of things.'

Nicholas rocked back on his heels and laughed. Still mindful of the watchful glints of the earrings, he then sneaked a careful kiss on the ridge of her collar-bone.

Though Nicholas by no means relished the thought of the slimy Jake getting his hands on his delectably nubile daughter, he could not help feeling some reassurance at the fact that it was Grace who was the subject of the flirtation and not Kate. It seemed ludicrous now that he could ever have regarded such a creature as a threat. Kate, he thought, with the bliss of conviction, simply wasn't the unfaithful type – and if she was it certainly wouldn't be with an aspiring model of a cameraman, with puffy hair and a ring in his ear. He sneaked a look at his wife's face, trying to read beyond the cocktail party serenity, wondering whether she minded about the attentions being paid to her daughter purely as a dutifully protective parent, or whether there was something of the competing woman lurking there too.

The biggest surprise of the evening was Joyce, who, thanks to some egging on from the indomitable Betsie, had taken the bold step of making the trip to London into something of a holiday. They appeared, full of reports about the amiability of their taxi driver and the cosiness of their Victoria hotel, wearing what were clearly their best frocks and with voluminous shawls draped across their shoulders. After a bit of awkward tottering and jostling amongst the increasingly unruly masses, Charlie, who was always something of a hit with old ladies, shoo-shooed them into the much emptier double room across the hall where he settled them with armchairs and footstools and glasses of sweet sherry. Rather than being left out, guests of all varieties drifted their way for conversations of every kind, drawn to the domineering poise of the armchairs like subjects to a throne. Betsie and Joyce, called upon to give their views on themes ranging from the age of sexual consent for homosexuals to the literary merits of performance art, were even more thrilled than they had been by the matinée of *Kiss Me Kate* which they had attended the afternoon before. Indeed, so engrossed were they by these entertainments, and by the sporadic but charming attentions of Charlie Hale, ever mindful of their appetites and general comfort, that members of Joyce's own family barely got a word in. Apart from Millie, who, secretly jealous of Grace's conversation with a man who looked glamorous enough to be a real live film-star and fed up with watching James show off to a very limited supply of spotty teenagers, flopped in between the old ladies' footstools and fell asleep – much to the delight of her grandmother – with her head on Joyce's lap.

Seeing the two old women having such a fine time allowed both Kate and Nicholas to wipe away the last vestiges of guilt about their failed attempts at granny-care earlier in the year. Thank God for Betsie, they said – as they had said many times already – shuddering at unvoiced recollections of the summer, thankful that the issue of aging parents had been scotched for the time being at least.

Last of all to arrive were Harry and Alicia, complete with a large portable carrycot and a bulging pink bag with the letters *Lilly A. M. Browning* embroidered on the side in red chain stitching. Alicia, in a hip-hugging cream cocktail dress, bore no discernible signs either of having been pregnant or of suffering from the sleep-deprivation commonly associated with newborn infants. Though Lilly was asleep in the cot, the golden down of her hair just peaking out from underneath the rim of a lacy cotton bed cap, she wasn't allowed to remain so for long. While Alicia looked on with admirable insouciance, sipping champagne and smiling, Harry bore his small daughter round the room in the crook of his arm, determined to recruit as many new members to the Lilly Anastasia fan-club as possible. Lilly herself, showing remarkable patience for one so small and sleepy, blinked sapphire eyes at the packs of inquisitive faces, showing a resilience and quiet charm which was to stand her in excellent stead in the years to come.

Both Kate and Nicholas rather dreaded Harry these days. The more Nicholas saw of his brother-in-law the harder he found it to conceal his intolerance of him. Any hopes regarding the mellowing effect of Alicia and fatherhood had been dashed almost at once: Lilly was like yet another acquisition, thought Nicholas bitterly, wishing the little blighter would puke or scream instead of allowing herself to be paraded round the smoky over-crowded room like a trophy. For Alicia, clearly bound by love and an overwhelming desire for unity, Nicholas felt nothing but pity. That the woman was attractive was beyond question; but she was flimsy too, Nicholas decided, far too mild and accommodating to do Harry any good at all.

Kate's reluctance to see her brother was for rather more complicated reasons. While part of her feared spotting some element of inquisition in his eyes, some mute reference back to his grisly nugget of information about Nicholas, another, stronger part of her, worried at how sharply she might reveal the cut of her lingering anger for the thoughtlessness of what he had done. Sometimes she still longed not to know what Harry had told her. Sometimes, in a few rare, bad moments she wished her concussion had been more severe, so that she could have stepped out of the car and out-stared those cows with the blankness of genuine ignorance. But mostly, she did not mind: it was an injury like any other, whose rawness would fade with the inexorable – the soothing – passage of time. Memory or no memory, the accident felt like the milestone for a fresh start; it was thereafter that her life had begun to glow once more, risen with all the basic ingredients of contentment which Kate swore she would never take for granted again.

'She's incredible, isn't she?' said Harry, having threaded his way back to his sister. Lilly was cradled in one arm, while his free hand managed the dextrous challenge of a cigarette and a glass together.

'Yes, she is,' replied Kate patiently, turning her head to avoid the jet-stream of smoke which Harry fired her way in an elaborate gesture of avoiding the area immediately around his daughter's head. When she turned back it was to meet her brother's eyes head-on for one of those rare moments which felt designed purely for the purpose of allowing him to say, well, what have you done about it? How is Nicholas to be punished?

But Harry said no such thing, and if it crossed his mind, he gave no sign of it. He talked instead of the new flat he was going to buy, a three-bedroomed ground-floor palace in Belgravia, with an enclosed south-facing garden all of its own, with plenty of room for Wendy houses and tricycles. As he talked, his eyes, instead of focusing on his sister's, began to roam the room, seeking the mother of his child, for Lilly was at last beginning to squirm, arching her back and screwing her face up at the unwelcome light and fuggy heat; his arm was beginning to ache from carrying her so long; he wanted the freedom to hold a glass and smoke a cigarette in comfort. Before alighting on Alicia, Harry's eye was caught by the figure of Grace, wiggling in what looked like coloured polythene, tossing a striking brush of spiked hair which reminded him, somewhat unsettlingly, of the young assistant who had joined their team the previous month: a ripe old executive of twenty-four, brimming with cocky self-belief and drive; the kind of twenty-four-year-old that Harry could not resist – had not resisted – and never would resist, no matter how alluring the pull of partners and daughters and flats with gardens. Given such preoccupations, any domestic problems of Kate's had long since slipped to the bottom of his personal agenda. The night in the hospital was memorable for the birth of his child and little else. Besides which, the two of them looked the same as usual – Nicholas his delightful surly self, Kate all sweet and making up for it –, there was no reason to believe that anything could or would ever change. In addition to which, given his own most recent executive exploits – admittedly his first for a while – there was no sense of any moral highground any more, no stance of relative fidelity from which to voice judgements regarding the predatory activity of others.

'Here, Kate, be a love and take Lilly, could you?' Harry's cigarette, lodged in one corner of his mouth, the burning tip dangerously near his lips, was smothering his face in smoke, making his eyes stream and his nose itch.

Kate, after only a fractional pause, took a step backwards. 'Sorry,' she said, seizing a clutch of lanced cocktail sausages and brandishing her glass, 'got both hands full. You'll just have to manage on your own, Harry.'

'I say – Kate – don't muck around, there's a good girl.'

Kate, while mindful of fire hazards and the safety of her niece, held her ground. 'This is my party, Harry – for the publication of my book – and you haven't even said well done.'

'Well done, congratulations – you're marvellous – and now please relieve me of this screaming babe. Come on, Kate, everyone's starting to stare.' By now he had regretfully jettisoned his cigarette into what remained of his champagne; the glass itself was wedged precariously between his knees so as to release both hands for the business of wrestling with his daughter who, every trace of patience now gone from her seven-week-old body, was howling with the abandonment of pure rage. Harry, who had so far mastered only one position for holding a baby without its head flopping and its limbs dangling, was fast losing the struggle to appear composed.

Just as the moment arrived when even Kate began to feel the stirrings of something like sympathy, Alicia appeared noiselessly at Harry's side with a bottle of warmed milk. She took the child without a word, settled the small head in the crook of her elbow, straightened the bonnet, which had flopped right over Lilly's button of a nose, and efficiently popped the teat into the furious cherry-mouth. Lilly latched on with a dainty slurp, sucking greedily, her glassy eyes blinking with relief, her tiny jaws working hard on the rubber nipple.

'You see, she was starving,' announced Harry in the tone of one under pressure to defend himself.

'That's better, my sweet, isn't it?' crowed Alicia. 'Breast-feeding didn't work out,' she added, a shade defensively; 'it just didn't suit any of us, did it Harry?' She turned for a nod of support, which Harry managed, just, before slipping off in search of a fresh drink and some conversation that had nothing to do with lactation or muling infants.

After Elizabeth had stood on the piano stool in her stockinged feet, suppressing all professional disappointment in Kate's lack of enthusiasm to produce another book, in order to deliver a short speech about publishers being nothing without their authors, the party quickly began to break up. Nicholas, who had volunteered to remain sober enough to pass a breathalyser test found himself longing to go home. His stomach ached from the quantities of designer fizzy water which he had forced into it, driven by a need to drink something at a party, however poor a substitute for alcohol. He had eaten a lot too, drawn to the platefuls of guileless looking pastry parcels which disappeared in one gulp but then seemed to expand inside, soaking up the heavy intake of bubbly water like sponges. Rubbing his stomach, he wandered through into the second sitting room on the other side of the hall, where he found both Millie and Joyce asleep, while, beside them, Betsie, showing no signs of wear at all, was making a feisty challenge about the ethics of boxing to the editor with flapping ears.

'. . . Nothing but brain-damaged vegetables,' she was saying as Nicholas approached. 'Think of their mothers, that's what I say – everyone's got a mother, you know – and believe me we suffer terribly, even when our children are all grown up and doing their own thing. I just thank God that neither of my two boys ever took a fancy to it – football's their thing, though Terence was always the better of the two – sturdier on his legs than Paul – but then that's the way, isn't it? – no two peas are the same, even if they come out of the same pod—'

'Excuse me, a moment please,' put in the editor a little desperately, as Betsie, whose threads of conversation had a tendency to zigzag out of control after a glass or two, paused for breath. He made a sort of introductory gesture with his arm at Nicholas, as if to say, she's all yours, before scuttling off towards the door.

'Time to take Mum back to the hotel by the looks of things,' remarked Nicholas amicably.

'And your little one needs her bed. There's a love.' Betsie,

neither of whose sons showed any signs of marrying or producing grandchildren, stroked Millie's mop of curls and gave a
deep sigh.

'Shall I call a taxi for you both then? Victoria, isn't it?'

Betsie nodded her head and closed her eyes. Her finger-dab
of blue eye-shadow had shrunk into a line of colour across
the middle of her eyelids. 'That would be nice. Thank you,
Nicholas.'

On the way to the telephone Nicholas was ensnared in
conversation by a young copy-writer who wrote novels in his
spare time. He was an intense, dreamy-eyed man, of the kind
who would once have made Nicholas feel edgy and dull. But on
this occasion, he found himself leaning patiently against the wall
letting the man talk, while he nodded his head like some elder
statesman who had long since passed through the undignified
tortures of soul-searching and creative angst. He used his glasses
to good effect while he posed, peering over the top of them
and feeling wise and greatly advantaged. The world – though
Nicholas' only obvious ocular alteration had been to throw his
contact lenses into the kitchen bin – had miraculously shifted
back into perspective, the edges of all its objects and themes
once again becoming beautifully dark and clear. Accompanying
this rejuvenated vision was the simple realisation that his own
writing need not be elevated above the status of a hobby, that it
was permissible for such an activity to be pursued for relaxation
and pleasure – like Kate's gardening or Millie's ballet.

The young man was becoming tiresome, talking in an increasingly garbled and abstract way about prose style, tying himself in
verbal knots through a painfully transparent desire to impress.
Though it was vaguely flattering to be adjudged worthy of
impressing, Nicholas felt that if he swallowed one more yawn
his jaw would snap somewhere around his ears. Interrupting as
politely as he could, with apologetic murmurings about taxis and
tiresome grannies, he finally slipped away.

By the time Nicholas returned to the armchairs, Betsie too had
fallen asleep, her mouth slightly open, her head flopped to one
side, pressing all the life out of her admirable bouffant of rich
grey curls. Kate was standing beside the sleeping trio, shaking
her head and smiling.

'Time to go, wouldn't you say?' said Nicholas gently, arriving at her side. 'I've called them a taxi. We're about the only ones left. Grace is picking at left-overs in the kitchen and James disappeared upstairs with that plump thing in a leather jacket.'

'Oh Lord, then it's definitely time to go,' giggled Kate, feeling suddenly weak from tiredness and too much fizzy wine. Somewhere at the back of her skull a headache lurked, a dull throb of a thing which she knew would get steadily worse. She yawned and leant up against Nicholas, putting both hands on one shoulder and looking fondly up into his face. I could say it now, she thought, I could just whisper, I know, I know what you did. I know and I no longer mind.

'Oh my – what's this – I say – I do believe I nodded off for a moment there.' Joyce, jolted awake by some silent trigger inside her head, was sitting up patting her hair and blowing out her cheeks, mortified at having allowed herself to fall asleep. 'Must have caught it from Millie.' She touched her granddaughter's cheek with the knuckles of her crooked fingers and looked up blinking at Nicholas and Kate, anxious to demonstrate that she was now wide awake. 'Lovely party, Kate – just lovely. And my, you look so pretty – I love those earrings. Where did you get those then?'

Nicholas stiffened. Kate feeling the tension charge through him took her hands from his shoulders and straightened herself. 'These earrings? Well actually they belong to—' She stopped and looked at Nicholas who, with an expression of studied neutrality, was staring at his mother. Not now, he was thinking, not this, not now.

Joyce was regarding the pair of them curiously. 'They're not yours then, Kate?'

'Surely you recognise them, Mum,' said Nicholas hoarsely, feeling like a man going through the motions of life when death is close at hand.

'Why should I? Kate hasn't worn them before, has she?' She frowned, wrinkling the powdered lines of her forehead into deep furrows of genuine puzzlement. 'I'm sure I'd remember a pair of beauties like that,' she began with conviction, though her voice trailed off as uncertainty crept in, her memory for things in the immediate past having deteriorated noticeably since Dick's death. Betsie was always ticking her off for being forgetful.

'Well, actually we thought they belonged to Alison . . .' began Kate, staring at the side of Nicholas' head, noticing a small blue vein twitch in his temple. A pebble of doubt was solidifying in her heart, pushing down, making it hard to breathe. Drawn by the silent force of her eyes, Nicholas slowly swivelled to face her, his eyes so full of anguished regret that Kate hesitated for a long second before speaking, hardly daring to let her mind proceed down the path upon which it had started.

So now he knows I know, she thought, the silent communication bringing with it a strange, physical shiver of something like power and relief.

'You're right, of course they are Alison's,' declared Joyce abruptly, unaware of the drama being enacted before her. 'I remember now – I'm absolutely sure of it.'

'You are?' Kate turned her head slowly back to her mother-in-law, torn between developing her silent conversation with Nicholas and letting the moment go.

'Oh yes.' Sensing only the interrogative intensity of the conversation but not its invisible theme, Joyce assumed it was her powers of recollection that were under scrutiny. 'Of course they are Alison's – I remember them now, clear as anything. Did she leave them at your house then?'

Kate let out a long slow breath. 'At yours actually. I found them when I popped in to do a check-up on it one day. I really ought to have sent them back, but I forgot. Then tonight I thought Alison wouldn't mind if I borrowed them just this once.' She swallowed. 'Naughty me.'

'Naughty you,' echoed Nicholas, his mouth dry, his eyes again fixed in the vice of his wife's, pleading.

'Oh, Alison won't have noticed,' chimed Joyce, 'you know Ally – drops things here and there – always has done – ever since she was a little girl—'

But Nicholas and Kate were not listening. 'If you won't mention it to your sister then neither will I,' said Kate; 'our secret.' Her voice was now no more than a whisper, not because she feared she might be heard, but because a pledge of forgiveness and silence could only be uttered in such tones.

The life was slowly returning to Nicholas' face. He blinked. 'Our secret.' He mouthed the words and bent his head, as if in deference to her new power.

Joyce had stopped talking and was fidgeting with her shawl to hide an urge to yawn which she feared might appear uncivil. Beside her, Betsie had woken up, and was applying flustered hands to her flattened hair. At their feet Millie blinked puffy eyes.

A sheepish James, looking raw-mouthed and tousled, appeared in the doorway behind them, followed closely by Grace, languidly chewing a stick of celery.

'Time to go home, I think,' said Kate, smiling at them all.

'Time to go home,' agreed Nicholas, picking up the dead weight of their sleepy daughter, who flopped in his arms like an invalid, frowning through her curly fringe at the unwelcome return to the real world.